Hell's Rejects

Chaos of the Covenant, Book One

M.R. Forbes

Quirky
Algorithms

Published by Quirky Algorithms
Seattle, Washington

Cover illustration by Tom Edwards
tomedwardsdesign.com

CHAPTER ONE

"FIRST TIME IN A DROPSHIP, Lieutenant?"

Lieutenant Abigail Cage glanced over at the Master Sergeant running the mission, a burly Curlatin who looked even more alien inside the shell of a Republic Marine battlesuit than he did outside of one. She wondered absently if the padded actuators in the flexible metal skin tugged at the abundance of hair the race was famous for before spitting out a quick response.

"My tour is up at the end of this deployment, Sergeant. I'm willing to bet I have more drop experience than you and your platoon combined."

She kept her eyes locked on the Sergeant, knowing that her words were being translated to his language through the implant that was standard issue for any government employee who would be heading off-world and every soldier in the Republic. She waited for his large round eyes to narrow slightly through the tinted glass of the battlesuit before pointedly looking away.

"My. My apologies, Lieutenant," Sergeant Coli said, clearly taken off-guard by the ferocity of her reply. "I meant no decrease."

Decrease? She hated when the translator fragged words as much as she hated being questioned on her drop experience. She suddenly felt like a bitch for biting at the Sergeant. She had mistaken his intentions, more accustomed to being attached to battalions filled with overly aggressive bouncers than genuinely curious chiefs.

Besides, the question itself wasn't totally out of bounds. Not all Breakers had the good fortune to ride the vomit comet into the shit. She was too accustomed to soldiers assuming she was nothing more than a desk monkey just because she held a commissioned officer's rank, an advanced degree, and a specialty in the relatively passive fields of linguistics and computer science. Most non-HSOCs didn't understand that while Breakers were commissioned officers, they were also the elastic in the Republic military's structural rigidity. Her training had been anything but typical, to the extent that she wasn't cleared to divulge even half of what she had learned.

"It's my fault, Sergeant," she replied. "I'm always a little defensive around a new crew."

"It must be difficult being shuffled from one part of the universe to another," Coli replied. "I am grateful to remain with my troop."

He motioned to the platoon arranged on either side of the dropship behind them, sixteen soldiers in nearly identical battlesuits holding fast to the walls of the craft to save them from getting too roughed up during the ingress. Coli was the largest of them, though Abbey knew there were two more Curlatins in the mix, along with a Fezzig.

"It can be," she said. "The upside is that I've seen a lot more worlds than most-" She paused before she said "people." There were a number of different species in the Republic, a network of nearly five hundred planets, and "people" was generally translated to mean humans. "Individuals," she finished.

"Have you been to Curlat?" Coli asked, hopefully.

"No, sir," Abbey replied. "I've spent a lot more time on the Fringe. That's where all the trouble seems to be these days."

Sergeant Coli emitted a heavy, monotone sound that the translator informed her was laughter. "Trouble is everywhere, Lieutenant. The Fringe is the worst of it. We have spent a lot of time out here ourselves. Enough that I would question your assertion that your experience is greater than ours."

"Fair enough. I guess there's always enough trouble to go around as long as the Outworlders keep pushing our borders."

"Indubitably."

Abbey winced at the word the software had chosen. She would have to tweak her implant to handle the Quiri dialect better when they got back to the *Nova*. It wasn't wrong, but it was annoying.

A loud tone interrupted the conversation, a signal to the platoon that they had reached the upper atmosphere of Gradin and things were about to get a little bumpy.

Abbey reached back, locating the attachments to her suit on the inner wall of the dropship. Unlike the rest of the soldiers, she was wearing a softsuit, a less bulky, more agile version of the standard powered armor. Hers contained a special issue embedded system on a chip and extra tightpacks to carry the tools of her trade. What it didn't have were magnetic connectors to stick her to the hull, and so she had to hook in manually.

No sooner had she gotten the last hook strapped to the suit than the dropship began shaking, rapidly rising and falling as it slammed into the planet's turbulent atmosphere.

Screw a little bumpy. She felt her arms strain against the tight material of the softsuit and her stomach shift with each jostle.

"Intel said it was going to be rough, but this is insane," she said.

"Affirmative," Coli agreed. "The storm must be more intense than the nerds on the *Nova* predicted. I've been in worse."

"So have I," Abbey replied, not to be outdone. And she had. Gradin was a Stage Four terraform, a planet with a breathable atmosphere and individuals already on the ground despite the continued output of the huge generators that created the powerful storms as a side effect of their atmospheric processing. She had been to a Stage Two before, three or four years earlier. The dropship had suffered extensive damage to the stabilizers on the way in, and it was a miracle they had been able to climb back out.

And that was with the Republic techs claiming the Spirit-class hoppers could handle Stage Two. Assholes.

She turned her head, watching the rest of the soldiers in the platoon. She knew how to identify different combat personalities by the way they reacted to a drop, though not because of the turbulence. While the shaking they were experiencing wasn't typical, it also shouldn't have been enough to unnerve any but the greenest cadet, and there were no green cadets in the Third Battalion. She was the closest in that regard, having only been transferred to the Nova two weeks prior.

Most of the male and females in the group were silent and static, riding out the rough seas without a hint of discomfort. Two had their eyes closed, and she shifted her eyes to manipulate her Tactical Command Unit, marking the bouncers with a small tilde. Closed eyes usually meant they would be the first to break or freeze if things went bad.

One of the soldiers, an average-sized grunt near the back, was smiling, and looking a little too pleased with himself. Abbey marked him with a karat, giving his suit a closer look so she would know how to find him. If she needed someone to do something crazy or stupid, he was the mark.

"Tell me, Lieutenant," Sergeant Coli said, nonplussed by the rocking. "Why did you volunteer for this drop? Gradin is a rock, and the colony here is composed of the worst kind of scum."

"Allegedly," Abbey said, smiling behind her helmet. "Let's just say I believe individuals are innocent until proven guilty."

"General Kett has been proven guilty," Coli replied, his large eyes lowering in distaste. "Not only of aiding the Outworlds, but of misappropriation of funds, embezzlement, and treason."

"The forensic evidence is questionable."

Coli shrugged, not wanting to get into an argument. "I only know what I've read on the Milnet."

Of course, you do.

Abbey looked away so the Sergeant wouldn't catch her rolling her eyes. The Third Battalion wasn't the military police. Neither was she, for that matter. But the support request in the Milnet had been for a Breaker, and when she had seen the job was to raid a purported Outworlder compound connected to the disgraced officer, her personal curiosity had gotten the better of her. She had seen and read the same media reports as Coli, but she had also read the full forensic breakdowns moving through intelligence. In her mind, all of the data didn't quite line up, and if there was a chance to either prove her hunch or resolve her own doubts, she was going to take it.

She had never quite been able to make up her mind if that tenacity was a gift or a flaw. It had gotten her into HSOC training, and it had helped make her one of the top Breakers in the Republic, but it had also cost her a husband and more than one friendship. She just hoped Gavin was taking good care of Hayley. Her daughter was the one and only reason she was giving up the military after a single tour, a situation that was especially rare among Breakers. Six years of intense training for only six years of active duty? She had made a mistake getting involved and getting pregnant, but it was her fault, not Hayley's. There was no reason she had to pay for her mother's indiscretion.

This was her last shot to satisfy her need to know. She wasn't going to waste it.

A new tone sounded in the rear of the dropship, signaling that they were closing in on the target. Sergeant Coli reached out and put a hand on her shoulder, dragging her from her head. Then he released himself from his tether, letting the battlesuit help him maintain balance as he made his way between the platoon to the back of the craft.

"Check your squad channels," he said over the platoon line. "One One, check."

Abbey didn't hear Sergeant Ray's squad check. She was attached to Coli's team.

"One Nine, check," she said, ensuring the others could hear her. The rest of the squad followed suit until they had all confirmed their links.

"We went over this back on the Nova, but here's the reminder for the morons in our midst," Coli said. "Sergeant Ray's squad is going to provide support while we make our move against the compound. Our job is to get Lieutenant Cage to a terminal so she can pull whatever intel she deems important. In exchange, the Lieutenant is going to get us into the compound in the first place. Do you copy?"

"Aye, sir," they all responded, including Abbey.

"Good."

They waited another ten seconds or so, for a third tone to sound in the rear of the ship.

"Form up!" Coli shouted over the platoon line.

Both squads detached themselves from their magnetic connectors. It took Abbey a few seconds more to get the softsuit unhooked, but she joined the ranks in plenty of time.

"Sergeant," Captain Yung, their pilot, said over the channel. "We've got incoming fire from the compound. We're going in hot. I repeat, we're going in hot."

"Roger," Coli said. "You're all Marines. You all know what to do."

"Ooh-rah," the platoon replied.

The dropship began to shake again. Not from the turbulence now, but from evasive maneuvers. They could hear the slugs pinging off the thick armor plating, followed by the high-pitched whine of the automated defense system spitting out thousands of pea-sized rounds to counter incoming missiles.

"Hot, Sarge?" The soldier she had marked with the karat, Private Illiard said. "These madar ghahbe aren't supposed to know we're coming."

"I didn't tell them," Coli replied.

A fourth tone sounded a dozen seconds later, and the soldiers instinctively braced themselves as the dropship decelerated sharply, the roar of thrusters growing so loud it made it through the armor and into the space. A second noise followed: the sound of the dropship's three chainguns laying down cover fire as they made a quick descent.

Abbey felt her stomach lifting in response to the maneuver, the artificial gravity of the dropship having slowly adjusted to give them a natural transition to the planet. She ignored the sensation, reaching back and finding her rifle, swinging it forward in unison with the rest of the platoon.

The hatch in front of them slid open with a sharp hiss, revealing wet, muddy, and rocky terrain layered in dense fog and being pummeled with heavy rain. Tracers from the dropship streaked out ahead of them, keeping their exodus clear. Her helmet's HUD switched at Coli's command, the TCU giving everyone in the unit marks for every tango the dropship's onboard computer had identified on the way in.

"Signal back for pickup, Sarge," Captain Yung said. "Good hunting."

"Roger," Coli replied.

He didn't need to give the command. The Marines were already on the move. Abbey followed as they charged from the cover of the dropship and out into the elements, making the five-meter leap from the ship to the surface. Their battlesuits made the height easy to manage, but her softsuit required a little more finesse. She pushed her rifle onto her back again, grabbing at her waist as she reached the lip of the dropship, hooking her fingers onto small straps there and pulling up and out.

Two gossamer wings spread from her as she dropped, catching the air and slowing her descent, allowing her to land gracefully behind the Sergeant. She released the line the moment she was down, the wings snapping back against her sides while she retrieved her rifle again.

One last time, and then she was going home.

CHAPTER TWO

NOW THAT THE PLATOON WAS out of the dropship, their advance on the target was steady. Second Squad moved to the flank, finding some poorly defended high ground and setting up a sniper position there, while First Squad made their way forward, bouncing from rock formation to rock formation, their battlesuits giving them all the power they needed to make it from one cover to the next in a long jump.

Abbey's jumps were shorter but quicker, aided by her own fit physique. She didn't as much bounce as skip across the terrain, making fifty meters in a low arc that put her out in the open for a split second before her boots brushed the surface and she sprang off again. That instant gave her a good view of the front of the compound, which was part of the original below ground bunker where the first round of colonists had made their home before the terraforming had given them air to breathe.

The individuals defending it weren't soldiers, at least not in the sense that the Republic Marines were soldiers. They didn't have powered armor, and they didn't look very organized. They were firing hand-me-down weapons, machine guns with low RPS scores and small magazines and ballistics that weren't even guided. It was the sort of cheap shit that was common among the Outworlds, mainly because it was cheap shit. It was the kind of thing that always left her wondering how the hell the war was coming up on its thirtieth year.

Oh, yeah. Because of the Shrikes.

The Outworld's ship-killers were faster and deadlier than anything in the Republic, and a handful of the things could break down a Goliath class battleship like the *Nova* in under two minutes. Meaning that it didn't matter too much if the units on the ground were inferior, because the Republic had a severe shortage of missions that made it to the ground.

"One Nine, watch your bounce," one of her squadmates said over the shared channel. "They're painting you."

"Roger," Abbey replied, taking a moment to peek out from behind the cover before making her next jump. Most of the squad was already across, holding position and waiting for her. "Two One, I'll pop them out, you cap them off."

"Roger," Sergeant Ray said. "We're in position."

Abbey took a breath before bending her knees and snapping her ankles, activating the thin strands of synthetic musculature attached to the inner side of the softsuit. They added their strength to her own, sending her out into the rain and fog. She kept her eyes to her left, to the compound there. Her helmet assisted her vision through the crap weather, allowing her to pinpoint the tangos popping from cover to shoot at her.

She tucked her body, adjusting her arc as the bullets whipped past her and below her, sending wet splatters up and around. She hit the ground on her shoulder, rolling, the mics in her gear picking up the two sharp cracks as Squad Two's snipers did their work. She came up, pushing off again, heading for cover and the rest of her team.

No more bullets followed behind her.

"One Nine, clear," Sergeant Ray said.

"Two One, thank you, thank you," she replied, hitting the ground again beside Sergeant Coli.

"We're four hundred meters," Coli said. "Four bounces to the base. It looks like that last hit convinced the tangos they're safer inside." He turned and looked at Abbey, his large eyes conveying his amusement. "They aren't, are they, Lieutenant?"

"No, sir," Abbey replied, patting one of the tightpacks on her thigh.

"One One, opposition is holed up in the target," Sergeant Ray said a moment later, confirming the Sergeant's observation.

"Roger," Coli said. "Two One, hold position. Squad one, standard leapfrog, reconvene at the front door. One Nine, line up behind me."

"Aye, sir," the squad replied.

"Aye, sir," Abbey said.

Coli went first, bouncing away, a long, high arc that brought him down closer to the front of the base. Abbey followed him, taking three quick hops to make the same distance. The rest of the squad trailed them, the second section pivoting and making an immediate second jump to the next available forward cover. They repeated the pattern until they were at the base of the compound, staring at a heavy blast door three meters in diameter.

"Blow it or break it, Sarge?" Abbey asked.

"We don't need a Breaker to blow a blast door," Coli replied.

Abbey smiled. "In that case, follow me."

"Lieutenant?"

"You have to know they're going to ambush us when we move in," she said. "Breaking the door will buy us a couple of seconds, but there's a better way. These places always have an escape hole."

"With no external access," Coli said. "Too small and too thick to blow."

"No external access for a standard Marine platoon," Abbey said. "But you have me."

Of course, that didn't mean the Sergeant was going to listen to her. Sometimes those same grunts who thought she was little more than a desk monkey found her capabilities threatening to their personal self-worth, to the point that they'd rather walk into an ambush than sneak in through the back door. Abbey didn't think Coli was that kind of bouncer, but she had been wrong before.

"My people can handle it, Lieutenant," Coli said. "Those shooters the tangos are using can't pierce a battlesuit."

Fool me once. Idiot.

"Aye, sir," Abbey said, moving in closer to the small control panel on the exterior of the blast door. She reached into one of the tightpacks on her softsuit and pulled out a small disc the size of a fingernail. She tapped the top of it and then placed it against the panel.

A new screen appeared inside her helmet as the extender intercepted the control panel's system and began filtering the commands to her. She put her left hand on her thigh, tapping her fingers against the suit on the invisible tactile receptors there. Those signals were sent to the control panel, appearing amidst the console output on her HUD.

"Twiddling your fingers, One Nine?" Private Illiard said.

"Shut your hole, One Six," Coli said.

"Aye, sir."

Abbey's eyes twitched as she watched the code, trying to match it up with the data she had on the particular make and model of the panel. It was Outworld manufactured, and much newer than the compound it was protecting.

"Lieutenant?" Coli said a few seconds later. "I'd rather not find out if there are reinforcements inbound the hard way."

"Aye, sir," she replied, getting frustrated with herself. She should have cracked this bastard by now.

She entered a few more commands, smiling when one of them finally yielded something she could use.

"Squad One," she said. "Prep for entry."

"You heard her," Coli said. "One Three, prep a flashbang. Standard ingress protocol."

"Aye, sir," Private Dis said, prepping the grenade launcher attached to her rifle. The other soldiers moved into position around the door, waiting for it to slide open.

Abbey raised her right hand, fingers open, using her left to keep entering commands. When she reached the system root, she closed it into a fist. When the door began to open, she dropped it.

Private Dis fired her grenade into the crack, the loud pop and bright light following a moment later. The other Marines filed past them, their TCUs painting targets, which passed immediately to Abbey's HUD. Pop. Pop. Pop. Pop. Pop. Three of them had fallen before the return fire started.

Abbey stood at the side of the entrance, gathering her rifle and prepping for entry. Coli motioned her to stay back and bring up the rear. She was supposed to survive to break into the compound's network and see if she could pull anything useful.

The firefight intensified in a hurry, the battle easy to follow on her HUD. Fifteen red dots appeared, spread in what was likely a large antechamber beyond the initial access tunnel. The eight members of First Squad moved in formation behind that, painted green, three of them with her added marks beside them.

"One Four, sweep left," Coli said. "One seven, cover."

"There's a lot more of them than we thought there would be, Sarge," one of the tildes said.

Six more red spots appeared on Abbey's HUD.

"Shit. Tango Twenty-one has an emgee," Illiard said.

"Duck and cover," Coli said, sounding a little nervous. "One Six, One Four, One Three, get on him."

"Aye, sir," the soldiers replied.

Abbey heard the high pitch of the electromagnetic railgun a moment later, spitting flechettes at nearly four times the speed of sound, easily packing enough kinetic punch to go right through both a battlesuit and the soldier in it. Handheld emgees were rare in the Republic military and unheard of among the Outworlds. What the hell had they just walked into?

"One Four is down," Illiard said a moment later.

"I'm hit," Private Dis said a moment later. "Shit, it hurts."

"Two One, we need backup," Coli said.

"Aye, sir," Sergeant Ray replied calmly. "We're on the way."

Abbey looked out to Second Squad's position, watching as the soldiers bounced to her at full speed.

"Sarge," she said as they passed her by. She hated being a bystander. "I can help."

"Negative, One Nine," Coli said. "Standby."

The firefight continued, the reinforcements forcing the opposition to begin retreating deeper into the compound.

"Position One is clear," Coli said. "One Nine, you're clear to move to Position One."

Abbey stood at the entrance to the compound. Something in her gut was telling her not to move, to consider another option. Nerves? Instinct? She took a step forward and hesitated. How much trouble could she get in? Technically, she wasn't required to follow Sergeant Coli's orders. Technically, she outranked him.

She watched the HUD for a few more seconds. It showed most of the remainder of the two squads moving down a corridor at the back of the first chamber, while Two Three and Two Four were coming back, likely pulling the dead out with them. Damn it; they could have avoided the casualties if Coli hadn't been such a stubborn furball.

She made her decision then, planting her feet and bouncing up the side of the compound, quickly scaling the rocky hill it had been planted below.

"One Nine, where the hell are you going?" Coli said a moment later, tracking her movement.

She didn't answer him, focusing on the terrain ahead. She hated to disobey, but he was wrong to have gone in the front door. Possibly dead wrong.

Her fears were realized a moment later. The channel burst with chatter, the platoon coming up against a second emgee dug in behind a steel barrier. Coli pulled them back, retreating to the first position, forced to wait to collect the three soldiers of the Fifth Platoon who died in the process.

Abbey slid down the far side of the hill, pausing at a bare spot on the ground and pulling a short, narrow cylinder from a tightpack. She stuck it into the earth, capturing the reading and then heading eighty meters to her right. She leaned over and pawed at the ground there, quickly uncovering the escape hatch beneath it.

"One One, I'm at the rear hatch," she said. "Hold tight."

"Does chain of command mean anything to you, Lieutenant?" Coli said.

"Not when our people are dying, sir," she replied.

CHAPTER THREE

SHE PULLED ANOTHER EXTENDER FROM her suit, slapping it onto the top of the hatch. It was much smaller than the main entrance; barely two meters across. It would have been a tight fit for a Sergeant Coli in the battlesuit, but he probably would have made it.

She brought the console up on her HUD, tapping her fingers rapidly on her thigh while crouched beside the hatch. Every few seconds she turned her head to look out at the landscape around her, making sure she hadn't been spotted. She could see the outside colony a few klicks in the distance. It was a small haven, a collection of low buildings with rounded tops beside a hastily constructed network of electrical connectors and drainage pipes. She doubted much of anything that occurred on Gradin was legal, but that had been one of the biggest negative side-effects to the proliferation of terraformers. You could get a used generator on the open market for a few million, and within a few years you could take a shitty rock in the middle of nowhere and make it your own private paradise.

If you considered mud, clouds, rain, and cold paradise.

The second hatch was easier to break than the first, now that she knew what to look for. She had it open within fifteen seconds, and it swung silently upward on damp hinges. The comm was quiet, the platoon pinned back behind the entrenched position. Maybe Coli was putting together a new plan. Maybe he was waiting on her. She didn't know and didn't care. She wasn't doing this to be a hero, or make herself look good. This was the sort of thing she had been trained to do, and if there was one thing she believed it was that if you were going to do a job, you did it to the best of your ability.

She reached down and tapped a receiver at the bottom of her boots. The material expanded, covering the soles with a soft gel, enabling her to slip into the hatch and onto the ladder leading to the compound without making a sound. She climbed in, closing the hatch behind her, and then scaled it quickly, sliding a few rungs at a time, dropping nearly fifty meters beneath the rocky terrain above until finally reaching a small, open space. The two tangos in the room were near the far door and facing away from her, weapons up and at the ready. They didn't notice her entrance, and they didn't notice the draft from the open hatch.

She ducked behind a stack of containers, pausing to read the labels. They were written in Plixian, a series of lines that looked more like scratches than writing. She cursed silently as she translated it. These assholes had more than two emgees. They had at least a dozen, though most were still in their boxes.

Arms dealers, then?

She reached into a tightpack near her breasts, pulling out a pair of soft, round balls. She pressed them between her fingers, activating the chemistry inside, and then stood and threw them forward. The aim didn't matter as much as the results. The balls hit the wall ahead of the two soldiers and began to glow brightly.

She vaulted the containers while the tangos were distracted by the light, bouncing to them in no time, producing a pair of nerve sticks as she did. They barely noticed her before she had slapped the sticks against their exposed skin, sending a jolt of electricity into them and knocking them out cold.

She disarmed them, turning back to the weapons crates and capturing a snapshot of them before heading out of the room. She knew from the TCU positioning where both her platoon and the enemy combatants were sitting, and she approached them cautiously from the rear.

The inside of the compound was as unspectacular as the outside. Bare metal walls producing warmth from the elements behind them, exposed pipes and wiring, heavy manual hatches and dim lighting. These places were meant to be temporary, built cheap and tough for bare necessities living.

Abbey navigated through it, pausing at each hatch and peering into the small slip of a window, noting the layout as she made her way across. She bypassed what appeared to be the command center, a room messy with wires and terminals spitting lines of data to nobody. She could hear the fighting now. The tangos had abandoned the use of the emgee, not wanting to waste the rounds if they couldn't kill anyone with them. The two sides were trading lighter fire, where lighter meant dense-tipped flechettes on the Republic side and small caliber whatever from the opposition. Only the threat of the railguns was keeping Coli and his Marines honest.

She froze when she heard a soft voice behind her, crouched and turning, bringing her rifle into her arms. A taller human with dark skin and a soft build crossed the corridor behind her with a shorter man. They didn't seem concerned that their base was under attack, or if they did they weren't showing it. She let herself exhale once they had passed without looking her way. Whoever those two were, they weren't the problem right now.

Enough stalling. She was moving too slow. Taking too long. She headed forward again, closing in on the enemy position. She reached the corner, peering around and finding a second blast door between her and the enemy. Damn. It would be hard to sneak up on them past that.

She leaned against the wall for a moment to think, and then padded across to the door, pushing herself into the corner while she dug a soft gray clay from a tightpack on her bicep. She began pressing it against the seams of the door as quickly as she could, doing her best to monitor the corridor while she did. It took nearly a minute to entrench the explosive, and she could hear running footsteps at her back as she pressed the last wad in place.

Had the two tangos in the storage room been discovered?

She bounced away from the door, pivoting as two soldiers turned the corner. They locked eyes with one another.

Then she tapped her thigh, triggering the detonator.

The explosion echoed through the compound, the force of the blast tearing the door off its moorings and sending it into the enemy force on the other side. Backwash flowed toward her, and she dropped to her stomach on the floor, letting the flames lick at the back of her softsuit while she aimed and fired, hitting the two soldiers in the chest. She was moving again before they had collapsed, getting to her feet and facing the no longer sealed doorway.

The blast created a lot of dust and smoke, but she could see the metal barrier beyond it, and the mounted emgee position ahead of that. The gunners behind it were on the ground and unmoving, as were the four other soldiers that had been defending the position with them.

"One One, you're clear," she said.

"Roger," Coli replied. He didn't sound happy, but he didn't sound angry either. His big form appeared in the haze a moment later at the opposite end of the corridor. "Definitely not your first drop, Lieutenant. Two One, take your men and sweep the compound. Clean up any trash you find. One Three-"

"Be careful Two One," Abbey said, interrupting. "Sergeant, I don't know what else is going on here, but they've got a pretty nasty cache of weapons in the rear storage area near the escape hatch. We can't be sure they aren't toting some of them."

"Roger," Coli replied. "Two One, use extreme caution. Unless you want to finish dismantling this compound for us, Lieutenant?"

Now his voice was dripping with anger. She had made him look bad, and he didn't like it. Too bad. They hadn't lost any more troops. That was more important than his ego.

"Negative, Sergeant," she replied. "I ID'ed the control center back that way. I'd like to go pick it for intel."

"Roger. One Six, One Four, go with her. You can use the

protection." Again, he made the loud monotone sound that her translator informed her was a laugh. Compensation for his anger?

Abbey let the two soldiers escort her back the way she had come. They took a guard position outside the command center as she entered and headed to the most central terminal. She put her hand on the seat as she neared. It was still warm. She tapped the small mat in front of it, and a holographic display rose ahead of her. She reached into a tightpack and removed a silver puck, placing it on the mat. The projection wavered for a moment before stabilizing.

Inside her helmet, she began to receive the unfiltered computer commands as they executed. There was too much activity for her to follow it, but she didn't need to. She started running the software embedded in her suit against it, filtering out the most common processes and damming the data river into first a stream, and then a trickle. Like all things military, there was a procedure involved, one that she could follow to a certain point before instinct and experience had to take over.

She isolated the data streams and then began using the projected interface, searching for data stores. She cursed under her breath after a few minutes of digging turned up nothing.

The data had been wiped.

She picked up the silver puck, putting it back in the tightpack, and then dropped onto the floor, finding the wire attached to the mat and following it into a small grate. She removed a laser cutter from her suit and sliced through the flooring, lifting a section up and reaching into where the main terminal was resting. She grabbed it and pulled it out, a small black box with a sharp pair of wings etched into it. The sight of the logo gave her pause. It was a Republic box, marked as black ops. If General Kett was involved, this was the kind of thing that would further his implication.

She disconnected the wires attached to it and stood, carrying it out of the room and heading back to Coli.

"One One, I'm finished here," she said on the way.

"Roger. Did you get what you came for, Lieutenant?"

"I don't know yet. The data was wiped during the standoff. I'll need the lab on the *Nova* to see if I can recover anything. I got eyes on two tangos on my way to you, a tall, dark man with a shorter, lighter skinned guy. Have you located them?" She had a feeling they knew a lot about whatever dealings were happening here.

"Negative," Coli replied. "The compound is clear. There were a lot fewer of them than our initial ingress would have suggested, though they did their fair share of damage. We lost four good Marines today."

"I'm sorry, Sergeant."

Coli grunted over the channel, unwilling to admit she had probably kept him from losing more. She was okay with that. They were alive regardless.

"What about the weapons cache?" she asked.

"What weapons cache?" Coli replied.

"I told you, sir, it was in the rear of the compound. Plixian writing. A dozen emgees, maybe more, among other things."

She turned the corner, reaching the Sergeant. He rotated to face her, his big eyes suggesting confusion.

"We didn't find any cache," he said. "The room was empty."

Abbey stared back at him. "Sir, that can't be possible. The arms were there thirty minutes ago."

"One One," Captain Yung said, his voice interrupting them on the platoon channel. "We've arrived at pickup station Delta, awaiting egress."

"It's time to go, Lieutenant," Coli said.

"Sir, we need to examine the storage room. If the weapons are missing-"

"I said, it's time to go, Lieutenant. The dropship is here; your mission is complete. Countering the dust-off puts our people at further risk, and we have casualties."

She didn't argue. How could she? "Aye, sir."

"Platoon, rendezvous at station Delta for dust-off," Coli announced.

Abbey fell in behind the Sergeant, following him out of the compound and back to the pickup point. She felt her stomach lurch at the sight of the four soldiers in dark bags. Then she looked down at the computer in her hand. Marines had died so that she could retrieve it.

It was her responsibility to make those deaths stand for something.

CHAPTER FOUR

VICE ADMIRAL EMIL CORTEZ STARED out of the shuttle's viewport, trying to force his eyes to function better than they actually did so that he could see past the glare of Sol Three to the star dock orbiting the planet Feru. His assistant, Petty Officer Smyra, had suggested that he might be able to catch a glimpse of the *Fire* and the *Brimstone* at rest out there, ahead of the other dignitaries and stakeholders that had been gathered for the demonstration of the starships.

The newest designs out of Eagan Heavyworks, he had heard the two ships were going to be the weapons that finally offered an effective counter to the Outworlder's Shrikes, providing the Republic with the tool they needed to end the conflict and return peace to the edge of the settled universe after nearly thirty years of tensions.

Then again, he had heard those kinds of claims before.

He gave up on trying to get a look at the ships ahead of time. The glare was hurting his eyes, and he would have his chance to see them soon enough. Instead, he settled back into his seat, picking up the drink that had been left beside him and putting it to his lips. It was a yellow, milky concoction. The server had called it 'blik' and claimed it was a Plixian delicacy. He was always open to trying new things.

"Admiral Cortez," Petty Officer Smyra said, returning from the front of the shuttle, where she had been conversing with the pilots. "You have an update from the *Charis*."

Cortez paused before tasting the drink. The *Charis* was near the Outworld border, running standard patrol, and due to remain there for six more weeks. What would they need from him?

He reached into the chest pocket of his jacket, retrieving a small silver disk from it. He held it in his palm while a projection appeared ahead of him.

"Sir," Captain Issiasi said, raising a tentacled appendage to salute him. "My apologies for the potential disruption, but my intelligence team has recently uncovered scattered disterium emissions that suggest a ship may have traveled through our jurisdiction from the Outworlds, and our mission directives were to contact you immediately in that event. Dating of the emissions is still in progress, but our early estimates put the incursion at one dot three EW. As always, I am your humble servant. Issiasi, out."

The projection faded. Cortez looked up at Smyra, who had raised her eyebrows in response to the missive.

"By-the-book, isn't he, Admiral?" she said.

Cortez smiled. "That's why the Rudin make good officers," he replied. "And Issiasi is a 'she.'" There were no outwardly visible signs of gender on the squidlike species, and the clicking tones their beaks made didn't provide many variations in vocalization patterns, so he wasn't surprised Smyra had guessed incorrectly.

"How can you tell, sir?" she asked.

"I've read her personnel file. I take it you haven't dealt with the Rudin much before?"

"No, sir. There weren't any at the Sol Academy."

"Their physiology requires a lot of modifications to our equipment," Cortez said. "It's a work in progress."

"Yes, sir."

It was the double-edged sword of being the more advanced species, he supposed. After all, it was humans who had been the first to develop faster than light technologies. Humans who had discovered the worlds of the Curlatin, the Gant, the Plixel, and the Rudin, among others. Humans who had started the Republic and built an empire that now spanned thousands of light years. He had read texts on some of Earth's more distant history. That they had managed to come so far as a species after nearly destroying themselves could only be accounted as a miracle.

"In any case, it isn't uncommon for smugglers to slip through our patrols. If the residual emissions are too small to date accurately, it's doubtful we have anything to be concerned about. I'll inform Issiasi of the same after the demonstration."

"Yes, sir."

Petty Officer Smyra saluted him, and then returned to her seat across the aisle. Admiral Cortez picked up his drink again, taking a small sip. It reminded him of blueberries and spices, with the kick of a nice vodka.

"Smyra," he said, "can you please have the server provide the details for this? It is fantastic."

"Yes, sir," Smyra replied.

Cortez looked out the viewport again. The shuttle was nearing the Heavywork's ring station. He could see dozens of other small ships already docked at the spokes that dotted the loop. Had any of the Republic's top military and civilian protectorate leaders not been invited to the demonstration?

And what kind of demonstration would it be? Director Mars Eagan, the CEO of the company that bore her father's name, had been tight-lipped about exactly what they were showing. Not that it was a surprise. Generations had passed without a design that could overcome the Outworld Shrike, and pressure had been mounting. While each iteration of military starship fared better and better, the Heavywork's stock had been plummeting, and newer companies like Tritium Heavy Industry had been eating them for lunch. The Apocalypse starfighter was the current cream of the small craft crop. In fact, the Admiral had seen to it that the Republic placed an order for two hundred of them just last week.

In other words, it was on the Heavyworks to impress him. Were they up to the task?

CHAPTER FIVE

URSIN GALL SMILED AS HE entered Grand Concourse A, the largest open space on Ring Station Feru, using his position at the main entrance to look down over the entire assembly of corporate snobs and military buffoons with a sense of satisfaction.

It wasn't a justified sense just yet, but it would be soon.

"Lovely party," the woman standing beside him said. She was a striking figure, her form long and narrow, her hair a deep, exotic blue. She wore a long dress that danced along the floor and opened at her wrists, draping her like an ancient Earth goddess .

Ursin could taste the sarcasm in her voice.

"Isn't it just?" he replied, taking it all in. They had burned a lot of good favor to get here for the event. Now they had to make it all worthwhile. "Do you see her?"

Her head shifted as she scanned the room. There were at least five hundred people gathered on the open floor of the concourse, surrounding tables of food and drink and raising a hum of sound as they made small talk with one another.

"No," she said. "She must still be in her office."

Ursin gazed out of the tall viewport at the side of the room, the rounded transparency covering the entire side of the one hundred meter wide ring. The design was a throwback to days long past when stations like this required centrifugal force to provide artificial gravity. It had been built long after those days were over; a retro-futuristic design meant to impress VIPs more than anything else.

"The demonstration starts in an hour," he said. "How do we know she isn't over there?" He pointed out to the star dock in the distance.

"Oh, Ursin," the woman said. "I don't think the Director has ever stepped foot on the star dock before. They turn the gravity off over there from time to time, you know."

"It beats the hell out of lifting heavy equipment," he said. "You memorized the schematics. Where do we need to go?"

She reached out her hand, taking his, as an older man joined them on the promenade. He was wearing a Republic Navy uniform, the hardware across his chest suggesting he had been around a while and had more likely than not been responsible for the deaths of a number of Outworlders. Ursin felt his eye twitch at the sight of him, and he had to squeeze his wife's hand tighter to get it under control.

"I don't believe I know you," the man said, approaching him and putting out his hand. "Admiral Emil Cortez, Republic Navy."

"Jason Smith," Ursin replied, forcing his voice into Earth Standard. It made him feel like he was speaking through his lips, instead of with them. "CEO of Hyperion Drive Systems." He took the hand and shook it, resisting the urge to crush it. Meanwhile, he could tell the Admiral was considering, trying to decide if he had heard of the company, and it's president, or not.

"A pleasure," the Admiral said a few seconds later, pulling his hand away. "This should be some demonstration."

"Do you know much about what we're going to see?" Ursin asked. "I heard was that there was some new drive technology involved, and I made sure to get myself on the guest list."

"You seem to know more about it than I do, Mr. Smith," Cortez said. "Military contractors don't like to share anything with us until we show them the coin."

Ursin faked a laugh. "It's a competitive environment, for certain.

We all have to be sure our secrets remain secure, especially when one good contract with the Republic can provide jobs and income for thousands over generations."

Cortez shrugged, dismissing the statement. "I suppose." He looked down at the party below. "If you'll excuse me."

"Of course," Ursin said, as the Admiral wandered away.

"He didn't even acknowledge me," Trin said.

"Just like a Republic Admiral to put himself so high on his proverbial horse," Ursin said. "He didn't want to acknowledge me either, but he couldn't get past without being a complete asshole. In any case, keep your eyes on the prize. Where to?"

"Follow me," Trin said, turning them back the way they had come.

They headed away from the concourse, into a corridor that ran along the edge of the ring. It was clean and sterile, with ambient lighting that aided in maintaining circadian rhythms and soft white noise providing a sense of place.

"If she's still in her office, we need to update to Operation B," Ursin said.

"I've already informed the team," Trin replied. "They're standing by."

"What about command?"

"Dak will loop them in."

"Good. I don't want any mistakes. We've already given up too much to get here."

"I know. No mistakes."

They continued through the corridors, turning left to take one of the spokes leading to the ring's central spire. It was the command and control center of the facility, a long, narrow structure that sat in the middle of the ring like the center of a gyroscope. It was where the Heavyworks employees were coordinating all of the incoming shuttles.

And where Director Mars Eagan would be preparing for her big moment.

"Ursin, wait," Trin said, pausing halfway down the corridor.

The ring was where the Heavyworks employees lived, and

composed mainly of apartments and recreational facilities. She had stopped him outside of one of the apartments, a nondescript hatch with the number displayed on the front. "321-9A."

He moved in close to her while she looked over his shoulder, finding the camera there. He smiled, reaching up and stroking her long blue hair, putting his hand behind her ear. He located the scrambling device behind it, tapping it to turn it on as he stared into her eyes.

"Clear," she whispered. Then she put her hand on the door, having produced a small disc from beneath the drapery of her sleeves. She tucked her other hand inside the front of the gown, and a moment later the door slid open.

The apartment was unoccupied. Most of them were at the moment. All of the Heavywork's employees were either prepping for the demonstration or waiting on Concourse B to witness it. They entered quickly, not wasting any time shrugging out of their formal attire and revealing the gear underneath. Two black, fitted softsuits, with tightpacks holding their equipment close to their bodies and making it easy to hide. Ursin opened one of them, pulling out a small monocle that he pressed to his left eye, the magnetic contact holding against the small implant beneath his skin. Trin copied the motion before opening two more tightpacks to reveal a pair of nerve sticks. They had wanted to bring guns, but while security on the ring was light, it wasn't quite that light.

"How far to the checkpoint?" Ursin asked, removing his own nerve sticks.

"Three hundred meters," Trin replied.

"How long until they notice their feed is fragged?"

"Best guess? Another seven seconds."

"Then why are we still standing here?"

Trin smiled, the way she always did when they were running together. Five years. Ever since that job on Manitou. He could still remember it like it was yesterday. She was the best fragging assassin he had ever seen.

The hatch slid open, and she darted through it, leaving him behind.

That reminded him of Manitou, too.

CHAPTER SIX

THEY DIDN'T SLOW AS THEY reached the security checkpoint, making it before any of the guards there had managed to check the feed from corridor 9A and catching the paid detail flat-footed and lazy.

Trin was a blur of motion, using the softsuit to vault the last ten meters to the checkpoint, where a surprised guard was trying to get to his feet and react to the incoming storm. She caught him hard on the temple with a nerve stick, sounding a sharp crack as it smacked his flesh and knocked him cold. She barely slowed, moving through the sensor grid and landing on the other side, reaching out and grabbing the guard there and pulling her in, bringing a knee up into her ribs before pushing her back and slapping her with a nerve stick as well.

Ursin trailed behind, slowing up as he reached the grid. It hadn't activated at her passing. Their contraband was manufactured to be invisible to the system.

"Did they hit the alarm?" he asked.

"Negative," she replied. "We're still ghosts."

"Help me get them propped up. Leave it to mercs to fall asleep on the job."

She smiled, grabbing the female guard below her shoulders and moving her back to her seat. Ursin couldn't make the other guard stand again, but he leaned him against the wall and out of sight. Then he produced a small device from his suit, putting it up against the guard's eye.

It made a soft humming noise as it reached behind the eye and efficiently cut it out.

"Trin," he said, tossing the device to his wife. She caught it and placed it in front of the scanner against the wall. The hatch guarding the access tunnel to the spire slid open.

"I could have cracked it," she said, slightly disgusted by the eye.

"Too slow," he replied.

They dashed along the corridor. It was completely transparent, giving him the feeling he was running across empty space. It might have been a fun experience if he weren't in the middle of a job.

They reached the other side, using the eye again to get into the spire. Once more the corridors were quiet, with most of the workers assembling in the ring to watch the demo, or already on the star dock to help organize it.

"This way," Trin said, leading him toward the center of the spire. There were cameras here, too, but the jammer behind her ear was overriding them as they neared, causing them to blink off and then on and hiding their approach.

They reached the center column, where a series of lifts were available to carry them to other levels of the spire.

"You're certain she's here?" Ursin asked again.

"Lestan is monitoring the feeds. If she wasn't already at the party, she has to be in the spire."

Ursin wondered if he had been wrong to let her take the transmitter. It was safer for only one of them to carry it, but if they got caught...

He threw that thought away. They weren't going to get caught. Not by these people. They had no idea what was coming.

"Which way?" Ursin asked.

Trin held up her hand to beg patience, turning slowly, her eyes half-closed. She was listening.

"Down," she said, darting away before he could react, heading toward the lifts.

He trailed behind her, catching up when she paused at the clear tube, pressing a patch against the sealed transparency. They both turned away as it flared and sparked, shorting the safety lock and allowing them to slide the clear wall aside.

Trin leaned in, looking down before facing him, a big smile on her face. "Thirty floors," she said.

Ursin looked up. The flat platform that was the actual lift was still high above their heads and not moving. She was suggesting they jump.

"You could have called the lift," he said.

"Too slow," she replied.

He breathed in, and then took her hand, jumping into the tube with her.

They dropped, keeping their bodies flat and straight. The fall took only seconds, and as they neared the lower level they reached out, putting their gloved hands to the glass sides. The rounded ends of their fingers began to elongate, shifting into sharp points that dug into the material, catching them and slowing their descent.

They nearly slid too far, reaching the lower floor still in motion. Ursin cursed, digging in harder and using his strength to get a firmer hold. He grabbed Trin's wrist, holding tight to her as he finally came to a stop.

She scaled his back, reaching the hatch attached to the tube and placing another patch against it. She put her hands over it to disguise the flare and then shoved the door aside and entered. Ursin climbed in behind her, waiting for her to direct him.

She pointed to the left, at the same time an older woman in a formal suit turned the corner, flanked on either side by a pair of bodyguards. They all made eye contact at the same time, transmitting their intentions in the briefest of moments before Ursin found himself running beside Trin, heading directly for the group.

The bodyguards moved to block Director Eagan, hands falling to their sides and drawing laser pistols. Too slow. Ursin and Trin pounced on them, grabbing them and throwing them into the walls, smashing their skulls against the hard metal and leaving them in a heap on the ground.

"Who are you?" The Director said, backpedaling. "This is a secure area."

"Clearly, it isn't, ma'am," Ursin said.

The Director raised her hand, tapping a band on her wrist.

"Nobody can hear you," Trin said. "The signal's being jammed."

"What do you want?" Director Eagan said, straightening herself and pausing her retreat. "Are you with Tritium? How did you get clearance onto my station?"

"It's nothing personal, ma'am," Ursin said, though that wasn't completely true. Anyone who built weapons for the Republic was complicit.

"We require the access codes for the *Fire* and the *Brimstone's* command terminals," Trin said.

"What? How do you know they have key code access?"

Most ships used biometric access. Eyeballs. Fingerprints. DNA. All of it could be faked. Codes were old-fashioned, but they worked because of it. With a code, it could be one and done with no external prompting. You either entered the numbers you had memorized correctly the first time, or you lost access. Simple.

"You should pay your people what they're worth, ma'am," Ursin said. "They won't take classified intel to the highest bidder if you take better care of them."

"A mole?" she said, indignant. "What else did they sell you?"

"Enough," Trin replied. "Give me the codes."

"What makes you think I have them?"

"Don't you?" Trin reached out, grabbing the Director's wrist and squeezing hard enough that she cried out in pain. "I can make it bad for you. Very bad."

The Director registered fear for the first time. "You. You won't be able to use them. You'll never get on the ships."

"No, we won't, ma'am," Ursin agreed. "But you see, we don't need to get on the ships." He glanced over at Trin, who nodded. "Our people already are."

CHAPTER SEVEN

"ADMIRAL CORTEZ."

THE VICE ADMIRAL turned around at the sound of his name, searching for the source. He found it a moment later in the form of a bald, heavyset man in a tuxedo, still a few meters back but approaching quickly, a wry smile on his round face.

Cortez did his best to disguise his disappointment at the sight of the man, while at the same time wishing he hadn't reacted to his name in the first place. It would make it harder for him to escape from the clutches of Tritium Heavy Industries' favorite envoy.

"Mister Toyo," he said, putting on his bravest face. "I hadn't realized that Mars invited competitors to this event."

"To gloat, no doubt," the man replied, holding out his hand. Cortez took it, shaking firmly and trying to ignore the dampness. "Congratulations on your purchase of the Apocalypse fighters, by the way."

"I don't have to like you or the people you work for to recognize quality," Cortez said, his eyes darting past the man, searching for a way out.

Toyo laughed. "That's my favorite way of doing business, Emil. Continue to make the buyer uncomfortable until they place an order, if only to get my fat ass out of their face."

The way he said it gave Cortez a chill. As a man who had been in the business of war for more than half of his life, it was an achievement.

"Oh. It looks like the demonstration may be starting," Toyo said. "Curious. I didn't think Mars would play it on the sly like this. She loves to talk too much to show and then tell."

"What?" Cortez said, turning to face the large viewport that ran the length and width of the concourse. He found the stardock in the distance, noting the movement from the other side of it.

"Really, an interesting approach," Toyo continued. "Certainly more dramatic this way."

The rest of the assembly was beginning to notice the movement as well, the buzz amongst them slowly fading as they stopped talking to look.

There was definitely movement at the far end of the star dock, Cortez decided. He started angling away from Toyo toward the viewport, trying to get a better view.

The bow of a starship appeared behind the dock, sliding slowly into view, framed by Sol Three. It was long and narrow, and a little bit rounded, much sleeker than any of their current starship iterations. It was also larger, at least one and a half times the size of a current generation battleship. He watched it intently, waiting for the bow to turn into an island, eager for the full reveal.

He was so intent that he didn't notice the second, smaller ship that made its way around the stardock from the other side, moving much more quickly, turning to face toward the station.

The other guests did, and they pointed and gawked at the glimmering sliver of metal as it headed their way.

An alarm began to sound.

The volume of it shocked the crowd into sudden silence, leaving a stillness on the concourse that seemed to hang, thick and timeless, as the ship in front of them opened its gills in a strong breath, releasing a handful of projectiles on the exhale.

It took Admiral Cortez two heartbeats to realize that the starship was firing on them. He was moving by the third, running from his position near the viewport toward the nearest exit from the space.

What the hell was happening?

He made it a dozen steps before the ring began to shake, the missiles striking some part of the structure and detonating. The guests shouted and cried out in alarm, starting to move in the same direction as him, pushing and shoving one another in an effort to escape. The alarm tone grew louder, a mechanized voice urging people not to panic, to file out of the space in an orderly fashion.

"It's firing again," someone shouted. Someone who was looking back at the starship.

Admiral Cortez reached the steps leading to the promenade, looking back toward the viewport as his head cleared the onrushing crowd. He looked just in time to see a half dozen missiles detonate early, breaking apart and revealing hundreds of smaller warheads. Those missiles streaked past the viewport, moving perpendicular to the ring and heading directly for one of the spokes where the shuttles were docked.

The projectiles tore into it, small explosions flaring in the space beyond, the force of them punching into the spoke and the ships docked there. Something happened after the detonation, and a moment later the spoke and the ships began to crumble as though they had suffered from instant and complete molecular degradation.

Cortez cursed, continuing his exodus up the steps to the promenade. The ship was nearly on top of the station now, the sharp front of it showing no signs of diverting from a collision with the ring. The second, larger starship followed behind it, hanging further back like a protective parent.

"It's cutting off our escape," the officer next to Cortez said. He was a Republic Marine. He looked shocked and confused.

Cortez reached into his pocket, removing his communicator. He clicked it on, a projection of Commander Cusp appearing an instant later. The big Curlatin looked confused.

"Admiral," he said. "What's happening?"

"We're under attack," Cortez replied. "Organize the fleet, Commander. All ships are to target the Fire and the Brimstone and destroy or disable them. Do you understand?" He didn't know why the ships were attacking, but it didn't matter right now.

"Yes, sir," Cusp replied. "It will be done."

Cortez reached the promenade, one of the first to make it to the top of the steps. The exit was clear ahead of him, and he ran for it at full speed, thankful he had made an effort to stay in shape despite his years.

A fresh round of screams rose up behind him. He whirled in time to see the starship almost right on top of the concourse, no further than four or five kilometers away. A line of darkness creased it, creating the visage of a dark, open mouth from which a third volley of projectiles emerged, streaking directly toward them.

The missiles hit the glass two seconds later, detonating against it and breaking through, immediately activating emergency protocols. Cortez looked away as the first of the guests were pulled out into the vacuum of space, pushing himself toward the exit. A heavy blast door was sliding down ahead of it, attempting to seal off the section.

The Marine cut in front of him, stretching out and grabbing the door and pulling himself toward it. Cortez reached him, taking hold of his shoulder and using it to pull himself ahead. He ducked under the closing blast door, turning and starting to stretch his hand toward the Marine. Too late. The door closed, a small glass slit in the center revealing the complete death and destruction behind it.

"May God help them," Cortez said, returning to his communicator. "Commander, what is your status?"

"We have engaged the larger ship, the *Fire*, sir."

"And?"

"Our weapons are ineffective."

Cortez froze, leaning against the wall. "Excuse me, Commander?"

"I said our weapons are ineffective, sir. The *Fire* has some manner of energy shield or something. She's coming about on us, sir. She's firing. Oh. The *Chrysalis* is hit. An energy weapon, it tore her right in half. Sir, the *Brimstone* is floating broadside to the ring. You need to get out of there, sir."

Cortez started to run, heading down one of the spokes leading to the center spire. He wasn't sure exactly where he was going, but he wanted to get away from the enemy at his back.

Too late. The ring began to shake again, another round of fire slamming into it. The metal frame was creaking and groaning now, the damage to the structure causing it to begin coming apart. The warning sounds and lights continued to flash as he raced ahead. There was no sign of survivors behind him.

"Commander, target the *Brimstone*," Cortez ordered. "Fire at will."

"Aye, sir," Cusp replied. "Fire torpedos on my mark." Tense seconds passed. "Fire."

Cortez couldn't see any of what was happening. He reached the end of the corridor, where a small guard station with a sensor array was waiting. If there had been guards there before, they had already abandoned their posts.

"Negative, sir," Cusp reported. "Two direct torpedo hits and they didn't leave a scratch."

"No damage at all?" Cortez replied, incredulous. That was impossible.

He ran through the sensor, ignoring the warnings as it identified the contraband beneath his coat. He always carried a sidearm, but he had forgotten it was there. He made it to the next hatch, which opened at his approach.

"No, sir. None," Cusp replied. "We just lost the *North*, sir, and the *Faraday* is reporting critical damage. Their weapons are tearing us to pieces, sir."

An entire fleet against two starships and they were losing? This couldn't be happening.

The station shuddered again. A sharp, echoing crack followed by a heavy vibration knocked Cortez from his feet. He rolled over, looking back the way he had come. The hatch was closed, and there was nothing but open space behind it.

"Commander, what does the ring look like from your position?" Cortez asked.

There was no answer. Cortez picked up his communicator. His

connection to the battleship had been severed, and there was only one outcome to explain it.

He felt a spear of sadness and dismay in the pit of his stomach. His greatest nightmare was becoming real. He got to his feet and sprinted ahead through the corridors, still headed inward. The ring had been destroyed, but the spire was still intact.

For how long?

CHAPTER EIGHT

"DID YOU FINISH ALL OF your school work?" Abbey asked.

"Yes," Hayley replied. "I finished it ten minutes after I got home from school. It's boring."

They were sitting on a park bench. There was a lake in front of them, ringed with evergreen trees. Boats dotted the water, some modern and barely touching the surface, others in the classic, centuries-old style with tall masts and deep keels. It was warm and sunny, and there was a pleasant breeze blowing in from the east.

Abbey leaned back against the bench, enjoying the time she had to spend with her daughter. The last week had been a hard one for her, dominated by her efforts to crack the computer she had recovered and come up with some kind of answers to something.

She wasn't used to being stymied, but the encryption on the server she retrieved was atypical and locked down harder than anything she had run across before. She had spent hours upon hours in the lab during the *Nova's* return trip to the nearest Republic base on Gannai, cross-referencing the schema with known encryption methods, and even turning to the Worldbrain for assistance. Not only had she found few clues, but the more she had examined the device forensically, the more her instinct had told her the whole thing was a trick, and the storage had been irreversibly wiped.

In other words, the Outworlders, or General Kett, or both, had left it there to waste her time and distract the Republic from the real prize.

It wouldn't have been the first time.

"Mom," Hayley said. "Are you okay? You seem distracted."

Abbey looked over. Ten years old, tall and lean, her daughter was almost the spitting image of herself when she was that age, save for the extra six inches or so in height. She was a pretty girl, not exceptional, but cute enough that the boys in her classes knew she existed. She was also intelligent, displaying the same boredom with regular curriculum that had brought Abbey to the Republic Armed Services to begin with. Maybe it shouldn't have been a surprise, but Hayley wanted to be an HSOC, just like her mother. Abbey wasn't sure about the choice. It was hard, dangerous work, and her protective instinct ran strong. She was also dead set on not being the kind of mom that didn't support their child's decisions regardless of her own personal preferences.

"Sorry, Hal," she replied, sitting up again. "The last mission didn't go the way I was hoping, and it left me with a bit of a conundrum."

Hayley looked thoughtful. "Maybe I can help," she offered.

"You probably could," Abbey replied. "But you know I'm not allowed to tell you anything about it. Everything I do is classified."

Hayley nodded. "I know. Hey, do you want to walk a bit? Maybe that will help clear your head?"

"Okay," Abbey said, standing up. "Who's teaching you to be so grown up, anyway? Aunt Liv?"

"I am grown up," Hayley replied. "Age is a number."

Abbey laughed. Hayley laughed with her. They walked along the edge of the lake, watching the sailboats and chatting.

"How long can you stay?" Hayley asked.

Abbey checked the time. "Another hour or so. You?"

"Dad's going to be calling me for dinner soon, but I'll stay as long as I can."

"Thanks, kiddo," Abbey replied. "You know, I've got two months left and then I'll be coming back to Earth. We can see each other for real, all the time."

"I'm excited about it," Hayley said. "I can't wait to have you here. I feel like you've been talking about it forever, but now it's so close."

"I feel the same way. I love you."

"I love you, too, Mom."

She reached out and took her daughter's hand, holding it as they walked. It was a good moment. A perfect moment.

Too perfect.

"Lieutenant Cage," a voice said, tickling the back of her ear.

"Hayley, give me a second," Abbey said.

She motioned with her hand, freezing the construct, including her daughter's avatar. Then she reached up and removed the small band from in front of her eyes, returning herself to the *Nova*. The ship's CO, Commander Kyle Ng, was standing in front of her in the darkness of the construct module, arms folded behind his back.

"Commander," she said, saluting him. "How can I help you, sir?"

It was odd that he had come down in person instead of pinging her communicator, but not unheard of. The Commander was a fit man, and he always said he kept that way by harassing his subordinates in the flesh, walking five to ten kilometers a day to cover the area of the battleship.

"I need you to come with me, Lieutenant."

There was an edge to his voice that put her on alert.

"Is something wrong, sir?" she asked.

"Please. Just come with me."

"I need to say goodbye to my daughter, sir. One minute, please."

She reached for the eyeband. Commander Ng shook his head.

"Immediately, Lieutenant."

Abbey looked up, noticing the soldiers flanking the door to her construct module. Something was definitely wrong, and it sent a chill down her spine. She took the band from her head. She hoped Hayley would understand her sudden departure. It wasn't the first time she had been forced to leave without a word.

"What is this about, Commander?" she asked.

"I'll let Major Klixix fill you in," Ng replied.

Klixix? That was Plixian. Likely Military Police. What the hell was going on?

Abbey let the Commander lead her from the construct module, through the wide corridors of the *Nova* and down toward the hangar. The two soldiers walked behind her, nerve batons in their hands. She didn't recognize either of them personally, but she did recognize the insignia on the shoulders of their uniforms. They were MPs.

They reached the hangar. The hatch slid open ahead of them, and when it did Abbey immediately noticed that Sergeant Coli was there, along with the surviving members of the Fifth Platoon. An entire platoon of military police were surrounding them.

The Sergeant's face was grim, his large eyes downcast and ashamed.

"Sir?" she said, still feeling uncertain.

Her eyes danced across the space, passing over the half-dozen dropships hanging neatly in their launch cradles, sweeping past the five squadrons of starfighters magnetically clamped to the floor. A smaller ship was sitting beyond the platoon, wide and sharp, and bearing the marks of the Republic. There was a stack of equipment resting beside it, being carefully cataloged by a six-legged Plixian who scuttled over at her arrival.

"Lieutenant Abigail Cage?" she said, her voice high and tight through the translator. Even their best software often had trouble with the clicks and clacks the Plixian used as speech.

"Yes, ma'am," Abbey replied, recognizing the hardware on the uniform that covered Major Klixix's segmented torso.

She recognized the inventory the officer was examining as well. It was the arms cache from Gradin that Sergeant Coli claimed had mysteriously vanished.

Her eyes darted over to the Sergeant as she began to put the pieces together. Coli and his platoon had planned on stealing the cache, and likely selling it on the black market themselves. It was a haul that would have made their retirement from the service very, very comfortable.

"Ma'am," she said, relaxing at the thought.

The Major probably wanted to know what she knew about the situation. She wasn't a snitch, but it didn't look like she would have to be. Just the truth of the mission from her perspective would be more than enough.

"You are under derailment for the illegal removal of contraband weapons with the intent of sale," Klixix said. "You will hand over your communicator and any weapons you may be carrying immediately. Then you will bracket the members of Fifth Platoon for proxilation."

Abbey stared at the Major, her heart beginning to race. What? She was still as she replayed the words in her mind. The translator had fragged a few of them, but it was clear what Klixix meant. They believed she was involved in the theft?

"Ma'am, I think there's been a misunderstanding," she said.

"Protocol is clear in this matter," Major Klixix said. "If there is a curious it will be regarded during due process." She held out two of her four hands, composed of three long, narrow fingers and an opposable thumb.

Abbey reached up to the neckline of her utility uniform and unclasped the small, silver pin there, dropping the communication device into one of Klixix's hands.

"I'm not armed," she said.

There was nothing she could do about this. Not now. If they believed she had a part in any illegal activities, she had to believe there was a reason for it. One that she could help them straighten out. It was an inconvenience, nothing more.

Besides, if Breaker training had taught her anything, it was how to stay calm and composed in any circumstance.

Even the ones that were the least expected.

CHAPTER NINE

LIEUTENANT ERLAN KRAG EASED HIS GRB forward, careful to maneuver around the debris instead of smacking into it. It was as essential that the evidence remained as unadulterated as possible, even while it was impossible to keep it all that way. The field was just too thick, the damage too complete.

"It's hard to believe there used to be two stations here," Lieutenant Jesop said. She was in the GRB a kilometer away, also picking through the wreckage.

He reached out with one of the ship's articulating arms, gently catching a larger piece of detritus in it, rotating it over and catching a snap of it before pushing it into a container at the rear of the vessel. There was a reason the GRB were more affectionately called 'grabbers.'

"It's hard to believe the fragging Outworlders managed to get this far into Republic space without being blown to shit," Krag replied.

He fixed his eyes further out in the field, where red and white painted GRBs were collecting bodies instead of evidence. There had been too many bodies. Way too many. Every time he thought about it or looked at the retrieval ships, he started to feel sick.

He was a native of Feru, the planet that Eagan Heavyworks had terraformed to help support the star dock and the ring station that orbited it. He had grown up with a view of the two stations in the sky, and as a lifeline to the colony they had been admired and revered. So had Mars Eagan. It was numbing to think that it was all gone. It was chilling to know that Mrs. Eagan was dead and that her legacy might die with her. As far as Erlan knew, the Director had little family. Just a Board who would likely wind up squabbling over what was left of the company.

If there was anything left to squabble over. Building two unstoppable starships and then allowing them to fall into enemy hands wasn't exactly good for business. And if Eagan Heavyworks went out of business, Feru was surely going to suffer as well.

"What's the count up to?" Jesop asked, her GRB crossing beyond his as she maneuvered toward a larger piece of debris.

"I've got ten, right now."

"I mean the casualties."

"Last I saw, it was over four thousand," he said. "I heard Ensign Polk lost half his family."

"I used to think space was beautiful," she replied sadly. "It isn't so beautiful today."

Krag scanned the horizon. The debris stretched as far as he could see. Thousands of kilometers and still expanding. It wasn't just the two stations. Fourteen Republic ships had been destroyed by the *Fire* and the *Brimstone*. Hundreds and hundreds of soldiers who he was certain hadn't expected to die so far from the Fringe.

His mother always told him he needed to make the most of his life because death could come from anywhere at anytime. It had never been more true.

"GRB Squadron Alpha," their commanding officer, Major Tow said. "We have communication from the Republic. They have ships inbound to assist with the investigation."

"Roger," Erlan said.

"Roger," Jesop said. "It'll be nice to get some help with this."

It would take months to get operations on the planet back to whatever the new normal was going to be. The Republic investigators would no doubt want to scour whatever they could to get more information about specifically who was behind the attack, and even once that was done they had to get the debris away from orbit if they were going to get any resupply or traders in. While most modern ships had shielding to protect from space junk, it burned a lot of energy and tended to make their captains pissed to have to use.

"I'm thinking about quitting the militia and enlisting formally with the Republic," Erlan said, the thought striking him suddenly.

"You want to leave Feru?"

"I want to see the bastards who did this pay."

"So do I, but the colony needs us more than ever now, don't you think? So many people lost so many people. I'd feel like I'm abandoning them."

Erlan considered. "Maybe. I'm just not sure how to handle this. I can't look out the viewport without feeling sick."

"Me neither, but somebody has to do this. At least you aren't collecting the corpses."

He couldn't argue with that. He had known a lot of the Heavyworks employees personally. A good portion of them would come down from the ring on off days, preferring the real outdoors to the constructs. Director Eagan even had a house overlooking the Feruvian Sea. To have to pick at their cold, lifeless bodies with an even colder metal arm? He didn't envy the retrieval crews, who until today had only rarely needed to recover a body from the grip of the universe.

A reflection further out caught his attention. A piece of debris that was larger than anything else he had captured so far.

"I'm going to head out that way," he said. "It looks like there might be a piece of the spire."

"Roger," Jesop said. "I see it. Do you want help with it?"

Erlan stared out at the reflective metal in the distance. "That might be a good idea. It looks big enough from here, and it's a good two hundred klicks out."

"Roger."

The two GRBs turned and headed toward the debris, small puffs of air constantly correcting their course and skirting them around the other damage. Smaller bits of matter smacked against the ship's shields, which in turn redirected it away from the hull or disintegrated it completely.

They approached their target slowly, watching it expand as they moved closer. They were halfway to it when it began to take on a more solid shape, changing from a lump of glimmering metal to something more defined.

Something intact.

"Feru Actual," Erlan said, feeling his heartbeat increasing in tempo. "Do you read me?"

"I read you, GRB Three," Major Tow said. "What's your status?"

"Sir, GRB Four and me are investigating a piece of debris we eyeballed at three hundred klicks." He paused, staring at the wreckage, confirming it was what he thought it was. "It appears to be the shuttle from Ring Station Feru. Sir, it appears to be undamaged."

"Roger, GRB Three. Have you scanned it?"

"Not yet, sir. We're approaching now."

"I'm dispatching an EMS to you in support, just in case."

"Yes, sir."

Erlan brought his GRB closer to the shuttle, while an emergency medical ship navigated its way toward them through the field. When he was within ten kilometers, he activated his scanning equipment.

A red beam pierced the black, sweeping along the length of the shuttle. Diagnostic information began flowing back as the GRB floated parallel to the craft, locking into a synchronous rotation with it.

Erlan watched the data stream into the terminal at the front of the ship. A summary of the diagnostics appeared a moment later.

Power: online.

Gravity: online.

Life support: online.

Life signs detected: 1.

CHAPTER TEN

"WHAT THE FRAG DID YOU do?" Abbey said, staring across the aisle at Sergeant Coli. "You told me the weapons were gone."

Coli was ignoring her, the same way he had been since Major Klixix and the MPs had picked them up and pulled them from the *Nova*, transferring them to the planet Belis, to a semi-comfortable facility she had heard the military police refer to as "Purgatory."

"Damn it, you hairy piece of shit; you've been pretending you can't hear me for days. I want some fragging answers, and I want them now."

She stood at the edge of her cell, wishing she could reach across to where the Curlatin was sitting less than three meters away.

"My tour is up in two months," she said. "Two damned months. I'm going home to my daughter. Do you understand that? She's waiting for me to come home."

Coli didn't reply. He continued staring at the ground, motionless.

Abbey stepped back, her entire body tense with her frustration. He wasn't listening to her. Damn it; nobody was listening to her. Even Major Klixix hadn't bothered to give her five minutes to hear her out during the six-day transfer.

"Frag. Why the hell did I volunteer for a job with your shit outfit?" she said, somewhat quietly.

"Hey, Lieutenant," Private Illiard said from his cell a few rows down. "I get that you're pissed, but I resent that accusation."

"Did you take the emgees to sell them on the black market?" she said, turning to look at the soldier.

Illiard didn't say anything. He wasn't about to confess. His reply was a resigned shrug. It was as much of an admission of guilt as she needed.

"Then my statement stands," she said.

She should have been back on the *Nova* by now. A quick round of questioning and the truth would set her free.

Wouldn't it?

She had believed it at first, but now she was starting to have her doubts. They had been brought here with hardly a word, stuck into confinement together while they waited for what, exactly? How could the Republic be treating her this way? She had given almost twelve years of her life to them. She was one of their top Breakers. It didn't make any sense.

She paced her cell, a four-meter square box with a mattress and a hatch in the rear that led to a private toilet. She could prove she was innocent. She had been trying to break the compound's network while the Fifth had allegedly been loading up a hidden storage compartment in the dropship, and she had the timestamps to prove it. Only they wouldn't let her prove it, despite her repeated requests. Guilty until proven innocent. She had already been judged by association, and it was driving her insane.

Sergeant Coli's silence didn't help. Every time she looked at him, she wanted to punch him in his teddy bear face.

The door at the end of the cell block slid open. Major Klixix scuttled in, her legs making a rapid clacking sound on the hard floor. She had another person behind her, a large man in a fancy suit. They both stopped in front of Abbey's cell.

"Major," Abbey said, coming to attention and saluting.

"At ease, Lieutenant," Klixix replied. "This is Mr. Davis. He's here to ask questions. Given your insistence that you had nothing to do with the attempted theft, he desires to speak to you forthwith."

Abbey could feel the tension begin to drain. Finally!

"Mr. Davis," Abbey said. "Thank you for coming."

Davis stared at her with dark eyes and a flat expression. "Save your thanks, Lieutenant. Depending on how you answer my questions, you may not be grateful when we're done."

The chill returned to her as instantly as it had faded. What the hell was that supposed to mean?

Klixix stepped on a small panel at the base of the cell, and the containment field around it dropped. Abbey stepped out, making sure to keep glaring at Coli. Not that he was going to look at her. The only thing worse than a criminal was a spineless criminal.

"Spot you later, Lieutenant," Illiard said as Davis led her from the room.

An MP joined them on the other side of the door, following behind her as she trailed Davis away from the cells. Major Klixix didn't join them, heading off down an adjacent corridor, probably back to her office.

"Mr. Davis," Abbey said. "This whole thing has been a huge misunderstanding. I-"

Davis put his hand up without turning around. "I'll ask the questions. You'll answer them. Are we clear, Lieutenant?"

Some choice words filled Abbey's head, but she decided to keep them to herself. Getting on the investigator's bad side wouldn't help her cause any.

"Yes, sir," she replied.

Davis brought her to a new room, with a small mirror, a simple table, and a chair. An interrogation room. Why? Did they really consider her a threat?

"Have a seat, Lieutenant," Davis said, motioning to the chair.

She sat without argument. This wasn't the time to lose her cool or to panic. Her training had taught her to stay calm in any circumstance. Of course, having the end of a gun pointed right at her face had been less unnerving than this. If she died in the line of duty, her daughter would get a nice dispensation, enough that she could get into any profession she wanted. If she was incarcerated? It would all go away. Everything she had worked for. Everything she had earned and saved. Gone.

Mr. Davis sat opposite her. He produced a folded mat from his pocket and then flattened it out on the table. A projection rose from it. She recognized the snap. She had taken it.

"The armaments in question," Davis said. "You provided this image."

"Yes, sir."

"You gave it to Sergeant Coli?"

"No, sir. I offered it to him as evidence of the munitions cache. He told me he hadn't seen a cache. I didn't understand why at the time. Now I do."

Davis looked considerate for a moment. Good. At least she was getting a chance to explain. They couldn't pin anything on her. She hadn't done anything.

"How did you come to be on the *Nova*, Lieutenant?" Davis asked.

"Standard HSOC procedure. My prior deployment ended, and after my week of rec time, I returned to the SpecNet to put in for a new deployment. I saw the *Nova* was asking for a Breaker for some work near the Fringe."

"There were seven companies requesting a Breaker at the time. Why did you choose the *Nova*?"

Abbey didn't answer right away. Her feelings on General Kett didn't line up with most of the Republic. They wanted to scapegoat him for all of their failures. It was easier that way.

"I was looking for a detail that would put me in a dropship," she replied. "If you look at my record, you'll see I'm not the type of Breaker who wants to sit on a battleship and stare at a projection."

Davis showed his first sign of emotion, cracking the smallest of smiles. "No, you aren't, are you?" He waved his hand over the mat, bringing up her file and flipping through it. "Your dossier is impressive. Very impressive. Even so, Lieutenant, I have to wonder what your interest is in General Sylvan Kett?"

"What do you mean?" The question took her off guard, leaving her feeling defensive. They knew?

Davis touched the edge of the mat, and a new projection appeared. It looked like a recording of a session she had in a construct module.

"I'm telling you, Liv," Abbey said on the recording, sitting a table with her sister in a fancy restaurant. "The Republic is looking the wrong way on this. Maybe Kett broke a few rules, but none of the evidence points to treason. Hell, his actions on Kyron saved an entire population center."

"You recorded my construct session?" Abbey said, fighting harder to contain her anger. "That's supposed to be confidential."

"The Republic reserves the right to surveil the activities of any and all of its people at any time. Especially Breakers who are sympathizing with the enemy."

"Sympathizing?" Abbey said, her ability to contain her anger vanishing as she stood up, violently pushing her chair back. "Sympathizing? A Breaker's job is to unlock things. Doors, computers, networks, you name it. Oh, and the truth. That isn't sympathy; that's justice. That's right."

"Right, or righteousness, Lieutenant?" Davis said, remaining calm. "The Republic offers some degree of freedom to its highly specialized operatives. You get a choice to your work, unlike most of your fellow soldiers. We've found that it improves performance across the board, and keeps our best returning our investment in them for years to come. It seems, however, that you've decided to take advantage of that freedom to settle your own personal interests, namely in General Kett, an enemy of the Republic. Am I wrong?"

Abbey stared at Davis; her hands clenched tightly. The shitty part of it was that Davis wasn't wrong. She had used her freedom to satisfy her curiosity. Not that it had gotten her anywhere.

"What does this have to do with the weapons?" she asked. "I just joined the Fifth two weeks ago. You can't possibly think I have anything to do with Sergeant Coli's actions? The hidden compartment on the dropship would have taken longer than that to make."

"Normally, I would agree with you, Lieutenant. Under regular circumstances, you would already be free to go."

"Except?"

"Except those arms were intended to be picked up by General Kett's people. And the server you recovered also belonged to the General. I'm very interested in why you haven't been able to break it. I've read your file top to bottom, Lieutenant. It appears that has never happened to you before."

Abbey closed her eyes. This couldn't be happening. She took a pair of long, deep breaths, and then retrieved her chair from behind her. She pulled it back to the table and sat down.

"The memory on the server was erased," she said. "I've been trying to piece it back together, but whatever algorithm they used has to be new. As far as I know, it isn't illegal for me to have a different opinion than the Republic Council. I've served loyally and to the best of my abilities for the last six years."

"Six years," Davis said. "Do you know what the average enlistment period for an HSOC is?"

"No, sir."

"Twenty-two years, Lieutenant. And that's including the operatives who die in the line of duty."

"Is that what this is about? My service time? I have a daughter. She's ten years old, and I've spent four EW per year in her actual presence. I've already missed so much; I don't want to miss everything. I never asked for anything. I never complained. I never let it affect my work. I accepted the responsibility and did what I had to do, and I have every intention of rejoining when she's an adult. Not that it should have anything to do with this discussion. You seem to be aggregating three distinct circumstances into a single conclusion, Mr. Davis, a single, completely wrong conclusion, and I resent that."

Davis leaned back in his seat for a moment. Then he reached forward and collected the mat, folding it closed and putting it back in his pocket. He stood up and walked over to the door.

"We're done here, Lieutenant," he said. "Thank you for your time."

Then he left.

Abbey stared at the door, mixed emotions flooding through her.

Did she just save herself?
Or damn herself?

CHAPTER ELEVEN

CAPTAIN OLUS MANN FELT HIS entire body turn cold the moment the *Driver* came out of FTL in the space beyond the planet Feru.

He had been told what to expect.

It hadn't helped.

"My God," he said.

While the planetary militia had sent crews out following the attack to begin collecting evidence and retrieving the bodies, a heavy field of debris remained trapped in the planet's orbit, a testament to the destruction that had occurred four days prior.

"Contact Planetary Command."

"Aye, sir," the communications officer, Ensign Korlov replied.

A projection appeared in the open space ahead of the bridge crew a moment later. Olus was surprised to see a Trover standing there, his three-meter, muscular frame threatening to tear right through his simple gray uniform.

"My name is Captain Olus Mann," Olus said, diverting attention away from the ship's commander, Usiari. "I've been appointed by the Republic Council to investigate the attack on Feru and the theft of the *Fire* and the *Brimstone*."

"Captain Mann," the Trover said, saluting with a hand that could wrap around his entire head. "Major Tow."

It took Olus a moment to remember that Trovers only had one name, typically translated into short, simple words. It wasn't a problem in most of the galaxy, where Trovers were still somewhat rare, but he had often wondered how anyone held a decent conversation with one on their homeworld, where a room full could lead to five or six of them responding to the same address.

"Captain," Major Tow said. "Welcome to Feru. Thank you for coming so quickly."

"This is a matter of Republic security," Olus replied. "I wish I could have gotten here sooner. How is she?"

"Director Eagan? She is recovering well from her ordeal."

"I'd like to speak with her as soon as I make landfall."

"I expected you would, Captain. She has already expressed a strong desire to speak with you as well, and have these criminals brought to justice. I'll have an escort awaiting your arrival at the star port."

"Thank you, Major. Mann out."

The projection vanished. Olus turned to Commander Usiari. "I'll need a shuttle."

"Of course, Captain," Usiari replied. "It will be ready by the time you reach the hangar."

"Thank you."

Olus looked out the viewport one more time before retreating from the bridge, headed for the hangar and the shuttle that would bring him down to Feru. He had read the reports, of course, but being here? Being here made it more real, and he could feel his anger growing. The Outworlds had been a problem for a long time, and by stealing the two prototype warships they had made a full-on declaration of war.

Of course, the Republic couldn't rush headlong into all-out war. Not now. Not when they had yet to prove it was the Outworlders who had taken the ships. Not when, if they had, they were now in control of weapons that could destroy an entire fleet singlehandedly. They had to be smart about their response. Clandestine. Underhanded. To fight fire with fire.

That was why the Committee had contacted him directly, their orders simple and straight to the point:

Recover the ships and kill the bastards who stole them.

He didn't offer any instructions on how to achieve that goal, nor would he. As the Director of the Office of Strategic Intelligence, it was up to Olus to figure it out and figure it out quickly. He would have full autonomy in the matter, with every resource in the Republic at his disposal, but it was imperative that he keep the operation top secret and that the Council, the Committee, and the military at large maintain plausible deniability.

In other words, he was on his own, and the Republic would sooner disavow him than risk further provoking the Outworlds. At least not until they were ready to do so on their own terms. At least not until the *Fire* and the *Brimstone* were accounted for.

First, he had to discover who was behind the attack. Right now the only lead he had was its sole survivor, the Director of Eagan Heavyworks, Mars Eagan. The fact that she had survived when nothing else had, including an entire fleet of armed starships, had raised alarms in his mind the moment he had heard the news. He didn't trust it. He didn't trust her. Which was why he had decided to go right to the source.

After that?

He had an idea for after that. One that the Council would probably blow up over if they ever found out about it.

Which they wouldn't.

The operation didn't exist.

CHAPTER TWELVE

TWO MEMBERS OF MAJOR TOW'S team were waiting when Olus arrived in Feru's spaceport. The Major surprised him by having the foresight to send the pair of grabber pilots who had found Director Eagan to escort him, giving him a chance to question them directly about the recovery.

The trip to the Eagan estate was the perfect opportunity for that, a ten minute atmospheric shuttle ride across the Feru countryside that would have otherwise left him more annoyed than he already was.

While the Major had been smart to give him the Lieutenants, he had been stupid to let the woman go back home. Olus wasn't going to rule her out as a suspect, and Tow shouldn't have either.

"Tell me how you came across the shuttle," he said, talking to the male pilot, Erlan.

"There isn't much to tell, sir," Erlan replied. "We were doing routine collection, picking up larger pieces of debris that looked like they might have damage marks on them, and scanning for bodies for EMS to recover. I noticed the reflection of Sol Three on the shuttle's hull. Of course, I didn't know it was a shuttle at the time. Anyway, I went to investigate. Lieutenant Jesop came with me."

Olus glanced at the other pilot, a pretty woman with blonde hair and a kind face. "And when you got close to the shuttle you recognized it immediately?"

"Yes, sir," she said. "We've gone by the ring station at least a thousand times. It was always sitting at the bottom, just in case."

"We picked up the life sign and Major Tow sent an EMS in to check it out. We didn't know Director Eagan was inside for a good twenty minutes after that, when the EMS boarded and found her."

"Was she awake when she was discovered?"

"No, sir. I've heard she was drugged. Knocked out on purpose."

Olus had read the same in his report. The single truth led to so many questions, but the foremost was always: why did they let her live, when everyone else died?

"We haven't really heard much about it since then, sir," Erlan said. "We've been scouring the field for the last four days, and I think all the bodies have been collected. Are you planning to look at the debris while you're here?"

He wasn't, but he nodded. They had put too much time and energy into the process for him to tell them it had been to help keep the colony focused, not because there was any forensic data for them to recover. They already knew what had happened.

"How well do you know Director Eagan?" he asked.

Erlan smiled. "Everyone on Feru knows Mrs. Eagan," he said. "She's the reason we're here. The colony supports the Heavyworks, and the Heavyworks supports the colony. I heard she was planning to rebuild."

Olus raised an eyebrow. "Oh? I didn't realize anyone had spoken to the Director."

"Word is she's been busy since she was released from Medical," Erlan said. "Always meeting with someone or another."

Olus grimaced. Why wasn't that in the report? If Mars Eagan was up to no good, she had all the time and opportunity in the world to capitalize on it.

He didn't ask the two pilots any more questions, preferring to stare out the window of the shuttle for the last few minutes of the trip. Feru was an interesting planet, a heavy mix of rocky terrain and thick vegetation that gave it a more exotic appearance than it deserved. The Eagan estate was in the middle of that, perched on a cliff overlooking a high waterfall that fed into the sea. It was in a classical style, square and stone and angled, with a large shuttle pad on the top of the highest tower.

That was where they landed. A younger woman in a crisp suit was waiting as Olus stepped out of the shuttle, putting her hand out as he approached.

"Captain Mann," she said.

He accepted the hand. Her grip was firm. "Miss?"

"Eagan," she replied, smiling. "Emily Eagan."

"Mars doesn't have any children," Olus said.

"I'm not her daughter," she replied. "I'm her wife."

Olus had imagined Mars' spouse would be the same age as Mars. He chided himself for not digging into her file more deeply.

"My apologies, Mrs. Eagan," he said.

"Don't worry about it. It happens a lot with off worlders, and I'm sure you've had little enough time to study family trees. What happened here is beyond tragic, and both Mars and I will do anything we can to help you get our property back."

"Your property?" Olus said.

"Of course. The *Fire* and *Brimstone* belong to Eagan Heavyworks."

"Not anymore. The articles are quite clear on situations like this. Once recovered, they'll become evidence, and as such will be legal property of the Republic."

"No offense, Captain, but the *Fire* and the *Brimstone* contain a raft of new, proprietary technology. Turning them over to the Republic is like asking for our IP to be stolen."

"No offense, Mrs. Eagan, but it already was stolen. From what I have read, it is most likely because of the lax security surrounding the Heavyworks."

Emily Eagan's face flushed. She bit her lip, likely to keep herself from saying something crude. Then she turned and waved him forward. "Follow me."

He did, letting her lead him in silence from the landing pad down into the estate. They navigated a few gaudily decorated corridors until they came to a pair of heavy, ornately carved wooden doors.

"Beautiful," Olus said, breaking his silence.

"They're from Terra," Emily replied. "Nineteenth Century."

Olus put his hand on one of them. He had never felt real wood from Earth before. "They probably cost more than a Republic battleship," he said.

"More than a dozen of them," she replied.

Her intentions weren't lost on him. She was trying to impress him with money, either to see if he could be bought or to see if he was afraid of the power Director Eagan could bring to bear against him if he weren't careful in his questioning.

It was a shame he didn't give a flying frag about her money or her power. He had been in the HSOC for over forty years. He had been in charge of the OSI for more than twenty. Maybe Mars thought she could threaten him. He hoped for her sake she didn't test that theory.

Emily pushed the door open enough for them to pass through, bringing him into a large sitting room. Mars Eagan was already seated on a large, cushioned chair, a tall glass of something in her hand. She stood as Olus entered.

"Captain Mann," she said, smiling as she took Emily's hand and accepted a kiss on the cheek. "Thank you for coming so quickly."

"It was only because of you," Olus replied sarcastically.

Mars laughed. "Cute, Captain. I had heard you have an interesting sense of humor."

"You've heard about me?"

"Of course. In my line of work, it doesn't pay to be uninformed."

"Then we have something in common."

"And yet you didn't know Emily was my wife."

Olus smiled. Of course she was listening in on him. "To err is human."

"And to forgive, divine," she replied.

"How are you feeling, Director Eagan?" Olus asked.

"Please, sit, Captain." She waved to the closest seat. "Emily, the

Captain and I require privacy."

"Yes, ma'am," Emily replied, retreating from the room.

Olus sat as he watched her go. "You have her well-trained."

"It's interesting what people will accept for money. A word from me, and she'll do anything I want. Anything, Captain."

The suggestion wasn't lost on him, but he didn't need to know.

"And power?"

"Power has to be earned."

"I appreciate your bluntness, so I'll return it with some of my own, Mrs. Eagan."

"Please, call me Mars. And before you say it, Captain, I'll put it forward for you. Being the only survivor of a terrorist attack makes me look guilty as sin, and because of that you think that maybe I am. Is that right?"

"Mars. Pretty much."

"Would you accept that this perception is precisely what the real perpetrators want?"

"I'm willing to accept anything."

"Then your next question is why."

"You're very astute. Did you go through HSOC training?"

"Please. I'll be two hundred and four years old in six weeks, Captain. I've been around long enough to know how this works."

"Stasis, or regen?" Olus asked. Humans were living longer than ever. Hell, he was almost seventy. Triple that was still a long, long time.

"Neither," she replied cryptically. "And also not relevant. What is relevant is that they wanted you wasting time bothering me while they get deeper into the Outworlds."

"Do you have proof of that?"

"No. Captain, I understand you're going to have me thoroughly investigated. I have no problem with that. In fact, I invite it. My house is your house, as they say. Send your people in, and my name will be cleared. But don't waste your personal, precious time targeting me. That's exactly what the real criminals, the real terrorists want. That's the only logical reason they left me alive."

"Not because you're working with them? I've gone over some of your records. The ring station didn't have much of a security force."

"Why should it? We're almost ten-thousand light years beyond the Outworld border, a border that your people are supposed to be protecting."

"You've never heard of corporate espionage?"

"Don't be ridiculous. I've got eyes and ears everywhere. The best defense is a good offense, is it not?"

"So they say. You saw the people who did this?"

"I saw two of them. Clearly, as they stole both ships and neither one of those perpetrators was on them, they didn't act alone."

"Clearly. What can you tell me about them?"

"Forget about that, Captain." She reached over to the table beside her, picking up a small, silver disc and tossing it to him. He caught it smoothly.

"What is it?" he asked.

"Lifestream," she said. "A recording of my life." She tapped her eye. "I cut out the important part for you and put it on that disc."

Olus smiled. "That's more than I was hoping for."

"I told you, I'll cooperate in any way I can, Captain. Do you have my personal communicator id?"

"No."

"It's on the disc. If you need to contact me with more questions, please do, but I expect that will be enough for you to start your investigation?"

"Okay," Olus said, getting back to his feet. "I see how you want to do this. My people will be in touch soon with follow-up requests. In the meantime, don't get too comfortable. If you're trying to hide something with your magnanimity, I'll figure it out."

"I have no doubt you would, if anything untoward was taking place. Those bastards killed thousands of my people, Captain. My family. I want them caught. I want them dead. And I want my ships back."

Olus caught her eyes with his for a moment. He didn't sense any dishonesty, but she wasn't the type of asshole he normally dealt with. He was willing to bet all of her lies had a ring of truth to them, and all of her truths were laced with lies.

"Thank you for this, Mars," he said. He started walking toward the ancient Earth doors, pausing halfway. "I forgot to ask you about the ships."

"What about them?"

"Everything. Defensive capabilities. Offensive capabilities. Weaknesses."

She smiled. "It's on the disc, Captain."

"Right. We'll be in touch."

Then he left.

He had somewhere else he needed to be.

CHAPTER THIRTEEN

THEY CAME THREE DAYS LATER, in the middle of the night.

At least, Abbey thought it was the middle of the night. It was difficult to be sure on the cell block, since there were no windows to look through. There was only the coming and going of the guards bringing them food and water, and Major Klixix and Mr. Davis taking each of the imprisoned members of the Fifth Platoon for questioning. None of them were gone very long, and when they came back they always looked more broken than when they left. Especially Sergeant Coli. Abbey had given up on trying to get him to talk to her. At times, she was tempted to give up on everything.

It was after lights out, so she knew it had to be some time during the night. She was awake, as she usually was until shortly before the lights came on again, going through a routine of exercises to keep her body fit while she challenged her mind by trying to work out new encryption algorithms. It was a habit she had gotten into during Breaker training, using it to memorize the countless different schemes that existed in the universe, from the Plixian ixilix-secure to the Rudin's niaisisisi-duplicator. It had worked, too, and now adding a new methodology was as simple as integrating it into the exercise a few times.

The lights went on too early, and were much, much brighter than usual. It was enough to both wake the Fifth and blind them at the same time, leaving all of them, including Abbey, with a sheet of white pulled over their eyes. She could hear the door open, and feel the energy field that held her drop. Then someone grabbed her arm, rewarded with a sharp elbow to the jaw for their effort before a second hand grabbed her, the two attackers holding her tight. She didn't know who they were or what their plan was, so she kept fighting, letting them give her balance while she lifted her legs and swung them sideways, catching one of her assailants in the gut. Her feet hit the tough shell of a battlesuit and she gave up. There was no point to even try, unarmed and wearing only a simple tank and pants.

"Lieutenant Cage, Stand down," Major Klixix said immediately following the decision.

"What the hell is this?" Private Illiard said. "Sarge?"

There was no sound from Coli.

"Take them," someone said. Abbey was pretty sure it was Mr. Davis.

Then something was draped over her head. Then she was being lifted and dragged away from her cell. She could hear the motion around the room, and she knew the same thing was happening to the others.

"Where are we going?" she said. "Major?"

"I'm sorry, Lieutenant," Klixix said. "You've been found guilty of treason. All of the members of Fifth Platoon have."

Abbey fell limp in the arms of the soldiers, her entire body first feeling a warm chill, and then falling completely numb. There was no thought to accompany it. No words to describe it. The emotions burned too quickly to capture in total. Fear. Anger. Sadness. Guilt. Hayley. She felt the tears spring to her eyes, suddenly thankful to have them covered so Mr. Davis wouldn't have the satisfaction of seeing them. What had just happened? How?

"Guilty?" she heard Illiard say. "How can we be guilty? What about a fragging trial?"

"Republic military code section ten fourteen, Private," she heard Davis say, his voice smug. "I'll paraphrase it so I don't confuse you, but you can look it up or ask someone smart like Lieutenant Cage later. It says that traitors don't get a fair trial, because they're sacks of shit and don't even deserve the air we're continuing to allow them to breathe."

He was enjoying himself, Abbey realized, the thought bringing some of the life back into her. The son of a bitch liked sending them away, sending her away, with little to no evidence of wrongdoing. Because he didn't like her? Because she wanted to be with her daughter?

She could feel the blood begin to flow through her body again. She licked her lips, tasting the tears that had run down to them. She had never been a quitter. She wasn't going to start now.

"Mr. Davis?" she said.

"You had your chance, Abbey," Davis said, not using her rank this time.

That was fine with her. She just wanted to know how close he was.

She jerked her arms, the speed of her reaction catching the soldiers holding her off-guard. They reached for her, but she ducked below them, somersaulting forward and to the right. She came up and threw her fist out, using her memory of Davis to guess his height, and gaining a satisfied smile as her fist cracked into his jaw.

She could hear him thump to the ground as Klixix grabbed her with four sharp hands, holding her until the guards could regain control.

"That wasn't wise, Lieutenant," the Major said.

"Frag you, too, Major," Abbey replied. "You're complicit in this mockery of justice. I hope you choke on your thorax."

"Wooo," Illiard shouted from the back. "You tell 'em, Lieutenant. Fragging shitholes."

The guards were extra-rough when they took her arms again, digging in hard enough she knew it would bruise. She didn't cry out.

"Screw you, too, Private," she said, instead.

"Anytime, anywhere," Illiard replied. "All you have to do is ask."

"Get Davis a medic," Klixix said. Abbey could sense the heat of the Major's face next to hers a moment later, and feel the thin hairs that surrounded the Plixian's face tickling her ear. "You knocked him unconscious. I'm sorry, Lieutenant. I tried to stand up for you. I did. He wouldn't hear it. I don't know why. There's no logic to this decision."

"Who the hell is he?" Abbey asked softly.

"I don't know. Someone from higher up in the chain, with clearance I will never have."

"Where are they taking us?"

"You know where they take traitors."

She did. It was almost enough to make her limp again.

"Cage," Mr. Davis said, his voice muffled. Hopefully she had cracked a few teeth, too. "I'd tell you that you would regret that, but there's nothing worse that I can do to you than what you're already on the docket for." He paused, groaning softly from the pain. "I'll see you in Hell, Cage."

CHAPTER FOURTEEN

THE SHIP THEY WERE DELIVERED on was a standard prison transport, composed of two rows of cells with heavy doors and only a small viewport out into the corridor between them, tucked at the edges of a long, flat, wide fuselage that hung behind a more comfortable wedge-shaped tug where the crew of the transport resided. There were no windows. There was hardly any light. It was a taste of what was to come. A small taste. An acclimation.

Abbey sat in the darkness of her cell, staring at the blank wall ahead of the mattress. The journey had given her a lot of time to think. Maybe too much time. The military had screwed her over. Davis had screwed her over. Was it really because of her plans to let her enlistment lapse so that she could go home to be with Hayley? Could the Republic really be that petty?

She had always been a loyal servant of their nation. A patriot. A believer. She had done her best to protect the Republic. To protect innocents from the Outworlders, and to help the Republic overcome the Outworlds, to bring law and peace and justice to the planets beyond the Fringe.

And now?

She was angry. Beyond angry. The Republic had used her and then thrown her away the moment she lost that usefulness. No, they had done more than throw her away. They had sent her away, to a place that she wouldn't have wished on her greatest enemy. A place that soldiers feared to wind up, even if some of them did. When your military was as large as the Republic's, it was no surprise to have some bad seeds in the bunch, regardless of the destination that awaited them.

She was afraid. She would have been stupid not to be. She had heard the stories. The rumors. She knew why the Republic sent people here. She knew what her life was going to become.

She should have been stuck in her despair, the way Sergeant Coli seemed to be. She couldn't see the Curlatin, but she could hear him from time to time, his high-pitched calls registering as crying in her translator. He was a mess. A pathetic mess. The most idiotic part of it all was that he was the cause of the whole damn thing. Or at least part of the cause. He was complicit, if not the ringleader, and she didn't feel sorry for him despite his whining. In fact, given the chance she still wanted to kick his fragging teeth in.

She should have been ready to lose hope, ready to fall apart, ready to die. She wasn't made that way. She had never given up, no matter how shitty things seemed to be. No matter what mistakes she made along the way. It wasn't in her to lie down. Especially now. Especially when Hayley was out there, surely wondering where her mother had gone. She had been cut off without a word. No goodbye. No I'm sorry. She knew the kid would understand. She was strong like her mom. That wasn't the point. They were trying to steal her family. They were trying to steal her spirit. They were trying to break her. It seemed fitting in a way.

She wasn't going to let them. If the only means she had to fight back was to keep her head up and her spirit intact, then that was what she was going to do. Frag them.

She sat up when she heard the sharp clang of the main tug detaching from the barge. The separation meant one of two things: either they had arrived or they were under attack and were being left to die. There was still a guard posted at the end of the corridor, so she had to assume it meant they had arrived.

Her heart began to thump a little faster, despite her earlier thoughts. She could be strong and still be afraid. Fear was strength when used the right way. She got to her feet, moving to the door to her cell and looking out. She could see fingers on a few of the other doors, and hear Coli begin another round of bitching.

The cries of the damned.

She stayed silent, backing away from the door. She didn't want to be the others. Not in any way. She was going to outlive them. Outlast them. She returned to her mattress and sat back down. The transport began to shiver as it hit the atmosphere. There would be a pilot at the back of the barge, guiding it down to the surface. He did an impressive job, and the shaking stopped within seconds. It felt almost as if they had been carried back up into space.

Another two minutes passed. Then she felt the slight force of the transport's inertia changing, the ship leveling out in its descent. The sound of thrusters grew louder, and the pressure from the anti-gravity coils increased.

So did the temperature.

The ship had heat shielding, of course. Either it wasn't powerful enough to block out the swelter, or the crew had opened the hold up to the outside air to allow it in. Another taste of what was to come? Either way, the interior of the ship went from comfortable to torrid within a matter of seconds, leaving Abbey sweating through her clothes.

Another minute passed. The ship's velocity slowed, and the heat faded away, replaced with a more temperate humidity. She heard the whine of the landing gear as it extended from the belly of the transport, and a moment later they touched down, the ship rocking slightly on the gear before coming to a rest. The lights in the corridor went on full-bore, causing her to squint her eyes. A hiss and groan as the main cargo hatch lowered at the rear. Soft clanks along the metal flooring signaling someone was coming in.

Then her door slid open. She stared at it for a second before getting back up and approaching it. She looked out toward the rear of the transport. A dozen guards in what looked like older-model battlesuits, the armor thicker and more bulky, the helmets wide. Tubes ran into them, suggesting they had some kind of climate control inside. They would need to. Even here, it was at least thirty-two degrees celsius, and still pretty humid.

One of the guards moved to the front of the line. His suit was slightly different, painted a darker navy. A small pop indicated that he had activated external speakers on the suit.

"My name is Warden Packard. I'd say it's nice to meet you, but you're all a bunch of shitbags and the truth is, I can barely stand the thought of looking at any of you. Even so, I'm going to give you orders, and I expect you to follow them. I want each of you out of your cells, standing single file in front of your cell. I want your hands at your sides. I want you to remain silent, still and at attention. Failure to comply will result in pain. Do you understand me?"

"Yes, sir," Abbey snapped, as loudly and sharply as she could.

She moved into the corridor, coming to stiff attention. The rest of the Fifth wasn't as prepared, and they eased out of their cells a disorganized mess.

"I see we have one real soldier in this bunch," Packard said, his helmet turning toward Abbey. "Private, grab that one." He pointed to Captain Yung. One of the soldiers moved forward and took him by the arm. "You all get one example because you're new here."

The soldier punched Yung in the gut, hard enough that Abbey could hear his ribs crack under the blow. Then he punched Yung in the face, breaking his jaw and knocking him to the floor. Abbey didn't move, holding herself at attention while the rest of the Fifth fell in line.

"Private, take him to medical," Packard said.

The soldier lifted Yung easily and carried him off the transport.

"That's better," Packard said, looking them over. Then he paused. "We seem to be missing one."

Abbey glanced around without turning her head. She noticed Coli wasn't in the line. She looked back at Packard. She couldn't see his face. She imagined he wasn't happy.

She didn't know if she was going to get another chance. There was a slim possibility the Warden might even thank her for it.

She burst ahead, breaking attention and rounding the corner into Coli's cell. The guards reacted immediately, falling into a defensive stance at first until they saw she wasn't coming their way. Then she lost sight of them, finding Coli on his mattress in the corner, head lowered into his folded arms. She almost felt sorry for him then. Almost.

He raised his head as she approached, just in time to catch her fist on the side of it. His head rocked to the side, and then he reached out for her, trying to grab her.

"You son of a bitch," she said, finally letting herself lose her temper. Finally getting the chance to act out on her anger and frustration. She hit him again, ducking away from is arms, coming in quick and punching him in the chest, and then the side. The blows were weak against a Curlatin without wearing a suit of any kind. She didn't care. She kept hitting him, cursing at him while she landing punch after punch, evading his too-slow defenses.

She could hear the guards coming up behind her. She saved the best for last, getting one good punch in at one of Coli's large round eyes, hitting the soft material and feeling it press in. Coli roared in pain, reaching up to hold the eye as the guards grabbed her from behind, throwing her backward and into the rear wall with enough force that it knocked the air out of her.

"Stay down," Packard said, standing above her as she tried to get up. "If you want to make it out of this ship with all of your bones intact."

She was tempted to test him. She was furious beyond words, beyond logic. She could see Coli holding his eye and howling.

"Get him to medical," Packard said. It took two guards to lift him by the arms and carry him away.

Abbey started to calm the minute Coli was out of her sight, her rapid heartbeat slowing. She stayed on the ground, motionless, waiting for Packard to speak.

"Cage, is it?" Packard said.

"Yes, sir," Abbey replied.

"Mr. Davis told me to keep an eye out for you. He said you're a firebrand. A real demon."

He bent down, grabbing her by the hair and pulling her to her feet before turning her around to face him. She could see his face behind the helmet, old and weathered and scarred. He smiled at her then, his teeth crooked and brown.

"We'll see how long that fire lasts down here. Welcome to Hell, Cage. You're going to be here for a long, long time."

CHAPTER FIFTEEN

HELL.

THE PLANET WAS THE site of one of humankind's first efforts at terraforming. It was an effort that only partially succeeded, leaving it with a breathable atmosphere, but turning it into a lifeless inferno in the process. The external temperatures remained above one hundred degrees at all times, making it impossible to live there. Instead, caverns had been bored underground - thousands of caverns that allowed the residents there to live like ants.

Why?

Because the interior of Hell was rich in all kinds of rare minerals, most importantly the disterium that enabled faster-than-light travel. That made it inherently valuable. Maybe the most valuable planet in the galaxy. Which also made it important to keep as a pretty good secret. That, in turn, meant that having paid employees mining the minerals was a less than optimal arrangement, which in turn meant having to source those workers from somewhere else.

And now Abbey was one of those workers. A miner in the pits of Hell, sentenced to a lifetime of hard labor until she died, either naturally or by finding a way to take her own life. It was illegal to sentence civilians to a place like Hell, but she wasn't a civilian. The military had their own rules, and those rules weren't always pretty.

She had never had a problem with what she had heard about Hell. Soldiers who broke the rules needed to be punished and the Republic needed the disterium to continue heading out among the stars and protecting all of the planets under its domain.

Then again, she had never planned to be one of the assholes incarcerated here.

Packard led her and the undamaged members of the Fifth out of the transport, down the ramp and into a large, rough hangar. It was nothing more than hollowed out stone with a grated metal floor. She lifted her arm and wiped her forehead, noting that it didn't do anything to reduce the sheen on her brow and deciding not to bother again. Her clothes were clinging to her skin, and it was more difficult to breathe. Damn the guards for their climate controlled suits.

In fact, everyone in the hangar was wearing a suit, though the mechanics and technicians were wearing something closer to a softsuit. They were cool and comfortable as could be, and she already hated them for it.

They were brought out of the hangar and into a large, metal lift. The guards surrounded them while it descended, keeping up the silence that had followed her altercation with Coli. It took nearly three minutes to reach the bottom, and while Abbey expected the temperature to decrease further from the surface, it actually seemed to get hotter.

She could tell the others were as uncomfortable as she was, and she was grateful for it. She hoped they burned down here. Lost hope. Killed themselves. Frag them.

The lift stopped. They filed out in a single column, the guards walking next to them. Packard stayed in front, beside her, keeping an eye on her until they were brought to a stop at the end of the corridor. Then Packard positioned himself between her and a heavy steel door with a biometric control pad on the side of it.

"Okay, you shitbags. Clothes come off." He looked at Abbey and smiled. "You too, darlin'."

She stared back at him as she pulled off her tank, keeping her eyes up when she bent to remove her pants and underwear. She heard a faint whistle from behind as she did.

Packard unlocked his eyes from her body, looking toward the back of the line. "Think you're funny?" he said, pointing. "I said the punishment for non-compliance was pain. I guess you like pain."

She didn't need to look to know it was Illiard who had whistled. She could tell by his grunts as the guards laid into him.

"Get him to medical," Packard said. Then he turned and put his palm on the control pad. The door slid open. "One at a time. You'll get cut, branded, and outfitted. You first, Cage."

She kept her eyes straight as she moved into the new room, taking in her surroundings. A small room. Simple. A chair. Another soldier in a climate-controlled suit.

"Have a seat," he said.

She moved to the chair, keeping her face straight as she sat. Somehow, the metal was cold despite the heat. The man approached, holding what looked like a cap of some kind. He put it on her head, pressed a button on the side of it, and then took it off. Her hair tumbled away from her onto her shoulders and chest. A few seconds later she felt a burning at the base of her skull. She was tempted to reach back to feel the area, but Packard had said branded, and that had to be the source of the pain.

"Stand up," the man said.

She did.

"Face me."

She did.

He was holding a red jumpsuit. No underwear. Just one piece of thin material. He held it out to her. She took it and put it on, feeling it stretch around her as she brought it up and put her arms in. The material merged as she brought it together in the front, creating a second skin around her. At least the genitals were padded. She didn't need everyone in Hell to get a full outline of her vagina, and she certainly didn't want a look at every male prisoner's package.

"Now that you've closed it, the material is coded to you," the tech said. "Only you can open it or take it off. It's safe to urinate in during the work shift, and a washer is provided in your cell to clean it. I recommend only removing it after lockdown. Head on to the next room. You'll be given your cell assignment and work orders."

She didn't need to ask why he was suggesting she stay in it until she was alone. She expected as much from a place like this. She followed his instructions, moving out of the room as the next victim entered. The second area was composed of a desk with a woman sitting behind it.

"Oh," she said when she saw Abbey. "We don't get too many females in here. You must be Cage?"

"Yes, ma'am," Abbey replied. Was this woman another one of Davis' cronies?

The woman looked down into one of the drawers and then lifted out a bracelet. "This one's yours," she said. "It will guide you to your cell."

"Instead of a guard?"

"Trust me, Miss Cage, once you have that on we won't need the guards."

Abbey took the bracelet and clasped it over her wrist. It beeped three times and then locked.

"If you try to move out of your assigned area, it'll deliver enough of a shock to knock out a Trover."

"Assigned area?"

She looked down at her desk. "Looks like you've been assigned to-" she paused and then looked at her. "Somebody out there must hate you."

Abbey felt her heart start to pound again. She swallowed the fear, focusing on keeping her face straight. "What do you mean?" she asked, as level as she could.

"Level Twenty," the woman said. "The deepest part of the pit. What did you do to deserve that?"

Abbey stared at the woman for a few seconds. The woman pushed her chair back, her eyes falling to Abbey's bracelet.

"I just give them out," she said. "G-G-G-Go through that door, it'll guide you from there."

A new door opened to her left. She turned on her heel and followed it out.

CHAPTER SIXTEEN

ABBEY TRAILED THE PROJECTION PROVIDED by the bracelet, walking behind a phantom figure of a guard through the corridors of the facility. It brought her directly to a second lift, equally large as the first, which left her in darkness when it closed and carried her down to Level Twenty. The deepest part of the pit. She would be mining disterium there.

For the rest of her life.

She tried not think about that. She had to live one second at a time or she wouldn't be able to live at all. She had to keep hope when everything told her she shouldn't, if only to get back at Mr. Davis and whoever had put him up to his bullshit.

The lift opened and dumped her out into a darker corridor than the last. It was at least another three or four degrees hotter down here, the air so thick she felt like she could hardly breathe. Of course, the Republic could use bots to mine this part of the pit, and all of the mines on Hell, but this was supposed to be a punishment as well as an operational enterprise. There was nothing punishing about letting machines do all of the work.

She kept following the projection. It brought her past other inmates who were also walking the halls. They kept their eyes down most of the time, but when they saw the newcomer, they glanced up. When they saw a woman, their eyes stayed that way, their expressions changing. How many women were down here anyway?

She was brought to a large, open area. The cell block. Nearly a hundred doors on each of a dozen floors, all arranged in a square around a central station, which rose up from the ground like a spike. Looking down, she could see a number of inmates sitting at tables at eating a thick wedge of something dark. Not all of them were human. She noticed a few other Curlatins, a couple of Plixians, a handful of Trovers, and even a Gant. That surprised her. She had never seen a Gant in person before. They rarely left their homeworld, and their enlistment numbers were already pretty low. To find one incarcerated down here?

Her bracelet buzzed slightly, sending a light shock into her arm. It stung a bit, reminding her to get moving. She did, following the projection up three flights of steps to a door at the corner of the block. It slid open at her approach, revealing a six-meter-square cell. There was a mattress, a toilet, a slim shower, and a small, square device which she assumed was the washer for her suit. She trailed the projection inside, at which point the door behind her closed, and it disappeared.

"Now what?" she said aloud.

A projection rose near the center of the room. Packard.

"Today is going to be the last easy day of your old life," he said. "Tomorrow, you'll begin your new one as a disterium miner. It's a difficult, thankless job, but then again, you're a murderous or traitorous shitbag, and you're lucky the Republic doesn't believe in wasting any of its resources. Don't worry that you have no idea what to do. Follow your bracelet, watch the others, and you'll figure it out soon enough."

The pre-recorded projection vanished. That was it?

The door to her cell opened again. Abbey looked at the bracelet. It wasn't giving her any directions. She moved to the door and looked out. She could see a number of the other cells were open, too. She looked over the edge, down to the tables below. Most of the inmates had finished eating and were just sitting. A few were talking, but most looked hollow and tired. Was that going to be her fate?

She headed back to the steps, taking them all the way down to the ground. Eighty heads turned toward her as she entered the area, every convict interested in the newcomer.

"Where do I get some food?" she asked, making eye contact with them. She knew better than to show any weakness.

"There," a Trover said, pointing to a small machine against the wall. "Touch your bracelet to it."

Abbey went to the machine. She could feel the eyes on her back as she did. How many of them were staring at her ass? She suddenly felt naked despite the suit. It was something she would have to learn to deal with.

She tapped her bracelet against the machine, and a single bar of dark brown material extended from the front. She took it and lifted it to her nose. She had expected something awful, but it didn't smell all that bad. She took a bite of it. It tasted pretty good. She turned around again, looking for a seat. She found one near the guard tower, next to the Gant.

The Gant was the only one in the room who hadn't stared at her. In fact, it hadn't looked at her at all. It's back was turned to her, facing the table. It was sitting alone, and hunched over it in a secretive way. She briefly considered finding another seat, but she had to make a statement that she wasn't afraid of anything about this place, even if she was afraid of all of it.

"Is anyone sitting here?" she asked, circling the table and sitting opposite the Gant.

It looked up at her. Most of it was covered by the red jail suit, but she almost smiled at the sight of its face. Gant bore a strong resemblance to an Earth mammal, the sloth, sharing a similar bone structure and fur pattern, although at a size that was about half of her own. It was holding a slim piece of bent metal between two fingers and two opposable thumbs, which it quickly tucked out of sight.

"Why did you just ask me if anyone was sitting here?" it said. "What was the point?"

She could make out the soft barking of its true voice behind her translator. It was almost cute. "I was being polite."

"Polite?" The bark turned into a chitter that her translator called laughter. "Look around, Greenie. Polite will last you about ten seconds down here. Besides, if you were being polite, you would have taken note of my body language, which was clearly suggestive to all comers that they should frag the hell off."

He stared at her, making an expression that she took as an attempt to look angry. Instead, it only made him look more cuddly.

"I've never met a Gant before," she said. "Are you male or female?"

"That's pretty forward of you, don't you think? We only just met and you're asking me questions like that? Polite? Do you even know what the word means? You want to know if I'm a boy or a girl? I'll show you mine if you show me yours."

He stuck his tongue out. It looked ridiculous, and she had to force herself not to laugh.

"You're amused?" it said. "Maybe you think because I'm small I can't keep up? You definitely don't know enough about Gants. Terrans don't call us space rabbits for nothing."

"Do you have a name?" Abbey asked, shifting the topic.

"It doesn't translate," he replied. "The rest of the losers down here just call me Gant. Now go away."

Abbey took another bite of the food bar. "I'm sitting here now," she said after she swallowed it. "You don't like it? You go away."

Gant hummed his amusement. "Fine. I don't need this kind of bullshit today." He stood up on the bench. "Watch your six, Greenie." Then he hopped down and wandered away.

Abbey watched him for a second before swiveling around on the bench. A group of inmates had gathered behind her, a Trover and three Terrans. She glanced up at the guard tower, noting that the guards had vanished from her sight.

"Hey, Greenie," the Trover said. "You're in my seat. You going to move, or do I have to move you?"

"Your seat? I don't see your name on it," Abbey replied. "Let me guess. It's Dik, isn't it?"

The Trover smiled. "A female on Level Twenty. Why am I not surprised you're a smart ass? You're new around here, so I'm going to give you a quick lesson in Level Twenty etiquette. Number one, on Level Twenty you get punished three ways: by the work, by the bracelet, and by my orders. Number two, I'm in charge down here, and I've got Packard's blessing to run this place how I see fit. That means if I want something, you give it to me, and nobody gets too hurt. You see, I could kill you, and the Warden wouldn't bat an eye. I wouldn't though. That would be the easy way out for you. Number three, if you earn my favor, I can get you things. Drugs. Vids. Extra food bars. Are you copacetic?"

"How did you get Packard's ear?" she asked. "Did you do him some favors?" She raised her eyebrow, her suggestive tone not lost in the translation.

He grunted. "Packard told me you were coming. He told me to rough you up a bit, one way or another. I do what he asks, and he looks the other way. That's how things are down here. Now, we can do this easy, or we can do this hard. I don't give a shit which."

Packard told this asshole to rough her up? She was willing to bet Davis had given that order to the Warden first. Was this really how it was going to be? She would rather get beaten than let him have the satisfaction.

She stood up on the bench. The rest of the cons had moved to the fringe of the room, sensing the oncoming altercation. "Come on then," she said. "Are you big enough to do it on your own?"

He smiled and moved forward without his lackeys, extending a long arm to grab her. She sidestepped it, reaching down and taking the huge forearm and bringing her knee up into it.

It bounced off like it was hitting steel, and the Trover laughed as he grabbed her arm with his free hand and pulled her from the bench, sending her sliding across the floor. The other inmates laughed at the move.

Abbey bounced up as the Trover charged, shoulder out to slam her back and into the wall. She rolled to the side, surprised at his agility as he stopped himself, bringing a leg up and spinning, catching her with his calf. The blow knocked her down again.

"I heard you were a Breaker up top," the Trover said. "Have you ever even been in a fight before?"

She heard murmurs from the other cons. They were probably wondering how a desk monkey wound up on Level Twenty.

She pushed herself up as the Trover approached. She couldn't hurt him one on one; she just wasn't strong enough. She shifted her eyes over to the food dispenser in the wall. What if a con tried to use their bracelet to get more than their allotment of food?

She ducked away from one punch, then another, rolling to the side, coming up and punching him in the bicep. It wouldn't hurt him, but it would keep him distracted while she backed toward the machine.

He followed, joining the dance as they traded blows. She was able to stay away from him as long as she didn't get too close, dodging his flailing appendages and leading him back. He was smiling at the workout, enjoying the challenge.

"You're a slippery little demon," he said, laughing.

She glanced back. She was getting close to the dispenser. Now she had to get him to touch his bracelet to it.

She ducked low, lining him up and waiting for him to punch.

Someone grabbed her from the side, pulling her away.

"I don't think so," the inmate said before throwing her back towards the center of the room.

Son. Of. A. Bitch.

She glared at the con in question, a younger, muscular Terran with an angled face, for a second before getting hit by the Trover again, his ham fist catching her in the ribs. She felt at least one of them crack as she was thrown backward, landing on the floor.

"Sneaky," he said, moving toward her.

She forced herself up despite the pain. It was so damn hot and hard to breathe, and she hated being here already. A new round of curses ran through her mind as she braced herself against the Trover's next attack, trying to move around him and finding her reactions slowed by the injury. It only took a few seconds for him to grab her again, and he pushed her to the floor, putting his weight on top of her.

"I can break your jaw, or you can open your suit," he said.

"Frag you," Abbey replied.

He punched her in the ribs, just hard enough to make them flare with fiery pain.

"Second chance," he said.

"Go to hell."

He punched her again.

"I'm already there. One more chance, Cage. I should tell you, medical will patch you up, but they don't care if they do it right. You want to live down here with chronic pain on top of this bullshit heat? Or do you want to just let me do what I was told?"

"Until Packard orders you to do it again."

"We're all living minute to minute down here. It isn't personal."

"Greenie."

Both Abbey and the Trover looked to the side, where Gant was standing. He bent down, sliding the metal he had been playing with across the floor, right into her waiting hand.

She took it, looking back at the Trover at the same time he looked at her.

Then she brought it up into his eye.

Deep into his eye.

He froze, looking down at her with his remaining eye, suddenly confused. The weight on her grew heavier, and she cursed as she pushed him off. He rolled away, still alive and awake, but barely alert.

"That's fragging cheating," one of his lackeys said. The three of them were coming toward her.

She struggled to get to her feet.

"He cheated first," Gant said, moving to stand at her side, pointing at the man who had pulled her away from the machine.

"I didn't do anything," the man said.

The guards suddenly reappeared at the windows to the tower, and a red light began to flash.

"Better get back to your cell, Greenie," Gant said. "Packard's going to be down here, and he isn't going to be happy."

"Why did you help me?" she asked.

He chittered in laughter again. "Just trying to be polite."

Then he left with the rest of the cons. Abbey wasn't far behind.

CHAPTER SEVENTEEN

THE BOTS IN MEDICAL DID a pretty good job of patching the cracked ribs, but then again the injury wasn't too serious. The Trover, Pok, as Abbey learned his name was, didn't fare as well, suffering from a brain hemorrhage that wound up killing him. In another place he probably would have been saved, but the damage had been done and he was never going to work again, so they just let him go.

Initially, Abbey expected that she would be punished for killing him. It was a perfect excuse for Packard to inflict more pain on her. He didn't. He never said anything about it at all, and nobody came for her. She didn't feel bad about doing it, either. She wanted to make a statement, and with Gant's help she had.

Losing Pok did create a bit of a power vacuum on Level Twenty, one that Abbey was forced to navigate without knowing much at all about how the pecking order worked in the deepest pit of Hell. There were a few fights, all of them broken up by shocks from the bracelet, visits from Packard, and plenty of broken bones and bruises. There were a couple of inmates killed. She stayed out of it, keeping to herself for the most part, working the mines during her shift and sitting by herself in her cell afterward. The other cons didn't bother her. They didn't even talk to her, except for Gant. It seemed that by siding with him, she had excluded herself from every other circle.

She was okay with that. Gant was crude, but he was also the smartest individual on the level by a long mile. He made things out of the bits and pieces of material he managed to squirrel away under his hellsuit or stuff into his cheeks. He had a whole collection of weapons hidden within the circuitry of his washer, where the guards would never find them. For what purpose? He didn't even know, or if he did he wouldn't say.

There was no relief from the heat. No relief from the heaviness. Working in the mines only made it worse. They had laser cutters to dig into the rock, but then they had to lift the chunks out and break them by hand, carefully so that they wouldn't damage the disterium within. It was grueling work. Not even as much physically as she had expected, but mentally. It took patience to get the crystalline material out unharmed. As much as she hated doing it, that aspect made her good at it.

She could feel herself wilting under the oppression. She could sense her hope trickling away, diminishing day by day, hour by hour. This was going to be the rest her life, and she was only thirty-one in a time when even the poorest Terrans lived into their early hundreds. She was sure she wouldn't last that long down here, but ten years? Twenty years? She had been here for three weeks and she was starting to give in. She had caught herself crying at the end of her shift the other night, sitting alone and naked in her cell while her hellsuit was wiped clean of the dirt and sweat and urine that accumulated within. She missed Hayley. She missed the sky, the stars, the light. She missed cool air, normal uniforms, and freedom.

All of her earlier thoughts about staying strong to prove something to Davis seemed so stupid now. Maybe she could hold out for a few months, but then what? Whatever the game was, he had won it. She knew herself well enough to know she would break eventually.

She picked up her cutter. It was an old thing, dented and rusted. It didn't put out enough power for her to harm herself with it before the bracelet would shock her unconscious, though she had heard plenty of inmates tried. She carried it from the staging room out into the mine, making the long walk along three kilometers of tunnels to her assigned section. Gant had worked beside her for the first couple of weeks, but Packard had noticed they were getting chummy and had changed the Gant's shift, forcing them to work opposite. Now she found herself setting up beside Private Illiard.

"Lieutenant," he said mockingly as she put the cutter down and put on her work gloves. "What's a nice girl like you doing in a place like this?"

Abbey glared at him. She hadn't seen him since their first day in Hell. "Did you just get out of medical?" she asked.

"Yup. It took a while for the mechanicals to reassemble all of my broken bones, and for the healing agents to knit them back together. I still have pain in my ankles when I walk."

"Do you want to go back?"

He put up his hands. "Whoa. Hold on there, Lieutenant. I may be giving you shit, but I had nothing to do with your situation. You got the raw end of the deal, I agree, but that wasn't me."

"Do you know who it was?"

He shrugged. "Would it matter if I did? You've been erased from the universe. We both have. We're ghosts, Cage. Demons. We have no voice beyond these caverns. We're going to rot here, whether the work kills us, Packard kills us, or we kill ourselves. That's reality."

"You seem to be okay with that."

"It is what it is, and I am where I am. I told Coli we were going to get caught. Fragging baby. If I had known he was going to crumble like that, I would have ratted him out."

"The guns. Were you selling them to the Outworlds? Are you really traitors?"

He started to step toward her until his bracelet buzzed a warning. He settled for turning his head instead. "To be honest, yeah."

"Why? You could have made just as much without getting sent down here."

"It isn't all about the money." He paused, looking around. "The Republic doesn't want anyone to know the shit that they're into. The level of corruption." He paused again. "It isn't what it used to be, is all I'm saying."

"What do you mean?"

"It doesn't matter. Not down here."

"So tell me."

"Nothing good happens to people who know things. Nothing good happens to people who try to do the right thing. Does the name Sylvan Kett mean anything to you?"

Abbey nodded. "You were selling the guns to Kett?"

"Not exactly." He paused when both of their bracelets began to buzz. "Time to work," he said. "I'll give you more tomorrow. Same place, okay?"

"For free?" Abbey asked.

Illiard laughed. "If you're offering, I'm taking, but otherwise for free. I know you weren't involved with the shit we were into. It's the least I can do. I'm an asshole, Lieutenant, but I'm not a heartless asshole."

"Tomorrow then."

She picked up the cutter and turned it on. One minute at a time. One day at a time. That was the only way to survive down here.

CHAPTER EIGHTEEN

ILLIARD DIDN'T SHOW THE NEXT day.

He didn't show the day after that or the day after that.

It took Abbey another day to find a minute to drop in on Gant, leaving her shift as soon as her bracelet buzzed her off and running full-speed through the tunnels and back to the cell block. The other inmates looked away as she sped through, and she briefly entertained the idea that they would be reporting back to Packard about her strange activity.

Maybe they would, but so what?

There was nothing anybody could do to her down here that was worse than being down here. Even Pok's attempted molestation paled in comparison to the daily grind of life on Level Twenty, and she was starting to believe the only thing keeping her going was the thought of getting some answers about what the Fifth Platoon and Gradin had to do with Sylvan Kett, and maybe why Davis had buried her down here in the first place. It was information that might never make it to the surface, but she was still driven by a need to know.

And right now that curiosity was tuned to finding out where Illiard had gone.

Gant was on his mattress facing the wall when Abbey arrived. She knocked as she entered, startling him and causing him to hunch over a little more, concealing whatever contraband he was working with at the moment.

"Gant," she said.

"Shit on a quasar," Gant said, her translator completely failing on his curse. "I could have been playing with myself over here. What would you have done then?"

"Probably laughed at the size," she replied as he turned around. His hellsuit was sealed, though she noticed there was a slight bulge around the wrist.

"Laughed in amazement, maybe. You missed me so much you ran?"

"Have you heard anything about Private Illiard?"

"I have competition?"

"I'm serious. What do you know?"

"He's gone," Gant said.

"What do you mean, gone?"

"I didn't think that was a vague statement. This is Hell, Greenie. Cons disappear all the time."

"Dead, then?"

"That's usually the case. He probably found a way to off himself. Or maybe Packard decided he wanted a piece of him."

"I didn't think Packard got involved down here unless there was a problem?"

"Maybe Illiard was causing a problem. You wouldn't know how that could be, would you?"

He raised his forehead, the motion making him look like a toy. Abbey opened her mouth to tell him about the conversation she had with Illiard but stopped short. What if the Private was missing because of the things he had told her? What if the Warden was listening in on every word they said? She remembered the recording Davis had shown of her private conversation with her sister in the construct. Nothing was safe. Nothing was secret. Packard was probably listening in right now.

Maybe, but again, so what? The worst he could do would be to kill her. She was already in Hell. She was already as good as dead. It would be a gift.

"No," she said. "I don't know anything."

Gant nodded, putting his hand to the side of his head, suggesting she was getting smarter. Abbey nodded back.

"I might need to think of a different name for you. You know, the other cons are calling you the 'Demon Queen of Level Twenty.'"

"Why?"

"In case you hadn't noticed, you're the only female down here. I've been here six standard years, and I've never seen another. And after what happened with Pok? Why do you think nobody else will go near you, or talk to you, or even look at you?"

Abbey had noticed she was the only woman currently on the level, but she had assumed there had been others before.

"I thought it was because we were friends. I couldn't have beaten Pok without your help."

Gant chittered in laughter. "Pok had a reputation for killing people with one hit. You held out against him, and if that asshole Bastion hadn't screwed you over you would have knocked him cold. Or rather, he would have knocked himself cold. They're afraid of you, Queenie."

"You're telling me that being down here, working in the mines, not everyone here wants to die? Six years?"

Gant made a sound that her translator named ambivalence. "Maybe we're just too stupid to realize we'd be better off not being here. Or maybe we're hoping the Outworlds will find this place and set us free. They try to keep the location secret, but everyone here knows we aren't that far from the Fringe."

"Does that mean you're a traitor, too?"

Level Twenty was reserved for traitors and mass murderers.

"No," he replied simply, sending a chill down Abbey's spine.

"They're afraid of you, too," she said.

"Size isn't everything." Gant's bracelet buzzed, and he hopped off the mattress and headed toward her and the door. "Time for my shift."

He brushed up against her as he passed, and she found herself holding a sharp, wedge-shaped piece of disterium crystal. It was large enough to be worth a fortune. Large enough that if Packard knew Gant had taken it, she wouldn't be seeing him again either.

She knew why he had given it to her. Not for protection from others. For protection from herself. If she used it to kill herself, they might trace it back to him and either mess him up or kill him, too, and he had made it clear he didn't want to die.

She used her fingers to push the crystal up under the sleeve of her hellsuit. Then she headed back to her cell before her bracelet decided she wasn't following the rules.

She sat on her mattress, staring at the wall ahead of her. Packard had killed Illiard before he could tell her what he knew about Kett and the dirty side of the Republic. Whatever the truth was, it all ran deeper than she had realized. All the way down to Hell, in fact. The thought only made her hunger for the answers deepen. But how could she learn anything without the Warden knowing about it?

She was still thinking about it when her bracelet buzzed, and a heavy clank at her door signaled that she was on lockdown. She immediately stood and went over to her washer, hunching over it and removing the small access panel on the side the way she had seen Gant do it. She slid the crystal shard from her suit and dropped it in, quickly putting the cover back in place. Then she stood and put her fingers to the front of her suit, pulling lightly at the invisible seam. The material spread apart and she removed the suit, enjoying the momentary sensation of slight coolness on her naked flesh before her brain adjusted to the heat once more. She placed the suit in the washer and turned it on before retreating to her mattress and lying down. Lockdown lasted four hours, and she had to use that time to maximize her sleep.

She turned onto her side facing the wall and closed her eyes. She could feel the sweat on her forehead, between her knees, her legs, her buttocks, and breasts. She would have given anything to be cold, if only for a second or two.

A bead of the sweat ran onto her nose. She was sleeping before it slid off and onto the mattress.

CHAPTER NINETEEN

ABBEY'S CELL DOOR UNLOCKED WITH a loud clang that jolted her awake.

She turned over as she sat up. There was only one person who could open her cell while it was on lockdown, and she wasn't that surprised he had come for her.

She was surprised to find Packard out of his battlesuit; however, wearing standard issue blue utilities, the high neck of them making his head look too big for his slim frame. He had a satisfied smile on his face as he entered.

"Cage," he said.

She put an arm over her chest. It was a stupid thing to do. She had no doubt there were cameras in every cell, and he had already seen her naked anyway. She lowered it, getting to her feet and standing in front of him.

"Did you come to make good on your threats?" she asked, edging slightly toward the washer.

"Please," he replied. "There's an order to everything, Cage. A hierarchy. Pok had his orders. I have mine. Davis has his. They don't include anything as banal as rape. There has been a change of plans, though. A miscalculation. They want you to do more than rot down here."

Abbey was both relieved and confused by the statement. "You...

You're going to let me out?"

"Yes. They have need of you somewhere else. It's your lucky day."

She felt her heart begin to thump harder, a sudden feeling of elation working its way through her, along with a greater sense of fear. She didn't feel very lucky.

"I don't understand."

A second person joined them in the room. A woman. She was tall and thin, and wearing a softsuit. She had something in her hand, but Abbey couldn't see it that well.

"This is Clyo," Packard said. "She's going to prepare you."

"Prepare me?" Abbey said. "For what?"

Packard didn't answer. He stepped back, closer to her cell door, touching a hidden control panel on it that caused it to close and lock once more. Then he leaned back against it while the woman, Clyo, approached her.

"What the hell is this?" Abbey asked. There was something about the woman that wasn't sitting right. A coldness, despite the overbearing heat.

"You should be honored," Clyo said. "They've noticed you."

"Who has?"

"You'll find out soon enough," Packard said.

"Please," Clyo said. "Lie down. It's easier if you don't resist."

Abbey tried to get a glimpse of whatever Clyo was holding. It looked like a small, black piece of metal. "What are you going to do to me?"

"Give you more than you ever dreamed you would have. A chance to get back at those who put you here. A chance to find the answers that you seek."

"Davis put me here, and Packard works for Davis. You work for Packard."

"I don't work for Packard. Davis? He is expendable if you'd like to expend him." She smiled, glancing back at Packard. His expression was flat. Empty. Submissive. "Please. Lie down."

Abbey glanced over at the washer. She had left the panel loose enough that it would fall off if she hit it hard enough, giving her access to the shiv. Could she take the woman in a fight? Against a softsuit? Probably not, unless the woman had no fighting skills at all. By the way she carried herself, Abbey doubted that was the case.

What would be the point of resisting, anyway? Packard had told her she was going to get out of here. Go free.

No. Not free. There was a price to pay to get out of Hell. She would be beholden to whoever Clyo worked for, individuals that she knew absolutely nothing about. Was that better than staying down here? Was that better than being dead?

The devil you know?

She returned to her mattress, lying down on it, arms at her sides.

"Thank you," Clyo said, approaching her. She climbed up onto the mattress before lowering herself on top of Abbey's hips. "This will hurt. My weight will keep you from convulsing too wildly and harming yourself."

Abbey didn't like the sound of that.

"Stay calm," Clyo said, leaning forward so that they were embracing like lovers before moving her hand toward Abbey's neck.

Abbey glanced over. She could see the device better now. It was black metal, wrapped partially around a clear cylinder filled with what appeared to be blood. Two needle tips extended from a flat surface.

Whatever it was for, she didn't want any part of it.

She never had. She just wanted to get the woman close. The only way to take her was to take her by surprise.

She closed her eyes as she jerked her head up, slamming Clyo in the nose with her forehead. She could hear it crack and feel it crumble beneath the blow, causing Clyo to cry out, distracted by the sudden pain. Abbey grabbed the woman's wrists, pulling them away and forcing the woman further down on top of her. She got a face full of blood as she rolled them both to the side and off the mattress, coming down on top of the other woman before trying to crawl away.

Clyo recovered quickly, grabbing Abbey by the leg as she lunged for the washer. She fell a little bit short of the machine, looking back and lashing out the woman with her feet. Her blows landed on the softsuit, the light armor easily absorbing the attack and giving Clyo the edge once more. The woman pulled Abbey to her, holding her down and climbing onto her back.

"I told you it was easier if you didn't resist," Clyo said. Then she jabbed the device into Abbey's neck.

Abbey felt a sudden coldness at the site, as though the tip of the device was frozen despite the heat. It lasted a second or two before starting to burn. Clyo placed herself across the top of her then, her mouth right beside Abbey's ear.

"Be glad they want you, Cage, or I would gladly cut your throat for what you just did to me."

Abbey blinked her eyes. Everything was turning cold again. She had thought it would be a blessing to feel after all of these days in Hell. It turned out she was wrong.

Her muscles began to spasm, her arms and legs convulsing, pushing her up and back, sending her to rock against Clyo's weight. The other woman held her down, shifting to cradle her neck as she bounced and writhed, the coldness spreading across her skin and diving deeper into her lungs. What had the woman done to her? What the frag was going on?

She clenched her teeth. She had to get away.

Her body spasmed again, her arm slamming itself into the ground, so hard it left a crack in the stone. What? That wasn't possible. Was it? She bucked again, noticing that Clyo was struggling to keep her down. She was getting dizzy. The room was starting to spin. Her entire body was cold, so cold there were bumps on her arms.

Focus, damn it.

Her arm shook as she fought to bring it under control. She would only have one chance. She rocked it back, hitting Clyo solidly in the ribs. The strike would have done nothing before, but now? Now it hit with enough force that the softsuit couldn't absorb it, and she felt the bones break beneath the blow, right before Clyo was thrown from her, back onto the mattress and into the wall.

She was free. She reached out, clawing her way forward, half a meter to the washer. She grabbed the panel, tearing it away, reaching in and taking hold of the shiv. Clyo was coming at her again, more prepared now. There were three of the woman behind her, holding out their hands as if they could grab her from two meters away.

She felt something touching her, pulling at her, bringing her toward Clyo though she was still out of range. Everything was spinning and blurry. Was any of this real? She turned over onto her back again, using her feet to try to push herself away from the woman and fighting the grip that had taken hold of her.

"No wonder they want you," Clyo said. "Too bad. They should have sent someone else if they wanted a demon like you alive."

Whatever was pulling at her subsided, and Abbey suddenly felt something choking her. She gasped, trying to draw air and finding that none would come, her esophagus constricted by an immediate pressure.

"They'll understand it was an accident. You put up such a fight; it was either you or me. Self-preservation, Cage."

Abbey stared at the blurred vision of Clyo, feeling more and more lightheaded with each passing second. Her entire body was shaking and rubbery, each motion exaggerated and difficult to control. She had thought she would be thankful to die after spending a month down here. Now she realized that she was just as dumb as the others on Level Twenty, living in Hell but still wanting to live.

And this bitch was trying to take that away.

She growled softly, concentrating on bringing her arm forward. It moved at her command, and as it extended she opened her hand, throwing the shiv, hurtling it toward Clyo.

The other woman clearly wasn't expecting it. She jerked, the pressure against Abbey's neck immediately vanishing as her hand moved toward the shaped crystal. She managed to get it into the blade's trajectory, but it didn't matter. It sliced right through the palm of her hand, cutting in, powering through the bone and exploding out the other side. It finally came to rest buried deep in her neck.

She gasped, reaching up to try to pull it out, her face wearing an expression of disbelief. Then she stumbled and fell onto the mattress and didn't move again.

Abbey picked herself up, turning toward Packard. The Warden had a look of fear in his eyes. He hadn't expected her to survive the fight. He put his hand to the control panel, unlocking the cell door. He tried to duck under it as it slid open, eager to put it back between them.

She couldn't reach him in time. Not in this state. She reached out anyway, grabbing for him, wishing she could pull him back.

His forward momentum stopped. Then he was headed her way, falling over backward and coming to rest on the ground right in front of her. She reached down, putting her hand on his neck and squeezing.

"Lieutenant," he gasped. "Wait."

"Who?" she asked. It was the only thing she was able to say. Her entire body hurt, and she could barely see at all.

He made gurgling, choking noises, unable to answer her question. She tried to ease up her grip, but her muscles spasmed again, forcing her to grip him harder. She felt his spine break beneath her fingers, and she knew he was dead.

She picked herself up, turning toward the open door to her cell and trying to walk to it. Her legs struggled to carry her, and she fell over three times before she reached the threshold. Where was she going? She wasn't sure. To Gant's cell, maybe. She needed help.

She used the frame to pull herself back up. She took another step and stumbled again. She heard a buzzing noise but wasn't able to place it, realizing too late that it was coming from her bracelet. She was on lockdown. She wasn't supposed to be out of her cell.

She didn't have the strength or energy or mental presence to throw herself back into her module. A moment later, the bracelet began sending thousands of volts of energy coursing through her body.

Everything went dark.

CHAPTER TWENTY

CAPTAIN ISSIASI OF THE REPUBLIC Intergalactic Navy stared out into the blackness of space, her large, oblong eyes focusing with an acuity that was beyond unaugmented human capability. A small, dark planet sat off the starboard bow of her battleship, the *Charis*. It was a Fringe planet known as Seta, a newer terraforming project that was still in Stage One and therefore lightly populated. The billowing clouds from the massive machines on the surface were visible to anyone. The machines themselves were visible only to her and the other four Rudin who complemented the ship's crew.

"We have uncovered the path of the disterium trail, Captain," her First Officer, Commander Dorn said, adjusting the main projection at the front of the bridge to show a map of nearby space. A thin, translucent red overlay appeared on it, showing the direction that the FTL traveling vessel had been moving in.

"Thank you, Lieutenant," Issiasi said, shifting her eyes until she found a second, much smaller vessel within her fleet of nine ships. An unarmed support patroller, the Hound Class sensor ship *Bose* would be able to detect traces of passing ships across a much wider field than the *Charis*' limited scanners. "Commander Sixiy, please confirm."

"Confirmed, Captain," the Plixian replied. "Forensic results suggest a single ship matching the engine profile of the incursion two EW past."

Issiasi tapped her beak in a tight cadence. It was as she had started to fear the moment she saw the trail was leading back into the Outworlds. The ship that had entered Republic space earlier had now left it.

The ship that was suspected to be involved in the destruction of Eagan Heavyworks and the theft of two of the most powerful starships ever built.

"Can we date it, Commander?" she asked.

"We are already processing," Sixiy replied. "We will have results in three EH."

Issiasi leaned down on her tentacles, taking a more relaxed, patient posture. They had dropped from FTL when the *Bose* had detected the emissions, an immediate pause to their overall mission of patrolling a long stretch of the Fringe. Space was a very big place, and it was often difficult to come upon ships in the act of passing from one side to the other, but the very understanding that the potential existed was enough to cause all but the most hardened or desperate to try. Especially when Republic sensor nets and passing Hound class ships would at the very least be able to track speed and vector and make a judgment of destination from there. While plenty of ships crossed the Fringe, it was rare that they managed to accomplish more than a little black market trading without being hunted down.

"Then we must wait," Issiassi said. "I want to know where we believe that ship was headed. Command will want to know as well."

"Aye, Captain," Sixiy said.

Whoever was on that ship, they had successfully run that gauntlet, slipping through the cracks of the Republic's patrols and making it to Feru unpursued. The fact that her ship had been the first to notice them made her consider that it was at least partially her fault that they had gotten away with it. At the same time, she didn't feel remorse the way a Terran might. She had followed her orders to the letter. If they did not prevent this tragedy, better orders would need to be provided.

In the meantime, she would report in on anything out of the

ordinary, as she had been ordered to do. She knew how badly the Republic wanted to catch up to the thieves, not only to mete justice for the death of thousands but perhaps more importantly to recover the stolen vessels. It may have seemed a cold motivation to some, but the Republic was home to hundreds of worlds, and billions of intelligent individuals. A few thousand was sad, but also barely a single star in the entirety of the universe.

She put her attention back on the planet, watching the terraformer do its work of emitting a breathable atmosphere around it. Another Terran planet, no doubt. There were so many of them compared to the other races. She wondered when they might terraform another Rudin world, one that was predominantly oceanic. She had heard there was a company interested in investing in such a venture, but it was difficult to find Rudin with enough spirit of adventure to want to head off-world.

Her internal musing was brought to an abrupt end by a split-second flash of orange light out of the viewport to her right. By the time she shifted her attention there, the *Bose* was already nothing more than a battered mess of bent framing, twisted metal, and expanding debris.

"Shields up," she shouted, opening the fleet-wide communications channel. "Full power. All ships, red alert. Battle stations."

The *Charis* shuddered as something slammed into the side of it before the shields could be raised.

"We're hit," Commander Dorn said. "Decks four through twelve."

"Rerouting shields," Ensign Praan said. "Weapons systems online."

"Who are we going to shoot at?" Ensign Sia said. "There's nothing-"

One moment the scanners were clear. The next, a dot had appeared on them, a ship materializing from the black. It was small and sleek, the front of it suggestive of a hungry animal. Issiasi recognized it immediately as the *Brimstone*.

"Fire at will," she said. "Ensign Sia, send an emergency message to Command. The *Brimstone* has been located off the planet Seta."

"Aye, Captain," the ensign replied, turning in his seat to send the transmission.

The *Brimstone* jerked forward, accelerating at sublight speed faster than any ship she had ever seen before, moving from one end of the fleet to the other as lasers and missiles flashed through the area where she had just been.

"Stay on target," Issiasi said. "Come about, thirty degrees."

The *Charis* began to turn while the other ships in the fleet started to spread away from one another. The *Brimstone* fired a single projectile that was barely visible as it crossed the distance from the ship to its destination. An instant flare of white light was followed by the silent explosion of the *Locus*, one of three smaller cruisers in the fleet.

"One hit," Dorn said. "She punched right through the shields with one hit."

"Remain focused," Issiasi said. "Fire."

The *Charis* opened fire, sending a dozen lasers lancing out from her port side. They slapped against the *Brimstone*, creating a flare of light around the ship as the shields absorbed the energy of the attack. The other ships in the fleet were moving into position, but before they could fire the *Brimstone* had moved again, flashing from one side of the fight to another, sending a second projectile out and destroying another cruiser.

"Send retreat coordinates to the fleet," Issiasi said. "This is a fight we cannot win."

"Aye, Captain," Ensign Sia said.

"Fifteen seconds to FTL," Commander Dorn said.

It felt like an eternity.

The *Brimstone* was facing their way and bringing her weapons to bear.

"Ten seconds," Dorn said.

Two torpedos burst from the front of the starship, reaching a half cee in less than a second and slamming into either end of the *Charis* a half second after that. Between the impact velocity and the explosive warhead each weapon carried, there was nothing the battleship could do to defend itself.

The *Charis* rocked from the impact, warning tones blaring at the death of a dozen systems. Issiasi began to rise from the deck, the gravity generators losing power, right before the force against the inner part of the ship shoved it against the outer part of the ship, and the entire thing bent and burned and crumbled, leaving her dead before she could even consider chattering her beak in fear.

CHAPTER TWENTY-ONE

CAPTAIN OLUS MANN SAT BACK in his chair, watching the projection of Mars Eagan's lifestream for what was probably the hundredth time. He had already captured every detail of the two perpetrators who had attacked the Director of Eagan Heavyworks, extracting their profiles from the projection and passing all of the data back to the OSI Command Center on Earth, but no matter how many times he watched the recording he still felt like something was out of place.

Of course, the data profile on the man and woman who had attacked Mars had turned up nothing. That was no surprise, considering the two were Outworlders. He had held a distant hope that maybe one of them was a defector, but could hardly allow himself to be disappointed when that didn't work out.

He leaned forward, waving his hand to move more quickly through the stream. He paused it at the same place every time, in the split-second when the ring station's shuttle was picked up by a larger, cloaked starship. She hadn't gotten a look at the outside of the craft, but there was a sliver of the interior hold visible through the shuttle's viewport, and he had spent most of the last week picking it apart bit by bit for even the smallest clue that might lead him to it. It was likely an Outworld vessel as well, meaning there would be nothing to match it in the Republic archives. Then again, if even one scrap of it was of Republic origin, he might be able to tracc it back. That was part of what his department did, after all.

He spent a few more minutes staring at it before forwarding ahead again. For some reason, Mars Eagan had given him more of her stream than he needed, allowing him a peek inside her private life after she had been rescued. To prove her innocence or to cover her guilt? It followed her as she was brought home, in full detail as she took comm after comm, immediately getting to work on shoring up the stability of her company and getting Republic Command involved.

She had even requested him by name.

That surprised him. Then again, what was the old saying? Keep your friends close and your enemies closer? He didn't trust the woman, and for as much as he supposed the stream was supposed to earn his confidence, every time he watched it he felt a little less so.

Not that Mars Eagan cared. His investigators had turned up nothing suspicious from her end, other than the fact that she was still alive. Everything was exactly as the woman had claimed it would be, which only unsettled him more.

It was too clean. Too perfect. Like the uncanny valley of the most humanoid of bots, it was so believable it was unbelievable. Nobody was that spotless, least of all the Director of an arms manufacturing corporation. Unless he had proof of something, there was nothing he could do.

A chirp from the pin in his collar signaled him that he was receiving a communication. He closed Mars Eagan's projection and replaced it with the incoming transmission.

"General Soto," Olus said, sitting up stiff in his seat.

"Relax, Olus," the General replied. She was an older woman, with streaks of gray intermingling with short, black hair that sat tight against a wide face. "The Council asked me to check in on your progress. It's been three weeks, and we have nothing to offer the populace."

"I know, Iti," Mann replied. They had known one another long enough to be on a first name basis once formalities were dropped. "You understand this kind of work isn't quick and easy."

"Of course I do. Many others don't. I need to tell them something."

"Did you fill the acquisition request I made?"

She smiled. "It took a little extra effort to find something suitable for you, but yes. I don't suppose you're ready to tell me what you're planning? It isn't everyday someone asks for a near derelict starship and no crew to fly it."

"I requested a crew," Mann said.

"A single SI-10. That isn't a crew."

"It will do for now. I can't tell you what I'm up to, Iti. An Outworld starship doesn't get this deep into Republic space without help, and right now it isn't smart for me to give anything away. That's why I came to you directly."

"I'm telling you now, Olus, you need to be quick about cleaning up this mess. The rumor is that the Council is going to pin this one on the highest ranks and start rotating positions if this isn't dealt with adequately."

"They don't have the authority."

"They do. Section Fifty-three was passed six months ago, remember?"

"Coincidentally."

General Iti covered her mouth to hide her laugh. "You're cynical about everything and everyone."

"Except for you," he replied.

"Maybe you should be cynical about me, too?"

"I know you well enough to know I can trust you."

"Getting back on point, Olus. I need something to give the Council that they can pass on to the representatives. More than one planet is concerned that the *Fire* and *Brimstone* will be used against them."

"Directly? That's ridiculous."

"Most worlds away from the Fringe think the Outworlders are nothing more than glorified pirates. That's what our media teaches them."

"I'm sorry, Iti. I would give you something if I had anything, but right now I'm stuck. Eagan is as clean as freshly processed oxygen, and the only other clue I have is a limited view of an Outworld starship's cargo hold. I've got my people tracing the components we've identified as we speak."

"Then that's what I'll tell the Council," General Soto replied.

"I would prefer you keep quiet for now," Mann said. "We-"

"Hold on," the General said, raising her hand and turning her head away. Her brow wrinkled in concern, and she motioned in the air with her fingers, passing whatever she was listening to on to him.

"This is the Republic Battleship *Charis*," a calm voice was saying. "We are under attack. I repeat, we are under attack. We have positive identification of the *Brimstone*. She's tearing our ships apart. Transmitting coordinates now."

"Their distress signal is active," Soto said, receiving more information than he was privy to. "On the Fringe near Seta."

He had expected they would take the ships back to the Outworlds. He hadn't guessed they would stop to destroy more Republic assets first. It was almost as though they were trying to pull the Republic into all-out war.

General Soto's eyes narrowed, her face tightening. She turned back to him. "Their beacon just went dark, Captain," she said. "You know what that means."

He nodded. It meant the *Charis* was no more.

"I don't care what you have to do. We need to get a jump on this, and we need to do it now, or many, many more individuals are going to die."

"Understood, ma'am," Olus replied, sensing that things had become formal again. "Please have the SI-10 contact me so that I can provide rendezvous coordinates."

"I will take care of it immediately. I'm counting on you, Captain."

"Yes, ma'am," Olus said.

The projection vanished, leaving him staring at an empty surface. He didn't have any more time to delay.

"Commander Usiari," he said, contacting the captain of the *Driver*.

"Yes, Captain?" Usiari replied.

"Set a course for Hell."

CHAPTER TWENTY-TWO

"CAPTAIN MANN," WARDEN LURIN SAID, raising a long, narrow hand to his forehead in salute. "Welcome to Hell, sir."

"Thank you, Sergeant," Olus replied as the ramp to the shuttle closed behind him. "You'll have to excuse me, but I thought Master Sergeant Packard was still running this place? I was communicating with him directly as of three days ago."

Lurin nodded before looking at the ground. The Sergeant was an Atmo, the first extra-terrestrial species to travel faster-than-light but the last to emerge from hiding. He was small and thin, with a large head and spindly arms that ended with two fingers and a thumb.

"Yes, he was. My apologies, Captain, but he was killed two nights ago. Murdered by one of the inmates."

"Really?" Olus said. "How did that happen?"

"Nobody is completely sure. The feeds in the cell block were offline at the time. An equipment malfunction, or so the technicians tell me. Quite common."

Olus raised his eyebrow to that but decided to drop the subject. There was no reason to suspect anything out of the ordinary. Not here. Not in a place where murder was almost ordinary.

"You have everything prepared as I requested?"

"Of course, sir. I reviewed the instructions you delivered to Warden Packard and made the proper arrangements. Sir, I imagine you would prefer a coolsuit?"

Olus absently wiped some of the moisture from his head. He knew Hell was going to be oppressive, but the stories he had heard didn't do it justice.

"A coolsuit is a good idea," he said.

"This way," Lurin said, leading him from the hangar to a large lift.

They took it two floors down to the administration level, a floor that was thankfully climate-controlled. Olus didn't realize how labored his breathing had become until he was able to draw in the cooler air.

"Suit storage is there, sir," Lurin said, pointing to a door on their left. "I'll retrieve the files while you prepare."

"That'll be fine, thank you, Sergeant."

Lurin saluted and headed down an adjacent corridor, while Olus opened the door to the storage room. A number of suits were hanging from a rack along the wall, marked by species. He searched through the Terran section until he found his size, taking a suit from the rack and holding it. He wasn't sure if he was supposed to wear it clothed or not, so he stripped to his underwear and put it on. He began to feel an immediate chill from the suit reacting with the cooler air in this section. It was a chill he knew wasn't going to last.

Lurin was waiting for him when he emerged, a small silver disc held between his thumb and forefinger.

"Sir," he said, saluting again. "The files you requested."

"Thank you," Olus replied, taking the disc.

"Sir, are you sure you want to speak with these individuals? I don't know what benefit it will have to the Republic. They are criminals, indeed. Larcenists. Rapists. Murderers. Soldiers don't get assigned to Hell lightly."

"I know how Hell works, Sergeant," Olus replied. "I've been ordered directly by the Council to investigate the destruction of Eagan Heavyworks and the theft of two prototype starships. I believe that one or more of the individuals whose detailed files I requested may have information that is vital to carrying out these orders. Not that I need to explain myself to you. Do you understand?"

"Yes, sir," Lurin said. "I wasn't questioning your competence, sir. Instead, I am concerned for your well-being. The prisoners can be violent, and I observed that in the case of Bastion Marrett you were responsible for his incarceration."

"I can take care of myself," Olus said. He couldn't help but wonder why the prison's new Warden was trying to dissuade him from meeting with some of the inmates. What was he worried about?

"Of course, sir. There's an interrogation room on Level Fifteen. I've arranged for the first prisoner to be brought there for questioning."

"Thank you, Sergeant. Have your people standing by to retrieve the next inmate as I finish my interviews. I intend to have everything I need by the end of the day."

"Yes, sir," Lurin replied. "Follow me, sir."

Olus trailed behind the Sergeant, back into the lift and down to Level Fifteen. He could feel the air getting hotter on his face as they descended, thankful for the second skin that was helping to keep his temperature static.

They walked a dim, narrow corridor to the interrogation room, situated at the base of the guard tower that sat in the center of the cell block. The prisoners had all been cleared from the area for his arrival, allowing him to enter the space without having to see or hear them. Even so, he knew they were there. The scum of the galaxy. Deserters. Killers. Thieves. Individuals who had sworn to defend the Republic and instead had taken advantage of it, using their positions of power in the military for their own personal gain. The select few whose files he was carrying didn't deserve what he was planning to offer them, but he didn't see another option.

He had to fight fire with fire.

"I'll take it from here, Sergeant," Olus said as they reached the door to the interrogation room. It was flanked by a pair of guards in battlesuits. "I trust you'll be available if I need you?"

"Yes, sir. I'll be back on Level Two, continuing my work on the transition. Master Sergeant Packard was not a terribly organized individual."

Olus smilcd, returning Sergeant Lurin's offered salute. Then he turned to the door, which one of the guards opened for him before saluting.

"Captain," the guard said.

"Private," Olus replied.

He entered the room. It was small and barren, save for a chair and small table placed in front of a thick transparency. A prisoner in a tight red suit was on the other side of the divider, watching him as he entered.

"You," the inmate said, immediately turning angry. "What the frag are you doing here, you piece of shit? What the frag do you want with me?" He began banging on the glass. "Haven't you done enough to me, you fragger? Haven't you gotten your pound of flesh? Whatever the frag you want, I'm not interested."

Olus didn't waver, continuing to the table and chair without changing his posture or cadence. He tossed the disc onto the surface, which responded by displaying a control interface for the device. He tapped it on, projecting the soldier's record in the air between them.

"Bastion Marrett," Olus said. "Call sign, Worm. Former Lieutenant Commander in the Republic Intergalactic Navy. A Vomit Comet Bouncehead. Sentenced to life in Hell for assaulting a superior officer-"

"Does it still hurt?" Bastion asked.

Olus did his best not to react. He couldn't help but remember how the man had attacked him. The HSOC needed a drop onto some backwater planet in the Fringe. Bastion had sworn it was suicide, and the pilot decided that beating the shit out of him would save the lives of his fellow soldiers. It was a desperate act that might have been almost understandable if he hadn't left Olus a breath away from death.

"Assigned to Level Twenty for acts of treason," Olus finished. It didn't matter if he was trying to help his crew. He had gone way over the line. In the end, they had attempted the drop without him. In the end, the inexperience of the replacement pilot cost everyone on board their lives. "You've been here for four years."

"Thanks to you," Bastion said.

Olus flipped through the file. "You've been to medical eight times since you arrived here for a variety of broken bones and cuts. You've also been responsible for nearly twenty injuries to other inmates." He looked past the projection. "You were running with Pok's crew?"

"Until he got himself dead, yeah," Bastion said. "I did what he asked, and he took care of me. Him and Packard both. That's how things work in this shithole."

"You know that Packard is dead?"

"I heard. It was that bitch that did it. The Demon Queen."

"Demon Queen?"

"That's what us L20s have taken to calling her. First girl I've ever seen down here. She did Pok her first hour. Packard had it in for her before that, though. I don't know why. I guess he got what was coming to him. Him and Pok both." He laughed uncomfortably.

Olus absorbed the information, filing it away in another part of his brain. He knew who Lieutenant Cage was. It was hard to believe a Breaker with her record would wind up down here, and even harder to believe she had turned so easily to murder. First Pok, and now Packard. She was somewhere in his list of inmates to interview, but in light of her recent history he was going to have to take her out.

There was a delicate balance between dangerous and out of control, and he couldn't afford the latter.

"That isn't why you wanted to talk to me, though," Bastion said. "A guy like you doesn't come to Hell for minor shit like that. So, what's your deal?"

"My deal is your deal, Worm," Olus said. "I came to offer you a chance to go free."

CHAPTER TWENTY-THREE

SO IT WENT FOR THE next four hours. Prisoners were cycled into the interrogation room one at a time, where Olus reviewed their files and interviewed them both on their time in Hell, and their life before it. It had taken weeks to get to this point. Weeks of sifting through hundreds of records to come up with a suitable list of potentials, a process that had left him exhausted. He was on his own, forced to secrecy for the sake of his plan, a plan he knew the Council would never approve. A plan he knew General Soto would probably hate him for having ever considered. The Council wasn't HSOC or OSI. They hadn't seen the things he had seen or done the things he had done before he had gotten caught up in politics and management. He knew what the universe was like. He knew what the Fringe was like.

There was no other way.

It was a dangerous line he was trying to walk. A dangerous game he needed to play. For the sake of the Republic and the safety of millions. It wasn't necessarily a responsibility he wanted, but it was a responsibility he had.

He stood up, stretching his body. Four hours to speak with twelve individuals. He had already cut more than half of them because they were too far gone, their minds destroyed by this place, leaving them either too weak or too unstable to be of any use. Was it the heat that did it? The work? Or was it something else? As he had spoken to the prisoners, he began to form an image of this place in his mind. It was cut and dry on the surface. A disterium mine powered by soldiers gone wrong. He couldn't shake the feeling that there was an undercurrent of something beneath the hot, sweaty, dirty, and violent exterior. Like there was something else happening here that wasn't in any of the official documentation.

He didn't like secrets. For as much as he was required to keep them, he hated the trouble they brought. Secrets were for skeletons, to keep them hidden away. He had collected an entire ship full during his career, and he was preparing to add another. He had a feeling this was going to be the biggest and grimiest of them all.

The door on the other side of the transparency opened. One of the guards moved in first, checking the room, before backing to the side. The second guard walked behind the prisoner, keeping a rifle trained on his back. Olus was intrigued. As he understood it, the bracelets the prisoners wore were usually more than enough to keep them in line, and he hadn't seen them treat any of the other inmates with this much concern.

The prisoner glanced up at him as he entered, a shared look of curiosity on a smallish, fur-covered face. Olus was intrigued by that, too. The others had all either greeted him with anger, disdain, fear, or distrust.

"Prylshhharrnavramm," Olus said, doing his best to get the inflection correct. It hurt his throat, but the prisoner perked up at the attempt.

"Pretty close," Gant said. "What can I do for you, Captain Mann?"

"You know who I am?"

"Rumors travel fast around here. You've already pulled three other cons from L20. Is this about Feru?"

Olus was surprised again. "You know about Feru?"

"News doesn't travel as fast, but I have pretty good sources. I know about Feru. I was thinking that maybe you were talking to individuals who knew other individuals, who might have some ideas on who could have done such a thing." Gant walked up to the transparency, rubbing his chin between his two fingers and two thumbs. "Then the guards came for me, and I realized I was wrong. You have to know that I wouldn't know anything about it."

"Prylshhharrnavramm," Olus said again, despite the strain on his vocal chords. "Everyone here calls you Gant. Former Chief Petty Officer in the Republic Intergalactic Navy. You're an engineer."

"I was an engineer."

"Sentenced to life in Hell for-"

"We don't need to go over that. We both know why I'm here."

Olus didn't push.

"You're saying you aren't an engineer anymore?" he asked.

"Everyone is a miner down here."

"And you don't make things?"

"No."

"You're sure?"

"Look, Captain, I've been here for six years. That's long enough that most of the fur under this suit has been worn away by the chafing. You can only imagine what I look like naked nowadays. Point being, there's no point to being obtuse. Tell me what you want from me, or let me go back to my cell. I only get four hours to sleep, and you're cutting into it."

Olus stopped talking. He regarded the Gant. "You know about Feru," he said again.

"I told you I did," Gant replied. Then his expression changed, and an almost threatening half-smile formed on his face, revealing a few sharp teeth. "Oh. I get it." His voice became a loud bark, which Olus' translator announced was 'strong laughter.' "You're in deep, aren't you Captain?"

"Very," Olus replied.

Gant was quiet for a minute as he paced along the partition. "This isn't a good idea," he said at last.

"Do you have something better for me?"

Gant paced for another minute.

"No. But that doesn't make this a good idea." He stopped and looked at Olus. "I can understand why you wanted to talk to me. What do I get if I agree?"

"A chance at freedom."

"Only a chance? I'd be better off waiting for the Outworlders."

"They'll never find Hell. It isn't where the rumors claim it is."

"The OSI started those rumors?"

Olus nodded.

Gant laughed again. "I should have known." He started pacing again.

"I'm in a bit of a hurry," Olus said.

"You should know Gant don't make quick decisions. We're a contemplative bunch."

"This isn't a difficult decision to make."

"Maybe for you. You're already on the outside. Being in here isn't much of life, but it's a life that I'm accustomed to. A life I know. Going back out there? I didn't do too well out there, or I wouldn't have wound up here."

Olus closed the projection of Gant's file. He knew there was a risk to his participation, but the whole thing was a risk, and he needed someone who was good at fixing things. Someone who would stand out in all of the right ways.

"I need an answer," he said.

Gant growled softly, his eyes locked on Olus, studying him.

"One condition," Gant said.

"We aren't bargaining," Olus replied.

"Yes, we are."

"No, we aren't."

"Yes. We are," Gant insisted. "I'm good at reading faces. Especially human faces. Tell me something, Captain. Do you have Lieutenant Abigail Cage on your list?"

"I'm not at liberty to discuss who is and isn't on my list."

"You're the head of the OSI," Gant replied, taking him off guard for the third time. "You can discuss whatever you decide you want to discuss. You didn't think I knew that, did you? I know a lot of things, Captain. That's why you want me on your side. The question is: how badly?"

"I had Lieutenant Cage on my original list," Olus said, giving in. "I took her off. I was told she murdered Warden Packard."

"Murder?" Gant said. "Who the hell told you that? Warden Lurin?" His eyes shifted toward the corner of the room before sweeping back.

Olus flinched, starting to turn to look before realizing what Gant was suggesting. He moved forward, crouching down next to the division, positioned to block the feed.

"I'll do what you want, Captain," Gant said softly. "But Cage comes with me. We're a package deal."

"Why?" Olus replied. "You can't have known her more than a few weeks. Why is she so important to you?"

"I like looking at her. She's the only thing here that's hotter than the air." He laughed.

"What's the real reason?"

"Six years, Captain, and only one person in this place has ever accepted me without question. Another thing about Gant: we're loyal to a fault."

Olus already knew that. If this one had decided to take an alpha, it was going to increase the risk even more. At the same time, there was no way Gant was going to accept without her. Not now.

"What's going on in this place?" Olus asked. "What really happened with Packard and Cage?"

"Why are you asking me?" Gant replied. "You're OSI. You're supposed to know."

"I have an entire galaxy to cover."

"Yeah, like that's an excuse. I don't know everything, Captain, despite how it might seem to you. I can tell you that the others are whispering that there was a second body in the room. A woman's body. There aren't any other women on Level Twenty, and I've never seen a female guard down here."

"Who was she?"

"No idea. Maybe Packard was into some sort of kink? I don't think so. We have an expression on my world, Captain. Where there are drugrum, there is food. And there's a lot of drugrum scurrying around down here, if you get my meaning."

"I think I do." He stood up. "Wait to hear back from me. I'll see what I can do."

"Yes, sir," Gant said, giving him a sloppy salute.

Olus turned on his heel and headed out of the room, pausing between the two guards. "I'm done with him. Bring him back to his cell."

"Yes, sir," one of them said.

"Warden Lurin," Olus said, tapping his communicator.

"Captain?" the Warden replied a moment later. "How can I be of assistance?"

"Lieutenant Cage. She was on my list. I want to speak with her."

"Sir, Lieutenant Cage is being held in connection with the murder of Warden Packard."

"So I've heard, but not from you. She's also not in the personnel files you gave me. Why is that?"

"Sir, I didn't think you would still want to speak to her in light of recent developments."

"I didn't ask you to think for me, Sergeant," Olus said.

"Yes, Captain. My apologies, Captain. Lieutenant Cage isn't well, sir. I can't in good conscience allow you to put yourself at risk. Whatever you think she might know, sir, she won't be able to tell you anything."

"I'll decide that for myself, Sergeant."

"Sir-" Lurin started.

"I'm getting the distinct impression that you're trying to interfere with my investigation, Sergeant," Olus snapped. "Would you like to explain to me why that would be?"

Lurin hesitated before responding. "My apologies, sir. I've been put into a difficult situation these past few days. I'll have the guards escort you back to Level Two. Lieutenant Cage is in isolation in the medical ward. I will meet you there."

"That's quite all right, Sergeant," Olus said. "I can find my way. I'd like to speak with her alone."

"Sir, if I may?"

"You may not," Olus said. "My safety and well-being is my own problem, and I take full responsibility for it."

"Yes, Captain."

Olus disconnected the comm. Then he glanced at the two guards, half-expecting them to try to stop him. He wasn't sure exactly what the Gant's proverb had meant, but he had the distinct feeling it was spot on. If they wanted to keep Cage, whatever the reason, he was going to make it his new life's mission to get her out.

CHAPTER TWENTY-FOUR

WHEN ABBEY OPENED HER EYES, a spindly-armed medical bot was standing over her, the end of one of its appendages touched to her abdomen. The device it was using to scan the injury was cold, and she jerked away in surprise and discomfort.

"Please, do not make any sudden movements," the bot said, its synthesized voice so close to human it was within a hair's breadth of being real.

"I already did," Abbey replied, turning her head to look around. Where was she? What had happened to her? "I'm cold."

"It is expected," the bot replied. "I will provide fresh linens after I complete the examination."

She let her eyes travel the room. It didn't take long. It was simple and sparse. A raised mattress, a small table with a glass of water on it. That was all.

"How am I doing?" she asked, still not sure what had happened.

"You are healing well," the bot replied. "You are young and resilient."

"I'm not that young. Where am I?"

"The penal colony on the planet Hell. Level Two medical ward. Isolation."

Penal colony? Hell? It all came rushing back to her. Packard. Clyo. The fight. Fear.

"If you will excuse me," the bot said, walking from the room on mechanical legs. The door closed behind it, the familiar sound of it locking causing her to flinch.

She forced herself to sit up. Cold. She was cold. It should have been a welcome change, but not under these circumstances. She put her hand to her neck, expecting to feel bumps where the strange device Clyo was carrying had been jabbed into her skin. It was smooth and flat, leaving her wondering if she had imagined the whole thing.

That couldn't be possible. Something had caused her to wind up here.

The door opened and the medical bot walked back in, a light silvery material folded beneath an arm. It took it with a second appendage and held it out to her.

"This will keep you warm."

Abbey took it, looking down at herself. "Clothes would help, too," she said, draping it over her chest.

"You have not been authorized for clothing," the bot replied.

"What?"

"You are at risk for self-homicide. You are not to be provided with objects which enable self-harm."

"I could choke myself with this blanket."

"It will tear very easily. Your uniform would not, and has been restricted."

"Uniform? You mean the hellsuit?"

"That is what I said."

"Warden Packard. Do you know where he is?"

"Master Sergeant Packard is deceased," the bot answered. "If you will excuse me, I will take my leave of you."

It turned and walked back out, the door locking behind it once more.

"Damn bots," Abbey said, standing and wrapping the flimsy material around herself. Then she picked up the glass of water, dumping out the contents and slamming it against the table. She wasn't surprised when it didn't shatter.

She sat back down, leaning over to put her head in her hands. What was all of this about? What had they been trying to do to her? What had they done to her?

She remembered how Clyo had held out her hand, causing her to choke with nothing but a gesture. She also remembered cracking the stone floor of her cell with her hand during one of her convulsions. Both actions were impossible, weren't they?

She looked down at the glass. Then she tightened her grip on it, squeezing as hard as she could. She gave up when her hand began to cramp.

She put it back on the table and stood up, approaching the wall. She closed her right hand into a fist, drawing it back and then hesitating. She was pretty sure her mind was embellishing the truth of things, but how far should she go to prove it?

She decided on one more test, throwing her fist forward in a well-practiced punch. Her knuckles hit the wall hard, scraping open along them, a shockwave of pain running up her wrist at the impact.

"Ahh," she cried, clutching her right hand in her left. Damn, that hurt.

At least it confirmed her suspicion. Even if Packard and Clyo had been real, the stranger aspects of the encounter weren't.

She sat again, shifting her thoughts from actions to words, trying to remember Packard's exchange with her. He had said that someone needed her for something. Who? For what? Did it have anything to do with Private Illiard's disappearance? Did it have anything to do with Sylvan Kett?

She looked at the sealed door. She was being kept separate from the other prisoners in the ward. Because she had killed Packard? Were they going to punish her for that? How? She was already in Hell.

"Just because Packard failed doesn't mean nobody else is trying," she said to herself, chilled by the thought.

Packard said he was following orders, the same as everyone else.

He was a link in the chain, not the head of it. This was a Republic facility. Illiard had warned her that the Republic was more corrupt than she had ever considered. Did that mean her own people were responsible? She had declined the enlistment renewal. They knew she wanted out, and she had already suspected that was the reason for all of this. Were Packard's actions confirmation?

That would explain a lot, but it wouldn't explain what had been in the vial Clyo was holding. The vial that had been emptied into her neck.

She reached up and touched the area again. If there had been a vial to begin with. It was all too damn confusing.

She leaned back against the wall. What was she supposed to do now? She was as much a prisoner as she had been before she woke up here. The only difference was the temperature. At least she could enjoy that for as long as it lasted.

She closed her eyes, focusing on the ease of her breath and the lightness of her being after the oppressive weight of Hell's fetid air.

The lock on the door clanked again. She opened her eyes as it slid open. The medical bot was back. Someone new was with it. An Atmo in a Republic Intergalactic Army dress uniform.

"Lieutenant Cage," he said. "I was informed that you had woken. I'm Warden Lurin."

Abbey eyed him cautiously. "Warden?" she said, forcing herself to stay calm. Nothing about this was going to be good.

"You've caused a bit of trouble here, Lieutenant," Lurin said. "Master Sergeant Packard was a friend of mine."

"He was an asshole," Abbey replied. "He tried to kill me."

"Nobody tried to kill you. We were doing you a favor. Giving you a gift. You murdered two people in thanks for that honor."

The medical bot stepped toward her. One of its appendages was holding a needle.

"What is that?" she asked.

"A sedative. I was hoping you would stay unconscious for another hour or two, but of course, you had to ruin that plan as well."

"That's one of my best qualities," Abbey said, pushing herself toward the edge of the table. The medical bot put out two of its arms, grabbing her by the shoulders and shoving her back.

"Please," it said. "Do not make any sudden movements." A third hand took hold of her wrist, turning her arm over with inhuman strength.

"Fortunately for you, murder isn't a way out. Your services are still required."

The bot sank the needle into her vein. She could feel warm liquid slipping into her bloodstream as she started growing lightheaded almost immediately.

"That should keep you in proper shape for your visitor," Lurin said. He flashed her a cold smile and exited the room again.

Abbey looked at the bot, her head becoming heavier with each breath. It eased her gently down, into a lying position with the blanket draped over her.

"If you will excuse me," it said. Then it too abandoned her, the door locking behind it and leaving her alone once more.

CHAPTER TWENTY-FIVE

OLUS STOOD AT THE ENTRANCE to the lift that would bring him back to Level Two and tapped his communicator.

"Warden Lurin," he said angrily.

"Captain," the Warden said a moment later.

"What's wrong with the lift?" Olus asked.

"I apologize, Captain. There was a minor malfunction. We had to restart the operational services. It should be back online any moment."

Choice comments streamed through Olus' head. "A common occurrence down here?" he asked.

"I'm afraid so. The moisture in the air wreaks havoc on our electronics, which as you can probably guess are massively outdated. The Republic doesn't tend to pass much funding to penal worlds."

"It must be a hardship."

"There are worse positions in the RIA, I assure you."

A loud thump sounded, followed by a buzz as the lift began to lower.

"Here it comes now, Captain," Lurin said. "Is there anything else you require?"

"Not at the moment," he replied, closing the connection.

He jumped into the lift the moment it arrived, directing it back to

Level Two. It dropped him off there soon after, and he crossed the corridors of the facility as briskly as he could, pausing twice to request directions. He reached the medical ward a few minutes later, making his way past a row of mostly empty mattresses to the first bot in the line.

"Captain Mann," the bot said, scanning his face and matching it up with its internal personnel identification records. "How may I be of assistance."

"I want to speak with Lieutenant Abigail Cage. Warden Lurin told me I could find her here."

"Yes, Captain. Abigail Cage is in Isolation Room Three. She is currently asleep."

Why was he not surprised?

"I'd like to see her, anyway," Olus said.

"Of course, Captain. This way."

The bot walked ahead of him, leading him to the isolation room. It was one of five, located near the center.

"Is there anyone in any of the other rooms?" Olus asked.

"No, Captain."

"Open the door."

"Yes, Captain."

The bot extended a pin-sized spike from one of its hands, sticking it into a matching receptacle on the wall and turning it. The door slid open.

Olus paused at the threshold, staring in at the woman asleep on a raised mattress at the back end of the small room. He couldn't see much of her under a light blanket, but he could judge from her features that she had a well-proportioned face.

"Lieutenant Cage," he said.

She didn't stir.

He watched the blanket for a moment. Her breaths were smooth and even, and very, very light.

"Lieutenant Cage," he repeated, a little louder.

She still didn't respond.

"I informed you that she was sleeping, Captain," the bot said.

"I know," Olus replied. He walked over to her.

"Captain, I am sorry, but she should not be disturbed."

"Will her health be compromised if she's disturbed?"

"No, Captain."

"Then shut up."

He leaned over her, studying her face from a different angle. She might have been pretty to some, not pretty to others. It was all a matter of taste, and he didn't care one way or another. He was old enough to be her great-great-great-grandfather, if not more.

"Lieutenant Cage," he said again.

Nothing.

He lowered himself, coming closer to her, putting his face near hers. He breathed in as she breathed out, furrowing his brow as the smell of her breath reached him. He shifted his eyes, glancing over at the bot.

Lurin had given her a sedative. He had suspected as much, but he knew it was true. He could smell it on her. The Warden wouldn't know he had that kind of training. The HSOC didn't advertise the skills it imparted on its members.

"Lieutenant Cage," he said again, futilely. If Lurin had slipped her the drug while the lift was out of commission, it would be at least six hours before she was alert enough to respond.

Her head turned slightly, and a soft groan escaped. What? Had he been wrong? Maybe Lurin had given her the drug before his arrival.

"Lieutenant."

Her eyes opened a millimeter or two. They shifted rapidly back and forth. She was starting to come out of it.

"What?" she said softly.

"My name is Captain Olus - ooph!"

He was thrown backward as her hand shot up from beneath the blanket, hitting him square in the chest. He hit the ground, rolling over into a squat.

Lieutenant Cage was sitting up, staring straight ahead. "No," she said. "No. Don't."

He got back to his feet. His chest hurt, and he had lost his breath.

"Lieutenant," he said as strongly as he could.

"No!" she shouted, turning her head to look at him. Her body was shaking.

"Captain, I believe you should allow the patient to rest," the bot said, reaching for him.

Olus shrugged himself away, moving toward her. "Abigail," he said.

"Leave me alone!" she cried, putting her hand up toward him.

He wasn't sure what happened next, but he found himself against the wall beside the doorway.

"Captain," the bot said again, forever calm.

She was staring at him. Watching him like a predator. He turned his head away, sliding up the wall and moving toward the door. She seemed to relax as he backed away.

He exited the room. The bot followed behind him, closing and locking the door.

Lurin had warned him that she wasn't well, but this? Something was happening here. Something that made his skin crawl.

He didn't know what to make of it. What he did know was that with all the authority he did have, it didn't include removing mentally unfit prisoners from treatment.

If he was going to get Lieutenant Cage out, he was going to have to do it the hard way.

CHAPTER TWENTY-SIX

OLUS HADN'T TOLD THE WARDEN why he really wanted to meet with the prisoners, but he knew from Gant that the Warden had been listening in during his interviews and monitoring everything that was said. He had been careful not to reveal too much - years in the field had taught him to be smarter than that - but he had suggested aloud that he was going to order transfers for the convicts he had selected. Transfers to his command, under his control, with his authority.

Earlier, he had thought that maybe he had made a mistake. That he should have been even more cryptic and careful, although that would have made the selection process that much harder. Now, he was almost grateful for the reveal.

It was going to make what came next that much more of a surprise.

He left the medical ward, finding his way to Lurin's office. He entered without knocking, catching the Warden with a large mass of written documentation projected at eye level, forms he recognized immediately as requisition requests.

"Captain," Lurin said, dismissing the projection. "I warned you about Lieutenant Cage, sir."

"You did," Olus agreed. "I'm sorry I didn't listen. What happened to her?"

"Post-traumatic stress, I believe, but I'm not a physician. I've requested a specialist be sent in to analyze her and document her case. It's a shame, really. She was a good miner."

Olus kept his expression flat. "Will she be transferred out to a rehabilitation center?" He already knew the answer. He wanted to see and hear how the Sergeant responded.

"No, Captain," Lurin replied. "You should know, the only way out of Hell is death." Lurin tried to smile, a difficult maneuver for an Atmo. It was more comical than anything, his lips forming an oval, his tiny teeth hidden behind them.

"You might have overheard that I was planning on changing that rule," Olus said. "I came to Hell to locate recruits."

"Recruits?" Lurin said, acting surprised. "What for?"

"That's classified. The point is, I've decided against it. This episode with Cage has shown me that it was a bad idea. I just stopped by to thank you for the use of your facility, and for your patience while I undertook this process."

"Oh. Of course, Captain. We are both servants of the Republic, and I was honored to be of assistance to you." Lurin stood up and circled his desk, pausing in front of Olus to salute. Olus returned the gesture. "I'll escort you back to the hangar, sir."

"That isn't necessary," Olus replied. "I can see you have quite a bit of bureaucracy to catch up on."

Lurin shook his head. "You have no idea. Master Sergeant Packard was not a fan of red tape."

"Is anybody?" Olus asked. "Goodbye, Sergeant."

"Goodbye, Captain."

Olus left the office, tapping his communicator as he did.

"Commander Usiari," he said.

"Captain," the commander of the *Driver* said a moment later. "What do you need, sir?"

"I'm ready for pickup. Can you please send a shuttle down?"

"Immediately, sir."

"Thank you."

He closed the connection, heading for the lift and taking it up to the hangar. He was overwhelmed the moment he left the climate controlled confines of the administrative level, having forgotten how hot it was while wearing the coolsuit. He was amazed all over again that anything could live in it with no hope of relief. He could have waited on Level Two for the shuttle, but he wanted to experience the heat, as oppressive as it was.

He stood sweating in the hangar for twenty minutes, climbing into the shuttle and closing his eyes as a raft of cool air washed over him once more. He wiped the sweat from his forehead with the sleeve of his uniform and then waited patiently while they made the return trip to the *Driver*, floating in orbit around the planet.

He didn't waste any time once he was back on board, summoning Commander Usiari to meet with him in his quarters, not even bothering to change from his sweaty clothes or clean himself up before he arrived.

"Captain," Usiari said. "You wanted to see me?"

"Yes, Commander," Olus replied. "Please, come in."

The door to his quarters opened and Usiari entered.

"Sir?"

"Commander. You understand that my mission and the means by which I carry out that mission are top secret, do you not?"

"Aye, sir."

"You also understand that I have complete authority over the *Driver* and all of the assets within, including yourself?"

"Aye, sir."

Olus watched him for signs of tension or concern. Meeting with Lurin had raised his suspicion, and he wasn't going to release it lightly.

"If you don't mind, sir, why do you ask?"

"I have a few requirements, Commander, and I'm going to ask a small number of your crew to act in a manner that could be viewed as treasonous without a full appreciation of the circumstances surrounding my requests, circumstances which I am not at liberty to describe in full. I will make it clearly known that this operation falls under my jurisdiction and comes under my orders, but it must be clear to both you and the affected crew members that one, no word of my requests shall ever leave them or this ship under penalty of court-martial and imprisonment, and two, orders will be carried out without question. Do you understand?"

"Aye, sir," Usiari said without hesitation. "My orders are clear in that regard. I am to do as you ask. My crew will do the same."

Olus nodded, convinced by the Commander's reaction that he was an honest soldier. "Good. Who on your ship is the most skilled with networking?"

"I'm sorry, sir. We don't have a Breaker in our manifest."

"I know, but you must have a tech or three in charge of maintaining onboard systems?"

"Aye, sir. That would be Petty Officer Nort, sir."

"Please have him come and see me in thirty EM. Do you have any softsuits available?"

"I'll have to check, Captain. We don't have any Marines on board either. We're running zero atmosphere this tour. What do you need it for?" Olus made a face, and the Commander lowered his head. "None of my concern. Aye, sir. My apologies. I will resolve your request shortly."

"Thank you. There are a few other things I'll need. Hopefully, you'll have them. We need to make this quick, Commander. Time is definitely not on our side."

"Aye, sir."

Olus began rattling off a list of equipment, his mind working furiously to round out the fullness of his plan. He was supposed to be retired from active combat duty.

It seemed that fate had something else in mind.

CHAPTER TWENTY-SEVEN

"I'M IN, CAPTAIN," PETTY OFFICER Lohse said, a little too excited over his successful hacking of a private Republic MilNet. Olus didn't think anyone should be that happy to commit what amounted to treason, but then again, what he was about to do was much, much worse.

"Go now," Olus said, reaching over from the rear seat of the small Shuriken starfighter and tapping the pilot on the shoulder.

"Roger," the pilot replied, sliding his finger along the throttle to push it to the max.

Olus was shoved back into his seat as the agile craft was jerked forward by sudden, massive ionic thrust, shooting through the *Driver's* shields and out into space, immediately altering direction and turning to face the planet below.

Hell was just as ugly from space as it was from the surface, a brown and orange blob of jagged rock and flowing lava streams. He hoped that when he was done with this place, he would never have to see it again.

"Orbital sensors are offline, Captain," Lohse reported. "I'm ready to open the hangar shields at your command."

"Standby," Olus replied, checking the feed to his helmet. Commander Usiari hadn't let him down, locating a softsuit in the ship's inventory. It was a little smaller than he would have preferred, but he had managed to fit himself into it.

"Two minutes to ingress," Lieutenant Holt said. "Hold onto your lunch."

The Shuriken began to bounce a little as it hit the atmosphere, its angled shape punching through the sudden influx of air and hurtling toward the planet. It broke through a dozen seconds later, smoothing out as it descended, coming down hard toward the rough terrain below. Olus held himself steady, trying not to flinch as they neared the floor, gripping the seat between his legs tightly while Holt broke the fall, firing vectoring thrusters and increasing power to the anti-gravity modules. The fighter shuddered and complained as it pulled out of the drop, rolled to port and then gained a little altitude back, nearly striking the side of a cliff as the pilot brought it back under control.

"One minute to ingress," Holt said as if the prior maneuver was nothing. "On target."

"Officer Lohse, prepare for shield deactivation," Olus said.

"Ready and waiting, sir," Lohse replied.

"Is there any indication they know what's happening?"

"No, sir. It doesn't seem that anyone is actively monitoring the system. Even the passcodes were outdated."

Olus smiled. He had been counting on Packard's laziness to work to his benefit, and so far it was.

"Thirty seconds," Holt said, navigating the fighter a hundred meters above the surface, shifting it back and forth to avoid taller obstacles.

The added stealth measures were unnecessary in light of their control over the colony's network, but Olus wasn't one to leave things to chance.

He counted his breaths until he reached eight. "Lower the shields," he ordered.

"Aye, sir," Lohse replied. Three more seconds passed. "Shields down."

"I'm going in," Holt said, altering the starfighter's path again, rising into the atmosphere and then rolling over and turning toward the open mouth of the entrancc to Hell. He didn't slow the ship as he approached it, blasting through and into the tunnels leading down to the facility.

"Lohse, I want lights out and every internal feed offline," Olus said.

"Aye, sir."

The Shuriken slowed slightly as it reached the hangar, sweeping around the back of it before decelerating quickly, pushing Olus forward in his seat. The lighting vanished a moment later, leaving them in pitch black. Both helmets adjusted a moment later, switching to infrared and giving them a view of their surroundings that the guards wouldn't have. The starfighter touched down, the canopy above the cockpit sliding back as it did. Olus unbuckled himself from it, picking up his rifle and vaulting over the lip of the cockpit, onto the side of the craft where he slid off and to the floor.

The Shuriken was ascending before he had taken more than a handful of steps, hurrying toward the pair of techs who had been left blind. He pulled a pair of nerve sticks from the softsuit, hitting each of them in the neck with the devices and knocking them unconscious. Then he rushed to the lift, removing a small disc from a tightpack and putting it to the controls. Lohse was doing a good job so far, but there were a few systems he had to handle himself.

He tapped the tactile controls on the suit, the terminal commands for the lift service slipping into the corner of his helmet's visor. He broke into it easily, finding the software hadn't been patched in nearly four years, leaving it vulnerable. He triggered the commands to send it downward. Level Twenty to start, then Eighteen and Fifteen.

He could hardly believe he was about to help some of the most dangerous individuals in the galaxy break out of one of the Republic's worst prisons, and that he was doing it in the name of the same Republic.

"Sir, we have local activity on the network," Lohse said. "I'm losing access."

The lift reached Level Twenty. "I expected you would. You've done well. Get out before you're identified."

"Aye, sir."

It was unlikely that Lurin wouldn't guess who was behind this, but the Warden wouldn't dare report it to Republic Command. There would be too many questions about why the head of the OSI felt the need to break into a facility he had authority over, and if there was something dirty going on here the increased scrutiny was highly likely to expose it.

And he was experienced enough to be certain there was something dirty going on here. The only question was: what?

It was a question for another time. He had enough to worry about already.

The lights suddenly came back on, an alert signal sounding throughout the prison. He could hear the synthetic voice instructing the prisoners to return to their cells immediately, and he allowed himself a small grin as the lift shuddered behind him, trying to follow the instructions coming from the mainframe and being overridden by his local patch.

He raised his rifle to his shoulder, flipping the toggle next to the trigger to switch the munitions type being loaded into the chamber. It had been at least ten standard since he had last made a combat drop, but the muscle memory had remained, and he felt like he hadn't missed a beat.

He moved deeper into the level, his clothes already soaking through beneath the softsuit, the lightweight armor holding in the gathering heat. He had to be quick if he had any hope of getting out before he cooked himself.

A guard in a battlesuit came around the corner ahead of him, his helmet marking the target before he made visual contact. He reacted from experience, shifting himself to the opposite side of the corridor and taking aim, squeezing off a round in the space of a heartbeat. The munition smacked into the battlesuit and flashed, the localized electromagnetic pulse cutting through the weaker shielding of the older model of the armor and disabling it, leaving its wearer trapped inside.

"Thanks again, Packard," Olus said as he moved past the guard, waving to him on the way.

He ran down the corridor, nearing the central cell block a moment later. Not only were the cells on lockdown, but the entire block was sealed off, a heavy blast door stopping him from entering.

It was too bad for them he didn't need to get inside.

Not yet, anyway.

He removed another disc from a tightpack and slapped it on the controls, quickly breaking into the system. He didn't use the access to open the blast door. Instead, he used the network connection to move further into the systems, deeper into the door controls. It was trivial to navigate his way to Level Twenty, searching for specific cell doors.

He found them a moment later:

2015: Merrett, B.

2315: Pik.

2401: Gant.

He entered the override command, and they all unlocked and slid open. Then he found the controls to the security door at the base of the guard spike.

He opened that one, too.

He held the connection to the disc, watching his back as he counted up to one hundred. Then he toggled the blast door, switching munitions as it slid aside, just in case.

Bastion was just coming out of the tower, one of the guards' rifles in his hands. Pik was with him, the nearly four meter tall Trover hulking over the back of the pilot. When he saw Olus, he squared the weapon off, ready to fire.

"Hold your fire, Worm," Olus snapped.

"Captain Mann?" Bastion replied, momentarily confused. He started to lower the rifle before changing his mind. "Give me one good reason, you son of a bitch."

"One," Gant said, rounding the side of the spike and pointing at Bastion's bracelet. It had started to buzz a delayed warning.

"They've regained control of the deterrence system," Olus said. "You have about twenty seconds to either kill me or escape with me."

"But you can't have both," Gant said, shaking a furry wrist. His bracelet was gone. "Captain, I thought you changed your mind?"

"No, but I needed a different approach. Lurin is as crooked as Packard was, and I'm a man of my word."

"Damn it," Bastion said, lowering the rifle. "Get this thing off me."

Gant walked over to him, a small, shaped sliver of metal in his hand. "Hold still," he said, putting the metal below the bracelet. He made a practiced motion with his hand, and the bracelet clicked and fell off. He did the same for Pik.

"How long?" Pik asked.

"Have I been able to take the bracelet off ?" Gant asked. "About two weeks after I got here." He turned to Olus. "Where is she?"

"Level Two," Olus replied. "We have a couple of stops to make first."

"If they know you're here, they'll be aiming to move her before you can collect."

"Move her where? I've got a bird circling the complex. They won't make it out without me knowing."

"Collect who?" Bastion asked before figuring it out for himself. "Cage? You can't be fragging serious. She's a demon, Captain. She's out of control."

"What the frag do you know, Bastion?" Gant said. "You think every whisper you hear is the cold truth. You probably think Santa Claus is real."

"First, mind your business about Terran customs, you little freak-monkey. Second, Santa Claus is real, isn't he, Captain?"

"Let's go," Olus said.

CHAPTER TWENTY-EIGHT

"IS IT COOLER UP HERE?" Bastion asked. "It feels cooler. At least five degrees."

"That makes a difference down here?" Pik asked.

"Sure does. My balls are only half as sweaty."

"Shut it," Olus said, scanning the corridor ahead of them. They had moved up to Level Eighteen, heading for the cell block. It was noticeably cooler two levels up, but it was hardly what anyone would describe as comfortable.

He was approaching the floor more slowly and more cautiously than he had on Level Twenty. He had used up the element of surprise, and now that the bracelets were back under the prison's control it wouldn't do any good to let the prisoners out. Even so, he could imagine someone was working feverishly to try to bypass his lift patch and get reinforcements down to their position, and he was amused by the inherent futility. If Hell didn't have the budget for newer equipment, it certainly didn't have room on the payroll for anything more than a generally competent systems admin.

"Who's the mark?" Gant asked, remaining close to Olus' side.

"Benhil Visani," Olus replied. "Also known as Joker. Cell 1847."

"Joker?" Bastion said. "Aren't there enough clowns in this outfit already?"

"There's you," Gant said. "So, more than enough."

"Funny."

"Joker's a former HSOC," Olus said. "Espionage. He spent three years in the Outworlds and knows them as well as anyone in the Republic. That makes him valuable."

"How'd he wind up in Hell?" Bastion said.

"You'd have to ask him yourself. Stay alert; we're almost there."

They reached the corridor leading to the cells. As Olus had expected, the blast door had stayed open, revealing a number of hastily abandoned tables ahead of the guard spike.

"Chow time already?" Pik asked. "No wonder I'm hungry."

"You're always hungry," Bastion said.

"It's muscle," the Trover replied, patting a bulging roundness in his gut.

"Yeah, right. How the frag do you manage to get fat on rationed meal bars and daily labor in the mines?"

"Trade," Pik replied.

"Yeah? Like what?"

"I said to stay alert," Olus said. "Shut your hole, Worm, or I'll leave your ass here."

Bastion fell silent. It didn't matter how long any of them had spent in Hell, responding to sharply barked commands was ingrained in their DNA.

Olus scanned the area ahead of them, picking up three targets through his helmet's infrared. They were sitting at the top of the spike, ready to fire down on anyone who went into the room.

"I'm guessing there's no other way in," he said.

"No," Gant replied.

"Here," Olus said, holding out his rifle. "I'm going to hit the control panel. I'll open the door to the tower. Pik, I want you to make a break for it."

"Yes, sir," Pik said.

"I can't help you with that," Gant said, wiggling his two fingers and thumbs. "Gant don't carry guns for a reason."

Olus realized that he might be able to work the trigger, but the shape of his hand wouldn't let him grip the weapon strongly enough to deal with the weight or the recoil.

"Right. You go with Pik. Worm, you cover."

"Yes, sir," Bastion said.

Olus slid along the wall, staying clear of the line of fire through the open blast doors. He made it to the control panel, pulling out another extender and attaching it to the pad. Lines of code ran down one side of his helmet, and he tapped at his hip, quickly reaching the door access. He looked back at the rest of his team and gave them the thumbs up.

Pik charged forward, while Gant jumped up and grabbed the back of his shoulders, riding along behind him. Bastion slipped out from cover, firing on the top of the guard spike. The rounds echoed in the tight space, drowning out any other potential noise. Olus watched the Trover approach the tower door, triggering it to open as he neared.

The Trover burst into the spike and vanished, Gant still clinging to his back. Bastion cursed and ducked back into the corridor, throwing his stolen rifle to the floor.

"It's empty," he said.

A short commotion followed. Then a voice came over the local speakers.

"Clear, Captain," Gant said.

Olus and Bastion moved into the block. Olus headed up the steps to Benhil's cell, pulling another item from a tightpack and attaching it to the door. It sparked and fizzled, and the door unlocked and slid open.

"What the hell is this?" its occupant said. He was sitting on his mattress, an array of crumbs spread out in front of him in an obvious but unrecognizable pattern. He was a lanky man, with dark skin and darker eyes that glanced up at him in curiosity.

"Time to go, Benhil," Olus said.

"You know that prison breaks are illegal, don't you, Captain?"

"Nothing is illegal until you get caught," Olus replied. "At least, that's what you said at your trial."

Benhil laughed, deep and hearty as he got to his feet. "It's true." Then he held up his wrist. "You have a cure for what ails me?"

Olus was going to call for Gant, but the Gant was already there. Benhil backed up at the sight of him.

"Whoa. What the frag is that?"

"You've never seen a Gant before?" Gant asked.

"A what?"

"A Gant. From the planet Ganemant."

"You look like a squirrel."

"I do not."

"You're furry."

"So are oxen. Would you say an ox looks like a squirrel?"

"I've never seen an ox, so yeah, probably."

"I bet you think Rudin look like octopuses, too."

"No. They look like squids. And isn't it octopi?"

Gant shook his head. "No, it's octopuses. Just give me your wrist."

Benhil held out his wrist. Gant retrieved his bent metal device and quickly undid the bracelet.

"Nice!" Benhil exclaimed, rubbing at the wrist. "Thanks, squirrel-man."

"You really need this guy?" Gant asked.

Olus nodded. "Come on."

They regrouped at the base of the spike, making quick introductions before heading back to the lift and coming up short.

It was gone.

"Well," Gant said, turning to Olus. "Now what?"

CHAPTER TWENTY-NINE

ABBEY KEPT HER EYES CLOSED. She didn't want the Warden to know she was awake.

She didn't want anyone to know she was alert.

She had already made that mistake once. It was one she wasn't going to make again.

She wasn't sure what was happening to her. She wasn't sure what was real and what wasn't. She knew that Hell was all that she had expected it to be, but it was also something else. Something darker. Something that felt cold and evil and wrong. She knew she only had two choices left in her life.

Get out, or die trying.

Lurin would be back. She knew he would. If he wasn't, someone would be. They hadn't sedated her to keep her here. They were going to move her at some point. Not that anyone would ever know it. She had already been removed from the universe. Erased from existence. Framed and convicted and buried.

She was still alive because she had value to someone, but she knew what would happen once her value had waned. If her life was going to end, then it would end on her terms. She had decided not to let Hell destroy her. She wasn't going to let anyone or anything else do it, either.

She didn't know how long she had been lying there. Two hours? Three? Four? She vaguely remembered someone coming to her cell, and then the medical bot giving her another injection of the sedative. It had put her out for an hour or two, but it had worn off in a hurry, leaving her awake, alert, ready, and waiting.

She heard the soft hiss of her cell door sliding open. She kept her eyes closed, listening. Metal feet on the tiled floor. The medical bot. Two other pairs of booted feet. Guards?

"Be careful with her," she heard Lurin say. "She isn't to be harmed."

She fought to keep herself still as the blanket was pulled away. Someone gripped her legs, lifting them and sliding something over them. She recognized the familiar feel of the hellsuit as she was repositioned to get it beneath her. Then her arms were lifted, the sleeves pulled on, the front closed. At least they had the decency to clothe her before taking her away.

When that was done, she was lifted and moved to another platform. She could feel her orientation change as it adjusted to exit the room. She could sense the soldiers behind her head and in front of her feet. Lurin had to be somewhere nearby.

A cold hand gripped her wrist. The medical bot. She resisted every temptation to panic, using what she had learned in training to maintain her calm and keep her heart rate slow. She was supposed to be unconscious.

"Vital signs are stable. Heart rate is slightly elevated but within acceptable parameters."

"Honorant," a voice said through a communicator. "I've regained command of the lift controls. I'm bringing it up now."

"Thank you, Agitant," Lurin said. "I expected you would succeed where my poor excuse for a systems technician failed." A short tone signaled the disconnect. "High Honorant Ward."

"Honorant Lurin," a new voice said.

"The rogue Republic operative is contained, along with the escaping prisoners. When can I expect your arrival?"

"We will arrive within two standard," Ward replied. "I trust you can keep things under control for that long?"

"Of course, sir. You are aware there's a Goliath class battleship orbiting the planet, and a Shuriken patrolling the surface?"

"I don't expect either to be a problem."

"What about the council, sir? We need to clean up this mess quickly before any word of unrest can make it back to them."

"Don't concern yourself with the Council, Lurin. It will be handled as usual. We've already put a plan in motion to purify our position there."

"Yes, sir. As you command."

Another disconnect tone sounded, slightly different than the first, signaling the connection was dropped from the other end.

Agitant? Honorant? They sounded like titles or ranks, but they were nothing Abbey had ever heard of before. A rogue Republic operative? Escaping prisoners? She didn't like the sound of any of it.

She needed to get out.

"Take her to my office. I want her close to the lift and ready for transfer as soon as the High Honorant arrives."

"Yes, sir," the guard said.

The platform began to move. She could hear the boots of the guards on either side of it, leading it out of the isolation room and into the medical ward. The ward itself was silent. Empty? She didn't dare open her eyes to look.

They left the medical ward, moving at a steady pace. She could feel it when the platform she was riding on changed direction, and she tried to memorize the path. Not that she wanted to go back to medical, but she had no idea how easily navigated the layout was.

They stopped a few minutes later. They must have reached the Warden's office.

Abbey kept her eyes shut. The guards remained in position on either end of the platform, surprising her with their rigid attention as a few more minutes passed. A lot of soldiers would have been tempted to sit down, relax, or otherwise lose focus on the task at hand. Especially the guards in Hell, who didn't tend to be the most successful members of the RIA.

But these weren't Republic Intergalactic Army soldiers. They were something else, going by different titles and following a different order. Did they have anything to do with Private Illiard's warning? She had a feeling they did.

First things first. This was the best chance she was going to get. She had to take it.

She opened her eyes slowly, leaving just the smallest slit through which she could see a blurred image of the guard ahead of her. He was wearing a lightsuit, similar to a softsuit but without the embedded tech that allowed Breakers to do what they did. That was good. It would be much easier to take a soldier in a lightsuit. She had to assume the other guard was equipped similarly.

She flexed her hands a few times. Slowly, so she wouldn't be noticed. Despite everything that had happened, her body felt strong. Loose. Ready. She needed to knock the forward guard down quickly, taking him by surprise before the rear guard could stop her. One on one, she had a fighting chance.

Take him down with what? She didn't have any weapons. HSOC training taught every operative to kill unarmed, but she had never had to do it before. That wasn't completely true. She had killed Pok with nothing more than a sliver of metal, and she had done it without hesitation, an act that had made the other L20s wary of her. It was her or them. Besides, who would she be killing, anyway? If anything, these individuals were the real traitors to the Republic.

And they were responsible for her being here.

Bastards.

She allowed herself one more light breath in. Then she made her move, tucking her legs beneath her as she sat up, pushing off, wrapping her arms around the forward guard's neck as her momentum carried them both away from the rear guard.

He stumbled forward, trying to regain his balance from her surprise assault, reaching out to get his hand on something to help him stay upright. She continued wrapping herself around him, turning her body and using her weight to pull him to the side. He tripped and fell, coming down hard on top of her, pressing against her freshly healed ribs. She heard a crack at the same time, and his head fell limp.

One down.

She looked past him, along the length of his body. He had a nerve baton holstered at his side, and she reached down and grabbed it as the second guard rounded the platform in pursuit. She shoved the body away while she rolled out from under it, barely evading the guard's boot when he tried to kick her in the stomach.

"Doesn't unharmed mean anything to you?" she asked, spinning from her knees to her feet and lashing out with the baton. It struck harmlessly against the side of the guard's helmet, and he reached out for her, trying to grab her wrist.

She backed away, holding the baton out. The guard pulled his own baton, trailing her as she put Lurin's desk between them.

"Who are you?" she said, pissed at herself for getting stuck here.

The guard didn't answer. She could see his lips moving, though. Calling for reinforcements.

Get out or die trying.

She glanced down at the desk. Then she pounced forward, using her arms to vault off it, leading with her legs. The guard hit her in the right knee with the nerve baton, but he didn't knock her off course. Both feet slammed into his chest, knocking him backward and into the gurney. He tripped over it and onto the floor.

She kept moving forward, landing on the other side, almost falling herself as her deadened knee threatened to give out. She shifted her balance, using her left leg to spring forward toward the guard, who was reaching for his sidearm.

She smacked his hand with the baton, dropping it away from the weapon. Then she came down on top of him, grabbing the gun for herself.

She put it to the clear visor of his helmet and pulled the trigger, turning away as the round blasted through the transparency and into his head.

It was ugly, but it had worked.

She pushed herself back up, noticing the feeling already returning to her knee. Getting hit with a nerve baton like that should have deadened the area for at least an hour, even if the jolt wasn't enough to knock her out. She didn't know why it hadn't, but she was grateful.

She stepped over the dead guard, heading toward the door, stopping when she saw an entire squad of guards in battlesuits bearing down. Damn it. She eyed the frame of the Warden's door, noting that it was reinforced. Probably to protect the prison's most visible sign of authority in the case of an emergency. She smiled. Perfect. Now it would protect her.

She tapped the control pad. There was no security on it from the inside, and the door closed with a sharp hiss and a bang as it sealed in place. Then she hurried back to the Warden's desk, activating his terminal, coughing out a laugh when the projection appeared over it. The idiot hadn't even locked it.

Her fingers began moving across the interface, quickly navigating to the subsystems hidden beneath the dumbed-down display. A rogue Republic operative caught without a ride up?

Not for long.

CHAPTER THIRTY

"SHIT," OLUS CURSED, HIS LATEST effort to recall the lift failing spectacularly, a shower of sparks reaching out and burning the fingers of his softsuit. Trying to override the override hadn't worked, and so he had made an effort to alter the wiring, opting for a manual hack instead.

"It was a good try, Captain," Bastion said. "As much as I hate you, I have to admit."

"Better to die on the road to freedom than to die quietly," Benhil said. "Although I suppose I can go back to my cell to wait this out." He laughed again. "Nice meeting you all. Enjoy your executions."

He took a few steps toward the cell block before Pik blocked his path.

"I don't think so," the Trover said.

Benhil put up his hands. "Fine. Have it your way. We can all die here together."

"We aren't going to die," Olus said. "I'll get it working."

"You said that five minutes ago," Bastion said. "Freak-monkey, you know how to take the bracelets off but not how to hotwire a lift?"

"It's Gant," Gant said. "Call me freak-monkey again, and I'll kill you."

Bastion looked at the floor, backing up a few steps. "Uh. Yeah.

Right. Well?"

"I've never studied the wiring diagrams of a Republic military penal colony," Gant said. "I had two weeks to study the bracelet. I can try?"

Olus checked the wires. They were dark brown at the ends. Burned. He pulled on them, trying to get enough slack to splice again. "Standby," he said.

How had the Warden managed to bypass his patch? His hack should have been beyond the aptitude of any non-HSOC.

He tugged on one of the wires, another spark firing as a result and forcing him to back away.

"Damn it."

A light hum followed. The lift started to descend.

"You did it," Benhil said.

"I didn't do anything," Olus replied, surprised at the result.

"Hello?" a female voice said, generated from the wall to his left. "Is anyone there?"

"Abbey?" Gant said. "Is that you, Queenie?"

"Gant?" Abbey replied. "Gant, what the frag is going on?"

"What do you think? We're rescuing you."

"You're doing a bang-up job."

"Lieutenant Cage," Olus said. "My name is Captain Olus Mann, Republic Office of Strategic Intelligence."

"OSI?" Abbey said. "Are you here about the assholes who are running this place?"

"Not exactly," Olus replied. "Where are you?"

"Barricaded in the Warden's office. I've got a patch on the door, but they're going to burn through it sooner or later. I've got the lift coming down to you. You can finish rescuing me."

"It's good to hear your voice, Queenie," Gant said. "I was worried about you."

"That's sweet," Abbey said. "Get the hell up here."

"We need to make a stop on Level Fifteen," Olus said.

"Are you serious?" Abbey asked.

"It's important. If you can help disable security there, it would speed things up."

"You are serious. I'll see what I can do. Make it quick."

The lift reached them, and they piled in. It ascended three floors to Fifteen before coming to a stop.

"They've got the burners on the door," Abbey said, her voice coming from the wall near the lift. "I give it five minutes, six if they're cautious. They seem to want me alive."

"Who does?" Olus said.

"I was hoping you could tell me."

"Three minutes, then get the lift moving." Olus turned to the others. "Wait here. I'll get Razor and then we're gone. Lieutenant, if you can open the door to cell 1515 and disable the occupant's bracelet, it would go a long way."

"Aye, Captain," Abbey said. "Is there anything you want me to tell her?"

Olus smiled. "Just tell her the bracelet is inactive, and it's time to go."

"Affirmative."

Olus started running, heading down the corridor at full speed. He wasn't worried about opposition. Not now. The only thing he was racing was the clock.

He reached the cell block inside of a minute, his rifle up as he cleared the blast doors, aiming toward the top of the guard spike. He didn't see any guards. He also didn't hear anything.

"Razor?" he said, turning slowly, his helmet assisting him in scanning the area. He kept the rifle ready. His heart was thumping, and he could feel the sweat running down his chest.

Something pressed against his neck, finding the space between the helmet and the softsuit.

"I'm here," Razor said.

Olus glanced down. Where had she gotten a knife?

"Razor," he said. "Is this necessary?"

"I don't know, Captain," she replied. "Is it?"

"I told you I would get you out of here."

"I'm out, sir. That makes you expendable."

"We had a deal."

She laughed. "I had a deal with my commander of the *Singularity*, too, Captain. That didn't keep me out of Hell."

"I know," Olus said. "I can't help you fix that if I'm dead."

"Fix it? You can't fix it, sir. You can't fix me."

"I can give you a chance at a new life. One that isn't spent down here."

"Like I said, I'm out already, sir."

"There's another soldier I'm trying to get out. Lieutenant Abigail Cage."

"I've never heard of her."

"She's the one who let you out. She's in trouble. The same kind of trouble you were in when nobody helped you. When you were blamed instead. Help me help her."

"How do I know you aren't bullshitting me?"

"Come and see, Airi."

The blade remained for a few more seconds. Then she pulled it away. "Very well."

Olus turned to look at the petite woman. Her face and hellsuit were both glistening with blood. None of it was hers. He bowed to her, locking his eyes on hers.

She stared at him for a moment, surprised he knew the custom. She bowed in return.

They ran back to the lift together.

CHAPTER THIRTY-ONE

ABBEY WATCHED AIRI SOTO'S NEWLY-disarmed bracelet move through the corridors of Level Fifteen, headed back toward the lift where she assumed the others were waiting. Captain Mann had promised three minutes, and with her help, he had delivered, retrieving the RIA soldier from her perdition and bringing her along.

For what purpose? Why was he collecting prisoners? Why was he helping them escape? And why had they been coming to save her?

Captain Mann knew about the Warden, and about the prison. It was clear the Republic's command over it was tenuous at best. At least, the part of the Republic she was still loyal to, and still willing to fight for. The other thing that had become apparent was that at least part of the nation was compromised, infiltrated by individuals like Lurin who went by alternate titles and bowed to alternate masters.

She glanced up at the bright flame that was piercing through the blast door. They were burning it instead of blowing it, still not wanting to risk hurting her. What the frag did they want with her, that they were willing to take the trouble? Why hadn't they killed her after she had killed two of theirs?

The job was almost complete, the flame three-quarters of the way through the door, a neat line of slagged metal showing the new outline of their efforts. Abbey looked back to the terminal. The lift was on the move, coming up. She checked one of the feeds near it on Level Two. Lurin had sent two full squads to defend it, knowing she had conquered his terminal and seized control of the facility.

She let herself smile at the thought. The Warden probably didn't know everything that she could do from here.

She navigated deeper into the systems, finding gravity control. Hell was dense and had some gravity of its own, but it was only about one-fifth standard, which was enough that they could live with it if they had to, but not enough to be comfortable for most. Nobody wanted to be banging their heads every time they moved.

"Captain Mann," she said, contacting his communicator. She had found the address in the Warden's records. The two had spoken multiple times over the last day. She wondered what about.

"Lieutenant Cage?" he replied.

"I'm going to turn off the gravitational equalizers," she said. "If you're ready for it and the guards aren't, it will give you an edge."

"Roger. Good thinking. We'll be ready."

"I'm also going to cut the ventilation. It's going to get hot in here in a hurry, but the inmates can handle it. Can you?"

"Do it, Lieutenant."

Abbey did, taking it one step further and reversing the airflow, pulling the hot air in faster while shutting down the cooling units. She was sure Lurin's lackey was watching it all, but she had already locked out his access and deleted permissions to every terminal that wasn't the Warden's. All he could do was watch.

That would teach them to screw with a Breaker.

The flame continued to burn through the door for a few more seconds. Then, surprisingly, it stopped, too early for them to break it down, even with a battlesuit.

Abbey checked the lift. It was nearly up. She cut the gravity equalizers.

She was close enough that she heard the gunfire when it started, and the shouting as guards found themselves overexerting, trying to move and winding up going too high or too far, having to recalculate to keep themselves from hitting the ceiling or bouncing off the walls. It wasn't that Captain Mann and the others wouldn't be affected, but since they knew it was going to happen, they were already prepared. Plus, she had a feeling the Captain was more than a little bit seasoned with alternate warfare and uncommon theaters. She had no doubt he was HSOC or had been at some point. Cadets who had gone through the training could always pick out like-trained individuals.

She started to lean back in the Warden's seat. It was only a matter of time before the inmates and the Captain broke through. The volume of gunfire was slowing already. She just had to be patient for another minutes or two and-

She barely threw herself out of the way as the blast door was ripped from the small bit of metal still holding it together, the larger piece of alloy tumbling toward the desk. It hit it with the force of a missile, causing it to explode so fiercely it was turned into little more than dust, the door itself cracking into the stone wall and becoming embedded in it.

Abbey looked up from her hands and knees, at the figure who had caused the damage. A man in a black lightsuit, holding a nerve baton in each hand, standing between her and freedom.

He wasn't wearing a helmet, and she recognized him immediately.

"Illiard?" she said. "What the frag?"

He didn't speak. He charged toward her, leading with the batons.

She pushed herself to her feet, barely jumping out of the way as the batons came in, using the reduced gravity to spring further than would have otherwise been possible. He adjusted quickly, lashing out and nearly hitting her in the temple. She could hear the whistle of the first baton past her ear, and she felt the numbing shock of the second as she blocked it with her forearm.

"You're working for them?" she said. "After you tried to warn me about this?"

He didn't answer, coming at her again. Her arm was already regaining feeling, which would have surprised her again if she had any time to think about it. Instead, she ducked low, moving in past his guard and hitting him in the gut with an elbow. The force was enough to lift him and push him back, and he threw himself over, hitting the ceiling with his feet and pushing back down, coming at her like a bullet.

She rolled aside, onto the body of the guard she had killed earlier, the one whose gun she hadn't taken. She reached for it now, pulling at it in desperation. Illiard was back on his feet, stalking toward her again in silence.

"What, did they turn you into some kind of fragging zombie?" she asked, struggling to pull the gun loose.

She cursed, digging her arms under the corpse and lifting, using the lightness to throw the body at Illiard. He ducked under it, catching two bullets in his forehead as he emerged.

"Shit, that was close," Abbey said, lowering the guard's gun.

She had almost lost her grip on the handle as the momentum helped her pull it free. Now she stood up again, looking down on Illiard. His eyes were a solid gray, like they were filled with metal. It was unnerving.

"What the hell happened to you?" she said.

His hand flinched. She felt something grab her ankle, and then she was down again, being pulled across the floor toward what should have been his dead body.

"Frag!" she shouted, firing the gun into Illiard.

He was still alive. Each movement of his body was jerky and out of sorts, but he was moving. There was no blood where she had shot him, only a small trickle of silver that plugged up the wound. The new holes she was putting in him didn't seem to have an effect.

He rose up, looming over her, bringing one of the nerve batons down at her chest. It hit her hard, sending jolts of pain through her body and leaving her momentarily paralyzed. The gun fell from her hand again, and he brought the other baton down on her thigh. She grunted in pain, unable to move while he raised the first baton and hit her in the chest again, and again, and again. She was numb to it by the fifth time, unable to move at all.

He stood up, reaching down and sliding his hands under her, lifting her easily as though she were a child. Her arms and legs were limp, her body out of commission. After that many hits from the batons, she shouldn't have even been alive.

He took a step forward. Then another. He was moving as though he were unsure of how to do it. He was trying to take her away.

A woman stepped into the doorway, blocking his path out. Abbey could barely see her in her peripheral vision, but she recognized the shape of the face. The woman charged in, leading with a blade of some kind. If Illiard tried to react, it wasn't obvious. The blade sank into his neck, and the woman shouted as she forced it to continue through.

Then Abbey was on the floor, the decapitated Illiard stumbling forward and depositing her there. She couldn't move her body. She could barely move her eyes.

"Queenie," she heard someone say. Then Gant was there, leaning over her. "Relax. It's going to be okay. We're getting out of here."

No!

She wanted to say it but couldn't. They had to find Lurin. They had to catch up to him and find out what he knew about everything that was happening here, and everything that had happened to her. There were questions, so many questions, and they needed him to answer them.

A new person entered the room. A huge Trover. She recognized Pik from the mess. He bent over her, lifting her gently into his massive arms.

"You have her?" Captain Mann said. She couldn't see him, but she recognized his voice.

"She was hit with a baton," Gant said.

"Then she'll live," Mann replied. "It's time to go. The *Driver's* picked up a disterium plume. Somebody's coming, and I don't think they're on our side."

"We're right behind you," Gant said.

Abbey tried to scream. She tried to wriggle. She tried to get free. She could sense some of the feeling coming back. She could wiggle the ends of her fingers. She needed to stop them. Five minutes. Lurin was hiding in here somewhere. He was nearly defenseless. She had to know why they had taken her. She had to know who they were, and what they wanted. She had to know how much trouble they were in.

It was no use. They carried her back to the lift, past a mix of dead guards and other soldiers in lightsuits. The lift didn't have far to go to reach the hangar, where one of the disterium transports was already online and waiting.

"Sir," someone's voice said through Mann's communicator. "We've just made contact. Republic vessels, sir. Two battleships. They're scrambling fighters to the surface and hailing us."

"Remember what I told you, Commander," Mann said.

"Aye, sir. Initiating zero contact protocol. Good luck, sir."

The connection closed.

"Zero contact protocol?" Gant said.

"It means we're on our own," Mann replied, leading them up the ramp into the transport. "Worm," he shouted. "Get us out of here. Now."

"Aye, Captain," Bastion replied, the ramp closing while the transport lifted and headed away from the hangar. "Anybody else here ever humped to FTL inside atmosphere before?"

Airi groaned, suggesting that she had. So had Abbey. She was paralyzed, and she still couldn't think of anything more unpleasant than accelerating faster than light so close to a planet's surface. She closed her eyes, the sudden pressure of the act threatening to squeeze her to death. The others cried out around her, all of them reacting with pained shouts which ended abruptly as the fiery agony cut them short. That intense pain lasted for nearly a minute, long after the transport had gone into FTL.

Long after they had left Hell behind.

CHAPTER THIRTY-TWO

BY THE TIME THE DISTERIUM transport came out of FTL twenty minutes later, Abbey had regained most of the use of her arms and was beginning to get feeling back into her legs. Her mouth was functional, and she had used it to thank Airi for cutting off Private Illiard's head and saving her.

Otherwise, she helped maintain the uncomfortable silence on the ship, relaxing against the side of the cargo hold next to one of four full disterium canisters, each containing enough of the refined crystalline powder to allow a battleship to spend nearly an entire month in FTL. Each one was worth more than she would ever see in her lifetime. Not that she cared all that much. She had other things on her mind. Things she wasn't going to discuss until she had more answers from Captain Mann, the foremost of which was who the frag he was, and why the frag had he just helped six cons from Hell break out of the penal colony.

And that was probably the easiest question.

She stowed it all for the moment. Time and place and this was neither. All of them were tired, sweaty, and on edge. She trusted Gant. She trusted Airi a little. The others? She and Bastion had never gotten along since he had helped Pok attack her, under Packard's order or not. Pik? She had never spoken to him, but he ran with Pok's gang of assholes, so that made him one, too. She didn't recognize the other inmate and didn't know his name. Captain Mann? He was Republic military. HSOC? A couple of months ago she would have followed him without hesitation. That was before people in the Republic, people like Davis, had fragged her.

"We're here," Mann said, announcing it directly to the five of them in the cargo hold, loud enough that Bastion could hear him from his position in the cockpit.

"Are you kidding me, Captain?" Bastion said, leaning over in the seat to look through the narrow corridor connecting the two parts of the vessel. "When you gave me the coordinates I thought we were headed for a battleship. A destroyer at least. Not whatever you want to call this hunk of space shit."

Abbey turned her head, trying to see out the viewport from her position. She got a small glimpse of what looked like the edge of a wing, decently sized but worn, with faded paint and burn marks along the top.

"Trust me, Worm," Mann said. "Where you're going, you'll be better off in the *Faust*."

"The *Faust*?" Gant said. "How apropos."

"I'm surprised you're familiar," Mann said.

"Ancient Terran history is part of my repertoire," Gant replied. "I can also make a mean omelet."

"Gant," Abbey said, her voice coming a little easier now.

"Yes, Queenie?"

"Shut up."

Gant chittered a laugh.

Captain Mann looked at her. "Feeling better?"

"Getting there," she replied. "Being hit six times with a nerve baton is not my idea of fun, and I was imprisoned in Hell."

She spoke the words deliberately, to judge his reaction. He bit part of his lip but didn't say anything. What did he know that she didn't?

"Six?" the inmate she didn't know said, whistling. "Damn. You're one lucky girl, Queenie. You should be dead."

Mann tapped on his communicator. "Ruby," he said.

"Yes, Captain," the voice came back. Female. Young. Synthetic. She could hear the slight distortion in the inflection.

"Move the *Faust* into sync and get us hooked up. I don't know if the incoming Republic forces are going to give chase, but if they do, I want us gone or close to it by the time they arrive."

"Yes, Captain," Ruby replied.

"Worm," Mann said. "Get us stationary. Ruby will take it from here."

"Aye, Captain," Bastion said.

"I don't get it," Pik said. "Why'd we have to break out of the prison? I thought you were going to get us out legal?"

"That was the plan," Mann said. "Don't worry. It's all legal or will be. I'll get everything straightened out."

"Straightened out?" Abbey said. "What's happening on Hell, Captain? And what kind of deal did you make with these other cons?"

"I don't know what's happening yet, Lieutenant," he replied. "I intend to find out, but to be honest I wasn't expecting to walk into the firestorm I found. Even so, it isn't my primary concern right now. As for the deal -"

Abbey cut him off. "Not your primary concern? Captain, I don't know who you are or what service you work for, but I have reason to believe that Warden Lurin, and Packard before him, and who knows who else, were abducting prisoners and either using them to conduct illegal experiments, or have been making illicit deals with them to bolster some kind of militant force."

"Kind of like you," the unknown inmate said. "I'm Benhil, by the way," he added, looking at Abbey.

"Abbey," she said. "Nice to meet you."

He laughed in response. "Likewise."

"There's nothing illicit about what I'm doing," Mann said. "To answer your question, Lieutenant, my name is Captain Olus Mann, Director of the Office of Strategic Intelligence. I have full, documented authority from General Iti Soto of the Republic Armed Services Committee to do anything necessary to complete my assigned mission. You and your crew were hand-selected to help me do just that, and as soon as I get in contact with General Soto, I intend to validate my actions and receive her final blessings for taking them. I'll also debrief her, not only on what I personally discovered during my time on Hell but also in reference to your experience."

Abbey stared at him. "You're Olus Mann?"

"You've heard of me?"

"Every Breaker wants to retire into OSI. Well, almost every Breaker. I'm sorry, sir, but I've been out of touch with the galaxy for awhile. What's going on that has you in the field?"

Whatever it was, it couldn't be good.

"That's right," Mann said. "You don't know. Four weeks ago, two prototype starships, the *Fire*, and the *Brimstone*, were taken from Eagan Heavyworks on Feru during a private demonstration of their new technology. Before leaving, the perpetrators responsible for the theft decided to demonstrate the capabilities of the ship by destroying the ring station orbiting the planet and everyone on it, as well as an entire Republic fleet."

Abbey felt a sudden coldness wash over her. "What?"

"A few days ago, one of the ships, the *Brimstone*, made an appearance in the Fringe. It confronted a Republic border patrol there, attacking and destroying every ship it encountered."

"On its own?" Abbey said.

"Yes, Lieutenant," Mann replied. "We have reason to believe the Fire was brought into the Outworlds so that it could be studied, its technologies replicated. We also believe that the Outworld Governance is behind the attack and that it is only a matter of time before they decide to use the ships to destabilize the Republic and break the stalemate that this conflict has become."

"The prison is connected," Abbey said. "It has to be."

"I do not doubt that you may be right," Mann said. "But as I said, it isn't and can't be my priority right now. The lives of a few disgraced, court-martialed soldiers versus hundreds of individuals in good standing? You can't in good conscience tell me that you would do any differently."

"No, sir," Abbey said.

A soft vibration ran throughout the ship, creating a low resonance.

"Docking synchronization complete, Captain," Ruby said.

"Thank you, Ruby," Captain Mann said. "Prepare for boarding."

"Yes, Captain."

"We can continue this discussion on the *Faust*," Mann said. The airlock between the cockpit and the cargo hold hissed and opened. "If you will?"

Abbey forced herself up, her legs still a little shaky. Airi moved in beside her, helping her stay upright.

"Thank you," Abbey said.

"You're welcome," she replied.

"Go into the airlock, enter the *Faust*, and wait in the de-con chamber," Mann said.

"Decontamination?" Abbey said. "What for?"

"I wouldn't call Hell the friendliest of atmospheres, would you?"

"You think we have some kind of disease on us or something?" Pik asked.

"Lieutenant Cage was in the medical ward as recently as a few hours ago. I can't discount the possibility, and the last thing I need to worry about is a sick crew."

"I guess a sterilization bath couldn't hurt," Benhil said. "It's just light."

Abbey followed the others to the airlock, and then over the threshold to the adjacent ship. The decontamination chamber was small, leaving the seven of them packed tightly into its confines. She had been through de-con plenty of times before. A blue light followed by a red light, the wavelengths able to penetrate and destroy most biohazards, as well as break grime and blood and sweat away in a hurry. The resultant particles would be sucked out of the chamber and evacuated into space. De-con was especially important after visits to foreign worlds, to prevent cross-contamination and inadvertent transportation of invasive organism that could really screw up another planet's ecosystem.

"Pik, that had better be your gun," Bastion said, standing in front of the Trover, who had to crouched to fit in the space.

"It's a gun all right," Pik replied.

"Can we make this quick?"

The hatches on either side of the chamber hissed as they sealed them in, the guide lights turning off and leaving them in total darkness. A moment later, the blue light came on, so bright it forced them to close their eyes.

It had been on for a few seconds when Abbey smelled something.

"Captain, what is that?" she asked.

"What is what?" Mann replied. His voice sounded different. Muffled slightly.

The smell was getting stronger.

"Gant, do you smell that?" she said.

"I don't smell anything," he replied.

She began to feel a little nauseous. She opened her eyes.

The light was being distorted through the haze of some kind of gas that was filling the chamber. She glanced at Gant. He was standing beside her with his eyes closed, undisturbed. She looked at Airi. She was just as calm. In fact, she looked almost too calm.

Pik was the first to crumple, dropping to the ground behind Bastion, who moved as if in slow motion in an effort to evade him, failing and being knocked to the ground as well. She shifted her attention to Captain Mann.

His helmet was on, his breathing steady. He was looking back at her, stone-faced.

"What the hell are you doing?" she said, starting to move toward him. Gant collapsed beside her. Airi and Benhil, too. She was the only one still upright.

"You're criminals, Lieutenant," he said calmly. "I'd be an idiot to expect compliance without a bit of leverage."

"What do you mean?"

"Murderers. Traitors. Thieves. What incentive do any of these individuals have to stay within mission parameters, especially now that they're fugitives with a ship designed to take them to the Outworlds, and enough disterium to live very, very comfortably for years? What incentive do you have to stay and fight instead of going home to your daughter? As far as the records from Hell are concerned, you're already dead."

Abbey made it to him, but shc could tell that her body was succumbing to the sedative.

"I'm not a traitor," she said. "I was set up."

"I don't care," he replied. "The Republic is on the brink of war. That's my concern, and now it's yours."

She reached out, grabbing him by the shoulders. He was wearing a softsuit. He could have overpowered her if he wanted to. He didn't make any moves to stop her.

"You son of a bitch."

"I can be," he agreed. "This isn't about you or me, Lieutenant. This is about the safety of the Republic."

He put his hands on her wrists, easing them away from him. She was getting lightheaded, unable to concentrate on standing any longer. He lowered her gently, placing on her on the floor with the others.

Her final thought before she passed out was that she was getting sick and fragging tired of being medicated.

CHAPTER THIRTY-THREE

"TAKE CARE OF LIEUTENANT CAGE first," Olus said, exiting the decontamination chamber and removing his helmet. "She probably won't be out for long. Send her to me when she wakes."

"Yes, Captain," Ruby said.

Olus looked the SI-10 over. Although he had been issuing instructions since General Soto had provided the synthetic intelligence, he hadn't seen her until now.

She was young and shapely in appearance, with a slightly disproportioned chest and long legs. Her face was heart-shaped, her lips full, her hair thick and wavy, cascading down to her shoulders in a soft wave.

"Where did Iti pick you up?" he asked. "The Red Light District on Centauri?"

"Your request was for an untraceable SI, Captain," Ruby replied. "My software has been updated with standard military protocols, and extended with the packages you requested."

It was as close to an affirmation as he was probably going to get. "Were you wiped first, or integrated?"

"Integrated, Captain. Wiping would have taken three days. You requested my availability within one."

"Disable those systems. Completely."

"Full disable will require a reboot."

"We don't have time for that. Take care of Cage. And when I say take care, I mean insert the kill switch."

The synthetic laughed, the sound of it likely provocative to some. "Yes, Captain."

Olus headed away from the chamber. He had studied the layout of the *Faust* on his way to Hell, and so he didn't have any trouble making his way from the docking airlock to the cockpit of the starship.

He could feel himself stiffen as he made his way into the control center. What the hell had Iti given him? He had asked for something untraceable and anonymous, but he had assumed she could have found something built in the last century. Instead, he was looking at a setup that predated his own flight training, a setup composed of multiple component boxes with separate displays, attached by wiring that ran exposed along the walls and ceiling of the space, leading forward to a small viewport and a pair of worn and torn seats that were barely big enough for an average sized Terran. They were positioned behind twin vectoring yoke systems, manual controls with no computer augmented guidance. In the center between them rested a larger box with a projection floating above it. The FTL master drive control unit, a computer capable of making the intense mathematical calculations needed for successfully navigating the stars at many, many times the speed of light. This one looked at though it had been carried over from an aging starship when this starship had been brand new.

Olus fell into the pilot's seat, spending half a minute searching for the comm. He found it behind his head, a manual toggle to activate the system, and then an interface on the control surface beside the yoke to select the communication service and frequency, and enter the receiver's identification. She already had a setting for Republic Milnet. He was surprised to find one for the Outworld's SyncSys as well.

He selected the Milnet and entered in his credentials and General Soto's identification sequence. The aging system didn't have projection capabilities, and it hissed and sputtered despite the fact that the entire thing was digital and nearly instantaneous.

"General Soto," he said.

He waited a few seconds for a response. She didn't answer. He tried a second time and again received no reply. It wasn't a cause for concern. As part of the Council, she was often busy and not in a position to respond directly to hails. His effort would be logged and noted, and he was sure she would get back to him as soon as she could.

He left the comm toggle active, examining the other switches and displays in the cockpit. Bastion was a highly-skilled pilot, but he had probably never flown something like this before. Then again, the controls were more akin to a dropship than a standard starship, which used positional calculations and computer algorithms for steering instead of direct, manual control.

"Captain Mann."

Lieutenant Cage's voice took him off-guard, and his head whipped back to where she was standing, framed in the entrance to the cockpit. There would be no outwardly visible sign of the implant, but he knew Ruby wouldn't have let her up without having completed the surgery.

"Lieutenant," he replied. "How are you feeling?"

"Pissed."

"Understandable. Have a seat." He motioned to the co-pilot's chair. She looked at it but didn't move.

"Leverage," she said. "What did you do?"

"Ruby inserted a small device into your head, behind your eye and up into your brain. She's duplicating the procedure on the others right now. It's a kill switch, a control module like the bracelets in Hell, only without the breakable centralized control system. Each module has an identifier and a short-range comm receiver built in, scanning system frequencies about fifty times per hour. As long as your identifier stays off the multitude of networks, you're safe. If it gets transmitted out, the first time you're within comm range it will break down and release a very, very nasty virus into your brain, one that will kill you quite painfully."

"So it's only effective in comm range?"

Olus smiled. "Try to find somewhere to survive that doesn't have a network within reach. It's effectively the same thing as killing you outright."

"Bioweapons are illegal."

"Their use against enemy combatants, prisoners of war, and civilians is illegal. There's nothing saying they can't be used on convicts."

Cage was silent for a moment, considering the implications. He appreciated her thoughtfulness. The others might not be as levelheaded.

"So, you decided to use inmates to help you with the starship problem," she said, moving over to the co-pilot's seat and dropping into it. "Why?"

"A few reasons," he replied. "Deniability, for one. I'm sending you into the Outworlds. If you get caught, the Republic doesn't have to worry about increasing tensions because you're not being supported by the Republic."

"Even if we are."

"Prove it. You're acting on your own, for your own gain."

"I don't think the Governance is stupid enough to believe that."

"Behind the scenes, maybe not, but there's enough of a question that they can't and won't make public accusations."

"And the other reasons?"

"Second, I can't just go to the Council and ask them for the best soldiers they have, regardless of where they're currently assigned. Not only would it circle back to my first reason, but let's face it, most Republic soldiers have too much at stake to do the things that will probably need to be done. I don't want moralization here, Lieutenant. I want results."

"And criminals have no morals?"

"I'm not saying that. What criminals who were sentenced to life in Hell don't have is anything to lose. No ties. No families."

"I have a family. A daughter."

"Technically. The moment you were sent to Hell you were as good as dead to her, and she's as good as dead to you." He paused while her face changed, growing more angry and tense. "I'm sorry to put it like that, Lieutenant, but we both know it's true. Reason three: I can give you the best motivation possible to get those results. For soldiers like Bastion and

Pik, freedom is enough. For you? I can dangle your daughter in front of you like a carrot. You want to get out? You want to see her again? You do what I ask."

"I'm nobody's slave," she said. "I'd rather die."

"I want you to help stop a growing threat against the Republic, which might also lead you to some answers regarding what you went through on Hell. If that's slavery then I would suggest it might be the best form of it."

She looked like she wanted to choke him. He didn't blame her.

"This has to be a better situation than what you would have had before," he said.

She laughed sardonically. "Are you kidding? I'm not a traitor, Captain Mann. I didn't do what they said I did. Packard worked for Davis, or at least for the same people as Davis. The same people who were trying to take me out of Hell so that I could be their slave instead. They set me up. They sent me away without a trial because the evidence was circumstantial at best. I shouldn't have been there, and I shouldn't be here. I'm certainly not going to be thanking you for giving me half a life."

"I'm not asking you to thank me. I'm asking you to follow my orders. If our mission is successful, you have a chance to be back with your daughter within weeks."

She didn't trust him. He didn't blame her for that, either.

"No bullshit?" she asked.

"No bullshit," he replied.

She was silent, staring out the viewport into space. He gave her a few seconds before speaking again.

"Tell me what happened on Hell," he said. "All of it, from the beginning."

"Why?"

"So I can help you."

"You just said you didn't care about helping me."

"I care about protecting the Republic. Do you?"

She looked over at him. "I used to. Now? I'm not so sure. I'm starting to feel like there are two Republics, Captain. The one that's visible to the majority of us, and the one that's really in control."

"You're talking about corruption?"

"The last person who used that word got up again after I shot him twice in the head, and didn't stop moving until Airi decapitated him. We've already gone way past corruption, Captain. We're moving headlong towards full-on chaos. In what form? I don't know. That depends on how deep this goes, but my instinct and my observations suggest it's pretty damn deep."

"All the more reason for you to tell me what happened."

"So you can bring it back to who? I don't trust you all that much, Captain. I'm not about to trust anyone else. Besides, when it comes to leverage, it's the only thing I have. When this mission is finished, I go free, and then you get your intel. You already said recovering the *Fire* and the *Brimstone* is your priority."

"What about the fate of the Republic?"

"The Republic that I've seen the last few weeks isn't a Republic I want to be part of. When this is done, I'm going to take Hayley, and I'm going to disappear as best I can. The Republic can go frag itself. Got it?"

Olus stared at her for a moment. She reminded him of a much younger version of himself.

"Fine. Have it your way, Lieutenant."

"I will." She paused. "I don't suppose there's a toilet on this thing?"

He laughed. "There is. Let me show you around. I know it doesn't look like much, but she'll get you into the Outworlds, and she does have a few tricks."

"Nothing but the best for us cons, Captain?"

"At least it isn't forty degrees in the shade," he said

The comment finally earned him a slight smile and a partial reduction in tensions.

"Finally, something I can't argue with you about."

CHAPTER THIRTY-FOUR

URSAN DIDN'T MAKE THE MISTAKE of being casual again, entering his quarters on the *Brimstone* with his head up and shoulders squared, posture stiff and at attention while General Thraven looked him over.

"General," Ursan said.

He had been expecting a communication from the General for the last three days, ever since he delivered the message that the Republic border patrol had been destroyed. He didn't know what had caused the delay in the General's response, but he was thankful the wait was finally over.

"Captain Gall," Thraven said. "Congratulations on your victory against the Republic. You've successfully delivered the first blows in what I am certain will be a glorious campaign. You should be proud."

Ursan bowed his head in response. "Thank you, General. It's an honor to serve the Outworlds in this time of transition. If you don't mind me asking, how are the efforts with the *Fire* coming along?"

Thraven smiled. "Better than we had hoped. She is a masterpiece of modern engineering, and will certainly become part of an unstoppable force in the days to come."

"Do you have new orders for me, sir? I'm eager to get back to Kell. To get back to my wife."

"Yes, Captain. I know. I admire your devotion. It is all too rare these days. I do have new orders for you."

Ursan leaned forward eagerly. He had enjoyed destroying the Republic patrol, but he would have enjoyed it much more with Trin at his side. He hated being away from her, and he was certain she felt the same.

"Yes, General?"

"You are to return the *Brimstone* to Kell. We are hoping to have unlocked the secrets of the *Fire's* torpedoes by the time you've arrived. I imagine the *Brimstone* could stand to be re-armed before its next encounter?"

"There are nine torpedoes remaining, General," Ursan said. "Though it typically only takes one to destroy most Republic ships. Two at most for a battleship."

"That's good to know, Captain." General Thraven began to turn away as though he was going to end the conversation. He paused halfway, facing Ursan once more. "Oh. You should know, Captain. Trin won't be here when you arrive."

"What do you mean?" Ursan asked, feeling a sudden wrenching in his gut.

"You have new orders, and so does she."

"Sir, what about once I've reached Kell? We're better together than we are separate, whatever the job is."

"I will consider the request, Captain. If it is in the best interests of the Outworlds, it will be honored."

"Thank you, sir. That's all I can hope for."

"Indeed," Thraven said.

Now he did turn away from the projection, the comm link disconnecting a moment later. Ursan didn't waste any time fleeing the quarters for the bridge.

"Dak, set a course for Kell," he said.

"New orders, Boss?" Dak said.

"To bring the *Brimstone* in."

"What about Trin?"

He shook his head. "Reassigned. He did it on purpose, the son of a bitch. You should have seen the smug smirk on his wrinkled mug when he told me she wouldn't be there."

"Starting to regret signing up for this?" Dak asked.

"I regretted it right after I did it," Ursan replied. "But Trin was convinced it was the best thing for us. Anyway, what's done is done. We follow orders; we ride this thing out. It'll be worthwhile in the end, especially when the Republic topples."

"I hope so. General Thraven scares the shit out of me. Especially when he does that magic bullshit."

"It isn't magic."

"Then what is it?"

Ursan shook his head. "I don't know."

"You have some of it in you, and you don't know what it is?"

Ursan tried not to think about it. There was a price to pay for the gift he had accepted. In servitude mainly, but not solely. He clenched his eyes tight, his mind returning him to that bad place where the fire was raining down, and he was covered in blood.

"Boss," Dak said, putting a big hand on his shoulder. "Sorry for asking."

Ursan shook off the flashback. "It's okay, my friend. Just get us to Kell."

"Yes, sir."

CHAPTER THIRTY-FIVE

IT TOOK TWO HOURS FOR the rest of the crew to wake up from the sedative. Pik was the last to revive, sitting up slowly and rubbing his bald head, his mouth hanging open and a glaze over his eyes.

"It's about damn time," Bastion said. "I thought I was going to die of boredom waiting for you."

"What?" Pik replied. "Where am I?"

"Deep space," Benhil said. "Middle of nowhere on an Outworld star hopper."

"That wasn't a dream?"

"Nope."

Pik smiled. "Good. I was afraid to wake up."

Abbey was standing in the corner of the small hangar with Gant, next to an orbital transport that had come with the starship. Like the *Faust*, it was an old thing, worn and tired looking. It was probably just big enough to carry them planetside, and though it appeared to be armed with a couple of small plasma cannons, she doubted it would be of much use for combat drops. It looked about as maneuverable as a terraformer.

She had toured the *Faust* with the Captain while the others had been sleeping. It was an interesting, eclectic design. Three levels in total accessed by one contiguous, large ladder clearly built with both Trovers and Rudin in mind. Level One was living space. Four separate sets of quarters branching off from a central sanitary station, which included the toilet. Considering there were six of them, it meant some of them would have to share. While Gant had suggested they bunk together, she had rejected the idea. She had gotten a glimpse of Airi's record when she deactivated her bracelet. She knew why the former RIA Master Chief had been sent to Hell. It was better for all of them if they joined forces.

Level Two was the main operational hub of the ship. The cockpit sat at the front, while most of the electronics - gravity generators, shield generators, communications equipment, and CPUs - were arranged along the center, leading back toward the hangar and the main engines, both sublight and FTL, in the rear.

Level Three was storage. In addition to a small armory that was decidedly higher-tech than anything else on the *Faust*, the Captain had also been savvy enough to provide less warlike equipment, such as a range of Outworld standard dress and various devices to help disguise their appearance, from basic headdress to follicaps. The time on Hell had left Abbey permanently bald, unless or until she could visit a medical facility to have it restored. It would have to be black market medicine, thanks to the prison branding she had received. No legitimate doctor would go near her as long as she bore that scar.

Level Three was also hiding a pair of additional cargo holds, both large enough to store a decent haul of black market goods, each invisible behind false walls along the hull, doubly shielded against scanning to prevent discovery of the goods within. Once Ruby had finished implanting them with their control chips, she had moved on to transferring the four disterium containers over to one of the holds. Each one of them was worth a fortune. "Operating capital," Captain Mann had said.

Abbey still wasn't quite sure what to make of the Director of the OSI. One part of her was in awe of him. His position, his reputation, and the reputation of the department. Another part of her was afraid of him. Not because he had the power to kill her, but because he had gone through so much effort to get them out in the first place. While his reasons were logical, she wasn't convinced that letting the lunatics out of the asylum was the best way to stop a war.

Were they really lunatics? She felt like one, especially now. Something was happening to her. Something she couldn't place or describe, but that she could feel at the edge of her mind and body in those brief moments when she wasn't thinking about anything else. It was as though she had hundreds of worms squirming just beneath her skin, creating a feeling of gross discomfort that she couldn't quite ignore.

She broke out of her head when Captain Mann moved to the center of the hangar.

"Attention," he snapped, as good as any Marine Drill Sergeant.

She reacted almost by instinct, coming up straight and stiff, her arms at her sides. The others did the same to various degrees of formality.

"I'm going to keep this short and simple," he said. "I spoke to most of you individually while you were still a bunch of incarcerated, pathetic remains of formerly promising soldiers." He paused, making eye contact with each of them wherever they were arranged in the hangar. "Right now, the only thing that's changed is that you aren't incarcerated anymore. You're on the outside now, and you have a second chance to atone for the mistakes you made and uphold your original oath to protect the Republic."

"Can we skip the bullshit speech?" Bastion asked. "I'm not here to protect the Republic. I'm here because here isn't Hell."

"Me too," Pik said.

Captain Mann glared at the pilot for a few seconds. "Okay, Worm. Here's the way it is. While you were all sleeping, my assistant Ruby was busy implanting a very nasty bug in your brains. You try to break orders; you try to run, you try to do anything that I don't like, I can drop you where you stand and leave you wishing you were back in prison." He looked at each of them again, one by one. "Before I continue, do any of you want to test me?"

None of them moved.

"Good. I've already briefed Lieutenant Cage on the parameters of your mission. It's the one and only reason I risked my own ass to get you off of Hell. She'll fill you in on the details, but the most important thing for you to know is this: when you finish the mission, you'll be released from duty. The implant will be removed, and you can do whatever frag-all you want with your lives from that point forward. That's your incentive to get the job done. Is that understood?"

"Yes, sir," they replied in ragged succession.

"Good. Ruby is my conduit to you, and your conduit to me. You can consider her your babysitter, your mommy, or whatever the frag else helps you comprehend that whatever you do, I'll know about it. With that being said, I picked you all because you're the best available at what you do. Maybe the best the Republic has in or out of incarceration. I expect you to do anything, and I mean anything, you have to in order to complete this mission. I don't care who you have to kill, torture, maim or otherwise put to harm. I don't care how many innocents die. I don't care what you have to destroy, as long as it's in line with mission parameters. Step over that line, and you're as good as dead. Is that understood?"

"Yes, sir," they said, more synchronized this time.

"Good. If you get in trouble, attract too much attention, or are caught in the act, the Republic doesn't know a fragging thing about you, and won't be coming to bail you out. Is that understood?"

"Yes, sir," they said, almost as one.

"Good. Does anyone have any questions?"

"Sir," Airi said. "Does this mean you aren't staying with us?"

"That's right," Mann replied. "Your mission is my mission, too, but I don't have the luxury of working anonymously. I'll be following up from my office, as well as working on determining if and how the mess at the prison is related to the stolen ships."

"Stolen ships?" Bastion said.

"Like I said, Lieutenant Cage will fill you in."

"Sir, what about our families?" Benhil said. "Are we allowed to contact them?"

"I can't stop you," Mann replied. "But keep in mind that they think you're gone for good. What would you be putting them through to turn up again, only to disappear if things go bad? Completing the mission means freedom, but that doesn't mean the mission is going to be easy. If it were, I wouldn't need individuals who are otherwise disposable."

Abbey flinched at the word, and at the response to the question. She had been considering trying to contact Hayley, to tell her what had happened. Now she was having second thoughts. It was obvious Captain Mann didn't have high expectations, or he wouldn't have come to Hell in the first place, and she couldn't adjust to the thought of getting Hayley's hopes up that she might be coming home and then dying on her. It was better to let her be crushed once and surprise her later than to risk crushing her twice. Of course, she would do anything to ensure she made it back to her.

Anything.

"Disposable?" Pik said angrily. "Who the hell are you calling disposable?"

"You need to manage your opinion of yourself, Pik," Mann replied. "You were all in Hell for one reason or another. You all broke the law. You were all court-martialed. That hasn't changed. Like I was trying to say before, being here doesn't make you any less of a frag-up. Not until you prove your worth."

"I'll prove something, you constipate," Pik muttered, Abbey's translator picking an interesting word for the Trover epithet.

"Any other questions?" Mann asked, looking at each of them again.

"Yeah," Bastion said. "If you're leaving, who's in charge?"

"I believe Lieutenant Cage is the ranking officer," Airi said.

"That may be so, but we aren't soldiers anymore. We can play at it as much as we want, but our ranks were stripped the moment we were shipped to Hell, and they sure as shit won't translate beyond the Fringe. Captain?"

"You're right about ranks," Mann replied. "They don't mean anything in the Outworlds, and you won't be doing yourselves any favors to use them. Republic military isn't well tolerated beyond Republic space. You're fugitives now. Dark ops. As far as chain of command goes, I trust you'll work out the details on your own."

Bastion smiled. "Yes, sir."

"Ruby," Mann said. "Is everything ready?"

"Yes, Captain."

"Good. I suggest you all get to know one another a little better. You can hate each other, but you need to be able to work together." He turned to Abbey. "If you decide you want to tell me more about what happened, talk to Ruby." Then he started toward the exit from the hangar.

"That's it?" Bastion said. "No goodbye?"

"What are you, a baby?" Gant said.

"Shut it, freak-monkey," Bastion replied.

"Didn't I warn you about calling me that?"

"What are you going to do about it?"

Abbey watched as Captain Mann slipped from the hangar without looking back. At that moment she wished that she could go with him. This crew was supposed to retrieve two stolen starships from the depths of the Outworlds? He hadn't even left yet, and they were already arguing.

She closed her eyes and took a few calming breaths. Then she moved forward, putting herself between Gant and Bastion. She knew she was going to regret it, but what other choice did she have?

"Queenie, don't," Gant said. "This one needs to be put in his place. He thinks now that he's out of Hell he doesn't need to be afraid of me anymore."

Bastion laughed. "I was never afraid of you."

Even Abbey knew that was bullshit. None of this was going to help.

"Gant, wait," she said. "Do you want to be in charge, Bastion?"

"It's not about want," he replied. "It's about who's the most qualified."

"Lieutenant Cage," Airi said.

"Shut up," Bastion replied.

Airi growled, rushing toward him. He smiled, turning toward her as she came in.

Abbey stopped her, catching her in the midriff and pushing back, throwing her to the floor. She couldn't believe she was defending that asshole, but the worst thing they could do would be to get into a brawl. It might settle the chain of command, but at what cost? The chain would be so weak it would break at the first sign of trouble.

"Airi, don't," Abbey snapped, pinning her arms. She looked back at Gant. "You stay there, too." She shifted her attention to Bastion. "You're in charge, Bastion," she said.

"We should at least vote," Benhil said. "That's the only fair way."

"Frag fair," Bastion said. "I'm not dying because you wanted a popularity contest. I don't care if any of you like me. I'll get the job done, and you'll all be thanking me when I do."

"You couldn't lead a whore to a bed," Gant said. "That's why you were always Pok's goon and not his competition."

"Gant," Abbey said. "Enough."

Gant didn't look happy to be told what to do, but he quieted.

"Any other dissent?" Bastion asked. He clapped his hands together when nobody responded. "In that case, it looks like I'm in command. The first order of business is-"

"Bastion," Abbey said, releasing her grip on Airi. "I challenge your authority."

"What?" Bastion said.

"You heard me. I don't believe you're fit to lead. How do you want to settle it?"

Bastion stared at her in silence for a moment. "But you just told me-"

"That you were in charge. You are. Do we all agree?" Abbey looked at the others, who affirmed the decision. Even Airi acquiesced, now that she understood what Abbey was up to. "If you're in charge, then I'm challenging it. That's how they handle this bullshit in the Outworlds, which I think is appropriate given our circumstances. Do any of you disagree?"

She looked at them all again. Even Pik shook his head. He couldn't argue with her logic.

"She's right," Benhil said. "If we're heading to the Outworlds, we should do as they do."

"How do you want to settle?" Abbey asked. " Do you want to fight or do you want to take your chances matching wits?"

Bastion's face paled. He was a pilot, not a Breaker. He was trapped, and he knew it. "Maybe Benhil was right the first time. We should probably vote."

"Fine. How do you vote?"

"I vote for myself."

"Of course you do. Benhil?"

"I vote for myself, too. Not because I want to be in charge, but it's more dramatic."

"Pik?"

The Trover was hesitant for a moment. Then he shrugged. "I vote for Bastion."

"Heh," Bastion said.

"Airi?"

"I vote for you."

"Gant?"

"I vote for you, too, Queenie."

Abbey glanced over at Bastion. "It looks like I'm the tie-breaker."

He lowered his eyes to the ground. "Okay. You win. You're in charge."

"Thank you," Abbey said. She didn't really want to be in command. She also wasn't about to pin her future on someone else. "Does anyone want to challenge my command?"

Nobody jumped at the opportunity.

"In that case, let me give you the grand tour of the *Faust*. Once we're settled, we can reconvene and talk about what we're going to do next. I've got a daughter on Earth waiting for me to come home, and I don't plan to keep her waiting long."

The statement was followed by mumbled affirmations.

"We may not officially be Republic soldiers. That doesn't mean you don't make it clear when you've heard and understand an order, understood?"

"Yes."

"Yes, what?"

"Yes, ma'am," Pik and Benhil said.

"Yes, Commander," Airi said.

"Yes," Bastion repeated.

"Yes, Queenie," Gant said.

Abbey shook her head. "We'll need to work on that."

She headed for the exit. Ruby was already waiting there, having observed the entire interaction.

"Well played, Lieutenant Cage," she said.

"You need to drop the rank, too, Ruby," Abbey replied. "It doesn't work anymore."

As much as she hated to give it up. It was part of her identity. Who she was. Past tense. Who was she now?

"As you request, Queenie," Ruby said, smiling.

Abbey frowned at the use of the nickname Gant had given her. "Not you, too?"

"I like it. It is suitable and appropriate."

What would she become?

At least she was still alive to find out.

CHAPTER THIRTY-SIX

THE SHIP WAS SMALL AND black, as dark as the space that surrounded it, coated with a layer of dampening material that would make it invisible to all but the most sensitive of sensor arrays.

It came out of FTL further back than Gloritant Thraven probably would have liked, back behind the two Republic warships still in stationary orbit around the dark, burning planet below. The planet the Republic had named Hell.

The battleships didn't respond to the appearance, unable to get a reading on the ship. They continued to hang above the nearly dead rock, where they had been awaiting new orders from their command for the last two days. Even when it maneuvered in close to them, crossing beneath the hull of one almost close enough to touch, it remained invisible. If anyone had been looking out that direction, they might have thought they saw something as the light behind it blacked out momentarily, but who paid that much attention to the near field of space when nothing was supposed to be there?

The Shrike continued past, accelerating toward the planet, slipping into the upper atmosphere, passing the thermosphere and continuing down, the size and shape and plating barely causing a disruption as it sank toward the earth. It flattened out close to the ground, duplicating the approach taken two days earlier by another ship seeking to do the unthinkable by breaking into a prison.

Trinity Gall allowed herself a small smile as she considered the Gloritant's briefing. The Republic's Director of Strategic Intelligence, Captain Olus Mann, had shown up on Hell at the worst possible time and interrupted the latest round of transfers. The particular shipment was supposed to include a high-value target in the form of a disgraced Breaker named Abigail Cage, a target that had shown even more promise than expected after receiving the first half of the Gift, using it to kill both the Venerant who had been sent to bestow it and the Warden himself. All of which would have been acceptable, except the Warden who replaced him was a fragging imbecile, and not only clued the Captain in on Cage's worth but also failed to secure the Breaker and prevent the once-great assassin from stealing her and a few of the other inmates away.

Stolen away for what?

It was a bold move on the part of the Captain. So bold in fact that it was the very reason she was there. Warden Lurin had put all of their work at risk with his stupidity. It was her job to put him back in line.

She guided the Shrike to the surface, to a deep canyon two kilometers from the prison's proper entrance. As she opened the canopy of the craft, the onboard computer chirped at her that the atmosphere was unsuitable for long-term survival, suggesting that she should remain inside. She picked herself up and jumped out, using a finger to increase the cooling output of her specialized softsuit to maximum. She still wouldn't last long without getting underground.

She sprinted from the position, the synthetic musculature of the suit allowing her to bounce across the surface, skipping from jagged stone to jagged stone, planting her feet and vectoring from one place to another. She covered a kilometer in less than a minute, coming to rest at the spot marked on her TCU's map. A small grate rested on the ground, overhung by the stone that obscured its existence. She put her hand over it, feeling the air.

Of course, the prison had to be circulating it from somewhere, pulling it in from the hangar and out here. Captain Mann had probably known about it, too, but what good would it have done him? He had come to bring others out. This path was only accessible to someone like him, or her, or maybe Abigail Cage.

She put her hand on the grate, feeling the writhing tingle as the Gift moved within her, extending outward to the metal and gripping it with an invisible hand. She pulled only with her mind, and the grate groaned and then snapped, breaking away from its anchor. She set it aside and slid her feet into the shaft.

She wasn't sure why, but at that moment she thought of Ursan. Where was he right now? What was he doing? Missing her, she was sure. He had always been that way. Strong enough to stand on his own, but so much stronger when she was at his side. It was an endearing quality most of the time. Frustrating at others, especially when she had other work that needed to be done. Ursan didn't know the truth about Thraven. Not the whole truth. He believed he was fighting solely for the Outworlds. For his homeworld, which had been attacked by the Republic and left in ruin. Even though he had accepted the Gift, she knew he would never fight with them otherwise, and so she had gained his love and loyalty with lies. She had tried to undo that decision so many times, but she was selfish that way.

She wanted it all.

She looked down into the shaft. It was too dark to see to the bottom. She breathed in, smiled, and let herself fall.

How far? Fifty meters. One hundred. Two hundred. Four hundred.

She felt the Gift again, slowing her descent as she neared what was supposed to be the bottom. She could see the light beyond the grate at the bottom of the shaft now, coming up to meet her. She landed silently above it before crouching down and peering through.

She was on Level Two, looking into a storage closet tucked into the rear corner of the facility. There was nobody present. Why would there be? It was a closet. She put her hand on the grate, pushing against it with the Gift. It too snapped off its moorings, and she caught it with her hand before it tumbled to the ground, holding it as she dropped silently to the floor. Only then did she place it aside.

She padded to the door. She didn't open it with the control pad. Instead, she dropped low, digging her fingers beneath the bottom and lifting, using the strength in the softsuit to force it to move slowly upward. She reached into a tightpack and removed a small tube from it, sticking it out of the opening. A small box appeared on her HUD, showing her a view of the hallway. It was empty.

She stuffed the tube back into the tightpack and stood up, pressing the control pad to open the door. She moved out into the corridor and away, letting it close behind her.

She had to be careful. While Lurin had created a mess, if she wasn't cautious she could make an even bigger one. Captain Mann would have every reason to return to the facility or to send more of his people back to it. Her job was to make sure that when they did, they found no evidence of anything out of the ordinary. Warden Packard never existed. Warden Lurin never existed. Neither did Abigail Cage or any of the other prisoners who had been removed. Mann knew the game as well as anyone. He would know what had happened. He was hamstrung by the laws of the Republic. Without proof, he would have no choice but to accept the outcome and move on.

She heard footsteps ahead of her, and she pushed off the floor, turning over and reaching up, her fingers and toes extending into claws that enabled her to cling to the top of the corridor above. A medical bot walked past, trailed by a guard who was leading a prisoner to the ward. She knew they wouldn't notice her. She dropped behind them and continued on.

She had to hide three more times before reaching Lurin's private quarters. She was amused to find his door was secured, as though he was afraid Captain Mann was going to come back for him, or maybe he knew how the Gloritant was going to respond to his failure, like a locked door could stop her. She withdrew a small disc and placed it on the control pad, breaking through the security in seconds. The whole effort only proved that Lurin had no business as Warden. Then again, even he probably hadn't expected Packard's sudden demise.

The door slid open. Trin stepped in, closing it immediately behind her. Lurin was on his feet near the back of the room, a gun already in hand.

"It wasn't my fault," he said.

She reached up and removed her helmet, shaking her head to allow her hair some freedom.

"It doesn't matter," she replied.

"Your Venerant was supposed to keep her under control. If she couldn't do it, how the hell was I going to?"

"She only has half the Gift and no idea how to use it. Your guards should have contained her."

"She killed two guards in lightsuits. She also managed to stop a convert."

Trin paused. Thraven hadn't told her about that. Interesting.

"It still doesn't matter. Olus Mann is going to be suspicious of what we've been doing here. Not only do we have to shut the operation down temporarily, but we also need to remove the evidence. You're part of the evidence."

"No," Lurin said. "I'm loyal. I did my best."

"Best or not, you still failed."

"An impossible task."

Trin felt a twinge of empathy for the Warden. She couldn't argue that he might be right in that. Not that it mattered.

She started raising her hand.

He fired his weapon.

The Gift stretched out to meet the slugs, pushing at them, stealing their energy and knocking them harmlessly to the floor.

"You're going to damage the room," she said, getting angry.

She pushed off, bouncing toward him. He dropped the gun, cowering as she came down. She pulled his arms aside and wrapped a hand around his delicate neck. A quick squeeze and he was dead.

She lowered him gently. It wasn't enough to just kill him. She had to find all of the soldiers who had been witness to the escape. Fortunately, the Warden had already provided a list.

To think that all of this was necessary because that damnable Kett had come up with an as-of-yet unbreakable erasure schema, using it to wipe a server that the Gloritant was certain contained the coordinates of the General's hidden base. They would never have needed to implicate the Breaker as one of Kett's disciples, and they would never have needed to try to bring her over to the cause to solve the algorithm.

She couldn't change history. What was done was done, and her orders were clear. She would finish up here, and then she would find Abigail Cage and either complete her conversion or complete her erasure.

Which one it was depended on her.

CHAPTER THIRTY-SEVEN

"So the Outworlders stole a pair of invincible starships," Bastion said, "and we're supposed to get them back?"

"Yes," Abbey replied.

"Two starships."

"Yes."

"You do realize; we only have one pilot?"

"I'm sure we can hire a temp or something," Gant said. "Pilots are a dime a dozen."

Bastion glared at Gant but didn't speak.

"We'll cross that black hole when we get to it," Abbey said. "We have to find the ships first. Any ideas?"

Abbey glanced around the small table where they had organized after a brief interlude, during which she had shown them around their new home and given them some time to convert themselves from prisoners back to soldiers.

Not soldiers. Regular individuals. Well, not quite regular.

The others had all swapped their hellsuits for something a little more comfortable, choosing from the selection Olus had left. Casual clothes. Clothes they would have never been allowed to wear as members of the Republic Armed Services, or as prisoners on Hell. The dress down had done a small wonder for the overall tension of being stuffed into a small starship with relative strangers and sent out on a suicidal mission after being broken out of prison. It had allowed the crew to start seeing one another as individuals instead of rivals, as thinking, feeling beings instead of slaves. It wasn't perfect, but it was something.

She had tried to do the same. She had taken a pair of loose knit pants, a shirt, boots, and underwear from the inventory. She had brought it back to the quarters she was sharing with Airi. She had taken off the hellsuit and put them on. She felt more naked in those clothes than she ever had in the suit.

She felt exposed and vulnerable. Was it that feeling of movement just below her skin? Was it her experience with Clyo and Packard? Was it a need to cling to a uniform of some kind? She wasn't sure. Whatever the reason, she had abandoned the fresh clothing for the suit, putting it back on before returning to the second deck where they had gathered. Nobody had questioned her on it yet, though she had noticed their surprise. She imagined Gant would quiz her later.

"Do we have their last known location?" Gant asked.

Abbey looked at Ruby.

"The *Brimstone's* second attack occurred near the planet Seta eight days ago," she replied.

"Seta is on the Fringe," Bastion said.

"Eight days is a long time," Airi said. "They could be on the other side of the Outworlds by now."

"Why did the Republic cross the Fringe?" Benhil said.

"Ugh," Gant replied, knowing the punchline.

"To get to the other side," he finished. It was old satire. The main reason the Republic continued pushing at the Outworlds was so they could punch through and keep expanding.

"Terrible," Pik said.

"Maybe the joke is bad, but the point is the same," Benhil said. "It doesn't matter where they were. That's old news. It matters where they are now."

"Mann pulled you out because you're supposed to be the expert on the Outworlds," Gant said. "If they took the *Fire* and the *Brimstone* there, what's the best place to start looking for them?"

"Why'd Mann pull you out, Gant?" Bastion said. "He wanted a new pet?"

"Who took your bracelet off, Worm?" Gant replied. "Not that I don't regret that decision now."

"Can you both shut up and stay focused?" Abbey said. "I want to be in FTL within the hour, headed somewhere that will lead us to something. Captain Mann picked each of us for whatever skills we have that can benefit the mission and the team."

"I don't have any skills," Pik said. "I'm just good at killing things."

"Killing things is a skill," Bastion said.

"Speaking of teams," Benhil said. "I-"

"You aren't going to give us another shitty joke, are you?" Bastion said.

"What's wrong with my jokes?"

"They suck."

"To each their own. I was going to say, speaking of teams, we can't go anywhere calling one another by our given names. Forget ranks. Our old selves don't exist anymore. We're ghosts. Shit, even our old nicknames could lead the wrong people backward in history."

"We came from Hell," Pik said. "We're more like demons."

"Demons who got kicked out," Bastion said. "Hell's rejects." He laughed. "Queenie over there can't even handle that part. How do you expect her to take a new name?"

"Why are you calling me Queenie now?" Abbey asked.

"Like you aren't lording over us like a Queen?" He raised his voice in pitch, mimicking her. "I challenge your authority. I'm in charge. Do what I say. I'm better than you because I was a Breaker. I can kick your ass with one buttcheek, and outsmart you with nothing but my pinkie."

Abbey wanted to be mad, but the outburst drew laughter from the rest of the crew except for Gant. He only smiled once she laughed along with them.

"Hmm, maybe there's a bit of human in you after all," Bastion said.

"Like it or not, I think you've inherited a new moniker," Airi said.

"Not," Abbey replied. "But maybe it'll grow on me. "What about the rest of you?"

"I don't count," Gant said. "I never had a nick, and nobody who isn't another Gant can pronounce my name. Gant is as generic as they come."

"True," Abbey said. "Benhil?"

"I don't know. I'm kind of partial to Joker. Give me some time to think about it?"

"You have until we drop somewhere."

"I want to be Lucifer," Bastion said.

"That's stupid," Gant replied.

"On what planet? We came from Hell, just like Lucifer. It fits."

"It does," Abbey said. "Lucifer it is. Luc for short."

"Shortening it already? You enjoy emasculating me, don't you, Queenie?"

Pik laughed. "Trover only have one name."

"Too bad," Bastion said. "You're a reject first, a Trover second. All of us are, like that or not."

"We're the walking dead unless we can get this job done," Benhil said.

"At least we aren't in Hell," Pik said. "I'd rather be here."

"Me, too," Bastion agreed. "And I hate most of you." He looked at Pik. "So pick something else."

"Okay."

They waited in silence for half a minute.

"Well?" Bastion said.

"I already said it. Okay."

"What?" Benhil said, laughing. "You can't be Okay."

"Why not?"

"For one, it's ridiculous."

Pik shrugged. "I like it."

"For another, it's four letters."

"It's two in Terran. O. K."

"It's four," Benhil argued.

"Two," Pik replied.

"Does it really matter?" Abbey asked.

"I like it," Pik said again.

"Then Okay it is," Abbey said. "We don't have time for this bullshit. Benhil, give me something we can use, will you?"

"You forgot about Airi," Gant said.

"I don't know," Airi said.

"I've got one for her," Bastion said. "Fury."

Airi smiled. "That will do."

"Who isn't fit to lead, Queenie? I just named half the people on this team, and the team itself."

"You didn't name the team," Gant said.

"Sure I did. You just didn't hear me because of all the fur in your ears. Hell's Rejects. Take that shit to the bank and deposit it."

"Hell's Rejects," Abbey said. "I admit, it has a certain ring to it."

"Works for me," Benhil said.

"I like it," Pik said.

"Deposit it," Bastion said.

"Well, now that we've got the important decisions out of the way," Abbey said. "Maybe we can start doing what we were brought here to do?"

"Find the ships," Bastion said.

"And kill the assholes who took them," Pik said.

"I can tell you one thing," Benhil said. "If you want to find something that doesn't want to be found in the Outworlds, there's only one place you go. Mamma Oissi's."

"I've never heard of it," Gant said.

"How much black market trading have you done in your life, Mr. Gant?"

"Admittedly, none."

"Mamma Oissi's," Benhil said again. "Deposit it."

Abbey smiled. "Give Ruby and Lucifer the coordinates, and let's get our asses moving."

CHAPTER THIRTY-EIGHT

ABBEY SAT IN THE DARK, in the small box that served as a conduit to the construct. The node had to be at least four or five generations old, lacking in both complete mobility simulation and the advanced realism engine that had made the communication system a suitable replacement to reality for some. She had been there for nearly an hour, with every key in Hayley's identification code typed into the system except for one.

She had tears in her eyes. Her heart was racing. She had told herself she wouldn't do that to her daughter, and at the same time, she missed her so much she could barely stand it. She had never said goodbye. She had never told Hayley she loved her. She knew her daughter knew, but she burned to say it, to speak the words. She wanted to tell her she was still alive, and she would be back.

She knew she couldn't.

She deleted the code for the fiftieth time, leaning back against the wall. She didn't know what to make of her life anymore. Nothing about it was organized. Nothing about it was consistent. Nothing about it was predictable. She had been in the military for too long for that to be easy to take.

Then there was the feeling that sat beneath the surface, the movement under her skin. It was growing more intense and harder to ignore. Was she sick? Dying? Had Clyo poisoned her? What about Illiard? They had done something to him. She had killed him, and he had kept coming. Or had he already been dead? It should have been impossible, but one thing the disterium had taught all of them was that nothing was impossible. The rules of science were only good until they were disproven or changed.

Just like the rules of life.

Captain Mann said he was going to look into it. She wished him luck. She had been a Breaker long enough to know how these things worked. If there was any evidence of wrongdoing at the prison, it would be cleaned before he got his people in. They wouldn't find a damn thing. Would Warden Lurin still be there by then? She had a feeling he wouldn't.

Illiard had grabbed her with nothing but air, pulling her back toward him. It lined up with her memory of her fight with Clyo, as spotty as that seemed to be. She had a vague idea that she had done something like it to Mann, throwing him backward without touching him. But that was impossible too.

Nothing was impossible.

She stood straight, putting out her hand. She could see her fingers shaking. She could feel the writhing beneath them, as though something alive was clawing at the underside of her skin. The sight was enough to frighten her, and she lowered her hand, turning and opening the hatch to leave the room.

Gant was sitting cross-legged on the floor, against the wall on the other side of the short corridor, beside the door to the armory. He had a small bit of material in his dextrous hands and was working on bending it into something or other.

"Queenie," he said as she emerged, getting to his feet.

"Were you waiting for me?" she asked.

"Waiting? No. I didn't even know you were in there. I came down here to be alone." His expression told her he was lying. "Six years. I had nothing else to do." He held out the bent metal.

"What is it?"

"Nothing. I had to use my hands to calm down. I needed

someplace small and dark. And I'm freezing in here. How are you?"

"Can you tell I was crying?"

"Crying? I hadn't noticed. Were you?"

She smiled. "I know when you're lying, Gant. They trained us to spot facial tics."

"I don't have a facial tic."

"Yes, you do."

"Yeah, well. I was worried about you, especially when you came out in the hellsuit. It's hard to let go, isn't it?"

"Harder for you, I imagine." She held out her arm. "I like the way it feels on my skin. I feel safer in it. More under control."

"Are you usually out of control?"

"I feel like I am more and more lately."

"What happened on Hell?"

Abbey shrugged. "They injected me with something. It looked like blood. Ever since then, I've felt like I have bugs or something crawling under my skin, and it's getting worse."

"There's a medical bot down the hall."

"It's at least thirty years old. Besides, it can't help. You really have no idea what the Warden was doing with the prisoners? You always seemed to know everything."

"I heard rumors about people disappearing, but in a place like Hell, what do you expect? We all figured they were offing themselves, or Packard was offing them. It was no loss."

"Private Illiard," she said. "He wasn't dead. They did something to him."

"What kind of something?"

"I shot him twice in the head. He didn't die. Not until Fury cut his head off."

"Are you serious?"

"Yes."

"You think this all has something to do with the ships?"

"I don't know. I heard Warden Lurin talking to someone else. They were using titles I've never heard before, not even in the Outworlds.

Honorant? Agitant?"

"I've never heard it. Did you tell Captain Mann about it?"

"No."

"Why not?"

"I don't trust him."

"What do you mean? He's OSI. He's your people."

She laughed. "Illiard said the Republic was corrupt. Davis was corrupt. Packard. Lurin."

"Mann saved you from them."

"I saved myself, thank you very much. And I saved you and Captain Mann."

"I'm not saying you're wrong, but Mann went out of his way to make sure you were on the team, and not only because I told him I wouldn't come unless you came too."

"You did what?"

Gant looked up at her, his eyes big. His face was adorable like that. He looked at the ground. "Lurin told him you were unstable. Dangerous. He would have believed it if I hadn't set him straight. Once he knew Lurin wanted to keep you, he risked his life to get you out."

"Gant, I don't understand. What if he had said to forget it, that you could stay in Hell and rot?"

"Then I would have stayed. Maybe I would have tried to get you out. I don't know."

"Why would you do that for me?"

"We're friends, aren't we?"

"Sure."

"Friendship for Gants isn't the same as it is for humans. It's non-negotiable and non-transferable."

"Like a dog?" she said, cringing as she did. She hated to put it that way.

He laughed. "Yeah, pretty much. That's why we're damn careful who we befriend because it's complete loyalty until death." He paused, his voice lowering. "And sometimes after." He was quiet for another few seconds before speaking again. "You're stuck with me, Queenie. I hope you can live with that."

She smiled. "I'm honored, Gant." She reached out, putting her hand on his cheek. He was ridiculously soft. He made a soft noise that sounded like a purr before pulling away. Her translator suggested it was pleasure.

"Don't ever tell anyone about this," he said. "Especially Bastion. He's an asshole."

"I won't. Thank you."

"For what?"

"I don't feel as alone now. That means a lot to me."

"Me, too."

"I hate you for getting everyone calling me Queenie, though."

He chittered in laughter. "I'd say I'm sorry, but I'm not."

"Who's the asshole?"

He laughed harder. Abbey laughed with him.

It felt good.

CHAPTER THIRTY-NINE

"JESTER," BENHIL SAID.

"WHAT?" ABBEY said.

"My new nick. Jester."

They were in the *Faust's* armory, picking out an assortment of equipment they thought they might need when they reached Orunel. A Fringe planet, Orunel was eighty percent water, with two main land masses positioned thousands of kilometers apart and a massive blue ocean between them. A terraformer rested on one of the islands, its job long completed, the area around it overgrown with imported vegetation and teeming with exotic animal life.

The other island was home to an Outworld settlement, a moderately populated center that was more popular for what happened beneath the surface of the white alloy and glass facade than it was for the legal trade that flowed through it, though there was plenty of that as well. The government of Orunel had decided to toe the line on the conflict with the Republic, choosing to allow trade between both nations and enforced a strict neutrality policy on its surface and in its spaceport. Such a thing was unheard of in the Republic, but all Outworld planets had their own government, social services, military and all the rest, and all of them made their own rules, coming together in unity as a diverse and massive delegation that pledged resources for the good of the collective.

"That's too close to Joker," Gant said, picking up a small box, opening it, closing it, and putting it back.

"That's the point. It's like Joker, but it isn't Joker," Benhil said.

"That's stupid."

"Bastion said the same thing about Okay," Pik said. The pilot wasn't there. He was running through diagnostics on the old shuttle that he had decided to call the *Imp*.

"And you said if you like it to keep it," Benhil said to Abbey.

She couldn't argue with that. "If you want to be Jester, you can be Jester," she said. "I thought you of all of us would come up with something a little more unique."

She picked up a small pistol from one of the racks, turning it over. It was a beam weapon. Normally she didn't care for them; reflective armor nowadays could handle most lasers without a problem. Then again, there was a benefit to nearly unlimited rounds. She held onto it, taking the thigh holster that accompanied it and wrapping it around her softsuit. The others were going in a little more discreetly, sticking with civilian clothing. While she had no choice but to give up the hellsuit, she needed the pressure against her body to keep her from going insane. Benhil had already told her that some Outworlders were augmented all of the time, even in non-combat situations. Some of them even had the upgrades embedded into their flesh.

"Good choice," Airi said, taking a matching weapon of her own. "Have you seen a lot of combat?"

"Enough," Abbey replied. "Six years of active duty. Seventeen combat drops. Twelve solo missions."

"I thought Breakers didn't do combat?" Benhil said.

"A lot of us don't. I never cared for desks."

He laughed. "I got that about you the first time I saw you."

"I couldn't move the first time you saw me."

"Doesn't matter. You have hardass written all over."

"What about you, Fury?" Benhil asked. "You know how to use a blade."

"Fifteen years active duty, Republic Intergalactic Army. Platoon combat, all on the straight edge, no special ops. I got used to the service knife, but when I realized how poorly designed it was, I went back to something more classic." She reached back, lifting the katana there slightly from its hilt. "Captain Mann must have expected me to come back with him. These things are hard to find."

"It looks custom printed," Gant said. "Rodrinium, if I'm not mistaken. It'll never lose its edge, and can probably cut through anything up to a battlesuit."

"Let's hope we don't need it," Abbey said.

"Queenie," Ruby said over the ship's loudspeakers. "We've received clearance from Orunel. Lucifer is ready to drop."

"Thank you, Ruby," Abbey said. "That's our call."

She led them out of the space and to the hangar, where the *Imp* was already humming, its reactor online. Bastion was visible through the cockpit's small viewport, watching them make the walk across the hangar.

Ruby was waiting outside.

"Queenie," she said, saluting.

"Not military," Abbey reminded her.

"My alternate programming is that of a pleasure bot," Ruby replied. "Would you prefer a kiss?"

"I would," Benhil said.

"Stick with the salute," Abbey said.

"As you command. I'll keep the *Faust* ready to receive you in the event of an emergency."

"You know how to fly this thing?" Benhil asked.

"Well enough not to crash."

"That's not very inspiring."

"A pilot's a pilot," Abbey said. "Let's go. Thank you, Ruby."

"My pleasure," she replied.

"What about my pleasure?" Benhil said as they climbed into the shuttle. "You didn't tell me we had a pleasure bot onboard."

"She's not a pleasure bot," Gant said. "She's Mann's assistant."

"I wonder what else she's assisted him with."

"Jester shut it," Abbey said, picking up a small, clear wad of material and shoving it into her ear. "Lucifer."

"Queenie," Bastion replied, his voice coming through the nearly invisible communicator. "Everybody strapped in back there?"

"Just about. You can seal us in and prep for launch."

"Yes, ma'am."

The ramp closed, the shuttle shuddering as the power was shifted to the thrusters.

"I'll have to take a look at the stabilizers when we get back," Gant said. "That shouldn't be happening."

"Ruby," Abbey said.

"Yes, Queenie?" she replied through the communicator.

"Whatever Jester says or does, the answer is always no."

Ruby's laughter was obviously tuned to attract, soft and slightly breathless. "Yes, Queenie."

"Hey," Benhil complained. "She's part of the crew. We should use her for what she was made for."

"She's here to support our mission."

"That is supporting our mission."

"You don't like it?" Abbey said. "Take it up with the person in charge."

He creased his eyebrows. "But, you are-" He paused. "Oh. I get it. Funny."

The shuttle vibrated more strongly as it lifted from the hangar floor and began moving toward the exit.

"I don't like this," Pik said in response to the shaking.

"I already said I would fix it later," Gant replied.

The shuttle passed through the force shield keeping space where it belonged, moving into the vacuum. The vastly blue world of Orunel was visible through the cockpit transparency ahead, the city glimmering on its island near the center. Dozens of other starships hung around them, a collection of miners and traders and transports from a number of worlds.

They were all pushed back slightly in their seats as Bastion punched the throttle, sending them rocketing forward.

"Oh shit," she heard Bastion say in excited response to the acceleration. "This baby is custom."

He rolled them a few times before leveling off and smacking into the atmosphere, pushing through and out into the air below. The shuttle quaked the entire time, and Abbey could see Gant was getting annoyed by the imperfection.

It took eight minutes to reach the spaceport. It was massive in scale, and already serving nearly a thousand ships of both Republic and Outworld design, segregated into separate sections of the area in an effort to avoid trouble. They were directed to the Outworld side, touching down in the midst of the other shuttles.

"Gear up," Abbey said, getting to her feet.

She picked up a long overcoat with a high collar from a small locker at the front of the shuttle, slipping it on and nearly hiding the entire softsuit. She checked her reflection there, turning her head to make sure the Hell brand was invisible beneath a patch of false skin. While Airi had put on a follicap to hide her baldness and grow a shoulder-length mane of synthetic black locks, Abbey hadn't bothered to cover up, figuring the lack of hair helped complete her overall look.

The others took their turns after her, finishing their outfits with jackets and hats, working to blend in with the population while setting up their nodes in the comm network.

"Roll call," Abbey said once they were all outfitted and waiting at the rear of the shuttle. "Queenie, check."

"Jester, check," Benhil said.

"Fury, check," Airi said.

"Lucifer, check," Bastion said.

"Gant, check," Gant said.

"Okay, check," Pik said.

Satisfied, Abbey tapped the control pad to lower the ramp.

"Let's go, Rejects."

CHAPTER FORTY

THEY TOOK A GROUND SHUTTLE from the spaceport to the city center, making sure to stay separated. Abbey paired up with Airi, while Gant sat nearby, alone. Pik was also by himself, close to Bastion and Benhil, who sat at the front of the transport. The other riders on the shuttle were as eclectic a bunch as they were. Republic soldiers in crisp uniforms, Outworld nomads in scuffed and worn starsuits, the wealthy in richly threaded clothes and the poor in dirty rags. It was an interesting, impressive mix, unlike anything she had ever witnessed on Earth, where people of different origins and classes tended to remain apart.

"We're getting off at the next stop," Benhil said to Bastion, his voice carrying across the team's network. "I know a good place to eat there."

They all stood when the shuttle reached their stop, disembarking to the side of a busy walkway. Benhil made short eye contact with Abbey before vanishing into the middle of the crowd.

Orunel was a unique place. Since most of the population was composed of incoming traders and tourists, the economy centered almost solely on catering to them, offering a broad reach of entertainment and dining options; a pleasure for every taste. The variety was extended by the number of races that frequented the location, and so not only were Terrans catered to, but Trovers, Rudin, Fizzigs, Atmo, and more could also find something of interest or something they might be missing from their homeworld. It meant there was a consistent buzz of energy in the air, an organic, ever-shifting force of life that made Orunel seem like the ideal place to be.

"Don't let it all fool you," Benhil said softly through the comm so that he wouldn't be overheard. "This place barely stays under control, and it's ready to blow up at any moment. There are too many Republics mixed with Outworlders here, and I have a feeling all of the bullshit with the stolen ships is going to be making it silently worse." He was quiet for a moment. "Not to mention, the whole damn thing is a front for the real business, which all happens underground. Everyone knows it. Nobody admits it."

"Mamma Oissi?" Abbey said.

"She's one of the biggest players. I don't know if I can get us to her personally, but even her third-degree lackeys know more than most."

"If she's got the answers, we'll get to her."

"How are you going to make that happen?"

"I'm a Breaker. It's what I do."

Benhil laughed. "I like the way you think, Queenie. Your confidence is infectious. But this isn't some second-rate Outworlder we're talking about here."

"Nothing ventured, nothing gained."

"I think my great-great-great-great grandfather used to say that."

Abbey continued trailing behind them, separated by more distance than would have been smart if they didn't have a Trover with them. Pik towered over most of the crowd, making him easy to spot and easy to follow, from the streets down into a subterranean network of fast-moving transports. She had to scan a payment card to get a pass into the underground system; thankful Captain Mann had thought all of that out, too. The cards were anonymous and untraceable. Most of the cards that got scanned here were probably the same.

They waited at the edge of an ultra-clean platform while a number of the underground transports paused ahead of them, allowing people on and off before rocketing away again. Abbey stayed close enough to Benhil and the others that she could keep up with them, but far enough that only the most seasoned operative might have guessed they were one unit.

"Are we going to stand here all day?" she asked.

"There's a system to this," Benhil said. "See how the shuttles are marked?"

Abbey watched one go by without slowing, barely catching a glimpse of a colored streak as it passed. "Color-coded?"

"Yeah. We want black. That one will stop where we want to go, as long as we tell the steward we want to stop."

"Sneaky. You're telling me the Republic does or doesn't know about this?"

"Yup. Of course, they do. But sometimes you need to let these things happen. Enterprises like Mamma Oissi's lead to better intel for everyone. You should understand that part of the game."

"I do, but I haven't had much occasion to operate in this sort of environment before."

"Which is why I was bailed out. Hey, here it comes now. Stay close once we board or I won't be able to include you in the group."

"Roger."

The shuttle stopped, the doors opening. It was a much lighter crowd than some of the other cars had carried. Abbey followed Benhil onto it, bringing them all back together once they were on board. She could feel the pressure of the inertial dampeners as the vehicle quickly accelerated.

"Excuse me, sir," she heard Benhil say to a taller Terran in a dark suit. "Do you have the time? In Earth Ordinary, if you don't mind. Is it after six?"

The suit lifted an arm. Abbey noticed his hand was metallic. An augmentation or a replacement?

"Fourteen seven three," he replied.

"Thank you," Benhil said. He glanced back at Abbey and winked.

They got off the third time the shuttle stopped, the steward watching carefully as they disembarked, counting their numbers. Only a few other individuals joined them, and they lowered their heads and went on their way without making eye contact.

"How far underground are we?" Gant asked.

"I'm not sure," Benhil replied. "Nobody knows exactly where Mamma Oissi's is. The car has all kinds of jamming tech on board to keep from being accurately positioned. I've heard a lot of rumors that the place is actually in the sediment beneath the ocean."

"I wouldn't doubt it," Airi said.

The shuttle platform led out into a large concourse, which itself was an open market of a kind Abbey had never witnessed before. There were vendors hawking food and clothes, sure, but there were just as many selling things that were illegal whichever nation you were from. Drugs, guns, augmentations, fake identification, even tech designed to hide away illicit cargo, like the kind the Fifth had used to steal the guns from Gradin. It was all there and out in the open, and she saw more than one Republic uniform amidst the crowds, taking a look at the gear, and in one case buying a patch of something.

"I don't fragging believe it," Gant said as they made their way through the throng.

By the time she turned to look at him, he had scurried across two rows to one of the smaller stalls.

"Rejects, hold up," she said, giving chase while the others came to a stop. She caught up to Gant at the display, surprised to find another Gant in charge of the wares.

"They really do have everything here," Gant said, picking up a gun. It had been modified to fit a Gant's two-thumbed grip.

"Watch where you point that thing," Abbey said as the barrel swung toward her.

"Shit. Sorry, Queenie." He lowered it. "How much?"

"Five hundred," the other Gant replied.

"Thousand?" Gant said, incredulous.

"Supply and demand."

"How much demand can there be for a Gant gun?" Gant said.

The other Gant said something Abbey's translator didn't

understand. Gant's lip curled, revealing sharp teeth. "You little piece of-"

"Gant," Abbey said. Both of them looked at her.

"Two-fifty," the other one said. "That's as low as I go."

"Include the holster, and we have a deal," Abbey said before Gant could continue arguing. She dropped her card on the table. The Gant took it and scanned it, and then handed it back.

"Deal. A pleasure doing business with you."

Gant held the gun, staring at it like it was the most incredible thing he had ever seen. A few seconds later, his eyes darkened.

"I don't know if you can trust me with this," he said.

"Why not?"

His mouth opened, but he didn't speak.

"You said we were friends," Abbey said.

"I know. That's the problem. The last time-" He paused. "Forget it. Thank you."

"Let's keep moving. We've got a lot of work to do."

"Yes, ma'am."

CHAPTER FORTY-ONE

MAMMA OISSI'S WASN'T WHAT ABBEY expected. It was crowded, but somehow it managed to keep an air of formality and a contained energy that separated it from what she had painted in her mind. It was no den of villainy. It wasn't home to the scum of the galaxy. It was organized, orchestrated, refined.

Maybe she shouldn't have been surprised. The Rudin were known for their attention to detail and their meticulous nature. There was order within the groups of individuals seated in booths or around open tables, sitting at one of a number of bars, participating in games of chance or watching the Terran singer in the color-changing long dress belting out songs Abbey had never heard before. There was a rhythm to it. A life of its own. Even the multitude of cleaning bots that wandered around the place picking up empty glasses and discarded trash were bright and shiny and perfectly maintained.

"What do you think?" Benhil asked.

"I feel underdressed," Abbey replied, looking down at herself. Maybe the style was unique, but it felt out of place amidst the individuals who were trying harder to look like they could afford whatever it was they came to buy or sell. Not that there weren't others in more standard Outworld dress, and even a few in armor, but they looked more like bodyguards than big dealers.

"You stand out. In a place like this, that's hard to do."

"In a place like this, I don't know if standing out is a good thing."

She looked around. She had no idea how far the reach of the High Honorant extended, whoever and whatever the hell he was. Being too obvious was more likely to get her noticed by the wrong individuals, as much as by the right ones.

"Where's Mamma Oissi?" she asked.

"She has a private suite up there." He pointed to a massive colored screen above the largest of the bars. "If you want to get up, you need to convince him." He shifted his finger to a Trover that made Pik look tiny in comparison. He was easily five meters tall, the largest humanoid she had ever seen.

"Got it," Abbey said. "Rejects spread out, keep an eye out for trouble. I'm going to see if I can get a word with Oissi."

"Hmm. This is boring," Pik said. "I should have stayed on the ship with Ruby."

"Not you too, Okay?" Abbey said.

"It's been a long time."

"She wasn't made for you," Bastion said. "I think you'd break her."

"I'm very gentle. That's another skill."

"One we don't need."

"Ruby needs it."

"Hopeless," Gant said.

"Enough," Abbey said. "Nobody touches Ruby. She's got a new directive. A military directive. Don't piss me off."

"Sorry, Queenie," Pik said.

"How can you be bored, anyway?" Bastion said. "You spent two years in Hell. Doesn't it feel good to get out, stretch your legs, have some activity around you?"

"It's okay, I guess. That singer is hurting my ears. Those ancient Terran songs are terrible. What does 'I'll keep holding on,' mean, anyway?"

Abbey shut out their banter, separating from Jester and moving toward the Trover. "Does that living mountain have a name?" she asked.

"Ill," Benhil replied.

"As in, sick?"

"In Terran, yeah."

He was being distracted by an Atmo by the time she reached him. The smaller humanoid was speaking quickly, and gesturing to the door behind the bouncer. He barely came up to the Trover's knee.

"I'll pass a message and let you know," Ill said. "Now frag off."

The Atmo groaned and turned away, rejected. Ill noticed Abbey approaching, turning his large bulk toward her and frowning.

"Mamma doesn't need another whatever the frag it is you think you are," he said.

Abbey smiled. "Who says I came to see Mamma?" she replied. "Maybe I came to see you."

"Yeah. I believe that. Frag off."

"You're the biggest Trover I've ever seen. How'd they even fit you through the tunnels?"

He softened slightly. "I've been here since I was a kid. Can't get out of here, now."

"Does that get lonely?"

"Nah. Mamma adopted me when I was your size. She's always got lots of indivs around. Look, we don't need to play games. You didn't come to flirt with me. Everyone wants to talk to Mamma. Everyone."

Abbey shrugged. "You've probably had a million individuals approach you in a million ways to speak to Mamma directly."

"That's right."

"Did any of them ever tell you they had information about Sylvan Kett and a potential Republic conspiracy?"

His face changed again. Curiosity. His left eye lowered as if he had a tic.

"Queenie, this is Lucifer," Bastion said. "I'm tailing two Outworlders who were acting a little funny. They're coming your way."

"It isn't two," Airi said. "I'm tracking three more. They look like they're networked."

"Are you calling for backup?" Abbey asked.

The Trover looked at her. "What? Do I look like I need backup to handle you?"

"No. I'm wondering, though. How do you keep order in a place like this? You've got lots of weapons for sale right outside."

"Is that a threat? Mamma and I don't like threats."

There was a bit of commotion coming from behind them.

"Queenie, I'm counting twelve at least," Pik said.

"More than that," Gant said. "They're coming from outside. What the frag?"

"Shit," Abbey said. "Will Mamma see me?"

He smiled and stepped aside. "It's your lucky day." The door behind him slid open. "She's been hoping someone would show up with some intel on Kett."

Abbey took a step toward the door.

All hell broke loose behind her.

CHAPTER FORTY-TWO

SHOTS ECHOED THROUGH THE SPACE as Abbey dropped to the ground, rolling over to find the targets that had painted her. They were closing in from all sides, shooting through anyone who got in their way, an assortment of individuals in a variety of dress that seemed to be producing weapons from every nook and cranny on their bodies.

Ill had just enough time to scream before a hundred rounds tore into him, digging deep into his flesh, some of them going completely through. His body wavered for a moment before toppling.

"Cut those assholes down," Abbey said, bunching herself and pushing off, the softsuit sending her bouncing toward the open door. Bullets hit the walls around her, somehow managing to miss as she slammed into the back of the lift.

"On it," Airi said.

"This is more like it," Pik said.

Abbey rolled over, pulling the laser pistol from her thigh. The first of the targets cleared the masses, and she squeezed off a pair of rounds, the laser quickly burning through his eye and into his skull. He was still falling as the lift doors slid closed and she started to rise.

She could hear the fighting intensify, even though she couldn't see it. She pulled herself to her feet, quickly checking herself to ensure she wasn't hit. She noticed a bullet hole in her coat, and she pushed it aside, revealing the softsuit beneath. It too had a hole, a stain of blood around it.

"Damn it," Abbey cursed. She wasn't hurting. She hadn't even felt the round hit her. She dug her finger into the hole, surprised when she couldn't find any torn skin and didn't feel any pain. What the hell?

The lift stopped. The doors opened. A pair of guards trained a pair of guns on her head.

"Drop the weapon," one of them said.

She did.

"I need to talk to Mamma," Abbey said.

"Mamma needs to talk to you."

The Rudin was at the back of the room, looking out through the one-way transparency to the space below. She didn't turn to look at Abbey. "Let her over."

The guards moved aside. Abbey made her way to the window. She looked out, checking on the fighting below. She found Pik first. He had one of the Outworlders in his grip, and she watched as he crushed the Terran, snapping his spine and tossing him away, ducking as bullets flew over his head. They smacked into the transparency right in front of her without leaving a mark.

She found Gant and Airi next, paired up and defending against a few more of the assholes, trading fire from behind an overturned table. Bastion was nearby, hunkered down and staying low while the munitions crossed overhead.

Where was Benhil?

"Do you bring this kind of chaos everywhere you go?" Mamma asked, still not looking at her. Abbey could hear her beak cracking beneath the translation.

"It seems like it lately," Abbey replied. "You don't seem concerned."

"I'm very concerned." That was the only thing she said about it. "Tell me what you know about Sylvan Kett."

"I need intel," Abbey said. "Two ships. The *Fire* and the *Brimstone*. Someone took them."

"His name is Ursan Gall. He's an Outworld mercenary."

"Which means he's working for someone."

"Yes."

"Who?"

Mamma didn't answer. Abbey knew the game.

"I was with the Fifth on Gradin," she said. "I'm a Breaker."

"What did you find?"

Abbey didn't respond.

"Ursan Gall works for an individual named Thraven. He's a very dangerous individual."

"He's an Outworlder?"

"He is in the Outworlds. He isn't an Outworlder. Though I suppose that depends on your definition."

Abbey watched as one of the cleaning bots she had seen earlier approached one of the targets from behind. Its fingers came together, creating a point, before lunging forward and into the man's back. She found another bot further away. It had produced a gun from somewhere and was shooting at the enemy. It sparked and hissed and sent up a plume of smoke as a round of fire from the rear of the space destroyed it.

"Queenie, where are you?" Bastion said. "We're not having the best time down here."

"I'm with Mamma. You need to hold the line. All of you."

"Roger," Gant said.

"Mamma," one of her guards said. "We need to get you out of here. Eln is reporting a problem in the tunnels, and an unmarked ship just showed up in orbit. It isn't responding to hails from Planetary Control."

"Who are you that he wants you so badly?" Mamma said, finally turning a large eye to her.

"I'm nobody," Abbey replied. "Just someone stuck in something they don't understand."

A pair of tentacles snapped out from Mamma, quickly wrapping themselves around her wrists and pulling tight.

"What do you know?" Mamma screamed, the snap of her beak so loud it hurt her ears.

"Not enough. That's why I came to you."

"About Kett. What do you know? Gradin? Hurry."

"I picked up a mainframe there. It was Republic, marked special ops. It had been erased before I grabbed it."

"Not erased, stupid girl," Mamma said. "Too valuable to erase."

"You know what was on it?"

"I know it belonged to Kett. You said you're a Breaker?"

"Yes. I tried to retrieve the data, but I got arrested before I was able to finish."

Her beak clattered together in laughter. "They took you." Another tentacle reached up, finding the false skin on her neck and pulling it away, revealing the brand beneath. "Hell."

The facility shook as a large explosion rocked it.

"Queenie," Bastion said, worried.

"Mamma, we have to go," the guard said.

"You don't know what you've gotten yourself into, girl. You should have stayed in Hell. You would have been-" She stopped talking, her eye falling on the hole in Abbey's softsuit. A fourth tentacle reached up and poked it. It immediately shot up to her face. "Oh."

"The ships," Abbey said. "I need to know where Ursan Gall took them."

"To Thraven," Mamma said.

"Where?"

"I don't know everything."

The facility shook again. Abbey turned her head to look down on the fighting. There was blood everywhere. Bodies everywhere. Broken pieces of beaten bots everywhere. Soldiers were moving in, in black lightsuits like the ones the guards on Hell had been wearing. The Rejects had closed ranks, part of the remaining opposition.

"Tell me what you do know, and make it fast. My team is down there. They're buying you time to escape. You fragging owe me."

"Thraven's been at the edge of the Outworlds for years. Nobody knows exactly where he came from. Some say unexplored space. He's been recruiting, building a military."

"And the Republic doesn't know about this?"

"I've heard that he has influence in the Republic as well. That his hand reaches everywhere. Like Hell."

"You know about Hell? Does the title High Honorant mean anything to you?"

"Thraven calls himself a Gloritant."

"So the theft of the *Fire* and *Brimstone* is related to the bullshit on Hell." She paused. "The way you reacted to my wound. You know what they did to me, don't you?"

"Not exactly. I've heard they've been taking people and making them harder to kill. Now I know it is true."

"How?"

"I told you, I don't know everything."

"Where did you get the intel from? I need a name. A location. Something."

"You aren't going to make it out of here alive."

"Don't tell me what I will and won't do. Give me a fragging name."

"I can't divulge my sources. My business will be ruined."

"Look around, you stupid squid. Your business is already ruined. I don't know Thraven, but you said he's building a military. He also just stole two of the most powerful starships in the universe. What does that say to you? Even if you rebuild, it isn't going to do much good without any customers."

Mamma stared at her a moment. "Drune," she said at last. "There's a Skink there named Yolem. He sold me the information about Thraven." She let Abbey go, pulling back her tentacles. "You brought this on us. You brought them here. He wants you. The mainframe. He wants you to finish decrypting it."

"Why?"

"Kett knows the truth. That's why the Republic turned on him."

"How do I find Kett?"

"Nobody finds Kett. We're done. I'm leaving."

"You have another way out?"

"My way out, girl. You find your own way. I told you that you're going to die."

Abbey glanced out again. More of Thraven's soldiers were arriving, shooting anything that moved. She couldn't allow herself to believe she had caused this mess, but she couldn't deny it either. Why had Thraven come here, now? Because she was here or because he had guessed someone would find their way to Mamma to ask about the ships? He didn't seem like someone who wanted to be found. Not yet, anyway.

"Gant," Abbey said.

"Queenie?"

"I need you to get the others up here."

"How?"

"There's a lift by the dead Trover."

"Looks locked."

"Come on, Gant."

"Fine. On it."

The two guards put their guns to her head again.

"You aren't coming with me," Mamma said. "You brought this destruction. This death. You've ruined me. You're a demon. You belong back in Hell." She turned away, heading for a secret door that opened at the side of the room. "Kill her."

CHAPTER FORTY-THREE

THE GUARD ON HER LEFT put his gun closer to her head, touching the barrel to it. Abbey surprised herself with her calm. She decided she wasn't going to die. Not today.

He began to squeeze the trigger. She could feel the motion beneath her skin, acute and almost painful, as though it was warning her of the impending shot. She snapped her head forward as the bullet fired, the heat of the muzzle flash burning the back of her neck. The bullet itself missed, the slug hitting the armored transparency and scuffing it before it fell to the ground.

She swung her arm back, catching the guard in the face, the power of her blow enhanced by the softsuit. His nose crumbled beneath the force, and he fell backward.

She was already shifting again, dropping low and spinning, bringing her leg around and into the other guard's ankles, knocking him over. She rolled on top of him as he hit the ground, punching him hard in the side of the head and putting him out, too.

She picked up the guard's gun, firing it into the wall beside Mamma Oissi.

"Wait up," she said.

Mamma rotated on her tentacles, half of them reaching up toward her robe. Abbey fired, hitting one of the tentacles, which exploded in bits of fatty flesh. Mamma shrieked, the other three appendages producing three separate guns. "Stupid girl."

Abbey bounced from her position, evading the Rudin's attack, rotating herself in the air and pushing off the nearby wall. Mamma tried to track her, rounds whizzing past, one of them clipping her shoulder and sending a momentary flare of pain from the spot. She landed, ducking down, firing again, hitting Mamma's robe, which absorbed the attack.

The lift doors slid aside, the rest of the Rejects piling out into the room. They were sweaty, dirty, and in Pik's case slightly bloody, but otherwise still in one piece.

"Queenie," Gant said. "We're-"

He saw Mamma turning one of the weapons toward him. He reacted like a gunslinger, the laser pistol he had bought coming up to his hip, the tight beam visible as it pierced her eye. A moment later, she vanished beneath a storm of fire from all of the Rejects.

"What the frag is going on out there?" Benhil said. "It's like fragging Armageddon."

"It might be worse than that," Abbey said, quickly checking her shoulder. Once more, there was the hint of damage, but no damage to be found.

"Mamma Oissi, I presume?" Gant said, waving his gun at the dead Rudin.

"She used to be," Abbey replied.

Something thunked into the transparency to their right, sticking to it. Abbey recognized the ordnance instantly.

"Get down."

She fell onto her stomach as the munition exploded, blowing out the transparency in thousands of small shards. She was up again in an instant, turning toward the broken shield as the first of the lightsuits began bouncing up to it.

She opened fire, knocking two of them to the ground as they arrived. "Let's go," she said, pointing toward the secret passage Mamma had opened.

A few more of the enemy soldiers bounced to the space, quickly knocked back by the combined firepower of the Rejects. They moved into the hallway together, Abbey waving them past as she lingered near the door. She shot one more of the soldiers before hitting a control pad there, closing the hatch and hopefully hiding them once more.

The Rejects ran along the hidden passage. They traveled a few hundred meters, spilling out into a separate shuttle passage, where a lone shuttle was waiting, another pair of guards waiting with it.

"Don't," Bastion said as they emerged. Five guns were trained on the guards, and they responded by putting up their hands. "Thank you for your cooperation."

They boarded the shuttle. Bastion found the controls, turning the craft on and getting it moving. They burst away, forward a few seconds before looping back and accelerating. The ride was short; no more than thirty seconds. It stopped in a much smaller station that fed out to a ramp.

"Where are we?" Benhil asked.

The ceiling above them shook, chunks of dirt spilling in a cloud of dust.

"Under the city?" Airi guessed. "I only see one way out."

"They're attacking the city?" Bastion said. "Damn. What the frag did I get myself into?"

"It's better than Hell," Pik said.

"Come on," Abbey said. It wasn't like they had a choice in direction.

They ran up the ramp to the round hatch at the end. It slid open, revealing a war zone behind it. Small, dark ships zoomed overhead, firing plasma cannons and projectile weapons, strafing the area as they passed. There was a large, rounded ship nearby, already on fire, sending plumes of smoke into the air.

"Spaceport," Gant said. "Nice."

"Ruby," Abbey said, hoping the *Faust* had slipped the attention of the invading force.

"Queenie," she replied. "The planet is under attack."

"I'm aware. What's your situation?"

"They are ignoring the unregistered ships in orbit and attacking planctary defense. Shrikes, but not like any I have in my database."

"Can you tell if the *Imp* is in one piece?"

"One moment. Checking. Yes. I'm able to reach its communications equipment."

"Great. We're on our way. Be ready to get the *Faust* away from here."

"Yes, Queenie."

"Queenie, you do realize the *Imp* is on the other side of the spaceport?" Bastion said.

Abbey looked up. There were at least a dozen Shrikes hovering near the spaceport, circling and strafing. Would they attack if they saw them running?

A plasma bolt whipped past them, making up her mind for her. She followed the path back to the shooter, another soldier in a black lightsuit. He was hit with a laser a moment later, falling to the ground and not moving.

"I like this gun," Gant said. "A little underpowered, maybe, but I can fix that."

"I thought Gant don't use guns," Bastion said.

"Most of us," Gant replied. "It's hard to find one with the right grip, and Queenie can tell you how expensive. But I was a Republic soldier too, or has that fact slipped your tiny little brain?"

"Come on," Abbey said, defusing their next round of insults.

She bounced ahead, using the softsuit to take long strides forward. She crouched as she came down, scanning the area before bouncing again. She made it nearly three hundred meters before spotting an incoming Shrike.

"Cover," she said, ducking beneath an already battered ship. The Shrike dove in, firing rounds of plasma across the area that hissed as they hit the ground.

Abbey waited for the others to catch up before moving out from the cover, keeping her gun ready and her eyes sharp. The air was hot from all of the fires. It reminded her of Hell.

"Three o'clock," Bastion announced, a stream of fire launching from his pistol.

Abbey shifted her weapon, finding a squad of soldiers moving in. They fired back, their bullets all aimed at her. If Mamma Oissi had thought Thraven wanted her alive, she was wrong. Maybe dead wrong.

The rounds whipped past her, whistling in her ears, striking the ground at her sides. Somehow, they missed their aim a little bit off, just long enough for a group of Outworlders to show up from nowhere, firing into the back of the soldiers.

"Serendipity," Gant said in response to the surprise defense, rushing up to Abbey's side. His face changed as he looked at her. "Oh. Uh. Queenie. You have. Oh."

Abbey looked down. She thought the slugs had missed her. They hadn't. She had four holes across her abdomen, all of them surrounded by fresh blood. She still didn't feel a thing.

"Whoa," Benhil said, seeing the damage. "Shit, Queenie. I'm sorry."

"Shut up," Abbey said. "I'm not dead. Keep moving."

"What? Are you kidding?"

"No," Abbey said. "Move, Reject."

She didn't know what the hell was happening, and there was a part of it that was scaring the shit out of her. There was also a part of her that was grateful for it. If whatever Clyo did had made her bulletproof, right now she would take it.

Then again, if she were bulletproof, that meant at least some portion of Thraven's followers were, too.

"There," Pik said, pointing as they crossed the spaceport. The *Imp* was visible ahead, slightly shrouded by smoke from a nearby ship.

"Hold up," Airi said, freezing them while a Shrike blew past, searching for targets. "Go."

They ran the last hundred meters, sprinting for the *Imp*. Abbey reached it first, entering the code to lower the ramp and waiting while the others piled in. She scanned the air one last time, noticing one of the Shrikes slowing and turning back toward them.

"We've been spotted, Luc. Cold launch."

"I don't know if this thing can hold up to a cold launch, the way she was shaking before," Bastion replied.

"I'm on it," Gant said, crouching in the area between the seats and working to unscrew the cover there with a small piece of metal he pulled from his pants pocket. He vanished below the floor as Abbey closed the ramp and the engines came online, making the whole ship shiver.

The *Imp* shrilled a sharp warning tone.

"Shit," Bastion said. "We're marked. Whatever you're doing down there freak-monkey, you better make it quick."

"How many times do I have to tell you not to call me that?" Gant said. "Give me a few seconds."

"We don't have a few seconds. I'm hitting the throttle."

"Wait," Gant said.

It was too late.

The *Imp* lurched forward, knocking Abbey back as she tried to reach a seat. The *Imp* vibrated harder than anything she had ever experienced, threatening to tear itself apart in the process.

"You asshole," Gant said.

Abbey grabbed hold of the side of the ship as they were bounced around, the stabilizers struggling to keep the ship level.

"Frag it's hard to fly her like this," Bastion said.

"I told you to wait," Gant shouted. "I'm going to break your face when we get back to the *Faust*."

Abbey pulled herself to the front of the shuttle, falling into the co-pilot's seat. The Shrikes were adjusting course, changing direction to attack them. A few of the other ships were starting to rise from the spaceport at the same time, attempting to escape.

"Use them as cover," Abbey said, pointing.

"I'm trying. I've got about fifty percent control like this."

"Gant," Abbey said. "Tell me you have something."

"I've got something," Gant said. "Don't get us killed for another five seconds or so."

A plasma bolt hit the side of the *Imp*, absorbed by the shields but still managing to knock it sideways.

"Ow," Gant shouted. "I said don't get us killed, you worthless piece of farble."

"Farble?" Bastion said, his translator glitching as badly as Abbey's.

"There," Gant said.

The *Imp* responded with an echoing clang, the vibration vanishing instantly. Bastion hit the throttle, changing vectors and swooping down toward one of the rising starships, two Shrikes giving chase.

"Wooo. Yeah," Bastion said, rolling the Imp and crossing beneath the ship, so closely that the top of the shuttle nearly brushed the hull. He snapped it up and over as one of the Shrikes slowed to make the maneuver, and the other crashed into the ship, passing through its shields and exploding.

Then they were streaking toward orbit, ascending in a smooth, straight line with the other Shrike still trailing. The smaller Outworld ships were deadly to slower maneuvering freighters and battleships and could go toe-to-toe with the best of the Republic's starfighters. Against the shuttle? It should have been no contest, but Bastion turned it into one.

The Imp slipped and rolled, the vibrations gone, the engines reacting with an acute sensitivity that belied the design. Wherever Captain Mann had gotten her, the engines had been tweaked, the computers updated, the vectoring thrusters overhauled. They spiraled and corkscrewed, evading the Shrike's plasma bolts as they streamed around them, threatening to put a well-placed bolt into their vulnerable rear.

"Ruby, we're coming in," Abbey said, contacting the synthetic.

"I'm tracking you," Ruby replied. "On an intercept course. Passing coordinates now."

"Got 'em," Bastion said. "ETA fifteen seconds."

The Imp continued to haul ass, through the upper edge of the atmosphere and into the vacuum beyond. Abbey could see the larger invading battleship now. It was unlike anything the Outworld was supposed to possess. Nearly two kilometers long, tall and wide, with a twin bow and a deep hull. It was stationary in space, unchallenged by the remaining ships around it. The battered remains of a Republic cruiser was sitting a few hundred kilometers off the port side.

Not the *Fire* or the *Brimstone*. That meant Thraven had more than just Shrikes under his control. Where had he gotten that ship?

It was a question for another time, one of the dozens that were floating around in Abbey's head. The order of the universe was unraveling before her eyes. Her personal order was twisting into chaotic knots. She absently ran her hand over her stomach, feeling the holes in the softsuit there. She should have been dead or dying on the tarmac of the spaceport, or back in Mamma Oissi's personal lounge. She shouldn't be here, now, on the verge of making it back to the *Faust*.

She snapped back to the present. The *Faust* was on their starboard side, cutting across on an intercept vector, rotated so the hangar was in line with them. The Shrike was still firing, the plasma bolts slapping the larger ship's shields, the turrets along the sides turning to fire back. Lasers pulsed around the Imp, invisible beams marked by flashes of light from the hull to help them evade the attack. Bastion sailed them smoothly around, leading the trailing enemy into the fire and laughing as it vanished from the shuttle's HUD.

"You stupid ass," he said. Then he slammed on the reverse thrusters, guiding the Imp into the hangar. Abbey felt the momentum shift, the gravity change, and then the shuttle dropped on heavy gear, dipping slightly before coming to rest.

"Lucifer," Abbey said.

"On my way," Bastion replied, ditching the pilot's seat and rushing to the rear of the craft. Gant had already hit the door controls, giving him room to slip through the crack.

"Ruby, Lucifer is on the way. Get us out of here."

"Aye, Queenie," Ruby said.

Abbey trailed Bastion from the shuttle. "The rest of you, get secured in case things get bumpy."

"Yes, ma'am," Pik replied for them.

Then Abbey was sprinting to the exit, through and to the central ladders, up and forward to the cockpit. Bastion was already there, seated beside Ruby. He was heading right at the unidentified ship.

"What the frag are you doing?" Abbey said.

"Ruby said Captain Mann might want a good look at that thing," he replied.

"Frag Captain Mann, get us out of here."

"You might be in local command of this crew, but Captain Mann is the Boss," Bastion said.

Abbey moved forward, wrapping her arm around Bastion's neck and pulling it back in his seat, choking him.

"Captain Mann left us with orders to do whatever we had to do to finish the mission. That doesn't include getting blasted by that ship. Now get us to safety, or I'll break your fragging neck."

"I.. can't... breathe..." Bastion choked.

"Ruby?" Abbey said. "I've already been shot six times today. I'm not in a good mood."

"Coordinates are set, Queenie," Ruby said.

"Lucifer, punch it."

Bastion reached forward, lowering his finger to the control pad just as the enemy ship started shooting. Abbey's eyes narrowed at the brightness of the plasma bolt nearly striking them right before they went into FTL, escaping Orunel in a flash.

CHAPTER FORTY-FOUR

ABBEY UNHOOKED HER ARM FROM Bastion's neck, getting back to her feet. The pilot leaned forward, choking and trying to regain his breath.

"You crazy bitch," he said, sputtering. "You could have fragging killed me. You're a demon. A damned fragging demon."

"Ruby," Abbey said, ignoring him. "Set a course for Drune."

"Drune?" Bastion said. "Frag. Why?"

"That's the direction Mamma pointed us. What are you so worried about?"

"Drune is shit. A dustball. Worthless."

"Not according to Oissi."

Bastion laughed. "The Rudin we killed because she was trying to kill you? It's just as likely a fragging trap."

"I don't think so, but if it is, it is. That's our lead."

"You're out of your damn mind."

"Ruby, set a course for Drune," Abbey repeated.

"Yes, Queenie," Ruby said, using the co-pilot station to begin entering the coordinates. They would have to come out of FTL to redirect, but that shouldn't be dangerous between planets.

"And get me a line to Captain Mann."

"Yes, Queenie."

"You should be dead," Bastion said, looking back at her, his eyes fixed on her stomach. "Why aren't you dead?"

"Because I'm a demon," Abbey replied. "Take us out of FTL and put us on course to Drune. When that's done, go find something to do to chill the frag out."

Bastion's eyes turned to Ruby.

"Something else," Abbey said. "Ruby, Captain Mann."

"I'm initializing the connection now," Ruby replied.

"Come with me."

Abbey left Bastion alone in the cockpit, Ruby following dutifully behind her. Gant and Airi were climbing the ladder into the central area of the Faust as they arrived.

"Queenie, you okay?" Gant said.

"I'll be fine," Abbey replied. "Where's Pik?"

"Already up top," Airi said. "He said he needed to use the bathroom." She raised an eye. "Where are you going with Ruby?"

"To speak to Captain Mann," Abbey replied, shaking her head. They needed to reset the synthetic as soon as they had the chance.

"You want to tell him what happened on Orunel?" Gant said.

"He probably already knows what happened on Orunel, or will soon. No, I want to tell him what happened to me, and what Oissi told me."

"I thought you didn't trust him."

"I don't, but I have a feeling he's going to be in trouble if I don't say anything, and he still has the keys to the kingdom." She tapped the side of her head.

Gant tapped his head, too. She had no doubt he was planning to see if he could do anything about that situation.

"What should we do in the meantime?" Airi asked.

"We're headed to Drune. Rest, recover, and prepare."

"As you say, Queenie."

Abbey continued down the ladder to the small construct module. It was the most isolated spot on the ship.

"I have Captain Mann linked," Ruby announced.

The small room forced them into close proximity. Abbey could smell the soft lilac scent embedded in the former pleasure synthetic's skin. No wipe and reset would be able to get rid of that.

"Captain Mann," Abbey said.

One of Ruby's eyes changed, projecting the Captain into the air between them.

"Lieutenant Cage," Mann said, pausing as he got a glimpse of her through Ruby's other eye. "Don't tell me. You were just on Orunel."

"As of about five minutes ago," Abbey said. "News travels fast."

"Especially when Republic ships are under assault by an unidentified warship. Do you know anything about it?"

"Unfortunately. Have you ever heard of Gloritant Thraven?"

"No. It sounds like a cocktail."

"Funny. He's a man. Actually, I don't know if he's a man. According to the late Mamma Oissi, he's been building up a military, and it looks like he's just about ready to make his move."

"The late Mamma Oissi? She was a valuable resource. What happened to her?"

"She tried to kill me," Abbey said. "She couldn't have been that valuable if you didn't know about any of this."

"Mamma doesn't sell Outworld secrets to the Republic, and vice versa. It would be... It would have been hard for her to stay in business otherwise. So, you're saying this Thraven took the *Fire* and the *Brimstone*?"

"His people did. He's the one who attacked Orunel, ostensibly to get to me, or to keep Mamma quiet about him. She divulged that there's a Skink on Drune who may know more about Thraven's operation. We're on our way now."

Captain Mann looked thoughtful. "Drune? There's nothing on Drune."

"That's what Bastion said. Thanks for busting him out by the way. He's a great pilot, even if he is an asshole. You seem to know Oissi. Can I trust her intel?"

"Did you have the gun to her head before or after she told you that?"

"She had a gun to my head. Two, actually. I killed her after."

"Then it's as good as it gets. Whether or not her source is reliable is another question, but they wouldn't have had time to set you up that way. Not unless they expected you to break out of Hell."

"Which they wouldn't have unless you have a leak."

"I don't. I'm on my own in this, Lieutenant, for that very reason. The only link back to Command is through General Soto, who is a highly trusted, personal friend of mine. She helped me procure the *Faust* and Ruby."

Abbey nodded, suddenly hesitant to tell Mann anything else. If he knew about her sudden inability to be killed, would he order her back and turn her into some kind of experiment?

"Lieutenant," Mann said. "Something isn't sitting well with you. Do you want to tell me about it?"

Abbey stared at him for a few seconds. "Is it that obvious?"

"No, but I have a lot of experience. I know you want to hold something you can exchange for your freedom later. I'm an honorable man, Lieutenant. I won't tell you that you'll be released and not follow through."

"Assuming you live that long," Abbey said, making up her mind. "I have reason to believe Thraven has been pulling the strings on Hell. Packard, Lurin, they both work for him. I overheard Lurin talking to someone else, calling him a High Honorant, a rank of some kind. If Thraven has control of Hell-"

"Then he knows about me," Mann said. "I was already suspicious of everyone."

"Suspicious enough to expect an assassin?"

"Like the ones who attacked Director Eagan? Keep this to yourself, Cage, but it takes one to know one, and I know one when I see one."

Abbey was surprised. "I understand." She paused again. There was no point to only giving him part of the information. "There's more. Mamma told me Thraven's been doing something to some of his soldiers that make them harder to kill. I told you about it already. One of the prisoners from the Fifth, Private Illiard. I shot him twice in the head. He didn't stop coming until Fury removed it."

"Fury?"

"Airi," Abbey said. "We settled on new callsigns."

"What's yours?"

"It doesn't matter."

"Mine was Killshot," Mann said.

"That's a lot better than Queenie. I hate nicks that end in a strong E. It makes me sound like a child."

Mann laughed. "You should have picked one for yourself sooner."

"Breakers don't have callsigns. I'm surprised killers do."

"Nobody's supposed to know who we are. It helps. Tell me more about Illiard. You're saying the head shots didn't kill him?"

"That's right. He seemed normal otherwise, other than the fact that he didn't speak. Oh, and his eyes. They were a solid gray."

"That isn't normal."

"No. It isn't. Then there's this."

She shifted her position, moving closer to Ruby so Mann could get a better look at her stomach.

"You were hit," he said.

"Six times. Four times in the stomach."

"But you're still standing."

"Whatever Thraven is doing, he did it to me, too. Back in my cell the night I killed Packard. At first, I thought it was a crazy dream. A hallucination. It wasn't. They injected me with something. It looked like blood."

"I can start to guess what this means for the bigger picture. But why you, Lieutenant? Of all the prisoners in Hell."

"Sylvan Kett," Abbey said.

"What? How does Kett tie in?"

"Mamma suggested the Fifth was on Gradin to steal something from Kett. Something he didn't want Thraven to get his hands on. He wiped the data as an added level of security, which it turns out was a good idea. The Fifth got busted for possession of Kett's contraband, and I got caught in the middle."

"You're saying you're innocent."

"Yes, but that's beside the point. I'm not stupid enough to think you're going to let me go just because I tell you the sob story."

"Good."

"The point is that Thraven wants the data on the mainframe I recovered. He tried to have his people break it, but they weren't up to the task."

"So they needed a professional."

"Yes."

"One who was easy to get control over."

"Who they thought would be easy to control. And who had already started working on the problem."

"Did you make any progress?"

"Not much, but I eliminated a lot of possibilities. That's a start. What do you know about Kett, Killshot?"

"I know the Republic thinks he's a traitor."

"Do you? As the head of the OSI?"

"The evidence suggests he is. Ferrying contraband?"

"What would you do, if you knew there was a threat to the Republic, but you couldn't tell anyone about it? If you couldn't ask for help? If you knew your chain of command was compromised?"

"I'd break an elite team of soldiers out of incarceration."

Abbey smiled at that. "I assume General Kett didn't have that option. Maybe he did the next best thing?"

"I'm open to the idea after everything else you've just told me. I'll see if I can dig anything up on Thraven. You stay the course, but be careful. Drune may be a trap."

"You don't want to pull me off the team?"

"Why would I do that?"

"To find out what Thraven did to me."

"You were already a weapon. If you're harder to kill, then you're a stronger weapon. Why the frag would I pull you out? We need all the help we can get."

"Yes, sir."

"Are you starting to feel a little better about the situation?"

"The one I should never have ended up in? Not at all. But if Thraven has designs on the Republic, he has designs on Earth. I'd rather he didn't have those ships to field in support of that. I have a daughter to protect."

"Good enough for me. Thank you for trusting me, Queenie."

"Don't make me regret it."

"I won't. Mann out."

Ruby's eye dimmed, the projection vanishing. Abbey closed her eyes for a moment, hopeful that she had made the right decision. Mann wasn't going to tell the Republic about her. What was he going to do with the intel?

"Ruby, how long until we reach Drune?"

"Forty-two hours, Queenie."

"Good. I need some time to unwind."

"I am skilled at massage," Ruby said. "Along with many other relaxation techniques."

"I can imagine," Abbey said. "You know what I do want?"

"I can provide many services."

"Nothing like that. Something to eat. I just realized I'm starving."

CHAPTER FORTY-FIVE

OLUS SAT BEHIND HIS DESK, in his quarters on the *Driver*. It had taken nearly three days for him to resync with the battleship after Usiari had been delayed by the Republic ships that arrived in orbit around Hell.

Ships that Warden Lurin had summoned.

Ships that were obviously not as loyal to the Republic as they might have thought.

Not that Olus trusted Usiari, either. After all, the Captain of the *Nebula* had allowed the Driver to leave without questioning her Commander too intensely. Because they knew he had given the gag order? Or because Usiari was helping to keep him in check?

He considered his conversation with Lieutenant Cage. He wasn't surprised that she had taken control of the mission. He knew from the moment he had decided he wasn't leaving without her that she was going to be vital to their success. He knew from the moment he had figured out that Lurin was a lying piece of shit, and the Republic was deep in it.

Even so, the future looked more and more like a black hole, gathering mass and threatening to swallow everything it neared. At the center of it, someone named Thraven, who had not only orchestrated the theft of the *Fire* and *Brimstone* but who had also been taking prisoners out of Hell and using them to bolster a secret army. More than that, he was experimenting on them. Olus still remembered how Cage had thrown him across the isolation room with nothing but a gesture, even if it seemed she couldn't remember it herself.

And now she was virtually bulletproof? He would never have believed it if he hadn't seen it. The thought worried him more than he had let on. Super soldiers had been a long dream of the Republic Armed Services. At one time, they had believed that bots and synthetics would be those soldiers until counter AI technologies had relegated them to peaceful servants. Then the battlesuits were supposed to be the next evolution of infantry warfare. While they had enhanced the combat effectiveness of a single soldier, making one as powerful as twenty or more used to be, they were still mortal. Still flesh and blood. Still able to feel pain, and to be killed.

If Abbey was right, and he had no reason to doubt her, all of that was going to change. Which would have been acceptable if it were the Republic who had made the leap. It wasn't. Gloritant Thraven was a step ahead of them. Maybe two or three.

Where the frag had he come from?

A short chirp indicated that someone was trying to communicate with him. Olus didn't hesitate, opening the link.

"What do you have?" he asked.

"Sir. I've completed the analysis of the lifestream you sent over," Ensign Klar said.

"Let me guess, no leads."

"Actually, sir, we may have something for you. I'm transmitting the results now."

Olus sat up straighter in his chair. He hadn't expected his investigators to turn anything up. He opened a second projection of the data the Ensign was sending him.

It was a single frame, a shot he had emblazoned in his memory. The inside of the starship that had picked up Eagan and her abductors. He watched as it zoomed in, from one hundred percent to one thousand, focusing on a small area behind Mars. The pixels were still relatively sharp at the high resolution, and they grew sharper as inferencing filters were applied.

"What am I looking at, Ensign?" he asked.

"Sir, there's a serial number on that power conduit."

"I assume you've already traced it?"

"Yes, sir."

He moved through the data to the report on the conduit. He wasn't overly surprised to discover it had been produced by Eagan Heavyworks, or that it had vanished from inventory two years prior.

Not stolen. Vanished. As though it had simply disappeared.

It was the kind of thing he might not have given a second thought under other circumstances. A company like the Heavyworks produced so many parts that losing a few thousand of them per year wasn't all that suspicious. To have that part turn up here and now? It was a piece of a puzzle he felt comfortable lowering into place.

"Ensign, delete everything you have on this immediately," Olus said. "Full wipe."

"Sir?"

"Local copies, and from the OSI datastore. If I could erase your memory of it, I would. Does anyone else know about it?"

"Lieutenant Platt," Ensign Klar replied.

"Give him the same orders, and watch your back, Ensign. This information is as volatile as it gets."

"Yes, sir."

Her voice was less confident, slightly shaken. Good. He needed her to be alert.

"Mann, out."

He closed the link, sitting back for a moment. He hadn't trusted Mars Eagan that much before. He trusted her even less now.

"General Iti Soto," he said, directing the communication system to send a signal out to her. He had been trying to reach her for days, frustrated and increasingly concerned with the lack of a response.

A Fizzig appeared, projected onto the desk. Short and wide, with big, heavy bones and thick, gray skin.

"General Omsala?" Olus said, recognizing him.

"Captain Mann," Omsala replied.

"Where is General Soto?"

Omsala cast his small, dark eyes downward. "I'm sorry, Captain. General Soto is dead."

Olus felt the chill run from the base of his feet, up along his entire body. For a moment, he could barely breathe. He had to compose himself. He could mourn later. Cry later.

"Dead? How?"

"An accident, Captain. A simple, stupid accident. A malfunction in a passing taxi caused it to veer out of control. It struck the shuttle she was riding in, damaging its stabilizers. Both vehicles crashed. There were no survivors."

He paused, waiting for Olus to speak. When he didn't, he continued.

"I've been put in charge of General Soto's responsibilities while a new General is sworn-in to the Committee. I haven't had much time to review her notes to this point, but I understand you've been assigned to investigate the theft of the *Fire* and the *Brimstone* from Eagan Heavyworks on Feru?"

"That's right, sir," Olus replied, his voice a whisper. Did Omsala know anything about Hell? Would he say so if he did?

"What is your status on that front?"

"I have a few leads, General."

"Such as?"

"I'm not at liberty to discuss them at the moment, sir."

"Did that sound like a request, Captain? I know the OSI is accustomed to operating independently from the Committee, but you still ultimately answer to it. I want a complete, detailed debriefing on your work and whereabouts since the *Fire* and *Brimstone* were taken. I expect it transferred to me by zero eight hundred Earth Standard tomorrow."

Olus stared at the General for a moment. He had told Lieutenant Cage he was good at reading people, and he was. He didn't like what he saw from Omsala, and he was beyond certain General Soto's death was no accident. He could feel the pain of it deeper down, waiting for the right moment to expose itself. Maybe he and Iti hadn't done that well as husband and wife, but he had always maintained his respect and admiration for her, and she for him.

"Yes, sir," he said.

Omsala cut the link without another word.

"Commander Usiari," Olus said.

"Aye, Captain?" the *Driver's* commander replied.

"Take me back to Feru." Would he?

"Aye, sir," Usiari said.

Olus closed the channel. Maybe Usiari would take him, but would he send a message out to Director Eagan to let her know he was coming?

Olus changed the view in the projection, digging into the Driver's onboard systems and tagging the communications subnet. If anyone sent anything externally, he wanted to know about it.

Omsala wanted a report delivered in sixteen hours. It was a report Olus had no intention of providing. He had to get to the root of this in a hurry and pass whatever he could glean on to Lieutenant Cage.

He could only hope she would stay on the mission whether or not he made it back off of Feru.

CHAPTER FORTY-SIX

"GLORITANT," TRIN SAID. "I'VE REACHED Mamma Oissi's. The Rudin is dead."

Gloritant Salvig Thraven observed his assassin kneeling ahead of the bloody mound of flesh that had once been Mamma Oissi. He considered the further reaching implications of the informant's death for a few seconds before speaking.

"And the Breaker?" he asked.

"Honorant Defay reports that a fugitive matching Lieutenant Cage's description was seen boarding a shuttle which evaded four of our Shrikes and boarded a larger, unmarked starship." She paused, hesitant to deliver the bad news. As if he would ever harm his finest Evolent. "The starship escaped."

"On the back of the skills of the escaped criminal Bastion Merrett, no doubt," Thraven said. "I knew Captain Mann was resourceful. This approach was unexpected, and is working well for him."

"So far," Trin said. "Most of the fugitives were in Hell for a reason. They also weren't selected for Conversion for a reason."

"Chaos can be a powerful weapon," Thraven replied. "Almost as powerful as subtlety."

"Was it a mistake to bring Captain Mann into this?" Trin asked.

Thraven stared at her for a long moment, until she shrank back slightly. "Mistake? No. Mann is a wild card in this endeavor. A man of power and morality, despite his shadowed past. That is precisely the type of adversary to keep on a short leash. The mistake was in trusting the word of the fools who promised they could get into Kett's mainframe. Lieutenant Cage should never have been implicated with the Fifth Platoon. She might have cracked the wipe by now and unwittingly given us what we are after." He could feel the muscles in his jaw clenching, and he got to his feet, his hands curling into fists. "Instead, we're chasing her around the universe."

"If she learns to control the Gift-"

Thraven lifted his hand, and Trin crumpled to the ground. "She only has half. Even if she learns to control it, she can never be as powerful as I have made you."

"Yes, Gloritant," Trin said.

He lowered his hand, letting her up. He didn't want to harm her, but sometimes she needed to be put back in her place.

"Is Mamma Oissi's gray matter still in one piece?"

"Yes, Gloritant," Trin replied.

"Good. I want to know what she said to Lieutenant Cage. Can you extract it?"

Trin smiled. "Of course."

She reached out to Mamma Oissi, her fingers elongating slightly as she reached for the dead Rudin's eye. She dug into the edge of it, her hand vanishing behind it before clawing it away. There was a large cavity through the soft skeletal structure in back of the eye socket; a direct path to the brain. Trin reached into a tightpack on her back, removing a single glove from it. Thousands of small, sharp protrusions lined it, and when she put it on, they began to glow softly.

She reached in with the gloved hand. Thraven couldn't see it once it vanished into Mamma, but he knew the procedure well. The glove was a conduit between the Gift and the flesh; a means to manipulate more than physically.

Trin closed her eyes when her hand touched the brain. She started speaking a moment later.

"There you are," she said. "They tried to kill her. Oh. She's fast. Very fast."

"The Gift," Thraven said.

"She used it. I don't know if she knows she did. Impressive. I can see why you want her."

"Where?"

Trin was silent for a few seconds. "Yalom?" she said.

Thraven recognized the name. He never forgot a name. "The Skink? Your husband's mechanic?"

"Former mechanic," Trin replied. "He left shortly after I introduced Ursan to you. He was afraid of you."

"We have been looking for him. He has reason to be afraid of me."

"It appears he sold what he knew about the operation to Mamma Oissi to pay for his escape."

"To where?"

"Drune. Cage is headed to Drune."

Thraven almost let himself smile. "Go."

Trin removed her hand, pulling off the glove and putting it back in the tightpack. "It will be done."

"Make every effort to meet her there. Show her the potential of what we have given her. Show her how she can become more than what she ever imagined. Show her the glory of the new Covenant."

"And if she refuses the glory?"

"None refuse the Gift in the end."

"And if she does?" Trin pushed.

"Kill her."

"As you command, Gloritant. I'll require additional resources, to take care of the other fugitives while I deal with Cage."

"Inform Honorant Defay that he is now under your command, on my order. His ship and support units are yours."

"Thank you, Gloritant."

Thraven closed the link, the projection vanishing. He lifted his head, turning it and looking out of the large transparency to his left. The massive open fields of Kell stretched beyond it, littered with thousands of pieces of heavy equipment being operated by many more thousands of his followers. A sea of starships, many near completion, rested among the machinery, waiting only for the final integration of the technologies proven by the ship docked at the head of the line.

The *Fire*. One of the keys to the glory of the Covenant. The beginning of the Great Return. How long had he waited to herald the next coming? How long had they been cast aside?

Too long.

Much too long.

He turned away from the view, heading to the rear of the chamber and passing through. A pair of guards stood stiffly on either side of the door, their dark armor making them nearly disappear against the equally dark alloy of the wall. They didn't as much as twitch as he passed them by, falling into lockstep behind him while he crossed the corridor to his private room. He entered without slowing, the hatch rising at his command. The guards turned on their heels, regaining the same waiting position with unmatched precision.

Thraven continued to the back of the room, where a dark pool of liquid rested, still but unreflective in the dim light. He shed his cape, his uniform, his boots, and the skin-tight layer of enriched cloth beneath until he was standing nude in front of the pool. His skin was mottled and scarred, beaten and battered. They were old wounds. Ancient wounds. He barely remembered them anymore.

He stepped into the pool. The thick liquid barely moved aside as he entered it. He could feel the charge in it. The energy. It soothed him. It eased the feeling of motion along his skin, as though something else was living just beneath it. He continued until he was submerged to his head.

As he had said to his assassin, none had ever refused the Gift once they had learned the true potential of it. Once they knew the truth about the past. Lieutenant Cage had surprised him twice already, something that was very, very difficult to do. Her command of the Gift seemed to be accelerated beyond any who had been fortunate enough to receive it, and without training.

"Let us see if you'll accept the glory of the Covenant," he said to himself. "Let us see if Trinity can defeat you if you refuse. If not?" He smiled now, his teeth growing into sharp points, more monster than man. "It has been too long since I had a protege. Much too long."

He lowered himself further, completely submerging himself in the liquid. He took a breath, letting it enter his mouth and soak into his lungs. He continued to breathe, feeling his energy returning, his body calming.

Whatever happened, he would be victorious in the end.

That promise had been made long ago.

CHAPTER FORTY-SEVEN

ABBEY WAS ALONE IN THE common area of the *Faust* when Bastion found her. A stack of wrappers for the simple rations Captain Mann had left them rested on the table in front of her, and she eagerly swallowed the last of her sixth bar. Or was it her seventh?

She didn't know. What she did know was that she had never eaten like this in her life, and she was still feeling hungry.

"How do you stay so thin eating like that?" Bastion said.

"Frag off, Lucifer," she replied.

He put up his hands. "Whoa. Sorry, Queenie. I'm not trying to offend. In fact, I was looking for you so that I could apologize."

"For what?"

"For not following your orders. For the things I called you after it was over. My adrenaline got the best of me. Can I sit?"

He put his hand on the back of the chair across from her.

"It's an open ship."

"I wanted to apologize for Hell, too," he said, sitting down. "For pushing you away from the food dispenser."

"Whatever. It worked out in the end."

"If you want to call it that. Anyway, I know you think I'm an asshole, and I can be, but I'm more of a part-time asshole. And if we're going to be stuck on this ship together, I'd rather we find some common ground."

She was going to give him another short, smart-ass response. She changed her mind. There was no reason to choke him with his olive branch.

"Okay," she said. "Apology accepted. Can you do me a favor and grab me another bar?"

He laughed. "Seriously?"

"Yes. I'm starving. I don't know why."

Bastion stood again, retrieving two of the food bars. He handed one to her and kept the other.

"How long have you been a pilot?" Abbey asked. "Before Hell, I mean."

"Eight years. Thirty-six live fire combat drops on twenty-two worlds."

"Impressive."

He shrugged. "It's all instinct. Some people have more of it than others. Anyway, that came to a crashing halt when I decided it would be a good idea to assault Captain Mann."

Abbey nearly spit her mouthful of food bar across the table.

"You did what?" she said.

"Yeah. He wanted to send my platoon into a hot zone. By hot, I mean hotter than Hell. I mean hotter than you." He paused, waiting to see how she reacted to his statement.

"Save the strafing; you have to do a lot more than apologize and make lame passes if you want to interest me."

"Like what?"

"Like finish the mission and help me get home to my daughter."

"And then I would have a shot?"

"I don't know. Would you still want one? I'm one of two right now, three if you count Ruby, which you can't. When I'm one in a million? I'm high cost. High maintenance. And I have baggage."

He laughed. "You're human, too, it seems. I was starting to have my doubts." He pointed at the torn bits of her softsuit. "That doesn't help."

"I didn't ask for this. Packard was doing some kind of experiments down there. They put something in me, and this is the result."

"I don't know if I want to know. Anyway, Mann was sending me on what I thought was a suicide run. I didn't want my friends killed, you know. I thought I could convince him it was a bad idea. When he wouldn't listen, I got pissed, and I decked him. He didn't fight back. He just let me beat him almost to death."

"Captain Mann?" Abbey said, not believing it. Mann told her he was a trained killer. She didn't believe he wouldn't have destroyed Bastion if he had wanted to.

"Yeah. When he came to see me in prison, I was ready to do it all over again. He's the reason I was in Hell."

"You're the reason you were in Hell."

He shrugged. "Yeah. It was stupid, but I couldn't sleep. Couldn't eat. All I could think about were my teammates dying." He paused again. "You know what the shittiest part is? They died anyway because I wasn't there to fly them out. They died because I tried to save them."

Abbey kept her eyes on Bastion's face. The memory was upsetting to him, even now. Maybe he wasn't as much of an asshole as she had thought.

"I'm sorry for that," she said.

He smiled. "I guess we're learning a little bit about one another, huh, Queenie? Maybe you won't be so quick to choke me in the future?"

"Maybe you won't be as much of a childish asshole, and I won't have to."

The ladder in the center of the room started to vibrate, cluing them in that someone was coming. Gant's head poked up through the hole in the floor a moment later, his eyes narrowing when he saw Bastion.

"You," he said, his hissing chitter loud enough to hurt her ears. "You stupid fragging son of a bitch." He finished climbing, approaching Bastion with his teeth bared. "Look at my arm, you shithead." He held up his arm. The fur was gone along the entire forearm down to his hand. "I told you to fragging wait a second."

"Gant," Abbey said. "Did you go to the medical bot?"

"Frag that. It isn't that bad. That's not that point. I told you to wait. You almost got me killed."

"I saved everybody's life," Bastion said. "If we stayed on the ground, we were as good as dead."

"I only needed a few seconds. I came this close to slamming into the containment unit." He held his two thumbs only a few centimeters apart. "Do you know what would have happened?"

"No."

"*Imp*. Boom!"

Bastion opened his mouth but didn't speak.

"And, you called me a freak-monkey again. I told you I was going to break your face." He jumped onto the table, getting to eye level with the pilot. "You want to let me, or you want to try to defend yourself?"

"Gant," Abbey said.

"Stay out of it, Queenie," Gant replied. "This asshole almost killed you."

"Stay out of it?" Abbey hissed. "Who the hell do you think you're talking to?"

Gant froze in place. He turned his head, all of the anger suddenly draining from him.

"Sorry, Queenie," he said. His lower lip was practically quivering. It was adorable. "I do want to break his face, though."

"Nobody is breaking anybody's face," Abbey said. "I know you two don't like one another. You both need to learn to deal with it. I don't have the time or the energy for your bullshit."

"I'm sorry, Gant," Bastion said. "We had to leave when we did, or we were going to die. It was nothing personal. I appreciate that you fixed the *Imp* in mid-flight. That was pretty damn badass."

Gant looked back at Bastion. "It was, wasn't it? So was your flying. You got us out of there."

"And we're still here, now," Abbey said. "Can we drop it?"

"Fine," Gant said, holding a hand out to Bastion. Bastion took it.

"Fine," he said.

"So, Queenie," Gant said, turning around again. "I've spent the last few hours going through some of our equipment. I tripled the beam density of the laser pistol I picked up. I also increased the *Imp's* maximum thrust twenty to thirty percent."

"You've been busy," Bastion said.

"I made you something, too."

"You made me something?" Abbey said.

"I'm not coming onto you or anything," Gant replied, jumping off the table. "Hold up one minute." He went over to the ladder. "Pik, bring it up."

"Coming," Pik replied.

"Pik helped you?" Bastion said. "Fragging traitor."

"I like Abbey," Pik said, his head appearing in the opening.

"Thanks, Pik," Abbey said.

"You're welcome."

He continued coming, his large frame barely clearing the opening. He was carrying what looked like a hellsuit in his right hand. It was way too small to be his.

"I took the liberty of pulling the synthetic musculature lining out of one of the softsuits and reattaching it inside your hellsuit," Gant said. "I also added some tightpacks for storage and integrated the tactile touchpad. I'm working on an upgraded HUD that won't require a full TCU and helmet, but it's going to take me a few more hours. You can also wear it full-time since it has the waste filtration built-in. I've scrounged enough parts to build a makeshift washer that won't short it out."

Pik held the suit out to her. She smiled as she ran her hand along it.

"It's okay with me if you want to change right here," Bastion said.

"Remember what I said earlier?" Abbey said.

"Yeah."

"That's strike one." She looked at Gant and Pik. "I'll put this on after I get cleaned up. Thank you both."

"Anytime, Boss," Pik said.

Abbey took the suit. "I'm going to excuse myself and go shower and try this on. Pik, keep these two away from each other's throats, will you?"

Pik smiled. "Of course, Boss."

Abbey climbed the ladder from the central common area to the living area. She went into the cleansing station, quickly stripping the damaged softsuit and her underwear, looking at her naked reflection. She ran her hands over her stomach. There was no sign that she had ever been shot, save for a small bit of dried blood. She could feel the movement beneath her skin, tickling her and making her uncomfortable. She stared at the flesh to see if she could catch something actually shifting below the surface. Failing that, she let the shower cleanse the blood away, emerging fresh, her energy level returning. She pulled on the hellsuit, grateful to have the pressure against her skin once more, reducing the overwhelming feeling that she was infested with parasites, if not something worse.

She headed to her quarters to lie down. Airi wasn't there. She had no idea where the soldier had gone. She laid flat, staring at the ceiling for a minute before closing her eyes. She gave herself twenty minutes before getting up again. She wasn't tired. In fact, she felt more awake than ever.

She made her way down to the lower deck. Bastion, Gant, and Pik had cleared the common area by then, likely going their separate ways. She expected to find Gant in a dark corner, trying to calm his nerves. She didn't. Somehow, they had managed to disperse out of her path. It hardly seemed possible on a ship the size of the Faust.

She went to the construct to sit in the darkness. She considered contacting her sister but came to the same conclusions she had with Hayley. If Liv believed she was dead, it was better that way, at least until she could go back home.

Would she ever be able to go home? Would she ever see Hayley again? For as much as she wanted to believe she would, the events on Orunel had made it feel as though she were back in Hell, rotting away. The Republic was in trouble. It seemed as though the Outworlds were, too, but she had no proof of that yet. Thraven's Shrikes had attacked the Republic frigates and left the Outworld starships alone. Maybe he was operating independently of the Outworld Governance, but she doubted they would be complaining.

Either way, even if they did somehow manage to recover the *Fire* and the *Brimstone*, she had a feeling that would only be the beginning, a singular, early victory in conflict that had yet to truly arrive.

A conflict she didn't want Hayley to grow up into.

Even if she did earn her freedom, would she take it?

CHAPTER FORTY-EIGHT

BASTION WAS AT THE CONTROLS of the *Faust* when the ship came out of FTL, blinking back into regular space a thousand AU away from Drune's orbit.

"Any sign of trouble?" Abbey asked from her position behind him.

"Negative," Ruby replied. "Only four ships in orbit. All Outworld make. Untagged."

She shifted her attention to the planet itself, grateful that they hadn't stepped directly into a trap. Then again, that didn't mean they weren't coming in at one from the side.

"Is there a colony down there?" she said, noting the mottled brown of the planet.

"I told you Drune was a shithole," Benhil said, listening in through his communicator. "No surface water. Hardly any rain. The H2O they do have gets pulled from the atmosphere, and even that's barely enough to keep anyone alive down there. Skinks do okay because they hardly use water anyway."

"Why would anyone come here?" Abbey said.

"Exactly the reason why I think Mamma Oissi was full of shit," Benhil replied. "If there was someone who knew anything about this guy, Thraven, I don't think he'd be here."

"Why not?" Airi asked. "It's easier to hide your scent in a pile of dung."

"And more disgusting," Gant said. "Nice simile though, Fury."

She laughed in reply.

"Here's how we do this," Abbey said as Bastion began angling the starship toward the planet. "After we land, Jester and I will head over to the colony and take a look around. We'll be posing as..."

"Arms dealers," Benhil said.

"...Arms dealers," she finished, feeling a little angry at the idea of posing as the very thing she had been sent to Hell for. "Gant, you'll trail behind us. Keep your distance, but stay close enough to warn us if you spot anything out of the ordinary, or back us up if we get in trouble."

"Yes, Queenie," Gant said.

"Fury, you and Okay will hang back with the *Faust*. If Yalom tries to run, your job is to stop him. If we get into really deep shit, you're the reinforcements."

"You bet, Queenie," Pik said.

"Lucifer, you're on the hot seat. God help us if we need air support or a quick extraction, but you know what to do."

"You're sure you don't want to take the *Imp* in and leave the *Faust* up here?" Bastion asked.

"Yes. If Thraven's forces turn up again, I want to make a quick getaway, not have to waste time regrouping."

"Roger," Bastion replied.

They fell silent as the *Faust* broke through the atmosphere. The small settlement didn't become visible until they were two kilometers from the surface, its position shrouded by a thick layer of dust that seemed to be a permanent fixture in the air. A single long transmission spike rose from within, climbing high above it.

"The dust is fragging up our sensors," Bastion said. "I don't like this, Queenie. If anything pops up in orbit, we won't be able to see it to react."

"They also won't be able to see us on the ground," Ruby said.

"We should go back, take the *Imp*."

"It wouldn't help," Ruby said. "Communications will be difficult. If I sent you a warning, you might not receive it."

"You're kidding? We can talk across thousands of light years, but not through a little bit of dirt?"

"Different systems," Gant said. "What works across the galaxy doesn't work as well nearby. It would be like trying to stop a starship on a plate."

"Damned if we do, damned if we don't," Benhil said. "You're the Queen of the Damned, Queenie, so it should work out in our favor."

"Let's hope so," Abbey replied, not bothering to take offense at the latest moniker.

The *Faust* shuddered as it entered the dirty air, chaotic currents challenging the stabilizers. Bastion got them through the mess, coming into slightly cleaner atmosphere a thousand meters from the ground. The colony was a few kilometers to the south, beyond a flat field of smaller rocks and sand where two other starships were already resting.

The *Faust* took roost nearby, the landing smooth and easy.

Abbey tapped Bastion on the shoulder. "Thanks for the ride," she said. He responded with a thumbs up, and then she turned and fled toward the lower level where the exit hatch was located. The others were already waiting for her, and Pik held out a long hooded trenchcoat, a scarf, and a pair of goggles when she reached them.

"Take this, too," Gant said, holding up a smaller monocle. "The goggles will hold it in for now."

"The HUD?" she asked.

"Yup. It'll give you limited infrared, and it's linked to your softsuit and the extenders if you need to hack anything."

"You're the best," Abbey said, accepting it and putting it over her left eye. It added a slight grain to her vision, but it also outlined her team, showing their body heat.

"I know," Gant replied. She could swear he was blushing.

She put on the goggles, scarf, and coat, raising the hood. She was covered from head to toe. So were the others.

"What's that?" she asked, pointing to the rifle Benhil was carrying.

"I don't recognize it."

"I modified a standard A70," Gant said. "Gave it a little more oomph and changed the profile to help you sell the cover story. Most of the extra hardware is useless garbage, but it looks aggressive."

"In case we need to demo our wares," Benhil said.

"Are we ready?" Abbey asked, moving to the open hatch. A ramp extended from it, three meters to the ground.

"I'm ready, Boss," Pik said.

"I'm ready," Benhil said, joining her at the hatch.

"I'm ready, Queenie," Gant said, tapping his laser pistol.

"Lucifer, stay alert. Fury, Okay, keep your ears open and be ready to move on my order."

"Yes, Queenie," they replied.

"Let's do this, Rejects."

CHAPTER FORTY-NINE

ABBEY MOVED DOWN THE RAMP with Benhil beside her. They started crossing the open space, heading for the colony. It was barely visible from their position, a series of smaller round buildings and a few taller rectangles hidden in the dust. She was grateful for the scarf and goggles as the dirt pelted them, seemingly from everywhere.

It was half a kilometer to the outskirts of the colony, marked by a few ramshackle stalls where tired-looking Terrans sat on the ground, selling ugly jewelry and what looked like old military rations. They stared at Abbey and Benhil as they passed, leaving her wondering what else they might be looking to sell.

Things started to get a little more active as they moved closer to the center of the outposts. The lean-to stalls turned into rounded huts dug halfway into the surface, with signs hanging outside to inform the visitor what they had to barter. Food, clothing, drugs. Not weapons. There probably wasn't much need for them out here. It made her wonder if their cover was the best choice.

Benhil had said Drune was a shithole, and he was right. He said there was nothing here, and he was right about that, too. The place looked like it was on permanent life-support. There was little worth trading here. Little worth coming to buy. The individuals who lived here had to be either stupid or on the run from something. With all of her experience, she couldn't guess how there could be another option.

And how was it that there was a building here that was nearly one hundred meters tall, rising from the ground and ending almost beyond the lousy visibility? It was the source of the spike they had seen from above. The transmission tower. It sat in the center of the colony, a beacon to everyone who lived and visited here. It was as dirty and worn as the others, but it was also brightly lit on the inside, and there was a flow of traffic in and out of it.

"I wish we knew what Yalom looks like," Benhil said. "Take your pick of Skinks."

It appeared that Drune was a popular destination for the lizard-like humanoids. Out of thirty individuals who went in and out of the central building, nearly half were Skinks. Thin, lean, covered in scales, with rounded, nearly featureless heads and faces and clawed hands and feet. They looked a little less downtrodden than the others. As though they enjoyed the dust.

"I don't know if this is better or worse than Hell," Abbey said.

"Yeah, Hell's just hot. This is depressing."

"Well, you're the expert on the Outworlds. Where's the most likely place to find Yalom without looking ridiculously suspicious?"

"I'm not sure that's even possible after seeing the colonists. Every settlement, no matter how big or small it is, has a place where everyone goes to relax and be social. We're all social animals, you know? Every intelligent species out there."

"On a planet like this, the individuals go where the water is," Abbey said.

"You're as sharp as you look, Queenie." He turned in a slow circle before pointing. "Follow the vapor condensers."

They did, tagging along behind a pair of Skinks who were also headed to the condensers. Abbey wished she had a full TCU and helmet; it would have let her eavesdrop on their conversation more easily. Instead, she settled for catching words and short phrases and staying extra alert for their target's name. Neither of the Skinks had mentioned it by the time they reached the dispensary.

There was a guard at the door, a large-bellied Terran holding a rifle that put Gant's creation to shame. He let the Skinks in without question but barred them from entering unchallenged.

"You come in on that bigger ship, looks sort of like a bird?" he asked.

"You know what a bird looks like?" Benhil replied. "I didn't think there were any here."

"There ain't," the guard said. "I've been to the Fringe. I've seen birds."

"We're from that ship, yes," Abbey said. "We're looking to do some trading."

"What have you got?"

Benhil held out the rifle. "An example," he said.

The guard smiled. "We don't get too many dealers out here. Market's pretty small, but supply and demand means you can get a pretty good price. You make a deal inside; house gets ten percent."

"For what?" Benhil said.

"For arranging a place to meet. Otherwise, you'd be chasing a sale every which way. Ten percent."

"It isn't a problem," Abbey said, smacking Benhil on the shoulder before he could argue again.

The guard laughed. "Your wife is feisty. By the way, you saw the other two ships when you came in?"

"Yes," Abbey said.

"One of them belongs to a Fizzig named Plusom. He might be in the market."

"Thanks for the tip."

"Why not? Helping you helps me."

He stepped aside, allowing them in. The dispensary was four steps down and through a narrow archway that opened up to a larger space inside. It was simply organized. Tables along the walls, pillows, and rugs in the center. Clear pipes carried water along the ceiling and down to each of the sitting areas, and more standard drinks were being served from behind what looked like the remains of a crossbar from a Republic battleship.

The mood was quiet. Private. A number of eyes turned their way as they entered, but nobody stopped what they were doing. They were used to travelers here. Used to guns. Used to individuals who looked a little different.

"That must be Plusom," Benhil said, tapping her shoulder and motioning to a Fizzig in the corner. He had a small entourage with him, two more of his kind and a Terran synthetic that bore a strong resemblance to Ruby. "I never could get into other species."

"Why do you think he has a synth?" she replied quietly. Xenophilia was considered an alternate orientation, one that mainstream society frowned on.

"Should we go talk to him?"

"No. I want to find Yalom and get the hell out of here. Something about this place is making my skin crawl." She didn't mean it figuratively either. Her skin felt like it was moving, the way it had at Mamma Oissi's.

"There's a Skink at nine o'clock who's staring at you like you're a piece of meat. That could be why."

She glanced over at the target. He was staring; his small, dark eyes focused on her. She turned and took a step toward him.

The skin at her back began to burn. She spun around just in time to see Benhil crumple to the ground.

Her eyes landed on a tall woman with blue hair, wearing a black softsuit. Her hand was out, palm up. Her eyes were sparkling gray.

Abbey reached for her gun, getting it halfway out before something tore it away from her, pulling it to the woman. She caught it smoothly and smiled.

"Lieutenant Cage," the woman said. "I've been waiting for you. Mamma told me you would be coming."

CHAPTER FIFTY

"Mamma Oissi is dead," Abbey said. She glanced beyond the woman to where the guard was standing, watching the exchange. He had sold them out. The other bystanders were remaining in their places, not eager to get in the middle of whatever this was going to be. "Is Jester?"

"Benhil Visani," the woman replied, tapping Benhil's body with her toe. "It's Jester now? No. He's sleeping. I'm aware the Rudin is dead. I saw her body, ten minutes after you fled Orunel. It was a daring escape. Impressive. I'm sorry it turned out to be such a waste."

"You're with Thraven?" Abbey asked, not surprised.

"My name is Trinity. Yes. I'm one of his."

"How did you get here ahead of me?"

"I told you. Mamma Oissi gave me directions, after her demise. It's part of the Gift, Abigail. May I call you Abigail?"

"Or Abbey. Why not?"

"It's part of the Gift, Abbey. The Blood of Life."

"I've never heard of it."

"I'm willing to bet there are a lot of things you've never heard of. The universe is too large for anyone to know everything. The point is, there is more to this existence than you know, Abbey. The true limits of possibility are still stretched beyond what our minds can handle. There is power beyond anything we've ever considered."

"Like reading a dead Rudin's mind?"

"A simple way to describe it, but yes. That's one of the abilities that comes with the Gift."

"If this Gift is so great, why did Thraven need to steal the *Fire* and the *Brimstone*? Why didn't he just wave his magic wand and have them poof right onto his doorstep? For that matter, why does he need a Breaker to help figure out where Sylvan Kett is hiding?"

Trin practically rolled her eyes. "It's a Gift, Abbey. Not magic. There are boundaries. It's science. Not fantasy."

Bitch.

"It seems pretty fantastic to me," Abbey said, holding her temper.

"Isn't anything we don't yet understand?"

"Okay. So if this Gift is science, why isn't Thraven's tech better? Why isn't the Outworlds'? Again, why does he need the ships? For what purpose? To what end?"

"Forget the ships," Trin said. "The ships are inconsequential."

"Not to me."

"They will be. You have the first part of the Gift, Abbey. It was given to you back on Hell. I understand that you thought it was an attack, but it wasn't. It was intended to be an honor. A glorious honor."

"I was naked and pinned down, and got stabbed with a fragging needle," Abbey said. "I still don't feel very honored about that. All I feel is like I have a million worms crawling under my skin."

"A side effect that we all learn to live with, to accept gratefully for the power that is unlocked. You have had a taste, but you can't understand the fullness that comes after receiving the second part. You can't begin to imagine the way the universe changes, the way your interaction with reality and existence changes. That's why Gloritant Thraven was trying so desperately to find you. That's why he sent me. To open your eyes to the glory of the Gift."

"Not so I could break Kett's mainframe for him?"

"At first, yes. Now? It would be little more than a fringe benefit. You're stronger than most who receive the Gift, Abbey. You have potential you don't realize. Thraven can help you understand what you're capable of."

"If your Gloritant has designs on the Republic, I'm not interested."

Trin's body language spoke of her frustration. She sighed as though she were talking to a child. "That's not a productive way to look at it. This isn't about governments and militaries. It's not about who controls what. It's about a promise made, and a promise kept."

Abbey smiled. "Funny, it's about that for me, too. I promised my daughter I would be home at the end of my tour. Do you know what happened instead? I got busted for trafficking guns to Sylvan Kett, I think. I'm not even completely sure who was doing what. I had no idea what the Fifth was involved in, and that asshole Mr. Davis had nothing on me. It didn't keep me out of Hell. I was there because Thraven wanted me there. He wants me to be honored for that? He wants me to what? Join him? No. I'm trying to keep a promise, too. One that's more important than being bulletproof, or waving my hand and making things fly around, or putting individuals to sleep or whatever the hell you did to Jester. So save your bullshit and frag off."

Abbey stared at Trin, pleased with herself for knocking the woman off her smug pedestal. Why had Thraven sent this woman to her, anyway? All blue hair was managing to do was piss her off. She could tell she had struck a nerve with Trin in return.

"Is it safe for me to assume that this Gift isn't free?" Abbey asked. "What did you have to agree to in exchange for your enlightenment? What part of your soul did you sell? Are you a follower or a slave?"

Trin froze for a moment, her eyes dropping toward the floor.

"What would you agree to do to save the ones you love?" Trin said. "What lengths would you go to? My husband, Ursan, lost his family to the Republic. He still has nightmares about what he saw and heard. Thraven promised him revenge. I don't want anything as complicated. I want peace, Abbey, believe it or not. Thraven promised me peace."

"While he sows the seeds of war?"

"Peace has a price. I'm willing to pay it."

"You say peace. Are you sure you don't mean power?"

Abbey noticed Trin's hand clench into a fist. Had she scored another hit?

"You can be a herald of the Great Return, Abbey," Trin said, speaking through her teeth, her anger bleeding into her words. "Or you can be nothing more than an escaped convict, a fugitive, a failure. You can die here on Drune, a shitty little rock in the middle of the universe, with no one, not even your daughter, to think of you as anything other than a waste. The choice is yours."

Abbey felt her anger flare, her body beginning to burn anew. Her skin writhed and shifted, the power she had been given becoming alert. Trinity sensed it, too, taking a step back and raising her hand as though to defend herself.

"Don't do this," Trin said. "Gloritant Thraven doesn't want you dead, but he will accept it if it's necessary."

Abbey laughed. A real, solid laugh. "So that's it? Sign up or die? I seem to be getting that shitty offer a lot lately. Sorry, I already signed the same fragging contract with the Republic. The devil you know, right?"

She wasn't sure how Trin's attack was going to come. She wasn't sure how she would possibly defend against it. Her body was on fire, her skin burning with an energy she had never felt before. Would the Gift defend her? Could she count on that?

She didn't have a chance to find out. Trin's hand started to rise, pausing halfway as the side of her head began to smoke.

The laser passed right through it, hitting the wall on the other side of the dispensary and spearing through that as well.

Trin's body collapsed on the floor beside Benhil.

"Shit," Gant said. "I think I pushed the power output a little too high."

CHAPTER FIFTY-ONE

"WE'RE NEARING THE PLANET, BOSS," Dak said.

Ursan was staring out of the *Brimstone's* viewport. He could see Kell ahead of them, a green and blue world that reminded him of home.

Except home was gone. A Republic military base was all that remained of it.

"Any contact from Thraven?" Ursan asked.

"No. If he knows we're here, he isn't saying."

Ursan smiled. He had brought the *Brimstone* out of FTL a few thousand AU beyond the planet, well past the reach of the orbital sensors that would detect any incoming starships. He had then activated the ship's cloaking mechanism, curious to explore the capabilities of the updated technology. He was surprised to find the power draw was minimal, and that efforts to locate him through standard anti-cloaking scans run by his own starship, the *Triune*, had failed.

That result had made him bold. Now he wanted to know if General Thraven, for all of his power, would be able to see him coming. He wasn't planning to betray the one who had promised him the downfall of the Republic, but the General acted as though he was the next closest thing to a God, and Ursan wanted to know if that act was on the mark. Maybe if he could prove the man was fallible, he wouldn't be so damn scared of him.

"Stay on course," Ursan said. "Take it slow. We'll slip past the outer defensive patrol, and if we still don't get called out, we'll move back and make a more standard entry."

"Okay," Dak said.

The *Brimstone* eased ahead, her velocity consistent as she drew nearer to the planet.

"What if Thraven is testing us testing him?" Dak asked, glancing back at him. He looked nervous.

"I'll tell him I was testing the cloaking system to see how effective it is," Ursan replied. "Maybe he'll appreciate that I took the initiative."

The outer defensive patrol was a group of fifty Shrikes, clustered together and sitting nearly dead in orbit around Kell. They were hard to see and small enough that without a larger power signature they were identified by sensors as ordinary space garbage instead of capable attack craft. Once a target moved within range, they would come alive and pound it with everything they had, which was more than enough to take down any Republic ship within a matter of seconds.

But probably not enough to take down the *Brimstone*.

"Make sure we don't run into any," Ursan said, watching them approach.

"I'm tracking them," Dak replied.

The *Brimstone* skirted the line, angling around the cluster. Ursan held his breath, watching the Shrikes intensely, waiting for them to react to their presence or for Thraven or some other officer from Command to put him to question.

It didn't happen. The *Brimstone* reached the other side of the first line of defense still undetected.

"I don't want to turn her in," Dak said, laughing at the results.

"She's amazing," Ursan replied. "But I prefer the comfort of the *Triune*. Let Thraven have his unstoppable killing machine." He paused, enjoying the invisibility of the *Brimstone* for a few more seconds. "Get us turned around and back out. We'll regroup with the *Triune* and come back in the clear."

"Okay, Boss," Dak replied.

"With any luck, whatever job Thraven sent Trin on will be finished soon, and she'll be -"

He froze as he felt a sudden chill throughout his body, causing him to shiver. He closed his eyes, a split-second vision crossing behind the lids.

Trinity was lying on the ground.

Dead.

"Contact General Thraven," Ursan said.

Dak turned around. "What? Boss-"

"I said open a fragging channel," he shouted in reply.

Dak did as he asked.

"Captain Gall," Thraven said a moment later, a projection of only his head appearing at the front of the bridge. "You felt it?" He sounded surprised.

"Where is she, General?" Ursan said.

"Where are you, Captain Gall?" Thraven replied. "You're nearby."

"I was testing the cloaking systems. I'm in orbit. Tell me where Trin is. Now. She needs me."

Ursan could feel the panic washing through him. This wasn't supposed to happen. Trinity couldn't die. She was stronger than him. Smarter than him. He couldn't accept it.

"Your orders are to bring the *Brimstone* in, Captain," Thraven said, remaining calm. "I expect you to follow them."

"Frag your orders, General," Ursan replied, forgetting himself. "I saw it. I saw her die. Tell me where she is, or I'm going to plant every torpedo this ship has left up your fragging asshole."

Thraven's eyebrows lifted. Ursan drew back in fear, expecting his outburst would result in being choked to death, surprised when he wasn't.

"Very well," Thraven said. "But understand this, Captain. Insubordination will not be tolerated. Expect consequences."

"I'll worry about it later. Where is she?"

"Drune," Thraven said. "You can find her on Drune."

"Dak," Ursan said.

"Already doing it," Dak replied.

Ursan's hands clenched against the command seat. He leaned forward, muscles tense as if that could hurry along the calculations needed to move into FTL. He was too worried and too frightened to wonder about Thraven's motives for giving him the location and allowing him to go. He knew there would be a price to pay. There always was. He didn't care.

The *Brimstone's* cloak fell away, the Shrikes in the outer defenses lighting up as they finally registered the presence of the ship. They turned toward it, ready to challenge its proximity.

Then it was gone again, vanishing into FTL in a dispersion of energy and gas, leaving the Shrikes to sleep once more.

Ursan remained upright in his seat, staring at the universe as it became a milky cloud around them, carrying them at what had once been thought an impossible speed.

Trin was dead. He couldn't stop that.

Would he get there in time to avenge her?

He would give anything to make it so.

"By going against Thraven's orders, maybe I already have."

CHAPTER FIFTY-TWO

ABBEY KNELT BESIDE BENHIL, PUTTING her fingers to his neck. Trin hadn't been lying. He was still alive.

She glanced over at the woman. Thraven's lackey wasn't moving. Her eyes were open and glassy, and still silver. Illiard hadn't been dead when he should have been. Was she?

"Jester," Abbey said. "Jester, come on."

The crowd inside the dispensary was moving out, heading for the exit, trying to escape the mayhem. Gant was blocking their path, and he fired his pistol through the top of the building as they neared.

"I'm looking for Yalom," he said. "Anybody seen him?"

"He isn't here," the guard said. It was his fault Gant had been able to slip in unnoticed. He had abandoned his post to watch the action, and now he was trapped with the others.

"Are you sure?" Gant asked, pointing the pistol at him.

"Jester," Abbey said again.

Benhil's eyes opened slowly. "Queenie? What the hell?"

"You need to get up, now." She looked back at Trin. The woman was still dead. Maybe Illiard had been something else, some other experiment. His eyes had been a dull gray, not silver, and it had been the entire things, not just the pupils.

"What happened?"

"Later."

"Queenie," Bastion said over the comm. "I hope... hear me. Ship... landed in... coming..."

Abbey smacked her ear as if that would clear up the signal. She didn't need the whole message to get the idea.

"Let's move, Jester," she said, standing up, holding his arm and yanking him to his feet. He wobbled slightly before getting his balance.

"Damn. One of you was bad enough," he said.

"None of you have seen him?" Gant said. "You." He pointed to another Skink. "You don't know Yalom?"

"I know him," the Skink replied. "His hut is that way." He motioned toward the southern wall. "He's usually here this time of day, but he hasn't shown."

"Let's go find him," Abbey said, heading toward the exit with Benhil.

"You all can stay put," Gant said. "We're leaving."

He lowered his pistol at the same time the stone of the doorway around him began to explode under the force of incoming gunfire.

Gant reacted quickly, diving into the building before rolling to his feet and facing the door. The bullets stopped coming, but a hum began to fill the air.

"Dropship," Benhil said. "Frag."

"Lucifer," Abbey said. "I don't know if you can hear me. We need backup now. Do you copy? We need backup now."

There was no response from the other end. She could only hope the message had gone through.

"We're dead to rights sitting in here," Benhil said.

"If they're after us," Abbey replied.

"Everyone is after you."

She couldn't argue with that.

"I can take a few hits, I think," she said. "I'll go out first and try to lead them away."

"Queenie, no," Gant said. "That's suicide."

"You have another idea?"

"You aren't going anywhere," the guard said, taking the opportunity to train his rifle on them as they argued. "Whoever wants you, they might pay a nice price for the honor."

Abbey looked at him. Then she bounced off, using her softsuit to power her leap. The guard fired, his first three rounds hitting her in the shoulder, turning her slightly sideways. She managed to stay on target, landing right in front of him and punching as she did, using the force of her momentum to drive hard into his chest. His bones cracked as his body was sent tumbling back and to the ground.

"Damn it," Abbey said, looking over at her shoulder, and then looking at the others gathered in the dispensary. They shied away from her, suddenly afraid. "That fragging hurt."

She rotated her shoulder a few times. Either there was no damage to begin with, or it was already healed. She wasn't going to complain either way.

"Queenie," Airi said. "We're approaching your position. You're surrounded. Three squads. A dropship landed half a klick away, and it looks like it's unloading heavy ordnance."

"Heavy ordnance? What the frag for?" Abbey said.

"They appear to be ready to raze the whole colony," Airi replied.

"Can you draw them away? Give us some cover?"

"Affirmative. Get ready to evacuate on my mark."

"Roger."

"What about Yalom?" Gant asked.

Abbey looked back at Trin one last time. She hadn't moved at all. At least something was going right.

"We have to find him. He may be the only one who can point us to Thraven and the ships."

"Whoa," Benhil said. "I'm pretty sure I heard Fury say heavy ordnance. How are we supposed to get around that?"

"Any way we can," Abbey replied. "Lucifer, come in. Lucifer."

There was no response. Bastion had probably sent Airi and the others when they picked up the dropship, not when she had pinged him.

They weren't about to get air support, not unless he decided to take the initiative again.

Gunfire echoed outside the building, thick and heavy. Some of it smacked against the walls, sending chunks of stone and dust into the air and causing the other patrons to take cover.

"Mark?" Abbey said, wondering why Airi hadn't alerted her to the attack.

"That isn't us, Boss," Pik said. "It's coming from the other side."

"What's happening out there?"

"I'm not-"

Pik's voice was cut off as a massive explosion lit up the landscape, so powerful that the shockwave shook the ground.

"Okay?" Abbey said. "Fury?"

"We're here, Queenie," Airi said. "Something just hit the dropship. Something ugly. All that's left is a dark spot."

"Fury, we've got incoming," Okay said. "Boss, we have two squads closing on us. Those bastards in the black lightsuits. Oh. Shit. Shrikes."

The top of the dispensary cracked as heavier caliber slugs tore into it from above, threatening to peel it apart. She could hear people shout outside the building, the strafing run hitting the units on the ground.

"We can't stay here," Abbey said. "Out the door. Now."

Gant and Benhil didn't question, heading through the door and out into the dust. She was right behind them, using the IR in the monocle Gant had given her to pick up targets before she could fully spot them. She reached the top step, aiming and firing, hitting a large soldier in a black lightsuit in the back. He was facing off against another target fifty meters distant, crouched at the corner of another building. She could barely get visual on that one. A Terran in a heavy cloak and wearing a full-face breathing mask. He fired into the front of the same soldier, his bullets cutting all the way through.

The target in the lightsuit didn't fall. He kept firing back at the other soldier until his rounds found their mark, cutting him down.

A rumble filled the air around them, and when Abbey looked up her HUD was filled with the heat signature of large thrusters. Two more dropships were landing to replace the first. If there was any question Thraven's battleship was in orbit, it was confirmed by the sight.

"Lucifer," Abbey said again, desperate to reach her pilot. "Damn it. Rejects, we're bugging out. We'll find another way to locate the ships."

"This way," Gant said, pointing down the street. "It's clear."

"Right behind you," Abbey said. "Fury, Okay, where the hell are you?"

"Pinned down, Queenie," Airi said. "Caught in the middle of a fragging war zone north of you."

"Gant, Jester, we're moving north," Abbey said. "We're on our way. Hold tight."

"There's nothing you can do for us," Airi said. "We're stuck. We know the blacksuits aren't friendlies. The others? I have no fragging clue who they are or where they came from, but they don't seem to care if they cut us down."

"If they aren't helping, they aren't friendly," Abbey said. "And either we all get out, or none of us get out."

"If you're still a real soldier, maybe," Airi said. "We're convicts, Queenie. Murder, in my case. We aren't worth the blood or the sweat."

"Frag that," Abbey said. "If nobody else gives a shit about us, then we need to take care of each other. It's the only way any one of us stands a chance."

"I see them," Gant said. "Next block over, hunkered down in one of those stalls."

Abbey scanned the area ahead of them. Soldiers from both sides had taken positions across the avenue, trading fire at one another. A Shrike passed overhead, strafing the foreign line, sending up clouds of dirt and hitting two of the fighters.

"The enemy of my enemy is my friend, right?" Benhil said.

"Until they aren't," Gant replied. He fired his pistol. The dust reduced the impact of the laser, but it was still powerful enough to take down one of the blacksuits.

"Lucifer," Abbey said again. Again, there was no reply. "Get down."

She spotted a Shrike swooping in, strafing the area ahead. She could see the bullets hitting the ground, throwing up chunks of dirt, creating a path that was leading right into them.

Shit.

She prepared to bounce off and spring away. A whistle sounded nearby, and then the Shrike exploded, the fireball and its debris passing overhead.

She looked to the right. A twelve-meter mech moved out from behind a building, its rifle arms rotating, tracking another target. It fired, the whine of the gauss rifle sending a heavy slug into a second Shrike, knocking it down.

The mech was a Republic asset, and not the kind of thing that came up for sale on the black market. Did that mean these were Republic soldiers?

She scanned the battlefield again. The arrival of the war machine had stolen the enemy's attention, breaking up the line that had seemed so solid only seconds ago. Airi and Pik were on their feet, running toward them.

"I can't get through to Lucifer," Abbey said as they arrived. "We need to make a break for the shipyard."

"The shipyard is that way," Gant said, pointing to where one of the new dropships had landed.

"Of course it is," Abbey said.

"We need Lucifer to come to us. I don't know why he hasn't yet."

"Probably too dangerous," Pik said. "He won't leave us here to die. Ruby won't let him."

"What should we do?" Airi said.

"Get a message to him," Gant said. "The comm tower is that way." He pointed further north. "The fighting isn't as bad that way, and that spike has more than enough amps to get through this shit."

"Good idea," Abbey said. "Let's go."

"Lieutenant Cage," a voice shouted at her back.

She turned slowly, feeling a spike of fear for the first time since the fighting had started. She should have known.

"We weren't done yet," Trin said.

CHAPTER FIFTY-THREE

"I KILLED YOU," GANT SAID. "I'm sure of it."

Trin was standing in the center of the street, flanked by a pair of blacksuits on either side. Billows of smoke mixed with the dust behind her and a pair of Shrikes rocketed overhead, passing by without attacking.

"The Gift, Abbey," Trin said. "It's power is limitless in the right hands. Life. Death. They become one and the same. The impossible made possible."

"Impossible this," Pik said, firing his rifle. The reports echoed across a suddenly dead silence, bullets whistling through the air.

Trin didn't move. Her fingers shifted slightly, and the slugs slammed to a stop in front of her as if they had struck an invisible wall. They hung there for an instant and then tumbled to the ground.

"Force field?" Gant said.

"I don't think so," Airi replied.

"Shit."

"Gant, get to the tower," Abbey said. "Get Lucifer here."

"I'm not leaving you," Gant replied.

"That wasn't asking. That was telling. Get your ass to the comm tower."

"Queenie," Gant said again, pleading.

"Now," Abbey shouted.

Gant turned and ran.

Abbey stared at Trin. How was she supposed to fight this?

"I can see your fear, Abbey," Trin said. "I can also see you're starting to believe in what I'm offering you. Anything I can do, you can do as well. Perhaps even more. All you have to do is come with me. Accept the Gift. Accept the glory and the honor. Be a part of the new eternal Covenant."

"I don't want to be part of some bullshit army," Abbey said. "I want to go home, to Earth, to be with my daughter. Maybe I'm thinking too small. Maybe my goals are too simple, but that's all I care about."

The ground shuddered. A moment later the Republic mech returned, emerging from the smoke behind Trin, its arms rotating to target the woman and her soldiers. Trin turned almost casually, putting up her hand as the mech's chest-mounted lasers began to fire.

They ricocheted against flashes of light that appeared ahead of Trin, reflective sparks that reversed the path of the bolts, sending them back into the mech. Its shields didn't cover the firing ports, and the exacting nature of the defense caused the attack to back up into the weapons, burning through their mechanisms deep inside the war machine. It began to smoke, the pilot opening the cockpit and climbing out, jumping from the mech as the top of it caught fire, flames licking through the gaps in the armored joints.

He landed on the ground, looking up at Trin in fear. A single round put a hole in his chest, and he fell over.

Abbey could feel her skin beginning to burn at the display. She didn't know what Thraven was, or what he wanted. Power, most likely. Wasn't that what invaders were always after? The Republic couldn't stand up to something like this. Not if Trin was only a single sample of a much larger mass of so-called Gifted individuals. If they attacked, if they made it to Earth, then what? The Republic would fall. What about Hayley? What would happen to her?

"Airi, may I borrow your sword?" Abbey said, putting her hand out.

Trin was turning back to them, a smile on her face.

"Power, Abbey," she said. "The impossible made possible. Honor. Glory. The Great Return. Your daughter can be the daughter of a queen. Think of how you could protect her then. I still don't want to kill you. I don't want to kill anyone, and neither does the Gloritant. Follow me. That is all that he asks. Follow me into a new future. Follow me to our rightful place in the universe."

"She's crazy," Pik said. "I have no idea what she's talking about."

"Me neither," Abbey said as Airi handed over her blade.

"Queenie, you can't fight her."

"Anyone can fight anyone. It doesn't mean they'll win. I'll slow her down; you get to the comm tower. Lucifer can pick you all up there. Tell Captain Mann I died to stop this bitch from advancing the ideals of a nutjob dictator, and he owes me to figure out what the frag is going on and how to put an end to it. I joined the Republic military to keep our way of life safe. It isn't perfect, but it's better than being under the boot of a psycho."

"I haven't known you that long, but I know you wouldn't leave me," Pik said. "I'm not leaving you either."

"I agree," Airi said. "All of us go, or none of us go."

"I'll stay too, I guess," Benhil said. "Why not? I always figured I was going to die in Hell. I guess I'll kick it on some waterless shithole in the corner of the galaxy, instead. It's as good a place as any."

Abbey smiled. "Gant's going to be pissed that he went to the tower."

"Then he shouldn't have left," Benhil said. "What the hell does the word loyalty mean to him, anyway?"

Abbey looked back at Trin. She was waiting calmly, patiently, for her to decide. She wasn't afraid of the sword. She wasn't afraid of the Rejects. Why should she be? Had anyone challenged her since she had been given the Gift?

Abbey's body was on fire. Her skin was burning, tingling, shifting and moving like it was alive and losing control. It was responding to her fear, her anger, her desperation. Maybe she couldn't control whatever power was inside of her the way Trin could.

Maybe she didn't have to.

"Keep those other assholes honest," Abbey said. "I'm going in."

"Yes, ma'am," they replied.

She closed her eyes, taking a breath. Her body felt like it wanted to explode, and the converted hellsuit was the only thing holding it together.

She flexed her legs and Jumped.

CHAPTER FIFTY-FOUR

THE *BRIMSTONE* BLINKED BACK INTO existence in a plume of gas, the disterium disbursing around the starship as it made orbit around Drune.

"Trin," Ursan said, trying to reach her through her communicator.

He had felt the change when she had revived, the sudden renewal of warmth within his soul. He was amazed that Thraven's Gift had allowed him to sense his wife so acutely and more grateful for it than anything else the General had done.

"Trin," he repeated. There was no reply.

"The atmosphere is too dense," Dak said. "Short-range signals can't punch through."

Ursan stared at the brown planet ahead of them. She was down there, somewhere. Was she still in trouble? She had to be. Why else would Thraven have let him come so easily?

"We're being hailed," Dak said.

"Who?"

"Captain Defay," Dak replied. "On board the Lahar."

"Defay," Ursan said.

"Captain Gall," Defay said. "General Thraven told me you were en route."

"Trin," Ursan said.

"We have everything well in hand, Captain," Defay said. "There has been some unexpected resistance from the surface, but our forces are winning the day."

"What kind of unexpected resistance?"

"Planetary defense of some kind. It may be that the Republic has been using Drune as a forward base, hoping to stockpile weapons and supplies inside Outworld space."

"And you didn't know that before you arrived? Then what are you doing here?"

"Following orders, Captain," Defay said. "Without question. Something you seem to struggle to do."

Ursan held his tongue, closing the link instead.

"Bolar," he said, contacting his shuttle pilot.

"What do you need, Captain?" the Outworlder replied.

"Prep the shuttle. Tik."

"Yes, Boss?" the Trover said.

"Get the ground team ready. We're going down there."

"Roger."

"Are you sure that's a good idea?" Dak asked. "Defay said they have everything under control."

"Frag Defay," Ursan replied, getting to his feet. "Someone killed Trin. It doesn't matter if the Gift brought her back or not, I want that asshole's head. Besides, I didn't challenge Thraven to sit up here and twiddle my thumbs. Get us in close so we can drop the shuttle."

"Okay, Boss."

"You have the bridge, Dak," Ursan said, fleeing the space.

He ran through the large corridors of the *Brimstone*, gaining the lift and taking it down to the hangar. His ground unit was already assembled by the time he had put on his lightsuit, headed by his Sergeant, Tik. The shuttle was behind the fifteen soldiers, lights on and reactor humming.

"We're ready to go, Boss," Tik said as he arrived, saluting him with the rest of his crew.

"Then stop standing around and get on the shuttle," Ursan said, hurrying past him and up the ramp extending from the ship.

"You heard him," Tik shouted. "Move out."

The soldiers piled into the shuttle behind him, quickly taking their positions and clamping themselves in.

"Locked and loaded, Boss," Tik said.

"Bolar, get us down there."

"Yes, sir," Bolar replied.

The ramp retracted, the hatch closing and sealing. The shuttle lifted off the floor of the hangar, thrusters firing and launching it out into space.

Ursan could see the Lahar to his right as the shuttle changed direction, diving toward Drune, the large, dark battleship barely visible save for the few lights coming from the hangar and the bridge. Defay wasn't stupid enough to challenge him, not while he was in control of the *Brimstone*. Was that why Thraven had deferred to him, too?

He could feel his skin start to burn as the shuttle hit the atmosphere, beginning to shudder slightly at the introduction of resistance. Wherever Trin was, he was certain she needed his help. Even if she didn't, he was going to give it anyway.

What the hell was the Gift good for otherwise?

CHAPTER FIFTY-FIVE

"FIVE O'CLOCK," RUBY SAID CALMLY, watching the *Faust's* HUD.

"I see him, thanks," Bastion replied.

The HUD lost the target to interference a moment later, leaving them flying blind to their attackers once more.

He couldn't hear the gunfire behind them, but he could see the results, the display to his right showing the shields activating, absorbing the rounds as the power continued to drain from the reactors.

Everything had been peaceful and quiet. He was kicking back, staring out the viewport of the starship's cockpit, daydreaming about Lieutenant Cage when first the onboard sensors, and then Ruby, had informed him that a dropship was coming in nearby.

An instant later and he was upright in the pilot's seat, monitoring the sensors and watching as the oddly configured ship crossed only a few thousand meters overhead, almost visible in the shrouded air. He hadn't wasted any time alerting Fury and Okay to the situation, and they had decided together that Abbey was about to be deep in the shit, and was going to need backup. He had tried to send a message to her as well, but Ruby questioned whether or not it would reach that far.

He had watched them go, and then he had waited. One minute stretched to five, which expanded to ten. The sensors had picked up the incoming Shrikes only seconds before they swept across the field, blasting one of the other starships parked nearby. That was all it took to get him airborne, trying desperately to find a vector that would get him to the colony in support of the Rejects and coming under heavy attack from the circling Outworld starfighters.

"We can't keep going like this," Bastion said, the shield monitor flashing every time a round hit the energy web. "I need visibility."

"We have to get Queenie and the others out," Ruby said.

"Damn it; I know that, I'm doing the best I can."

Bastion manipulated the control yoke, sending the ship into a tight bank. They would have been dead already if not for the long wings that extended from the starship's upper hull, making it more maneuverable in atmosphere than most vessels its size. It allowed the larger ship to fly more like a fighter, albeit a big, ugly fighter and had given him the opportunity to down two of the Shrikes already.

The only problem was that there were still two more behind them, with pilots who were skilled enough to match him turn for turn. He had managed to keep the *Faust* intact so far, but intact wasn't good enough. Whatever shitty fate had brought the Rejects together, they were still his team, and he wasn't about to let them die while he danced around in the sky.

"Do you have any useful strategies for a situation like this stored in that database of yours?" he asked, glancing over at Ruby. "Or are your memory banks overrun with sex positions?"

"I have a complete encyclopedia on both topics available, with adequate storage remaining," Ruby replied. "However, you don't want me to answer the first question."

"Why not?"

"There are no known documented examples of a starship outclassing Shrikes in atmosphere."

"Meaning?"

"You should consider yourself lucky for destroying two of them already. What you are attempting to do is bordering on the impossible."

"I'm sorry I asked."

"You should be."

Bastion rolled the *Faust* over. The starship shook slightly as it made the maneuver, the wings flexing and threatening to snap under the tension. Then he leveled out and raised the bow, moving into a sharp climb. Impossible?

He hated that idea.

The Shrikes held behind him, continuing to fire as they rose, switching from projectiles to beam weapons. They wouldn't do as much damage that way, but they could keep up the chase and the attack indefinitely, wearing at his shields, his patience, and his psyche until he made that final, fatal mistake.

He kept climbing, eager to escape from the dust and get the HUD locked onto the Shrikes once more. He couldn't hit them if he couldn't see them, and sensors were too unreliable close to the ground. At the same time, for as deadly as the Shrikes were in atmosphere, they were even deadlier out of it, their vectoring thrusters allowing them to make tight spins and rotations that a larger body simply couldn't match.

It was a delicate balance, but one that he had managed before. This wasn't the first time he had come up against the Outworlds' best line of defense, though it was his first time doing it on a ship as large as the *Faust*.

They broke through the dusty air, reaching clear atmosphere. The sky was darker above them, and he could see the outline of that damned dark battleship silhouetted against it, the source of the bastards who were trying to down him.

"What the," he said as his eyes landed on a second object in orbit near the first. A starship unlike any he had seen before, except in the data Captain Mann had provided them.

"The *Brimstone*," Ruby said. "It's here." She paused. "Why would that be?"

"I don't know, and I don't care. We have enough problems already."

The computer beeped at him, signaling another hit, this one passing through the shields and leaving a mark on one of the wings. A flesh wound. He was lucky.

"Hold on," Bastion said. "Either this is going to work, or we're going to die."

"I can't die," Ruby reminded him. "Only be destroyed."

"What's the difference?" Bastion asked.

Ruby was silent for a moment and then shrugged. "I can turn off my pain sensors," she offered.

"I can turn off my pain sensors," Bastion mimicked. "Whatever. Here goes."

He cut the power to the engines.

Completely.

He also cut the power to the anti-gravity, turning it off and allowing the *Faust* to become the heavy mass of alloy that it truly was.

"This is not a good idea," Ruby said, as the ship's climb came to an abrupt end, the nose beginning to roll over toward the ground.

The Shrikes were maneuverable, but not enough to stop that quickly. There was a brief moment where their vector and the changing vector of the *Faust* lined up. Bastion didn't waste it.

He triggered the ship's guns, heavy plasma lancing out from the two cannons mounted beside the cockpit and the two turrets over the top. Sharp red bolts speared one of the Shrikes, burning through it and cutting it in half, while the other banked and turned, peeling away from the assault.

"Damn," Bastion said, his stomach dropping when the *Faust* started to fall, the Shrike circling back behind them and peppering them while they regained momentum.

Warnings sounded in the cockpit, the shield display lighting up as he switched the thrusters back on, immediately pegging them to max. He kept the anti-gravity off, allowing the planet's pull to increase their acceleration.

"We won't be able to pull out of this," Ruby said.

"I'll worry about that when we get there," he replied.

"I believe you were correct. We are going to die."

"I thought you said you couldn't die?"

"Same difference."

"Synths," Bastion said, his body beginning to tense as he re-activated the anti-gravity. They were back into the dusty air, and even though he couldn't see the ground, he knew it was fast approaching.

"Lucifer."

Gant's voice took him by surprise, almost causing him to miss his mark. He clenched his teeth, beginning to pull the *Faust* up out of its dive.

"Gant. A little busy," he said, the combined activity causing the *Faust* to shake violently.

"With what?" Gant replied. "Queenie needs you, damn it."

"With not dying," Bastion shouted back. "I'm on my way, just get your ass off my back and let me do my job."

"Did you just call me a monkey again?"

"Stow it, Gant," Bastion replied, the computer blaring warnings about the oncoming surface of the planet.

He pushed himself back in his seat as if that would help level the ship, practically wetting himself as he saw the ground appear below. He was outside of the colony, looking down on a field where six mechs were squaring off, four on two. They seemed to pause at his approach, rotating to face him, noticing that he might not make it up in time.

Then he did, getting the *Faust* even and then on the rise, the exhaust of the ship's thrusters pushing against the mechs and knocking them off their feet. The trailing Shrike misjudged the floor, not quite making it up in time and slamming hard into the ground behind them.

"Woooooooo," he shouted, releasing the pent-up energy. "Am I good or what?" He glanced over at Ruby, sitting beside him with the same, calm demeanor. "Come on; you're a pleasure bot, can't you show a little bit of pleasure at not being destroyed?"

"I can simulate an orgasm if it will satisfy your need for validation and overall machismo," she replied.

Bastion closed his mouth, all of the excitement draining from him. "Gant, we're on our way. Gant?"

He was gone.

CHAPTER FIFTY-SIX

THE POWER OF THE SOFTSUIT'S synthetic musculature added to Abbey's own was enough to carry her about fifty meters in one bounce.

The Gift-enhanced Jump sent her across the entire distance at a much higher velocity than she would ever achieve on her own. She hurtled her through the air toward Trin, sword gripped in two hands and held over her head, ready to cut the woman in half.

She had no expectations that she was going to make it all the way across. She was certain the other woman would knock her out of the sky. The effort was foolish and probably wasted, but she wasn't going to submit, and she wasn't going to let Trin kill her without a fight.

Trin raised a hand at the approach, holding it out toward her. Abbey felt the Gift pushing up against her own, as though two giant invisible hands clapped together and pushed, strength against strength. She knew she wasn't as capable as Trin, but even so, she powered through the defense, surprising Thraven's assassin by landing within striking distance. She had never used a sword before. How many people in this century had? She had used nerve batons, though, and a stick was a stick, this one just had a sharp side. She swung it toward Trin, who slipped beneath it, the surprise evident on her face.

"A challenge then?" Trin said.

She moved in quickly, taking an angle around the blade, her movements fast and precise. She hit Abbey in the side, the blow forceful enough to send her tumbling sideways, rolling to a stop a dozen meters away.

Abbey tensed against the pain, pulling herself to her feet. The hit increased the burning in her skin, and she squared off with the blade as Trin came toward her, running so quickly her feet barely hit the ground. Abbey watched in surprise as the woman's fingers elongated into a set of sharp claws. Had her fingers grown, or was it some kind of augmentation built into her softsuit?

She didn't have time to think about it. She brought the blade up ahead of Trin's attack, catching the first swipe, then bringing it down and over to block the second. Ahead of her, she could see Pik and Airi attacking the blacksuits, sending rounds into the exposed soldiers, who absorbed the damage without falling.

The scene distracted her, giving Trin an opening. She felt the pain as the woman's claws tore into her stomach, ripping through her hellsuit and into flesh. She backed away, swinging the blade ahead of her to keep the other woman honest.

"You're a good fighter," Trin said. "You would have made an exemplary Evolent."

"Past tense already?" Abbey replied. "Try killing me first."

Trin smiled, more like a predator than a person.

"This is the power of the Gift," she said. "The power you could have. The power you refuse."

She spread her arms to her sides, her entire body flaring in heat and energy, surrounding her in flames.

"What the frag are you?" Abbey said.

"The past. The present. The future."

Trin held out her hand, and a stream of energy burst from it, heading for Abbey. She rolled aside, terrified as the attack hit the ground where she had been and tore a deep gash into the earth.

"This could be yours, Abbey," Trin said, pausing the attack. "This and more."

"How many times do I have to tell you to go frag yourself?" Abbey said, getting to her feet.

Trin moved in, coming at her so fast she barely had time to react. She got the sword up to block the first swipe from elongated fingers, only to find the other on her wrist, the touch burning into her flesh and forcing her to drop the weapon.

"Go frag yourself, Lieutenant," Trin said, reaching out and wrapping her other hand around Abbey's throat, lifting her easily off the ground.

Her skin smoked and burned where Trin's flesh touched her, and she couldn't breathe. She had part of the Gift. She needed it to *do* something. She punched, trying to increase the strength the same way she had when she had bounced. Her fist smacked harmlessly against Trin's chest.

Damn it.

She tried again, and again. It was no use. The Gift was failing her. Because Trin was stronger?

No. Because she was afraid.

She felt sharp claws punch through her hellsuit and sink into her stomach. Trin was smiling, enjoying the moment. Enjoying the kill.

A bright flash and a wave of heat flowed over them, leaving Trin cursing as a plasma bolt hit her in the back, throwing her away from Abbey. The *Faust* flashed overhead, appearing for an instant and gone just as soon. Abbey took a moment to gather herself, fighting to catch her breath, feeling her body recovering as she rolled to her feet. The blacksuits had been hit by the run as well, burned by the incoming plasma but getting back up.

An angry growl forced her attention back to Trin. The assassin was up again, still smoldering from the hit but healing quickly. Abbey saw Airi's sword laying a few meters away. She had to hold onto her anger, and bury her fear. She reached out to it, eager for it to be in her hand., eager to use it as a weapon to kill this flaming bitch.

Her skin burned as the Gift responded, extending to meet her needs, bringing the weapon to her. She caught the hilt, ready for round two.

"Come on," she said, waving Trin toward her. "You wanted a challenge, didn't you?"

Trin lashed out with a hand, sending another burst of energy forward. Abbey moved forward to meet it, bringing the sword up as she did, attacking the energy with the weapon as though it was a living thing she could kill. It burned around her, not even hitting the sword but moving to evade.

"Die, damn you," Trin shouted, bringing her hands together and then casting them out.

Abbey felt the force of Trin's power coming at her again, so much stronger this time. She thought of Hayley, and the idea that she might never see her daughter again. The anger spread across her flesh, the Gift threatening to tear her apart from the inside.

Trin's power hit her, but it didn't harm her. The Gift became a wall, completely deflecting the attack.

"How?" Trin said softly.

Then Abbey Jumped again, bursting forward, speeding ahead faster than even she could believe. The assassin put her hands up to block, but Abbey dropped early, spinning low, hopping in and coming up, bringing the blade behind her in a powerful uppercut. She could feel the sharp edge slicing into the flesh, cutting in deep as she wrenched it with her, bouncing straight up, pulling Trin with it until it finally tore out through the neck.

She landed, watching as Trin looked down at the wound. Her eyes were wide with shock, and she struggled to recover from the blow.

Abbey raised the sword again. Trin's flesh was already healing, knitting itself together, the blood along it thick and sticky and unlike any blood Abbey had ever seen before.

She was vaguely aware of something behind her, and the sound of a hatch opening on a shuttle she couldn't see.

"Ursan," Trin said softly.

Abbey wasn't taking any more chances. She cried out as she swung the blade, feeling the power of the Gift added to that of her hellsuit. The edge cut easily through Trin's neck, decapitating her in one smooth blow.

"Nooooo," someone shouted behind her. Abbey barely had time to turn around when she was thrown forward by an unseen hand, knocked away from Trin's body and sent tumbling once more. "Kill her."

She pushed herself to her feet, turning to face her attacker. A man, the only one in a lightsuit while the rest of his soldiers wore battlesuits. Their guns raised, all of them training on her at once.

She felt the bullets begin to hit her, tearing into her, digging in deep or going clean through, even as she watched the man rush over to the fallen assassin, kneeling in front of her head. He was crying out in agony, his pained howls nearly drowning out the reports from his soldier's rifles while he reached down and touched the face, stroking a lock of blue hair away from it.

More and more slugs poured into her, the force of them knocking her back and then finally off her feet, bringing her to the ground. Her eyes filled with blood, her face wet and throbbing, every part of her on fire.

She heard another howl then, unlike any other she had heard before. It was sharp and biting, the pitch high enough to cause pain if she hadn't already been drowning in it. She struggled to lift her head, to see what was causing it.

Then Gant was coming toward her, his laser pistol lighting up over and over again, a warning of the invisible flashes of dense energy he was firing, flashes that cut right through the visors of the enemy soldiers' battlesuits with unerring accuracy. One, two, three, they fell in rapid succession, one after another as the Gant charged, screaming the entire time. The man at the head of the group looked up, raising his hand as if to throw Gant aside, gaining a surprised expression as he kept coming. The man reached down and picked up Trin's head, cradling it as he ran back toward the shuttle, his soldiers following behind.

"Queenie," Gant said, reaching her. "Queenie!"

She tried to smile. She couldn't. Everything was dark. Everything hurt. There was only one gift she wanted right now.

Rest.

CHAPTER FIFTY-SEVEN

"LET'S GO, LET'S GO, LET'S go," Bastion shouted, standing at the ramp onto the *Faust* with Ruby beside him. It took him a few seconds before he realized that Pik was carrying someone, and a few more seconds to figure out who it was. "Oh, shit. Queenie?"

"What are you doing here?" Airi said, arriving ahead of the others. "We need to go, now."

She paused and pointed back to the soldiers in the field. They were burned and broken but still standing, their motions jerky but constant. Further away, a small mech was reaching the edge of the dust, turning to face their direction.

"Queenie," he said softly.

"I don't know," Airi replied. "She's in bad shape. Get us out of here."

Bastion recovered from his shock, racing back to the ladder and climbing it, hurrying to the cockpit. He found the incoming mech in the rear viewscreen, turning the wing mounted turrets toward it and firing. It sidestepped the first effort, returning fire that pinged against the craft's armor before a second volley hit a leg and knocked it to the ground.

"Everybody's in," Ruby said. "Let's go."

"Wait," Benhil said. "Where's Gant?"

"Damn," Airi said. "I'll find him."

"There's no time," Benhil said. "We have to go."

"We don't leave anyone behind."

"We don't have a choice."

Bastion scanned the rear viewscreen, and then put his eyes out of the forward transparency. The Gant was nowhere to be seen. Frag it. He hit the control to close the hatch, ending the argument in a hurry.

"Strap in," he said, pushing the thrust to max and increasing the anti-gravity. The *Faust* slid along the ground on its landers for a few hundred meters, kicking up a huge plume of dust before rising into the air and blasting away.

Bastion kept his eyes forward, trying not to think about Abbey. For as much as he had feared her when she had first arrived in Hell, for as much as he had disliked her when she challenged him for leadership of the Rejects, he couldn't argue that she was the solder that was holding them together, and the only reason they had managed to come together so quickly as a team. She had proven herself to each of them in individual ways. To him, as a decisive, strong leader who didn't hesitate to take point. It didn't matter if she was special. It didn't matter that she was somehow bulletproof. She hadn't known that when she took the lead on Orunel, and she certainly hadn't been able to count on it now. Not with the amount of blood he had seen on her body, and on Pik's battlesuit.

It was a strange thought for him to have. It was a thought he would never have expected to have the day he pushed her away from the food dispenser to help Pok get his hands on her. He didn't want her to die. If they were going to have any chance of survival, if they were going to have any chance at retrieving the *Fire* and *Brimstone* and being released, they needed her.

The *Faust* broke through the dust, continuing to climb. The atmosphere gave way to the vacuum of space, and he set FTL coordinates for anywhere but here.

The dark battleship was still in orbit, floating far enough away that Bastion didn't need to be concerned. He checked his sensors for signs of the *Brimstone*. It was already gone.

To where?

It didn't matter. The computer finished running its calculations, giving him the green light to make the acceleration. He hit the launch control, sending them blinking away.

Except they didn't blink away. They didn't go to FTL at all. A soft tone sounded, a light flashing in the cockpit.

"Oh, frag me," Bastion said. "Ruby. We've got a problem." He glanced to his left, watching Thraven's battleship. It wasn't paying them any mind.

"What's wrong?" Ruby asked, appearing in the cockpit.

"I'm not sure. According to the diagnostics, we're out of disterium."

"Now?"

He held his hands out. "I didn't do it. We've got four canisters in the hold. Ask Pik to help you replace it, and we'll be on our way. I'll keep an eye on the big ugly over there. Fortunately, he doesn't seem to give a shit about us."

"Roger," Ruby replied, vanishing from the cockpit again.

Bastion leaned back in the chair. "Fury, how's Queenie?" he asked.

"She's." Airi paused. "I don't know."

"What do you mean you don't know?"

"We brought her to medical and strapped her down. She wasn't breathing."

"You mean she's dead?" Bastion leaned forward resting his head in his hands. They were screwed.

"I don't know," Airi replied. "She wasn't breathing. But you saw those soldiers planetside. You hit them dead-on with heavy plasma, and they got back up. Maybe she'll get back up."

Bastion felt a chill. Would she? Could she? He doubted it.

"Son of a bitch," he said softly.

"Lucifer, we've got the canister," Ruby said. "We're bringing it back to the engine room now."

"Thanks. When you're done, see if you can get Captain Mann on the line." He had no idea what he was going to tell him, but he had to tell him something.

"Affirmative," Ruby replied.

He looked out the viewport again, finding the battleship in the distance. He could see the light of a thruster headed toward it, trailing behind one of the dropships. The battle had to be over then. But who the hell were the units already on the ground, the ones who had tried to defend the colony?

He didn't have a chance to think about it. One second, the space ahead of them was empty. The next, a ship shimmered into existence, the cloak that was hiding it falling away.

The *Brimstone*.

Why the frag hadn't the sensors picked it up?

He leaned forward, his hands at the controls, punching the *Faust* to max thrust as the starship opened fire, advanced railguns spewing heavy, piercing flechettes at almost point two cees, barely missing as they went up and over.

"Shit, shit, shit, shit, shit, shit, shit," Bastion said, repeating the mantra as he worked to escape the warship. Entire fleets had fallen to the *Brimstone*, and he was flying a starship that should have been broken down for salvage years ago, with no immediate hope of escape.

"Lucifer, what the hell is going on?" Ruby said.

"*Brimstone*," he replied. "She's still here, damn it. Strap in."

"We can't load the canister if we strap in."

"If we fly straight, we're sure to die. If we don't, maybe we can get away."

"How?"

"Back to the planet?" Bastion suggested. "I don't know. You're the synth. Give me something I can use."

"Queenie ordered me not to respond to those kinds of requests."

"Damn it, I'm serious. You've got to have something in your databanks."

"I can tell you the odds of survival."

"I can figure that out for myself. Hold on."

He threw the *Faust* into a tight vector, feeling the force despite the inertial dampeners. The *Brimstone* was larger and turned more slowly, shifting to get an angle to fire. The maneuver brought him in line with Thraven's battleship.

His mouth opened, his heart racing. "Oh, hot fragging damn. I've got an idea. Ruby, do your best to get the canister as close to the engine room as possible. Don't give me any shit about the rocking; you've got better balance than any Terran."

"Roger," Ruby said. "What are you going to do?"

"Hopefully put something between us that those assholes don't want to hit."

He couldn't increase the thrust, but by keeping it steady he continued to add velocity, moving away from the stolen starship. At least, he thought he was moving away. He cursed as the ship seemed to hop from one place in space to another, behind them one second, and ahead of them the next. He adjusted vectors as lasers lashed out, spearing the space around them so close he could almost feel the heat. It seemed impossible, but somehow they missed, tracing below them.

Bastion angled the *Faust* in close, dropping low and under the *Brimstone*, constantly changing paths in order to throw off any targeting efforts while keeping an eye out for more incoming fire. They were closing on the other ship in a hurry, and as they streaked ahead of the *Brimstone* he aligned them with the other ship's hull, hopeful the *Brimstone's* commander wasn't too eager to down a friendly.

That hope was short-lived. The *Brimstone* continued to fire, lasers lancing out behind them, one of them finally making contact. The *Faust* shook, the computer blaring out warnings, the shields overloaded by the assault. Bastion cursed, adjusting vectors, rising and falling, rolling left and right, doing everything he could think of to keep the enemy warship from getting a lock.

Then the laser fire stopped, the *Faust* drawing close to the battleship. Batteries from the other side took over, trying to get in one final volley before they were over and past, trying to score that one hit that would turn them into corpses and wreckage.

Bastion didn't know how they survived. He didn't know how the battleship continued to miss, often by the skin of their teeth. The *Faust* drew within one hundred kilometers of the ship, a journey that would take only seconds to cross.

The computer beeped again, indicating an enemy lock and the release of a torpedo.

Bastion watched the HUD, the projectile moving at an impossible speed, jumping from the front of the *Brimstone* to their tails in the span of milliseconds. He clenched his eyes, waiting for the sudden fury of death.

He opened them a second later when he realized he was still alive. Ahead of him, an explosion rocked the battleship, the torpedo slamming into it and detonating, the force sending debris out from the impact and causing secondary explosions along the hull.

"Lucifer, the canister is in place and connected," Ruby said, shaking him from his paralyzed amazement before it could get them killed.

He adjusted vectors instead, turning away from the crumbling battleship and hitting the launch control once more.

This time, the *Faust* disappeared.

CHAPTER FIFTY-EIGHT

OLUS STOOD OUTSIDE THE EAGAN estate, behind one of the large trees that composed the jungle canopy beyond the walls. It was late in the evening, the planet's sun having barely settled behind the water, a darkness beginning to fall over the property.

He had arrived on Feru two hours earlier, taking a shuttle from the Driver to the city before reaching out to Director Eagan to set up another meeting for the following day. He hadn't spoken to Mars, being first received by an assistant and then passed on to Emily instead, but it was just as well. He didn't need to speak to her. He only needed an excuse to be on the planet.

He also didn't know what was going to happen in the morning, when General Omsala asked after his report and he refused to respond to the request. Would the General go so far as to have him removed from his position as head of the OSI? Or would they prefer to keep him close, but not too close? The missing report could be forgiven depending on how the Committee, and by extension, the infiltrators who had gained control of the Committee, wanted to play their hand.

Whatever. He had another job to do first.

He pulled a small device from his softsuit, sticking it to the tree. The screen in the corner of his visor presented him with a detailed layout of the grounds, highlighting electronics the sensors in the device picked up, labeling each. Cameras, motion sensors, heat sensors, audio sensors. The estate was a fortress.

He had been in plenty of those before.

He memorized the pattern of the equipment, glancing at the buildings to get an idea of the positions. Then he removed the device from the tree and took out a second. He tossed it into the air, and it hung there a moment before moving ahead, taking a position a meter in front of him and sending data back to his TCU. The average grunt didn't have access to this kind of tech, but he wasn't the average grunt.

He moved to the wall, bouncing in his softsuit, rising ten meters and catching the lip of the wall. The bot stayed ahead of him as he moved, hugging the stone and sending out jamming signals within a thirty-meter radius. As long as he didn't get in line with the cameras, he would be safe.

He rolled to the other side and dropped onto the grounds, staying low and waiting to see if any alarms were tripped. He caught a bit of motion further off to his left and zoomed in to see a guard standing at a post near the corner of the mansion. He wouldn't be a problem.

Two quick hops across the grounds, carefully planned to avoid the cameras and motion sensors, and then he was at the wall of the mansion. The jamming bot hovered beside him, silent and dark, while he plotted his next course. He decided to head toward the guard, assuming there had to be an entrance there. He stayed low along the wall until he was close, and then he removed a small tube from a tightpack. He blew into it as the guard turned the corner, hitting him clean in the neck with a needle packing a concentrated sedative, jumping up and catching the man when he fell.

"Easy," he whispered, lowering the guard to the ground.

Then he approached the side door, pulling out an extender and placing it on the control pad. System code ran along his visor, and he quickly tapped commands along his thigh, seeking a bypass for the security. He had it within a minute, unlocking the door and slipping inside.

The visor switched itself to night vision, a clear view of the inside of the mansion coming into focus. The jamming bot still hovered beside him, disrupting signals to nearby equipment, including a camera pointed right at the door. The bot would be more effective inside where the ranges were shorter, as long as he moved quickly enough to prevent suspicion if the feeds were live-monitored.

He climbed three flights of steps, covering half the height of the mansion before a light went on and he had to duck into a dark corner while a servant passed by, carrying a tray of half-eaten food. He waited a minute for the woman to vanish, and then continued up, all the way to the top. If there was one thing he had learned in his years as a trained killer, it was that despite all of the property at their disposal, the powerful still kept a fairly tight radius, placing their most commonly used rooms in close proximity. What he wanted was Mars' office, and access to her mainframe. He wanted to check her messages, her logs, her data stores. He wanted to prove his hunch.

If he couldn't?

She would never know he had been there.

He padded across a long, open corridor, with a view all the way down to the ground floor. A massive chandelier hung in the center of the space, crystal and gold, probably another Earth relic. He checked each room quickly, scanning through for occupants and seeking the familiar signature of a terminal.

He knew he had found Mars' bedroom when his scanner picked up two bodies on infrared. They were awake and in motion, one on top of the other. Distracted. Good. He moved on, not surprised to find the Director's office, and her terminal, was only two doors down.

He slipped in and sat at the desk, running his hand over the surface to activate it while sending a signal to the bot to contain its jamming radius to the room and keep a watch for him. Then he took out another extender, placing it under the desk and connecting through his softsuit. The terminal was locked, and there was only one other way in.

Strong outer security usually meant weaker internal security, and Olus found that true in Mars Eagan's case as well. He cracked her password within seconds, making his way into her mainframe. He ran a query for the serial number of the part Ensign Klar had discovered. It turned up a short missive about a hijacked shipment. Not helpful, but also not surprising.

He moved on, seeking out the Director's lifestream storage. It was all organized by date, and that made it easy to find the footage recorded during her abduction. He was surprised to find there was nothing missing. What she had given him was honest and complete. Was he wrong about her? He dug a little deeper, finding his way into her messaging system and scanning the missives there. He found mention of the *Fire* and the *Brimstone*, but nothing that would suggest she had been in on the theft, or that she had any connection to anyone named Thraven.

He could hardly believe it. He had been distrustful of her because she was too clean. Now it seemed she really was spotless.

He looked at the code on his visor, and then at the projection rising from the desk, and then back again. There was still something about it that was rubbing him the wrong way. Something he didn't trust. How would an Outworld ship manage to get so close to Feru without being seen? How could they have the means and know-how to steal the ships without inside help?

He had already checked the employee manifests against the casualty reports. There was no one else who could have been responsible unless they had sacrificed themselves for the cause. While it was possible, it was a hard pill to swallow.

There was one other option. A long shot, maybe. Maybe not. All HSOCs were taught that things are rarely what they seem, and he had enough experience to know the accuracy of that lesson. He regained his momentum, digging through the mainframe until he found a second lifestream.

The one that belonged to Emily Eagan.

He didn't go to the date and time of the theft, or even right before it. He went back two weeks, quickly scanning through the retinal recordings. If she had anything to do with the attack, she would have needed to contact someone to plan it.

It only took a few seconds of scanning for him to reach the first moment he was sure Emily Eagan would have preferred to keep private.

She was with Mars in the bedroom, standing in front of the older woman. Mars was on the bed in some form of white lingerie. Olus didn't particularly care about either one of their sexual escapades, but he did care about what he caught as he moved through the stream at twenty seconds per frame, something that caused him to back the stream up. He scrubbed forward again more carefully this time, to the midst of their passion.

Only it wasn't passion, and despite what Mars had told him earlier, he discovered that it just wasn't true. The older woman laid on the bed, almost still, while the younger directed her in everything, controlling her as though she were a slave, not the owner of one of the most important companies in the Republic. And then, as Emily Eagan seemed to reach the height of her enjoyment, he watched as she leaned forward, tucking her face into Mars' neck. He could hear the sucking noises. He could hear Emily's pleasure. She was there for nearly five minutes. When she pulled away, Mars' neck had two clean puncture wounds in it, a small bruise around them. Emily reached up and wiped her mouth, her hand coming away with a small trickle of blood on it.

He filed the activity away, moving forward in the stream. The episode repeated itself the next night, and the night after that. He glanced over at the door. He had picked up the two bodies on top of one another. Was the same thing happening right now? It didn't matter. He needed something else. The activity was a curiosity but didn't prove a damn thing.

Not yet, anyway.

He stopped the stream again a few seconds later. Emily had finished with Mars and had gone to the bathroom to shower. She dressed, and then came into the room he was in, locking the door before turning on the terminal. Her terminal, not Mars'. She had glanced around slightly nervously before switching on the communications relay.

"Gloritant Thraven," she said.

Thraven appeared before her a moment later, projected to the other side of the desk. Olus thought he was a handsome man, though he found his age hard to place. He could have easily been well over one hundred, depending on whether he used stasis regeneration or not.

"Venerant Alloran," Thraven said. "Is everything ready?"

"Yes, Gloritant. The arrangements have been made. The assets are in position."

"And Director Eagan?"

"She has no idea what the ships really are." She smiled. "She has little idea of anything beyond what we want her to know. My control over her is complete." She paused. "They work, Gloritant. The ancient technologies. The blueprints of the Covenant. We have proven them."

"And once we have the *Fire* and the *Brimstone* in hand, we will begin to duplicate them," Thraven said. "The Great Return will be as it was promised. Remember, Venerant. There can be no witnesses."

"There won't be. I have arranged it with your Evolent, Trinity. Only Mars will survive. Her lack of complicity will be suspicious to the OSI, and will lead them away from the truth."

"Do not underestimate Olus Mann. Killshot. He is a worthy adversary. A true Hunter."

"It was your decision to get him involved."

"Do not question my decisions," Thraven snapped.

"Yes, Gloritant," Emily replied, shrinking back. "I trust your judgment explicitly."

Olus stopped the stream. As he had guessed, it was Emily Eagan who had betrayed Eagan Heavyworks and the Republic. She was working for Thraven and using a title like the ones Lieutenant Cage had described. Ancient technologies? Blueprints of the Covenant? No witnesses? What had they done here on Feru? What were the *Fire* and the *Brimstone*, exactly?

He abandoned the recording, moving through the mainframe in search of the answers to his questions. Had any of the data surrounding the construction of the two ships survived?

He went deeper, scanning through files stuffed with data. It could take a year or more to properly digest the contents of the system, and he had minutes at best. He needed to find something, fast.

His eyes paused on a collection amidst the sea of collections. Not for any other reason than because he didn't recognize the text of the label. He moved into it, revealing a list of simply numbered documents. He opened the first and froze, staring at what appeared to be a scan of a scrap something old and yellowed and faded, with dark symbols scratched across the surface in an alphabet he had never seen before.

"It predates humankind," a voice said behind him.

He turned, reaching for his sidearm as he did, getting it drawn and aimed by the time his eyes landed on Emily Eagan. She was wearing a light nightgown. A small stain of blood rested on her lip. Why the hell hadn't the bot alerted him that she was coming? For that matter, how the hell had she gotten in here?

"Thraven warned me not to underestimate you," she said, raising her hand. Immediately, he felt a pressure on his body that left him unable to move. "He had hoped our misdirection would be enough to satisfy, but then you went to Hell and got involved with Abigail Cage. It's a mistake you'll come to regret much more than we will."

Olus struggled against the pressure, but it was no use. For the first time in a long, storied career, he had been caught.

"Kill me and be done with it," he said, his lips barely able to move.

"Kill you?" Emily said. She shook her head. "No. That would be a waste, and I abhor waste. You'll make an excellent Convert, Olus. Even if you won't ever know it."

"The text," he said, shifting his eyes toward the terminal. "What does it say?"

Emily laughed. "Always the investigator, aren't you? It is the cover of a contract so old that it has been long forgotten by many, but not by all. It is the written Covenant between the first true children and our lord and master. The premonition of our Exile, and the promise of our Great Return. It has been carried throughout the millennia, away from the place of our creation and to the furthest reaches of the universe where we have waited for the fruit to ripen, the seeds of our eternal dominance planted and sewn.

We are the sons and daughters of the Slayer of God. We are the Nephilim, and our time has come."

CHAPTER FIFTY-NINE

GANT MOVED QUICKLY THROUGH THE corridors of the *Brimstone*, doing his best to keep himself out of sight. It wasn't that difficult, really. Not when the ship had so few crew members on board, and not when those crew members were mainly stationed on or near the bridge.

He was still struggling to calm himself, still fighting to let go of the torment that followed losing another alpha. Another friend. He still couldn't accept that he had listened to Abbey and gone to the comm tower, only to return and find her dead, gunned down by a line of soldiers and another one of *them*.

He still couldn't quite believe that he had made it to the shuttle before the ramp had finished retracting, squeezing on board and shoving himself into an access hatch in the back of the vessel while the enemy soldiers were still getting settled and clamped in. He wasn't quite sure how none of them had seen him. Everything was a dark blur since the moment he saw Abbey flailing, the bullets sending blood and flesh and cloth bursting away from her. Since he had felt the thing that reached out for him, trying to control him, to stop him. It had drawn near, and when it had sensed his anger, his resolve, his pure, unadulterated desire to kill, it had withdrawn.

In fear?

In pleasure?

Whatever.

He had done good work, killing five of the soldiers before the one with the power had stopped him and called the retreat. It had been a quick decision to hitch a ride, and at first he had done it so he could finish what he started, killing them as the opportunity came.

He still planned to, but not right away. Queenie wouldn't have wanted that. The mission was to recover both starships, and he was sure the commander of this one would know where the other one had gone. She would have wanted him to finish the mission, to earn his freedom, and to help the others earn theirs, too. It didn't matter if he only barely tolerated them, and outright disliked that asshole, Bastion. It was what she would have wanted, and so it was what he would try to do.

Now he was trying to find the engines, eager to dig into the mechanics and start fragging things up. Step one, force the *Brimstone* out of FTL. Step two, hijack the communications array and start transmitting a beacon that the *Faust* couldn't miss. Step three, disable the weapons systems. Step four, continue killing crew members until only the commander remained.

He couldn't wait to get to step four.

He continued running along the corridor, happy to find that the back of the ship was uninhabited and untended. It seemed the individuals that had stolen the ship didn't give a shit about how it worked or ensuring that it was operating efficiently. That it worked, that it was operating, seemed to be good enough, even after their targeting systems had somehow gone completely to hell, their torpedo missing the mark and hitting a friendly instead. He was planning to laugh about that one later when he related the story to Pik and Airi and the others. Not Abbey. He clenched his fists. Focus.

It took him nearly thirty minutes to locate the door to the engine room. It was a thick alloy blast door, but the control pad was surprisingly unsecured. Maybe not surprisingly. He doubted the builders thought anybody would ever get onto the ship if it was as nasty as Captain Mann claimed.

He checked the corridors before opening the hatch, slipping in and closing it again from the other side. The onboard systems would register the activity. Would the bridge crew notice? Would they think much of it? He hoped not.

Banks of computers sat on either side of him, a larger diagnostic terminal in the center. A second door sat behind it, another blast door with a small transparency at Terran eye level. The damn Republic insisted on putting things at human height, and it was especially annoying for the more vertically challenged species like himself. Even so, he made his way to the door and looked up at the window. He would need to get into the security systems before he would be able to gain entry, but maybe if he could see what reactor manufacturer Eagan had used he would be able to pre-plan his mischief. He was familiar with all of the latest designs, including the newer ones that had been produced while he was in Hell. He had good connections despite his lack of friendships, or maybe because of it. The other cons had always trusted him to keep his mouth shut.

He reached up, feeling a slight lip between the alloy and glass. He wouldn't be able to hold himself up for long, but it would only take a second to identify the reactors.

He put his other hand up and dug in with both, jumping and pulling at the same time. His face reached the window, his eyes barely clearing the lip.

He dropped to the ground, slumping against the door, his entire body shaking. He blinked a few times, trying to decide if he had just seen what he thought he had just seen, too terrified to look again.

CHAPTER SIXTY

THE MEDICAL BOT STOOD OVER its patient, looking down at her without moving. It had been programmed to deal with over two thousand potential injuries to over a dozen intelligent species, its understanding of Terran physiology the most complete of all.

It had no idea what to do.

The body strapped to the gurney in front of it barely looked like a Terran. It had so many wounds and so much shrapnel embedded into it that it appeared as a singular lump of flesh coated in a sheen of blood, and certainly not something that could ever be brought back to its prior condition. Even so, the individuals that had delivered it ordered the medical bot to do something, and so it had processed the instruction and come to a conclusion.

It decided to observe.

It had been observing for nearly an hour. The others had come and gone in turn. It registered that they appeared upset and unhappy, but it was a medical bot and not programmed with emotions. It was programmed with skills that were useful in most cases, but not in this one. It was obvious from the signs that this Terran was dead. How could it heal something dead?

Answer: it couldn't.

It would stand here and observe until it was ordered to stand down. That was the maximum that it could do. It didn't understand impatience, and so it remained still and unblinking for two hours more, eyes fixed on the patient. Somewhere in its systems, it registered that the flesh in front of it was changing, altering, but the impossibility made it struggle to compute.

By the time the patient opened her eyes, its operating system had crashed, and it was nothing more than a dead mass of mechanical parts.

CHAPTER SIXTY-ONE

THE WATCHERS RELEASED THE FOCUS, their hands lifting from the glowing blue orb that floated in the air at their center. The moment they did the glow subsided, the device powering down and sinking back to the pedestal from which it had risen. They looked at one another silently, knowingly, before dispersing back to their prior duties. Mainly, shoring up the damage that had been done to them and taking proper care of the bodies from the remains of the colony on Drune.

One of the Watchers, younger than the others, broke further away, retreating from Central Command and returning to his quarters. It was a simple space, a three-meter-square hewn into the rock, well-apart from the larger cavern where their hidden forces had been stashed. He took up a position in front of a small terminal there, turning it on and checking the connection to the colony's communications spike. He was pleased to find the spike had remained unharmed. It would have been a challenge to make his report otherwise.

"Sylvan Kett," the man said.

A projection of the Terran appeared a moment later. General Kett was hardly an imposing figure. His build was slight, his features delicate. That spoke only to his physical strength. It was his mind that was the dangerous tool.

"Jequn," Kett said. "It is over?"

"Yes, General."

"What about Cage?"

"She was badly wounded."

"She escaped?"

"We were forced to use the Focus to protect her, but yes, she escaped."

"Did the Evolent make the offer?"

"Yes, General."

"And she refused?"

"Yes, General."

Kett smiled. "And Yalom?"

"He was killed by the Evolent," Jequn said.

"He's a hero. If he hadn't come to us, we might have lost our only chance."

"Then he will be remembered that way." Jequn paused. "We lost an entire squad of mechs and two platoons. A dozen more are injured and will not fight for some time."

"The mechs are only machines. The soldiers? I will keep them in my thoughts. Today was a victory, one that was a long time coming."

"Has the time of change arrived?"

"The time to fight has arrived. Whether we win or lose depends on us."

"And on her?"

Kett smiled. "Yes. And on her."

17367275R00181

Printed in Poland
by Amazon Fulfillment
Poland Sp. z o.o., Wrocław